HABI
BY A.G. MANNY

ISBN: 979-8-9929174-0-6

Published by A.G. Manny

Cover Design by Muhammad Kaleem

For inquiries, contact: a.g.manny.author@gmail.com

Chapter One
EM 1138

In the heart of the desert, Koura—the hive city of trade and entertainment—transformed at night, its streets bathed in a golden glow from lanterns flickering against the darkness. The air thrummed with a medley of sounds—distant chatter, the clinking of coins, and the soft whisper of fabric stirred by the warm desert breeze. Sandstone buildings adorned with intricate carvings stood alongside sleek modern structures, crumbling ruins, and makeshift tents, all unified under the amber light that spilled across the city. The stark contrast between the ancient and the modern formed a tapestry bound by a shared rhythm—the unyielding pulse of life in the desert's core.

The streets teemed with a vibrant mix of people—merchants peddling their wares, nomads with weathered faces, and city dwellers weaving through the bustling crowds. Markets overflowed with shimmering jewelry, vibrant textiles, and exotic goods from distant lands, each stall a kaleidoscope of color. The air buzzed with haggling voices, the laughter of children darting between the legs of passersby, and the lilting melodies of street musicians playing instruments carved from wood and bone. Food vendors lined the streets, their grills crackling with the scent of spiced meats, while the sugary aroma of freshly baked pastries drifted through the air, tempting all who passed to savor their warmth.

Above, the sky stretched out like a vast indigo sea, scattered with countless stars that mirrored the flickering lanterns below. The ancient tower of the Sultan loomed over the city, its jagged silhouette rising against the night—a monument to Koura's enduring strength. Its weathered stone walls, marked by time and desert winds, stood as a testament to the resilience of the city and its people. Even as the darkness deepened, the city pulsed with life—music, laughter, and the sounds of celebration spilling from every corner, as if Koura's heart beat in defiance of the harsh desert surrounding it.

But this was the lower hive, where survival was a relentless struggle. The dwellers here lived by their wits and strength, doing whatever they could to scrape by. In the outer ring, life was a constant battle, with crime running rampant and danger lurking around every corner. Behind a stall, illegal deals unfolded in hushed exchanges, money slipping through hidden hands. Down shadowed alleys, the muffled sounds of a struggle were easily swallowed by the din of the streets, a mugging just another risk of city life. Amid the bustling crowds, pickpockets moved with practiced precision, their nimble fingers lifting pouches and purses unnoticed. And murder—murder was an old companion, as familiar to the residents of the slums as the cold indifference of the city itself.

The list went on.

HABI

A tiny figure draped in tattered khaki robes darted through the throngs of people, moving with surprising speed through the crowded streets. The towering figures around her loomed like shadows, their forms stretching beneath the amber glow of the lanterns, but they paid her no mind as she wove effortlessly through the living maze of the city. Her focus was fixed on a single destination: a bustling food stall, manned by two merchants and surrounded by eager onlookers drawn to the savory smells drifting through the air. The warm, tantalizing aroma of freshly baked bread mingled with hints of garlic and melted cheese, beckoning her. And she took it.

With quick, nimble fingers, she swiped two pieces of loaf, her slender arms moving like a shadow. The merchants, too preoccupied with other customers, failed to notice the missing pieces, and the buyers, their own pockets barely jingling, gave no sign of concern. Hunger dulled everyone's senses, leaving the small theft unnoticed in the haze of need.

The girl swiftly melted back into the masses, vanishing among the sea of bodies. With the stolen bread tucked tightly against her chest, she felt the weight of success settle over her. Her mission was complete—for tonight, at least.

—

3

After a grueling trek through the bustling marketplace, the girl finally reached a crumbling shed in the lower slums, nestled beside a busy street where the feet of pedestrians churned up clouds of sand with every step.

The slums sprawled like a patchwork of tattered tents, crumbling buildings, and rusted scraps, hastily thrown together to offer some semblance of shelter from the unrelenting elements. In this desolate wasteland, the homeless drifted aimlessly, like forgotten ghosts, seeking refuge beneath makeshift roofs that barely kept out the wind. Piles of refuse choked the narrow, dust-choked alleys, the silent remnants of a society that had long abandoned them. The stench of rot hung thick in the air, fusing with the oppressive heat to form a suffocating blanket that seemed to drain the very will to hope.

But for today, the girl carried a glimmer of hope, fragile but present.

She stepped into the dwelling, a place she called home. Inside, five other children stood gathered, their bags resting at their feet. They all appeared slightly older than the young thief, their eyes holding a mixture of curiosity and weariness as they regarded her.

The girl pulled back her ragged hood, revealing amber eyes that gleamed like polished gold. Her hair, dark and cropped short, was caked with dust, sand, and dirt. A single, stubborn lock of hair fell across her right eye, clinging to her brow. Sweat trickled down her forehead, tracing a path to her chin, catching the light against her olive skin.

"Habi, you're the last one again," the eldest of the group said, his voice young but carrying an unexpected maturity. He was lighter-skinned than Habi, taller, and stood with a quiet confidence that set him apart from the rest. His shaggy, dirty-blonde hair was just as tangled and littered as the others', but his sky-blue eyes—sharp and unwavering—radiated authority.

Habi pouted, "The market was busy tonight," she said with a soft, innocent tone. "Most of the food was being sold out."

The children giggled, their playful teasing filling the small space. Despite the banter, an unspoken bond tied them together—they were family. Not by blood, but by circumstance. Each one was homeless and orphaned, no different from countless others wandering the streets of the lower hive.

"It's not funny, guys," Habi retorted, her tone sharp. "Rafi, you know how hard it is!"

Rafi, the eldest, grinned and gave a quick signal to the group to cut it out. With a swift motion, he reached into his bag and pulled out several skewers, each loaded with juicy lamb, tender chicken, beef, pork, and a vibrant assortment of vegetables. The kids' eyes widened in awe, their mouths watering as they stared at his prize.

"It is indeed hard, right fellas?" Rafi was proud of his heist, yet humble as he handed a skewer to each child. Habi being the first.

Rafi patted her head, a faint smile on his face, as his eyes flicked to the bread she had tucked securely against her chest.

"At least this should finally put some meat on your bones, *twiggy*," Rafi chuckled, though his words carried a hint of truth. Habi was the most malnourished of the group, not just because of their scarce food options but because she rarely ate as much as the others. "You gotta eat right if you want to last down here, Habi," he added, his tone softening with a trace of concern.

"I can take her share again," another child volunteered, his gruff voice laced with humor. This boy was more solidly built than the others, his broad shoulders and thick arms a testament to the strength he had gained surviving in the slums. It was clear to anyone that he had claimed more than his fair share of food—perhaps a little more than his smaller companions.

"That's a no, Hamza. You're big enough already," Rafi said, shaking his head in firm disagreement.

"Oh, come on, man! I'm a growing boy!" Hamza roared with laughter, his booming voice filling the room.

The entire shed erupted in laughter as the children eagerly shared their spoils. Skewers, sizzling with tender meat and charred vegetables, were passed around with delight. Rice was ladled into wooden bowls, and pastries were carefully sliced into even portions. Habi's bread, still warm from the market, was torn into generous pieces and handed out, each child savoring the rare feast in their hands.

"Alright, we've got to finish all of this before Father gets back," Rafi warned, his tone serious. "You know how mad he gets if he finds out we swiped a bunch of stuff from the stalls."

"Then we should make it look like we found bits and scraps from the bins!" Hamza suggested, a mischievous grin spreading across his face.

Rafi sighed. "I don't think we'd find exotic cakes and shiny bread in these parts," he said, shaking his head.

Hamza frowned and raised his brows, conceding with a reluctant nod.

The children feasted, savoring every bite. This might have been their biggest haul in a while, but it was still a routine end to their day. It was just another way they survived in the lower hive—taking what they needed or waiting for someone else to do the same. With millions of hungry mouths to feed in the slums, survival was always a struggle, a constant fight against the odds.

Jokes flew between the children, some pulling faces that left others choking on their meals with laughter. A few boasted about their latest heists, while others simply listened, amused. Habi cherished these moments, as one should. She admired them all—their skill in the art of thievery and their uncanny ability to vanish into the bustling hive. But her breath caught when Rafi reached into the pocket of his ragged pants and pulled out an object that caught the flickering candlelight, its surface gleaming faintly in the dim room.

"Look what I managed to snatch today," Rafi announced, lifting a silver necklace toward the ceiling to display his prize. The pendant was adorned with delicate engravings along its edges, and at its center sat a brilliant sapphire gem, catching the light and holding everyone's attention.

"Better not let Father see that," another child said, her tone cautious. She was dark-skinned, with the same strong build as Rafi. Her long black hair cascaded around her shoulders like a ripple, spilling toward the ground as she leaned forward to get a closer look at the necklace.

"I know, Taliba. That's why I've got a hidden stash," Rafi said with a sly grin as he crawled to his feet. He made his way over to the cluster of bedrolls a few feet behind the huddle, the others following him with quiet curiosity. Kneeling, he lifted one of the bedrolls and folded it back, then tugged at a loose wooden plank beneath. With a soft creak, he revealed a small wooden box hidden underneath.

Everyone stared in awe as Rafi opened the box, revealing a treasure trove of jewelry none of them could have imagined seeing in this part of the city. Inside lay coins, gold, rings, and even glittering diamonds—each piece a testament to its worth. Anything small enough to fit in the box yet valuable enough to fetch a hefty price was there, gleaming under the dim light like a forbidden dream.

"Where did you even get all of that!?" Hamza hissed, his voice low but sharp enough to convey his disbelief and disapproval.

"The upper hives, *duh*," Rafi replied matter-of-factly. "You're not going to find rich people down in these parts."

"I don't think that's what he meant, Rafi," Taliba chimed in, her tone firm. "We all know where stuff like this comes from. It's more about the fact that we're *not* supposed to be going anywhere up there. You know the rules Father set for us, and this is literally number one!"

"Yeah, but he hasn't found out yet, has he?" Rafi said with a smirk, his confidence unwavering.

"I think it's brave," Habi added, her voice quiet but earnest.

Habi admired everyone, but she held a special soft spot for Rafi. Ever since Father had taken her in as an orphan, Rafi had been the one who cared for her the most. She looked up to him, yearning to be as brave and strong as he was. She longed to be closer to him, cherishing the kind of innocent love that only a young heart could feel.

"At least Habi understands me," Rafi said, his voice filled with determination. "Once I sell this haul, we won't have to worry about Father anymore. We'll be rich—living in the middle hive, maybe even higher. Who knows?" His ambition burned in his eyes, a fire that ignited both hope and unease within the group. Not everyone shared his vision. Taliba, for instance, was more cautious, preferring to stick to the routine and make small changes as needed. But Rafi was different. He had a goal—he didn't just want survival, he wanted change. He wanted something better for all of them. He dreamed of a life where his family could live comfortably in the upper hives, a place of wealth, luxury, and joy.

"He's coming!" another child, Tariq, called out, his voice sharp and urgent. Tariq was slender, quick on his feet, and the most observant of them all. He loved playing the role of lookout and messenger, knowing he could slip away before anyone had the chance to catch him. His carefree nature made him thrive in the chaos, always living in the moment.

As soon as the kids heard the message, they scrambled back to the bowls and dishes. Rafi immediately stored the silver necklace and placed the wooden board back into its place, covering it with his bedroll.

"The food!" Taliba whispered urgently, pointing at the leftovers that would catch the eye of any slum dweller.

Hamza stuffed as much food as he could into his mouth, nearly choking in the process. At least he managed to scrape it down enough to make it look like the remnants of a poor man's meal.

Taliba and another child, Naji, quickly cleaned up the scraps and poured them onto a rag, bundling the mess all together to conceal any evidence of their hidden feast.

Habi, the youngest, put on an act, pretending to wander out the door to use the restroom. Her real intention, however, was to distract Father for as long as she could. So, when the sound of loud boots shifting the sands and stomping toward her grew nearer, she quietly opened the door.

HABI

Before Habi stood a tall, gray-bearded man draped in dark robes. In his right hand, he held a lit candle lantern, its glow casting flickering shadows across his stern, weathered features. A brown leather bag hung from his other hand, while his scarred-shut left eye and the deep lines etched into his face lent him a menacing presence. His gaze slowly shifted to Habi, whose urgent trip to the restroom now seemed dangerously close to becoming a reality at the sight of Father's ominous return.

"Habi," Father grunted, his deep voice reverberating through her, making her freeze. "Where are you going?"

"Peepee," Habi answered quickly, then added with a shy smile, "I missed you, Father. Can I get a hug before I go?"

Father grinned as he knelt down to Habi's level, wrapping his arms around her in a slow deliberate embrace. She returned the gesture, but his attention was elsewhere. Despite the warmth of the moment, Father kept his one good eye open, glancing over her shoulder. There, his gaze landed on the mess behind her. Hamza had vomited, and the remnants of the food he'd stuffed into his mouth were now scattered across the floor. It wasn't from overeating, but rather from his stomach rebelling against the rich food he wasn't used to, a sharp contrast to his usual diet of raw potatoes and insects.

Father patted Habi's back and gave her a silent nod, signaling her to go ahead and use the restroom as requested.

"Go, my child," Father said.

Habi quickly darted out the door and headed toward the back of the shed, where the makeshift restroom was located. It consisted of a simple bucket with a wooden board placed on top. The board had a large hole in the center, offering both access and an outlet for waste.

As soon as Father stepped two feet into the shed, everyone froze. The air grew heavy with tension, though Hamza, oblivious, was still groaning in pain.

Father exhaled sharply through his nostrils, the sound like a warning, before demanding with a single booming word: "Rafi."

Chapter Two

Habi returned from the restroom and stepped back into the shed. What awaited her was nothing short of theatrical.

Rafi, Taliba, Tariq, and Naji were kneeling before Father, their heads bowed in silent submission. Behind them, Hamza lay sprawled on the ground, appearing lifeless. Habi, eager to blend in, wobbled over to Rafi's side and mimicked his posture. Between the children and Father, a messy pile of vomit lay, the remnants of what had once been a rare feast. Father's sharp eyes easily recognized the luxurious scraps—slices of beef, grains of rice, and bits of cake—that now lay discarded, reduced to nothing but refuse.

"Explain yourselves," Father commanded with his thundering voice. "Have you all been stealing from other people again?"

There was no point in hiding it—past attempts had only ended in failure.

Naji, one of the middle children, looked up at Father, his emerald eyes glinting with a mix of fear and resolve.

"We have, Father. We apologize," Naji said softly, his shy, raspy voice barely audible.

The children grimaced at his response, but soon resigned themselves to their fate. It wasn't often that they spoke the truth, but when they did, it earned them a lighter punishment.

"*We*? So, it is the fault of all of you?" Father concluded, his voice heavy with stern authority as his gaze swept over the group.

There was no verbal answer, but the frowns on their faces spoke volumes. Even poor Habi was deemed guilty, even though she was rightfully so. Father had always believed that if one child was to be punished, all should share in the consequence. It was a method of motivation, a way to keep each other in check at all times—especially given his years of experience in the harshness of the slums.

"You are all given food, water, and shelter. I took you under my wing to give you a better chance at life. All I ask is that you follow the rules and take care of your home," Father thundered, his voice laced with fury. The lecture was familiar, one they had heard countless times before whenever their misdeeds came to light.

The children knew they had the bare minimum to survive—food, water, and a roof over their heads—but it was a meager existence. Meals were simple: warm soup with bread, dirty water, and, on rare occasions, a raw potato. Sometimes, if luck was on their side, Father would add a chunk of meat to the potatoes. It wasn't much, but it kept them alive.

"Rafi," Father called, his voice steady but unmistakably commanding.

Rafi's head lifted, his eyes meeting Father's with reluctant defiance, the gravity of the moment settling heavily on him.

"What is the first rule?" Father asked.

"No one shall go to any upper hive," Rafi answered.

Father maintained his composure as he shifted his gaze toward Taliba, his expression unreadable.

"Taliba, what is the second rule?" Father asked.

Taliba mirrored Rafi's movements, lifting her head to meet Father's gaze. "Commit no crime," she answered confidently.

Father nodded, as that was the very rule they broke.

"Habi," Father said, his gaze now falling on her.

Habi was startled, her eyes widening as she looked up at Father, resembling a lost puppy caught off guard.

"What is the last rule?" Father asked.

Habi wasn't as fluent in the common tongue as the others, but the third rule held the most significance for her—it was the one that truly mattered.

She answered, "Take care of those around you."

Father nodded and then continued his lecture.

"These three rules are enough to keep you alive, and they are enough to make you decent human beings. Do you all understand that?" Father growled, his voice low and menacing, reverberating through the tense silence.

Almost in unison, the children replied with, "Yes, Father."

"Very well then," Father said, satisfied with their acknowledgment, though his tone hinted at the gravity of what was to come. He straightened, his stern gaze sweeping over them. "As punishment, I expect a full-page essay detailing your wrongdoings and what you will do to redeem yourselves in the future. The deadline is tomorrow night before dinner."

The kids groaned, well aware that their knowledge of literature was limited. Taliba and Naji were the exceptions—both had a keen interest in academics. For the others, however, this felt less like a punishment and more like an ordeal. Still, they knew that in some way, it was also an opportunity to hone their literacy.

"Is that clear?" Father asked.

"Yes, Father," the children replied.

"Good. Now clean this mess up and help Hamza," Father ordered firmly. "Afterward, I expect you all to be in bed. No one is staying up late tonight."

The children groaned again but complied with Father's orders without protest. They quickly set to work, using their brooms made of twigs and scraps of old rags to clean up the mess. As they worked, Hamza managed to regain his strength and shakily rose to his feet. Though he'd been dazed earlier, he now fully grasped the task at hand—and the consequences of their actions.

Within the hour, the children had curled up in their bedrolls, their bodies sinking into a deep, much-needed slumber. After a long day spent outside, it was no surprise to Father that they drifted off so quickly. The weight of their exhaustion, coupled with the warmth of full bellies, had caught up to them, and it showed in the way they moved sluggishly as they cleaned.

Once Father had checked on the children one final time, he snuffed out the flame of the lantern hanging from the ceiling, letting the cold, expansive darkness of Koura's desert night seep into the room.

HABI

—

The next morning, the children were up at first light, eager to get the task over with. They wasted no time borrowing scraps of paper, a jar of ink, and a handful of quills from Father's cluttered wooden desk. Each of them was determined to finish their essay quickly, hoping for enough free time to wander the streets and enjoy their fleeting youth.

They gathered in a tight circle, placing the ink jar at the center as they lay on their bellies, quills in hand. The pages they wrote on were tattered and worn—salvaged from the dusty shelves at the back of the shed. One by one, they dipped their quills into the ink and set to work, scribbling furiously on the fragile sheets.

Taliba was the closest to finishing. She wrote with a steady hand, her quill dancing across the paper as if the words flowed naturally from her mind. Her penmanship was immaculate—each letter neat and precise, her sentences well-structured. As she worked, her essay took shape like a masterwork, almost resembling the elegant scrolls one might find in the Sultan's own library.

Habi, on the other hand, was struggling. She sat between Rafi and Tariq, both of whom were scribbling their thoughts onto the paper with ease, the ink flowing smoothly beneath their quills. But for Habi, it wasn't just the essay that was difficult. More than anything, she wanted to be near Rafi. She ended up picking herself up and placing herself right beside him. Her gaze would drift over to him every now and then, watching him write, her thoughts scattered as she tried to focus on her own work.

"Rafi," Habi called out under her breath. Rafi stopped what he was doing and turned toward her, giving her his full attention. "How do you spell 'sorry'?" she asked, her eyes wide with uncertainty.

Rafi chuckled at her request and prepared to spell it out for her.

"S-O-R-R-Y. Sorry," Rafi answered.

Habi then blushed and let out a smile, "Thank you."

Rafi smiled warmly at her, but as his eyes drifted to her sheet, the smile faltered. His expression shifted from lighthearted amusement to one of confusion and concern.

On Habi's sheet of paper, she wrote:

I AM

SORRY

Those three words alone took up the entire sheet of paper, stretching from top to bottom. The letters were barely legible, scrawled in an uneven, almost frantic hand.

"Habi, that's not an essay," Rafi pointed out, nearly about to burst into laughter.

Habi frowned, raised a brow, and looked at her paper intensively.

"Is it not the full page?" Habi wondered.

The rest of the children began to notice their conversation and saw Habi's 'essay'. They all giggled, but no one really had a problem with it, because she was partly correct. It was indeed a full page.

"I think that'll pass," Hamza said, glancing over at Habi's paper with a shrug.

Habi wasn't embarrassed by her essay. To her, it was perfectly fine the way it was. She didn't know any better, and besides, she thought the little doodles of herself and Father holding hands at the bottom might earn her some extra points. It was a small, innocent gesture, but it made her feel like she'd done something special.

—

Rafi collected all the essays and stacked them on top of Father's desk.

As per usual, Father was absent, since he carried out his tasks part of the day and night. And to the children's knowledge, there were no restrictions to wandering about in the lower hive. So on this day, Rafi decided to make an impulsive decision.

As the children were conversing about what they wanted to do for fun, Rafi folded up his bedroll and lifted the loose board underneath, retrieving the wooden box.

"What are you doing?" Taliba inquired, noticing his actions.

"What do you think I'm doing?" Rafi grinned. "I'm going to go sell these and we are going to get out of this dump."

"You're absolutely crazy! You don't care about Father at all?"

The two began to argue as they drew in the rest of the kids to gather.

"Father is well off without us. In fact, I believe we're just a burden to him. I'm doing this for all of you," Rafi explained.

"And what if you don't make any money?" Taliban retorted. "Unless you go to the upper hives, which you better not—your only option would be to–"

"Sell them in the lower hive. That's exactly what I'm doing", Rafi interrupted. "I've already made up my mind ever since we got caught yesterday. You're either with me on this, or you can stay here and wait with the rats."

Taliba sighed and crossed her arms, "I'm staying."

Both Rafi and Taliba looked at the rest to see which sides they would take.

"I'm staying," Naji said.

"I'm staying," Tariq joined.

Hamza rubbed the back of his fuzzy head, astounded by a near unanimous decision to stay. Ultimately, he came up with the excuse of, "I'll go with you. If things go wrong out there, I'll pummel 'em for ya."

Almost after his decision, Habi chimed in.

"I'll go with you too," Habi said, her voice soft but filled with determination.

"No," Taliba interjected firmly. "You are not bringing Habi with you."

Rafi draped an arm around Habi, pulling her close as they stood side by side, his other hand still clutching the box of jewels.

"She's old enough to make her own decisions," Rafi insisted, his tone unwavering. "What good is she if she's not allowed to adapt to the outside world?"

"She's just a child, Rafi," Taliba pleaded, her voice tinged with desperation.

"A few years younger, but so are we."

Taliba stayed quiet, shaking her head in disapproval at the outcome. After a few moments of silence, she turned away and went to borrow a book from Father's desk. Tariq and Naji, feeling the sting of guilt from their refusal to join Rafi, bowed their heads in silent apology before retreating to retrieve a makeshift board game they had hidden beneath the desk.

Rafi glanced around, disappointed.

"Hamza. Habi. Let's go," Rafi commanded, his tone sharp and decisive as he headed for the door.

In a moment's notice, Rafi walked out of the shed, his steps deliberate. Hamza followed closely behind him without hesitation. Habi lingered for a moment, glancing back at the trio who stayed behind. Then, with a small, uncertain wobble, she turned and hurried after those who had departed, convincing herself that she had made the right decision.

—

During the day, the streets of the lower hive were scarcely different from their nighttime chaos. Dust hung heavy in the air, and lost souls clustered under makeshift shelters, seeking refuge from the relentless sun. The streets teemed with merchants and city-dwellers, moving ceaselessly as they struggled to make ends meet. Food vendors called out to passersby, hawking their wares and enticing anyone who walked within earshot. Rafi had to muster every ounce of his willpower to resist the urge to let his sticky fingers roam. In the stark light of day, his mischievous pursuits became far more perilous.

As Rafi and his crew roamed the lower hive, they frequently encountered vendors peddling exotic items like silk, furs, and tobacco. Yet, with his deep familiarity with the hive's reputation, Rafi knew these goods were often of questionable quality or outright forgeries. His sharp eye and experience allowed him to discern the difference, and more often than not, the items fell into the latter category. When goods were both poorly made and fake, it was an unmistakable sign that the merchants were struggling to keep their businesses afloat.

"We may have to go to the middle hive. There's no luck around here," Rafi suggested, glancing at the others.

With that, Habi hesitated before voicing her concerns. "But we promised that we wouldn't–"

Before Habi could finish her worries, Rafi said, "We never promised anything, Habi. Here, I'll teach you something."

Habi pouted and stared intensively at Rafi, awaiting his lesson.

"If no one finds out you've broken a rule, is it really breaking it?" Rafi said, a sly grin spreading across his face. "You've got to take chances, even the risky ones. How else do you expect to get anywhere if you don't make your own moves? When the moment's right, you go all in, yeah?"

Habi's eyes glistened as she took in the information.

"That's why I like ya, Rafi. You keep it real," Hamza said with a grin.

"If only Taliba agreed with this, we could be out of this dump already," Rafi muttered.

As the three continued conversing and walking, Habi, distracted and not paying attention, accidentally bumped into a large figure. The impact sent her stumbling backward, and she landed on her butt with a soft thud.

"Habi, are you okay?" Rafi asked, helping her up onto her feet.

"I'm okay," Habi said, brushing herself off and patting away the sand clinging to her tattered rags.

The three then looked up at the towering figure who obstructed their path.

The man's olive skin matched Habi's, but his long, braided brown beard set him apart. His head was wrapped in a turban, and his dark eyes glinted with a hint of violence. He wore a golden blouse and trousers, their rich fabric catching the sun's rays. Over his attire sat a steel chest plate emblazoned with an eight-pointed star at its center. A sheathed scimitar hung from his left hip, attached to his sword belt, while a brown leather satchel wrapped around his waist next to a hooked canteen. With each step, his brown leather boots kicked up dust and sand, sending it swirling into the faces of nearby children.

A.G. MANNY

This was one of the Sultan's men. A soldier of Koura.
They were called *Ghazi*.

Chapter Three

"Move," the Ghazi soldier commanded, his voice nearly as deep as Father's but laced with an edge that struck even greater fear into the children. This man had undoubtedly seen battle, and the acrid scent of tobacco clung to him, adding to his imposing presence.

The Ghazi could've maneuvered around the children, but he knew who he was. He knew what he represented. He asked himself, *Why should I spend my extra steps swerving around some rats in the slums*?

"Move," the Ghazi repeated, his tone sharp and unforgiving. Without warning, he pushed through the cluster of children, sending both Hamza and Rafi stumbling aside with the sheer force of his stride. He passed by Habi as if she were nothing more than debris that might scuff his boots. She escaped with only a face full of dust, which made her cough—a consequence of being the shortest of the group.

Rafi snickered as the trio reunited, glaring at the Ghazi who didn't bother to turn his head back at them.

"What's a *gold tongue* doing down here?" Hamza asked, hoping for a reliable answer from Rafi.

"He's here alone. You don't see many of the Sultan's foot lickers down here," Rafi said. "If he's here, then that either means they're doing their checks, or he's up to shady business."

Both Rafi and Hamza were accustomed to the occasional Ghazi soldier strolling through the lower hive, but for Habi, this was her first encounter—and her reaction was plainly written across her face.

"He looked scary," Habi whimpered, her voice trembling as she glanced nervously at the man who slowly disappeared into the crowd.

"Don't worry about it, Habi," Rafi said, reassuring her. "He's just another man, that's all. They bleed like we do." He patted her head with a small smile. "I'm here, after all. Nothing to fear."

Habi smiled back as Rafi took the lead, guiding them north along one of the main roads through the lower hive. With no opportunities to sell his box of valuables, they decided to head toward a massive iron gate embedded in a thick, towering sandstone wall. The wall rose high above the surrounding structures, dwarfing everything in its shadow. Flanking the gate, two Ghazi soldiers stood on guard, alternating between chatting with merchants unloading large wagon shipments and roughly shoving away those they deemed unworthy of passage.

At this point, Hamza and Habi knew that Rafi was trying to lead them out into the next hive.

The middle hive.

"Alright, Rafi, I know we agreed to do this, but *how* are we actually going to pull it off?" Hamza asked, his voice tinged with concern.

"I know a way," Rafi smirked confidently, his eyes scanning the surroundings. From the smug look on his face, Hamza could tell that he'd done this before.

Before the gate, the slums gave way to a large clearing, a bustling crossing point for those seeking to pass the border. The area was surrounded by tents, makeshift sheds, and crumbling buildings, though none came close to reaching the towering ledge of the massive sandstone wall looming above.

Rafi nodded toward the left of the clearing, where the crumbling remnants of an old building stood, just out of the Ghazis' line of sight. Without hesitation, Hamza and Habi followed his lead, swiftly weaving through the crowd of pedestrians to reach the discreet spot.

Around the foundation of the ancient building, several homeless people lay scattered, using whatever debris they could find for shelter. Some had set up tents and were cooking simple meals from tin cans over small bonfires. A few of them looked so still and motionless that they made the children wonder if they were even alive.

A few moments later, Rafi came to an abrupt stop and pointed to the ground. Beneath him lay a small iron manhole cover etched with an eight-point star emblem. The lid was so narrow that a full-grown adult couldn't hope to fit their chest through—but the trio weren't adults. However, Hamza's bulk made him the most questionable contender for squeezing through.

"This is how you get to the middle hive?" Hamza asked, knowing the answer.

"Yes," Rafi simply answered. "This is the only way that I could find. This manhole is linked to the sewage system, meaning the tunnels are going to be tight and nasty. The large manholes I found all lead to man-sized tunnels, but they are guarded by gold tongues. This is perfect for us."

"Yeah, but wouldn't this drain lead to the large main tunnel?"

"Of course," Rafi affirmed. "Just don't go that way."

"So you want me to dive into poop and trash—that's what you're saying?"

Rafi shook his head.

"No. Me and Habi are going in. You'll just get stuck," Rafi said firmly.

"I'm fine with that," Hamza said with a smile, shrugging off the decision.

"You're still opening the hatch though. I'm tired of doing it."

Hamza cursed under his breath, while Habi giggled, amused by his frustration.

Hamza stepped over the grate, hooked his fingers through the openings, and pulled with all his strength. At first, it resisted, but thanks to Rafi's prior tampering, it loosened and came free with ease, sending sand scattering from its surface and the surrounding ground.

"Alright," Hamza huffed, wiping his hands on his trousers. "Go make some money."

Rafi nodded at Hamza before turning toward Habi.

"Are you ready for an adventure, Habi?" Rafi asked, a hint of a grin tugging at his lips as he looked at her.

"Yes! I'm excited!" Habi exclaimed, her eyes lighting up with anticipation.

Without hesitation, Rafi jumped feet first into the five-foot-deep hole. Sewage and waste squelched around his worn, ragged shoes.

"Wait for me to crawl into the tunnel, and then you can follow, Habi," Rafi instructed. He turned to Hamza. "Hamza, you just stand guard and make sure no one messes with the hole, I guess."

Hamza pumped a fist to his heart, mimicking the salute of Ghazi soldiers.

Rafi dropped to his hands and knees, set the wooden box ahead of him, and began to crawl. Inch by inch, his body disappeared into the unseen tunnel below, viewed from above as if swallowed by darkness. The sound of slimy matter squelched and echoed from beneath him.

Following Rafi's lead, Habi waited until he vanished completely before lowering herself into the hole. The stench of rotting waste and an overwhelming mix of sewage hit her like a wall. Panic bubbled up, and for a moment, she almost turned back to call for Hamza's help to escape this foul pit. But then, she reminded herself of the most important rule.

Rule number three, take care of those around you.

And she whispered to herself, "I must stay with Rafi."

After her short ritual, she held her breath and finally began to crawl after him.

—

The tunnel was narrow, barely allowing Habi to stretch her arms out to the sides, but she pushed forward regardless. Ahead of her, Rafi's feet wiggled as he crawled deeper into the darkness. The ceiling pressed low, just enough to keep them hunched like worms inching forward. Each crawl brought her hands into contact with unidentifiable, slimy objects, but she forced herself not to react, focusing on the path ahead. The stench, once an overwhelming assault on her senses, had settled into an almost bearable background presence. This, without a doubt, ranked among the most disgusting experiences she'd endured in the lower hive.

"Having fun back there?" Rafi's voice came back to her, muffled and echoing slightly in the cramped tunnel.

Habi simply groaned in affirmation as she nearly puked within the first breath to let a word out.

"That's the spirit," Rafi added. "A turn is coming up. Don't go that way, since that leads to the main tunnel system."

"Oka–" Habi puked in her mouth, but immediately swallowed it back down.

Rafi laughed, completely immune to the atmosphere around him.

"I've been there too, don't worry," Rafi reassured her. "We're already close to the exit. Remember, we weren't that far from the gates."

Habi kept that in mind. She accepted that if she suffered for only a few more minutes, then she would be greeted with the unfamiliar air of the middle hive.

Before she realized it, Rafi was on his feet, waste dripping from his clothes. From just a short distance away, Habi watched as he pressed upward, straining against the grate that led to the middle hive. With a few firm shoves, the small beams of sunlight piercing through the manhole widened into a full ray, and Rafi hoisted himself up. He leaned down and extended an arm just as Habi neared the end of their treacherous path. Summoning every ounce of strength, she crawled faster and lunged to grab Rafi's hand. With a firm grip, he pulled her free from the muck below.

Habi took a long breath, exhaling as the unfamiliar air filled her lungs—a strange blend of the middle hive's cooler, cleaner scent mixed with the foul remnants of the lower hive clinging to her nostrils. The sewage stench lingered, stubborn and invasive. As she steadied herself and stood, Rafi patted her back and offered a quiet cheer.

"Now you're the second one to have made that journey! Congratulations!" Rafi praised quietly, a smile spreading across his face despite the streaks of discolored slime dripping down from the tunnel's grime.

Habi was speechless, caught between joy and disgust. The moment she finally rested, her body rebelled, and she retched up yesterday's dinner in a single heave of bile. Still feeling the burning sensation in her throat, she wiped her mouth and managed a shaky smile, joining Rafi in his triumph.

She made it and she couldn't believe it. She's actually in—

"Welcome to the middle hive," Rafi said, his voice filled with quiet triumph as he gestured to their new surroundings.

—

The contrast between the lower and middle hive was as stark as night and day. The streets were lined with low, flat-roofed houses made of wood and sandstone, their surfaces worn smooth by years of sand and wind. Locals moved at a more leisurely pace, seeking solace in the shade of modest shops and homes. The vendors, though similar to those in the lower hive, appeared more authentic, their goods displayed with pride. The streets were cleaner, the air fresher—a sharp departure from the choking stench of the slums. Laughter echoed through the winding, paved sandstone streets, a sound almost foreign to the lower hive. There, the roads were choked with open sand and dust, but here, life thrived, bustling with activity, and for once, no lifeless bodies lay discarded in the corners.

Fortunately, the manhole Rafi and Habi had emerged from was hidden from view. They found themselves in a narrow alley, pressed against the sandstone border, far from any doors or windows that might reveal them to prying eyes.

"Follow me," Rafi instructed, glancing back at Habi. "I know a place where we can wash. Walking into town looking like this is a surefire way to get caught."

Habi nodded, wiping the last traces of bile from her jaw before following Rafi into the maze-like neighborhood, her steps quick to keep up with his.

Around the next corner, tucked behind the homes, stood a water well crafted from smooth stone. Its base was surrounded by several wooden buckets, neatly arranged and ready for use.

"This is a luxury," Rafi said, gesturing to the well. "I've seen folks up here drink from it and wash up. There must be a well behind every complex in this part of the hive."

Without hesitation, Rafi grabbed a bucket, tied a rope around its handle, and lowered it into the well. He paused, listening for the faint splash of the water table, before swiftly pulling it back up. Retrieving the bucket, he wasted no time drenching himself with the cool water, letting it wash away the grime. Then, lifting the bucket to his lips, he drank the remaining water in desperate, satisfying gulps.

"Refreshing!" Rafi exclaimed with a grin, flashing his teeth as droplets of water dripped from his face.

"My turn! My turn!" Habi demanded eagerly.

Rafi laughed, handing her the bucket with a playful shrug. She quickly dipped it back into the well, pulling it up with a determined tug. Without hesitation, she poured the water over herself, giggling as the coolness washed over her, and then drank the remainder in quick gulps.

"Nice, isn't it?" Rafi said, grinning as he watched Habi enjoy the moment.

Habi jumped in delight, savoring the refreshing wash and the cool, fresh water. Without hesitation, she dipped the bucket back into the well, poured some over herself, drank a few mouthfuls, and then, with a mischievous grin, splashed Rafi with the remaining water.

The both of them were laughing, enjoying the opportunity to be here together.

"Hey, you kids! Stop wasting water!" a man yelled. He was middle-aged, dressed in clean, buttoned-up clothing—an uncommon sight in the slums. Two empty buckets dangled from his hands, and it almost looked as if he might throw one at the children.

"Run!" Rafi yelled, laughing along the way as he retreated from the scene.

Habi laughed along and hurried after him, letting the bucket fall beside the well with a clatter.

The man from the middle hive simply shook his head, muttering under his breath, before turning to fetch his share of water.

—

The duo ran until they reached the main stone-paved road, bustling with merchants and entertainers. Stalls overflowed with fresh produce and rare, exotic wares, their vibrant displays drawing eager buyers. Children—some darting about on their own, others trailing behind guardians—wove through the lively crowd. To Habi, it was almost unreal, like stepping into a dream.

"There, I see one!" Rafi exclaimed, pointing to a vendor displaying an array of jewelry. "Let's try our luck!"

Rafi dashed ahead, with Habi close on his heels. As they wove through the bustling crowd, heads turned briefly, noses wrinkling at an unpleasant scent that trailed after them. Yet, one by one, the locals shrugged it off and returned to their business.

The wooden stall wasn't crowded, but it had plenty of onlookers, drawn in by the temptation to flaunt their personal wealth. Two individuals manned the stall: a boy who spoke with customers already making purchases, and an elderly man who watched over him, answering any questions thrown his way. Both were modestly dressed, embodying the age-old practice of 'learning on the job'.

Rafi shoved his way to the front of the line, sparing no thought for decorum as he confronted the elderly man. Moments later, Habi appeared beside him, her head just peeking over the edge of the table.

"That's quite rude of you to cut in line, young lad," the elderly man remarked.

Rafi disregarded the man's words and slid the wooden box onto the counter, opening it to reveal its contents.

"I want to sell these," Rafi said, holding out his offering.

The man's eyes widened as he carefully examined the valuables inside the box. He picked up several pieces of jewelry, inspecting them closely, his practiced gaze assessing their quality. The boy beside him leaned in, equally surprised by the impressive haul.

The man carefully returned the jewelry to the box, then slowly scanned Rafi and Habi from head to toe, his gaze sharp and appraising.

"Now, where did you come by all this, young man?" the elder asked, his gaze narrowing.

Habi jumped in fear for a second until Rafi decided to begin his act.

"They were my mother's—" Rafi began, his voice faltering as he cast his eyes downward, a frown tugging at his lips. He sniffled softly, the sound heartbreakingly convincing. "She loved collecting jewelry. But she passed away after falling ill, and now my sister and I are just trying to help our father. He's doing everything he can to make ends meet. Please, sir, can you help us?"

Rafi blinked back a tear, quickly wiping his eyes. He wasn't concerned about Habi playing a role—she already looked like a lost puppy, and she didn't even have to try.

The elderly man frowned, his expression mirroring Rafi's, as he seemed to consider the story. After a long pause, he cast one final glance at the valuables and then, seemingly satisfied, came up with a solution.

"I'm sorry to hear that, lad," the man said gently. He reached into Rafi's box and lifted out two necklaces and a ring. None of the pieces matched the wares displayed at his stall. "I'll buy these three," he continued. "That way, it can help both of us out."

"That's fine, sir," Rafi agreed with a nod.

The old man smiled, satisfied with the trade. He tucked the three items away behind the desk before retrieving his money pouch.

"How does two hundred gald per item sound?" the man asked, his fingers already sifting through the coins in his pouch.

"That's more than perfect, sir!" Rafi said with a bright smile. "Please place it in the box—I forgot my pouch at home."

"Will do, lad."

Once the elderly man placed the gald coins inside the box, the transaction was finished, and the two were ready to move on to the next.

"Bless you, sir. The Sultan is great," Rafi proclaimed with a fervent tone.

"The Sultan is great," the elderly man echoed in agreement.

As soon as Rafi reclaimed his box of wonders, he departed swiftly with Habi close behind.

"Where did you learn to do that?" Habi asked, her eyes wide with amazement.

Rafi grinned, humming to himself. "Let's just say I've been watching how these middle-class folks operate for quite a while."

As the duo walked through the market, Rafi opened the box and pulled out a single gald coin, holding it up to the sky. The coin was crafted from gold, with a small mixture of silver and other alloys. One side featured the eight-pointed star, while the other displayed the Sultan's portrait. A jeweled crown rested upon his head, a third eye gleaming at the center of his forehead. He was depicted as strikingly handsome, with piercing eyes and sunken cheekbones. Around the Sultan's image, the edge of the coin was inscribed with the common tongue: *The Sultan. All Great. All Powerful. Long Live Koura.*

"I've never held a gald coin before," Rafi admitted, his tone laced with a mix of wonder and disbelief.

"I've never even *seen* one," Habi gasped, her voice filled with astonishment.

Rafi had let out a jolly laugh, patting Habi on the back.

"We already got six hundred gald, Habi! That's enough to feed us a proper meal for months! I can already feel the weight of the box in my hands!" Rafi was ecstatic. His plan was working.

Habi couldn't help but smile, watching the boy she so deeply admired bask in his happiness.

"On to the next!" Rafi cheered, his enthusiasm unwavering.

"Yes, sir!" Habi chimed in, mimicking the Ghazi salute playfully.

For the next hour, the duo carefully selected stalls—avoiding those too crowded or too empty—slowly collecting more gald as they moved deeper into the middle hive. Rafi spun a series of facades: tales of domestic violence, children fulfilling their parents' wishes, even being cast out of a home. As the box filled, it grew heavier with the weight of the coins. When it became too much for Rafi to carry, he suggested a rest near the manhole where they had entered the hive. Both Rafi and Habi collapsed by the water well where they had bathed earlier, exhausted but full of bliss.

"Here, Habi," Rafi said, opening his box and pulling out a single gald. He kissed it lightly before placing it into her palm. "Keep this one. Think of it as a good luck charm. We did good out here."

Habi stared at the single coin for a moment, then pressed it gently against her chest. She knew without a doubt she would be keeping it. A strong reminder of her time together with Rafi.

"Thank you, Rafi," Habi said with a warm smile. "How many coins do we have now?"

"I don't know," Rafi chuckled, still catching his breath. "Maybe I should buy a pouch."

"Maybe," Habi agreed with a small nod.

The two sat in silence as they laid on their backs, embracing the comfortable breeze the middle hive provided. They basked in the sun, letting their minds and dreams go wild.

"Rafi," Habi called softly, breaking the silence.

"Yes?" Rafi replied.

"What do you think the others are going to say about this?"

Rafi thought for a moment before coming up with an answer that could manifest into a possible theory.

"I believe—" Rafi breathed, "That they're all going to wish they joined us. This is proof that it's possible to escape from the lower hive. Sure, Taliba will probably yell at us, knowing that we broke the rules again, but maybe, just maybe, she'll be happy that we're trying."

"And Father?"

Rafi remained silent for a few seconds before answering.

"I have no idea", Rafi concluded.

Habi was satisfied with Rafi's answers, even though there were no guarantees. His efforts would either make or break the group, with the constant threat of Father expelling them from their adopted home. Still, Habi believed that as long as Rafi was by her side, she would be safe, no matter where they were.

"I knew something was up with you two!" a young voice shouted from around the corner, causing both Rafi and Habi to sit up, startled.

It was the boy who worked with the elderly man from the first vendor they sold at, and he looked furious.

"You're both lower hive *rats*!"

Chapter Four

The merchant boy, older than both Habi and Rafi, wore a plain gray tunic paired with neat indigo trousers. His shoes, though modest, were in far better condition than theirs.

Rafi snickered, his eyes narrowing as he studied the boy. Rising to his feet, he passed the wooden box to Habi, who stayed seated.

"What'd you call me, punk?" Rafi taunted, a mischievous edge in his voice.

The boy was momentarily caught off guard by Rafi's taunt, but quickly regained his composure.

"You heard me, street rat. They don't teach you manners down there, do they?" the boy growled, stepping closer to Rafi. "Oh *right*, there are no teachers down there."

"Keep talkin' and see what happens. You think you're tough? What, you stand 'round and clean daddy's boots all day? Lick the counter clean?" Rafi's accent began to slip as his blood started to boil. Poor Habi was only a spectator in this conflict.

"You rat—how about you just return the gald you cheated Pops out of?" the boy snarled, his tone dripping with contempt. "Unless you want me to call the Ghazi. Neither of you belong here," he threatened, his glare shifting between Rafi and Habi.

At this point, Rafi and the boy were face to face, although the latter had a slight height advantage.

"Call me *rat* again," Rafi warned, his tone low and dangerous.

The boy raised a brow before contemplating his next few words.

"Just hand over the gald, you *rat*," the boy repeated.

In the blink of an eye, Rafi swung his right arm, hooking a punch directly into the boy's jaw. The impact sent the boy stumbling backward, collapsing onto his knees.

The boy yelped in pain, clutching his face as he cried out, "Help! Ghazi!"

Rafi didn't stop his onslaught though. As the boy crumpled to the ground, Rafi swung a leg straight into the boy's face, ensuring that he stayed down. The boy cried in pain again as he saw Rafi go to retrieve an empty bucket nearby, lifting it over his head in preparation to strike.

"Rafi, no!" Habi cried out abruptly, her voice sharp with urgency. The plea made Rafi freeze, the bucket he had raised hovering ominously over his prey. He hesitated, sparing the boy from another painful blow. "Let's go back. Please," she begged, her eyes wide with desperation.

The neighborhood stirred as turmoil erupted. Footsteps echoed in the distance, growing louder, accompanied by the clanking of armor—the Ghazi were on their way. Rafi cast one last glance at the boy, who lay crumpled in a pitiful heap, before discarding the bucket with a sharp clatter. Without hesitation, he snatched the wooden box from Habi and gripped her hand tightly.

"Run to the hole!" Rafi commanded, urgency etched in his voice.

In the blink of an eye, the two vanished around a corner into a nearby alley, just as the Ghazi and curious onlookers arrived. They found the young boy on the ground, blood streaming from his nose and cheeks, tears staining his face. A few Ghazi cordoned off the area while one kneeled beside him.

"Who did this to you?" The soldier asked, more focused on answers rather than the boy's comfort.

The boy was incoherent, groaning and crying, unable to comprehend such harsh treatment—especially from other children.

"Search the area," the Ghazi ordered his peers.

As soon as the order was announced, they carried it out and scanned the section. Their scimitars were unsheathed, strongly grasped in their sword hand. Bystanders were pushed aside to prevent any obstruction to the search. Most of the onlookers departed, knowing the consequences of most incidents under Sultan law. They did not want any part of it.

One of the Ghazi, rounding a corner, noticed a small anomaly—a manhole slightly ajar. He gave it little thought, assuming a maintenance worker had failed to seal it properly. Refusing to investigate further, he stomped on it to close it.

Below him, the duo was already halfway through the toxic tunnel, crawling with frantic speed. Their eyes remained fixed ahead, determined not to glance back.

—

Habi led the way, as Rafi had hurriedly insisted she go first in case they were caught. The tunnel's toxic muck clung to them once more, covering them in a fresh layer of ooze and grime. Habi finally reached the opening where she could stand, her heart pounding with hope that Hamza would open the grate.

But he didn't.

The space above was eerily silent—Hamza was nowhere to be seen or heard between the grates. Panic surged through her as the thought of the Ghazi closing in pushed her to act. Desperately, she shoved at the grate with all her strength, over and over.

"Hamza!" she cried out, her voice trembling. "Hamza, help me!"

Rafi, wedged tightly in the cramped space behind her, could do nothing but watch helplessly.

At the time, Habi had no idea that Hamza was still by the manhole—he had simply fallen asleep. Her frantic shouts and the repeated clanging of the grate finally stirred him from his nap. Groggily, he sat up, rubbing his eyes and muttering curses under his breath.

"Habi! I'm coming!" Hamza called back, his voice sluggish but audible as he scrambled to his feet.

With Habi's help, Hamza lifted the grate effortlessly. He reached down, pulling her up and guiding her to a seat nearby as they waited for Rafi.

Moments later, Rafi emerged from the tunnel, his wooden box thrust upward first.

"Take it!" Rafi demanded, his voice sharp with urgency.

Hamza expected the box to be light, but as soon as he grabbed it, he realized it was anything but.

"What in the blazes did you put in this thing!?" Hamza gasped, carefully setting the box aside. With one swift pull, he helped Rafi climb out of the hole.

The duo collapsed nearby, panting heavily, nearly hyperventilating as adrenaline and disgust coursed through them.

"Boy, do you two *stink*! What happened back there?" Hamza asked, wrinkling his nose in disbelief.

"I'll tell you once we wash up," Rafi replied between gasps, retrieving the box with a faint grin. "We did it."

—

After a brief reprieve, Rafi and Habi were back in the lower hive, reunited with Hamza. The oppressive atmosphere of the slums hit them again, and for the first time, Habi understood why Rafi had worked so hard to sell those items—there was a better life beyond these walls.

Rafi led the way to a nearby murky pond surrounded by a scattering of tattered tents. The water, far from the freshness of the well in the middle hive, was clouded with mold, dirt, and traces of urine. It was the usual spot where slum dwellers came to quench their thirst or bathe. Despite the frequent urination and defecation contaminating it, in this place, a wash was still a wash.

Rafi handed the box to Hamza before he and Habi submerged themselves in the grimy pool. They quickly resurfaced, wiping the dirt from their faces and hair. This was the water they were used to, after all.

Rafi retrieved the box and washed it with him, removing all the dirt and slime from the tunnel.

Hamza squatted beside Rafi, leaning in close to whisper, "Are you telling me we actually have gald in that box? Like, real gald?"

Rafi quickly shushed him. "Keep your voice down. I'll show it to you once we get back home."

Hamza nodded, his excitement barely contained.

Habi, on the other hand, was exhausted. Though she had enjoyed her adventure with Rafi, the walking and crawling had drained her small frame.

"Can we go home now?" Habi asked softly, wishing, just for a moment, that home was somewhere in the middle hive.

"Of course," Rafi assured her with a nod.

Once Rafi and Habi had rinsed themselves off as best they could, the trio set off toward the place they called home.

—

Habi was the first to knock on the shed door while Rafi and Hamza stayed hidden out of sight. If Father happened to be home, they couldn't risk him getting even a glimpse—or a whiff—of the wooden box.

Fortunately, it was Taliba who answered the door.

HABI

"Habi? You look exhausted!" Taliba exclaimed, leaning in for a quick sniff before recoiling. "And you stink! Where are the others?"

"Is Father home?" Habi asked, her tone cautious.

Taliba shook her head. "He hasn't been home since he left."

"That's a good thing, then, because *boy*, do I have a surprise for you!" Rafi announced, appearing suddenly from around the corner, with Hamza following closely behind.

Taliba jumped, clutching her chest. "You scared the living daylights out of me! Don't do that!" she snapped, glaring at Rafi.

The trio laughed as they stepped into the shed. Inside, Tariq and Naji were huddled together over a book, their heads lifting as they noticed the others' return.

"Hey, welcome back, you guys!" Tariq greeted warmly.

"Barely gone for four hours, and now you're stinking up the place!" Naji added, wrinkling his nose in mock disgust.

Taliba closed the door behind them, moved to the center of the room, and crossed her arms with a curious look.

"So—how was the trip? Did you guys stay in the slums?" Taliba asked, her tone firm but inquisitive.

Rafi grinned widely. "We sure did! We even made a lot of–"

"The middle hive was so fun!" Habi interrupted, her face lighting up with excitement.

Rafi immediately pouted, and Hamza shook his head in mild exasperation, but they both allowed the little one to continue her excited rant.

"The water there was so yummy, and the air was so clean! People everywhere were smiling, and other kids were running around having fun! There were even—"

"You did *what*!?" Taliba interrupted sharply, cutting Habi off mid-sentence, her arms tightening across her chest.

Rafi quickly stepped between the two, shielding Habi from the barrage of words Taliba was clearly ready to unleash.

"Hear me out, Taliba," Rafi said, his tone calm but firm. "It was my idea, and it worked. There was no chance of selling those jewels in the slums, and you know that."

Taliba sighed, pinching the bridge of her nose before speaking again.

"You do understand that if Father were to—"

Rafi cut her off, his voice rising slightly. "Stop worrying about Father! Our world doesn't revolve around him!"

"It *kind of* does."

Rafi grew impatient and opened the box, revealing its contents. Stacks of golden gald gleamed under the light of the overhead lantern. Though some coins were stained with sewage residue, most remained untouched and pristine.

Everyone's eyes snapped open, except for Rafi and Habi, who already knew what to expect. Taliba even picked up a coin, her gaze fixed on it, mesmerized by its unfamiliar shine.

"Convincing, isn't it?" Rafi teased, a triumphant grin spreading across his face. "This is enough to feed us proper meals for months. If we had more, we could maybe even pay the fee and live in the middle hive. If this doesn't make you change your mind, then what will? My solution worked."

Tariq, Naji, and Hamza each pulled out a single coin, their eyes glued to the shimmering gald, falling into a shared state of mesmerization.

"And this is all because you stole from the lucky?" Naji asked, his voice tinged with curiosity as he turned the coin over in his palm, inspecting it closely.

Rafi nodded confidently. "Now imagine if we all did it." He then turned toward Taliba, a sly grin forming. "I know you're Father's pet, Taliba, but even you can't resist getting your hands dirty when it suits you."

Setting the box down to ease his cramping arms, Rafi stood tall and addressed the group.

"Tariq, I know you crave adventure, and the upper hives are the perfect place to move your feet," he began. "Naji, don't you want to explore the culture and technologies out there? All you've gotta do is take a step and make it happen!"

Rafi paused, catching his breath, before turning to Hamza with a knowing smirk. "And you—I already know you're crazy."

Hamza chuckled, shaking his head with amusement.

"And Habi—" Rafi said with a smirk, bending slightly to meet her gaze. "You're doing a good job. You keep being you."

Habi beamed, her smile stretching from cheek to cheek as she clutched the coin Rafi had given her tightly in her small hands.

"You can stop the cringe speech, Rafi," Taliba said, her tone flat but teasing.

Rafi sighed, his shoulders dropping as he frowned, turning his gaze back to her.

"I'll keep the idea in mind," Taliba added with a sly grin, flicking the gald coin back into the box with her thumb.

Rafi grinned back, a spark of hope igniting within him. He knew that if Taliba was on board, the rest of the crew would follow. His plan had worked, and this was just the beginning. They were one step closer to freedom.

Taliba crossed her arms, her expression turning serious. "If Father finds out about this—"

"He won't," Rafi interrupted confidently. "As long as the box stays hidden and all of our mouths stay shut, there won't be any problems."

The room fell silent, the only sound breaking the void was the howling of tunneled winds outside.

"Well, how about we celebrate and get some food already? I'm starving!" Hamza suggested, rubbing his stomach dramatically.

With that, the children erupted into cheers and laughter, their spirits lifting. They knew they were about to enjoy something rare—a warm meal, earned without the need to steal.

—

Each child received ten pieces of gald, more than enough for a hearty meal in the lower hive. Afterward, Rafi carefully tucked the wooden box beneath the floorboard. Taliba, ever cautious, fashioned makeshift pouches from scraps of rag and rope. These were tied securely around their necks, hidden beneath their shirts—kept out of sight from curious strangers and, most importantly, from Father.

In the lower hive, gald was a rare and precious commodity, something few could ever dream of possessing. Its value made it dangerous. Mugging—or worse—was a constant threat for anyone carrying it. That's why an unspoken rule existed: if you carried gald in the lower hive, you never traveled alone.

Once the children were all set up, they finally exited the shed together.

They spent the evening discussing their future plans, but the conversation kept circling back to how Rafi and Habi had escaped the Ghazi and the events leading up to that moment.

"There was this middle hive kid who wanted to pick a fight, so I gave him one," Rafi said with a smirk. "Knocked him right to the ground, and he cried like a baby. He was older than me too! Even called for help from some dust wipes!"

"I wish I was there with you," Hamza chimed in, his tone filled with excitement.

"That would've been awesome—until the Ghazi showed up. Me and Habi bolted so fast, they didn't even have time to catch the gas we left behind," Rafi added with a chuckle.

"I hope the boy is okay," Habi said softly, her voice full of concern.

Her words caught Rafi off guard. He glanced at her, then gave her a reassuring pat on the head, knowing how much she loved the gesture.

"He deserved it for talking to us like that," Rafi stated firmly. "Why should we worry about some middle-classed kid?"

Habi leaned into his touch but still pouted. "But he's still human. Maybe we could've been friends under different conditions."

Her words made Rafi pause, his expression softening as he began to pout as well. The sudden awkward silence threatened to settle, but Taliba, quick to sense the shift, stepped in to rescue the moment.

"Now who taught you those big words?" Taliba giggled, already knowing the answer.

"You," Habi replied with a shy smile.

"Good girl!" Taliba said, giving her a thumbs up and a playful wink.

That lighthearted moment was enough to ease the tension and spare Rafi from lingering guilt.

"What are we eating, anyway?" Tariq asked as the group wandered aimlessly through the streets.

"Good question," Rafi replied with a shrug.

"I want curry pork with rice!" Habi announced with a firm nod.

The dish was one of her favorites, a cherished memory tied to one of the rare occasions Father had treated her. She could almost taste the rich, creamy brown curry, its spices perfectly balanced, coating the grilled and fried pork pieces, all nestled atop a bed of fluffy white rice. It was a simple lower hive meal but always a top seller—and to Habi, pure comfort.

"You know what, let's all get that," Rafi agreed with a grin. "Let's head to the same spot Father used to take us to."

—

A short walk around the outer ring brought the children to their destination.

The curry shop was modestly successful, wealthy enough to display a sign above its counter with the simple name 'Curry'. A brilliantly innovative name, no doubt. Most shops in the lower hive didn't bother with branding, focusing solely on setting up and selling.

The shop itself featured a single long countertop with a wooden awning, offering seating for eight customers, though they served far more. Many others sat cross-legged on the ground, eagerly devouring their plates if they were fortunate enough to afford gald.

Despite the humble setup, the shop was known for its safety. Everyone came for one shared purpose: to eat.

Whatever grudges existed were left outside—settling them could wait for another day.

As expected, there were no seats available, and the line was so crowded it looped around the wooden booth. At least the tantalizing aroma of freshly boiled curry made the wait bearable, even exciting. The kids bounced with anticipation, their enthusiasm infectious, and no one seemed to mind the group of unsupervised children mucking about.

Patiently, they waited for their turn to receive a bowl of curry—the sole item on the menu. Thanks to the efficiency of the chefs, who prepared numerous bowls in advance to keep the line moving, the children eventually reached the ordering counter.

One of the chefs, a wrinkled middle-aged man whose face bore the wear of hard years, leaned over the counter, scanning the line until his eyes landed on the next group of customers—Rafi and his crew.

"What do you kids want?" the chef asked, his tone sharp and gruff. The children, however, knew better—it was just his way of speaking.

"Six curry, please!" Rafi ordered confidently.

"Right then. You lot got coin?"

Rafi nodded and reached beneath his shirt, pulling out the makeshift pouch. Carefully, he unwrapped the tie, revealing the shimmering gald pieces nestled inside.

"Six curry for six gald," the chef confirmed, his tone brisk.

"Yes, sir," Rafi replied, picking out six coins from his pouch. He glanced back at the others and added, "It's only six gald. I'll just use mine. It's fine."

"Thank you," Habi said softly, her gratitude evident despite her hunger.

Rafi handed the coins to the chef, who pocketed them with practiced efficiency. With a swift turn, the chef retrieved six wooden bowls of steaming curry, each filled to the brim and ready to eat.

"Six out!" the chef barked, handing a bowl to each child in an unexpectedly orderly fashion. Without pausing, he moved on to take the next customer's order, his rhythm unbroken.

The children wandered toward an open area with enough room to sit on the sandy ground. As soon as they settled, they dug into their bowls, the rich aroma and flavors of the curry making the feast all the more satisfying.

"Oh man, this is delicious!" Hamza exclaimed, his mouth full and grains of rice lodged in the nooks of his teeth.

The others were too engrossed in their meals to respond, but they all shared his enthusiasm.

Habi, in particular, relished every bite. She savored the tender crunch and chew of the grilled pork, the curry sauce igniting a delightful burst of flavor on her tongue. The fluffy white rice provided a perfect balance, cleansing her palate and preparing her for the next mouthful.

"We should invest in a canteen or something, because we forgot to get water," Tariq mentioned, coughing slightly as he nearly choked from eating too quickly.

Rafi cursed under his breath, realizing his mistake. Forgetting to order water was a rookie error.

"I'll get it," Habi volunteered cheerfully, standing up and swallowing her last bite. She skipped over to the counter, eager to help.

The others barely noticed Habi leaving, fully trusting her with the task as they remained engrossed in their meals. For a brief moment, they forgot their surroundings. Though the eating grounds were relatively safe, the possibility of trouble was never zero.

Rafi was the first to snap back to reality.

He realized, with a sinking feeling, that he'd just let a little girl wander off alone, carrying money in a place like this. His sharp eyes caught the subtle glances of other customers, their gazes predatory, like vultures sizing up their prey.

Panic surged through him. Rafi immediately set his bowl down and bolted toward Habi, who had already taken her place in line. Driven by fear, he positioned himself protectively beside her, standing tall—just as Father would have.

"Rafi?" Habi asked, glancing up at him as he stood beside her, still chewing his food.

"I don't think you can carry six cups by yourself," Rafi mumbled, swallowing his last bite.

Habi paused, unsure whether to feel joyful at his protective presence or offended by his remark. Either way, she couldn't help but enjoy his company.

When it was finally her turn, the same chef leaned over the counter and spotted her.

"Back in line? What you want?" he asked, his tone as gruff as before.

"Six cups of water, please," Habi said politely.

"Fresh water ain't free down here. Three coins," the chef replied without missing a beat.

Habi nodded and reached under her shirt, pulling out her pouch. Carefully, she began to untie it.

Without warning, Habi was yanked forward, falling face-first onto the ground as a man behind them tore the pouch from her neck. The chef cursed loudly as Habi let out a yelp, her small frame crumpling from the impact.

Rafi froze for a split second, his stomach sinking as the worst-case scenario unfolded before his eyes. He had known this could happen, even in pairs, yet he was still a moment too slow to act. The thief, much taller and faster than Rafi, was already darting down the alleyways, his long strides giving him a clear advantage.

Rafi clenched his fists, wanting to give chase but knowing it was futile. Instead, he knelt and helped Habi back to her feet.

"Hey, guys! Stop that guy!" Rafi shouted toward his family, his voice echoing across the eating grounds as he scanned for any sign of their response.

Tariq and Hamza lifted their heads from their bowls, their attention snapping to the man sprinting past them with a pouch clutched in his hand.

"You buffoons! Get him!" Rafi shouted again, his voice brimming with fury.

The urgency in his tone jolted them into action.

No other customer or bystander seemed to care; such incidents were all too common in the lower hive. However, Tariq and Hamza wasted no time and took off after the thief. Tariq, being the fastest, quickly closed the distance between himself and the man, his legs pumping furiously.

Just as Tariq prepared to tackle him, the thief suddenly stumbled and crashed onto his back as though struck by a horse. The reality wasn't far from it.

The thief scrambled to get back up, but another man, who now stood towering over him, shoved a knee into his chest, pinning him firmly to the ground.

"Get off of m–" The thief's protest was cut short as the man above him delivered a series of brutal punches to his face. Blow after blow, the relentless onslaught continued, leaving the thief dazed and defenseless.

Without breaking his pace, the attacker grabbed the crumpled figure by the collar of his tunic, hoisting him up effortlessly. He leaned in close, his eyes burning with fury as he stared into the thief's bloodied, tear-streaked face.

"Why are my children chasing you?" Father growled, his voice low and menacing.

Tariq's jaw hung open in disbelief as Hamza finally caught up, panting and out of breath. Neither of them could believe what they were witnessing.

The beaten man, too weak and dazed to respond, remained silent. Without hesitation, Father tore the man's tunic into shreds, fashioning the scraps into a makeshift rope. He looped it around the man's neck and began dragging his limp body toward the two boys.

Tariq gulped, forcing down his fear. "Fancy seeing you here, Father," he managed, his voice trembling.

"Where are the others?" Father demanded, his tone cold and authoritative as he gave the rope a sharp tug, making the man groan weakly.

Chapter Five

Back at the curry shop, Rafi helped Habi out of the line and guided her back to the group. The chef, showing an unexpected bit of kindness, brought over six cups of fresh water on the house. Perhaps he wasn't so gruff after all.

Habi was inconsolable, tears streaming down her face as she sobbed uncontrollably. The others surrounded her, gently brushing the dust from her clothes and wiping her scraped face. A red bruise had already begun to swell on her forehead, and a thin trickle of blood ran from her nostril.

"I'm so sorry!" Habi cried, her voice trembling as she rubbed her eyes. "I just wanted to be useful!"

The people nearby cast fleeting looks of pity at the child but quickly returned to their meals. Such scenes were commonplace, and Habi should've known better—this was life in the lower hive.

"It's okay, Habi. You couldn't have known," Taliba said softly, handing her a cup of water. "Drink. It'll make you feel better."

Habi took a few gulps, draining half the cup, before gasping and sinking further into her despair.

"He took the money from me," she sobbed, her voice breaking. "If I was stronger, like Rafi, then maybe—" Her words caught in her throat, and she buried her face in her hands, crying harder.

"It wasn't your fault," Rafi said, his voice steady yet tinged with guilt. "I should've been ready. I was right there next to you, and I couldn't stop it."

"Let's stop playing the blame game and focus on making Habi happy again," Naji interjected, his tone light but earnest.

As the trio worked together to comfort and clean Habi, Tariq and Hamza appeared in the distance, making their way back to the group.

"How'd the chase go?" Rafi asked, still holding Habi close.

"Oh, it went fine," Tariq replied, his tone casual but tense. "But we have a problem."

"A *big* problem," Hamza echoed, his expression grim.

Before the children could say another word, Father appeared, dragging the roped man behind him. A cloud of dust followed in his wake, swirling around the scene like a storm.

The children froze, holding their breath as the air grew heavy with tension. Habi's quiet sobs were the only sound that broke the silence.

"Did this man take something from one of you?" Father asked, his voice calm yet sharp, though he clearly already knew the answer.

The group glanced at the ragged man in Father's grip, confirming his identity with a quick nod.

"That's him," Rafi said firmly. "He hurt Habi and took something from her."

Father gave a single nod of acknowledgment, his face expressionless. Without hesitation, he dragged the man over to Habi, forcing him onto his knees so they were face to face.

"Apologize," Father snarled, his hand gripping the back of the man's neck like a vice.

"I'm sorry," the man mumbled weakly.

"She didn't hear you."

"I'm sorry!" the man repeated, his voice louder, shaking with fear.

"Habi," Father said, his tone softening slightly as he turned to her, "do you forgive him?"

Habi sniffled, her small body trembling as a tear rolled down her cheek. "I forgive you," she whimpered, her voice barely audible.

Rafi shook his head subtly, knowing that forgiveness wouldn't have been his answer if he were in Habi's shoes. But Habi had been raised closer to Father, and his lessons had clearly influenced her just as Rafi's drive had shaped him.

While Rafi lived by the belief of 'an eye for an eye, a tooth for a tooth', Father had always taught that 'only the strongest people learn how to forgive'. Rafi had never understood why Father would emphasize forgiveness in an environment as brutal as theirs.

But for a fleeting moment, as he looked at Habi's tear-streaked face, a thought flickered in his mind: *if we didn't forgive, then we weren't much different from anyone else.*

Father untied the strap around the man's neck and hoisted him to his feet with little effort. Leaning in close, he whispered coldly, "You should know the punishment for thievery in this city. You're lucky to keep a hand today." With that, he shoved the man forward, sending him stumbling. "Leave us."

The man remained silent, his head hung low as he shuffled off into the dark recesses of the hive. Bystanders chuckled and jeered at him, mocking his foolishness and lack of tact as he disappeared into the shadows.

Father turned back to the children, his stern gaze sweeping over them. "Why are you children here?" he demanded.

It wasn't unusual for the children to roam the hive and play freely, but this situation was different. The children knew Father's sharp instincts would immediately catch on to the truth. They had been caught at an establishment—an undeniable sign they had something of value.

Their curry bowls sat abandoned, forgotten amidst the chaos of the crime. But Father, as always, had his ways of uncovering the truth.

Without a word, he tossed a money pouch toward the group. Hamza's quick reflexes caught it before it hit the ground.

The children exchanged uneasy glances, already sensing the storm brewing. They knew better than to incriminate themselves, but their silence spoke volumes. Trouble was inevitable.

"Why do you have gald?" Father asked, his tone unreadable—a blend of disappointment, wonder, or perhaps both.

The children shifted uncomfortably, glancing at one another, silently hoping that either Taliba or Rafi would come up with a clever excuse. But deep down, they all knew the truth: no matter what answer they gave, Father would press further, dismantling their story piece by piece.

Father's method of interrogation was methodical, starting with the youngest—Habi. However, today, she was in no condition to speak, her composure still shattered from the incident. Seeing this, Father's sharp gaze would likely fall on the next youngest, Naji.

The young were his preferred targets, their naivety often leading to truth slipping through. Depending on Naji's answers, Father would then turn his focus to the eldest, Rafi and Taliba, dissecting their words with relentless precision.

Once satisfied with the information gathered, Father would deliver the consequences—shared by all, regardless of individual involvement.

"Saif Sabbah?" a young woman called out, her voice cutting through the tense air. She had fair olive skin, faintly dusted from the grime of the slums. A single brunette braid draped over her shoulder, hanging just above a toddler cradled in her arms. Her brown, tattered gown showed signs of wear, with a dingy white apron tied over it, frayed and stained.

Father turned sharply, his one good eye widening in recognition.

"It *is* you, Saif," the woman said, a soft smile forming on her lips.

"Sara," Father replied, his voice betraying a flicker of emotion, though it was unclear whether it was surprise, relief, or something else entirely.

The mutual recognition between Father and the woman left the children stunned. They had never seen him speak so casually with anyone before, and the unexpected familiarity was both surprising and intriguing. More importantly, the encounter had interrupted what promised to be a stern lecture, sparking a fleeting hope among the children that this distraction might make Father forget their predicament—though they knew better than to count on it.

"I saw everything, Saif," Sara said, her tone gentle but knowing. "Are these your children?"

"Yes," Father replied with a calm nod. "Yes, they are."

Sara smirked as she approached the children, her gaze soft but inquisitive as she examined each of them in turn.

"You saved each one of them? Just like how you saved me?" Sara asked, her voice laced with curiosity and a hint of nostalgia.

The children exchanged puzzled glances, lost in the conversation. This strange, unexpected interaction was enough to ease the tension, even calming Habi's shaken mood bit by bit.

"You children are lucky to have Saif as a father," Sara said, her tone warm but firm. "I was once in your shoes—almost quite literally."

The children, in unison, lifted their feet and glanced at their worn shoes, exchanging curious looks.

Sara chuckled softly before turning her attention back to Father. "May I tag along and visit your stead once more?" she asked, her tone hopeful yet respectful.

"Yes, you may," Father replied with a calm nod. "You are always welcome."

For now, the children were safe, quietly celebrating Sara as their unexpected savior in silence. Relief swept over them, but a sense of caution lingered. They remained on edge, their instincts sharp, because this would be the first time a stranger was about to step inside their home.

—

As the group made their way to the shed, the children spoke sparingly, exchanging only a few whispered words. Rafi gave a subtle signal—briefly covering his ears and pinching his fingers near his lips. The message was clear: *Hear nothing. Say nothing.*

Father and Sara walked ahead, leading the way, while the children followed closely behind. Sara carried most of the conversation, her voice filling the quiet air.

"Do the children adhere to your teachings?" she asked, glancing at Father.

"They do," Father replied evenly. "Some, better than others."

Sara giggled as she fixed the blanket around her toddler.

"Yours?" Father asked, his tone steady.

"Yes. Her name is Rosa. She's everything to me," Sara replied with a soft smile. "Me and the husband are slowly making a living down here—if you could call it that."

She let out a small laugh, but her jokes did nothing to break Father's neutral expression.

"Saif, do they know?" Sara asked, her voice dropping to a more serious tone.

"No, they do not," Father replied firmly. "And it is better that they do not know."

"Very well then," Sara said, letting the matter rest.

The group fell into silence after that, the only sounds accompanying them being the distant hum of the hive and the steady rhythm of their footsteps. Despite the tension, there was a glimmer of light—Habi's mood was beginning to lift. Hamza, ever the joker, pulled strange faces that coaxed soft giggles from her, her smile slowly returning.

—

Father held the shed door open as Sara and the children filed in, one by one. Once everyone was inside, he shut the door firmly behind them. The sun dipped below the horizon, casting a faint orange glow across the hive and cooling the air inside the shed.

Taliba moved without needing instruction, grabbing the small piece of flint and steel Father kept near his workspace. Striking them against a piece of paper, she created a small flame, which she carefully transferred to the candlestick inside the lantern. The soft glow spread across the room. With Rafi's help, she hung the lantern back onto its hook on the ceiling, casting dim but sufficient light.

Once the shed was lit, the children scattered to their bedrolls, huddling close as though performing a ritual. They aimed to give Father and Sara as much space as possible—but also to eavesdrop as much as they dared.

Sara quietly observed her surroundings, her gaze lingering on the makeshift furniture and scattered possessions. Meanwhile, Father approached his desk, his eye landing on the stack of essays written by the children. He picked them up, flipping through the pages slowly, his expression unreadable.

"Just like how I remembered," Sara said softly, breathing in the familiar, confined air of the shed. Her eyes wandered as nostalgia crept into her voice. "I wonder how the others are doing."

"They're at peace," Father replied.

Sara's brow furrowed slightly. "What do you mean by that? You know where they are?"

"I do," Father sighed, lowering himself onto the stool beside his workspace. "I buried them."

Sara's jaw dropped slightly, her grip tightening on her child's blanket.

"You're serious?" she asked, her voice barely above a whisper, a mix of disbelief and sorrow etched across her face.

"I do not joke," Father replied firmly. He opened a drawer and retrieved a tobacco pipe. With the flint and steel still nearby, he lit the already packed bowl and took a few deliberate puffs, drawing the smoke deep into his lungs.

After setting the tools aside, he reached for a large book on the desk, its pages partially filled. The text inside was written in a language no one else in the shed could decipher—except for Father. Dipping a quill into an inkwell, he began to write, his movements deliberate and unhurried.

"I have changed my ways since then, Sara," he said without looking up, his voice calm but carrying the weight of past regrets.

Sara stood frozen for a moment, shocked at how casually Father spoke of the situation. Meanwhile, the children huddled at the back of the shed, straining their ears to catch every word, piecing together the somber revelations.

"Assad, Karim, Lena? All of them?" Sara asked, her voice trembling as she took a few tentative steps toward Father, clutching her child tightly as though shielding her very heart.

"All of them," Father confirmed, his tone steady but heavy with regret. "You survived because you chose independence. You found love. You built your own path."

He paused, his eye fixed on the page as he wrote, though his mind seemed far away. "The others—they only wanted to follow in my footsteps. That was their mistake—a mistake I now know too well."

As the conversation continued, Father had already filled an entire page of his book. Setting his quill aside, he turned his attention to the stack of children's essays. The paper on top caught his eye—it was Habi's. His brow rose slightly as he read the bold, childlike letters scrawled across it: *I AM SORRY.*

A faint smirk tugged at the corner of his mouth. He decided she would pass the examination—not for eloquence, but for her creativity and sincerity.

"What do you do now, since you've forsaken the old ways?" Sara asked, breaking the silence.

"I am simply a scholar. Nothing more," Father replied, puffing on his pipe as he flipped through the next few essays. He paused briefly, scanning the contents with a practiced eye.

"I will soon depart once more for the evening," he continued. "You may stay, or you may go. It is your decision."

After skimming through the stack of essays, Father stood up from his stool, methodically placing his tools and pipe back in their designated spots. He moved with deliberate steps toward the center of the room, stopping directly under the faint glow of the ceiling lantern. Turning his head, he fixed his gaze on the cowering children.

"You all passed," Father announced.

The children's faces lit up in unison, their smiles spreading quickly—until he continued.

"But don't think I've forgotten about the gald situation. I will address that after I return."

The smiles vanished, replaced by frowns and nervous glances.

Without another word, Father opened the shed door and stepped into the looming darkness outside, leaving the children to their uneasy thoughts.

The shed remained still for a moment after Father's departure, the weight of his presence lingering in the air. The children sat in silence, unsure how to interact with the stranger who now shared their space.

Sara, sensing their unease, decided to break the ice. She approached the group and knelt down to their level, offering a gentle smile.

"Cold as ever," she began, her voice steady despite the lingering grief of Father's revelations. "You all must be Saif's children. My name is Sara, and this little one here is Rosa," she said, gesturing to the toddler nestled in her arms.

Though her voice carried a trace of the sorrow she tried to suppress, Sara's composure shone through as she attempted to make a connection.

"I'm Rafi," Rafi began, stepping forward. "The big one is Hamza. The long-haired one is Taliba. Tariq is the skinny one. Naji is the nerdy-looking one. And Habi is the small one." He gestured toward each of them with a casual wave as he spoke their names.

"You must be the leader of the pack then?" Sara said with a smile.

"You bet," Rafi replied confidently, grinning, while Taliba rolled her eyes in mild exasperation.

Sara's eyes softened as she scanned the group, her friendly expression unwavering. "I used to be just like you guys, long ago," she said warmly. "The same shed. A familiar family. The same Father."

The children exchanged uncertain glances, unsure how to respond.

"I overheard that you're also in trouble for possessing gald, no?" Sara added, her tone curious but kind.

The children flinched, their unease growing as they wondered if Father had left Sara behind to deliver their punishment.

"Don't be afraid," Sara said, her soft giggle easing some of the tension. "We got in trouble for the same thing once. Our eldest, Assad, admired Father from the moment he took him in. He wanted to be just like him when he grew up. Back then, our only rule was 'take care of those around you'. So, we got our riches by pickpocketing and running around like deranged little rats in the upper hives."

"Then how'd you guys get in trouble?" Taliba asked, her voice laced with curiosity.

Sara coughed lightly, pausing for a moment. "I apologize—I should've been clearer. We weren't in trouble for possessing gald. It was about how we *came* to possess it."

The children, now more curious and intrigued by Sara's stories, leaned forward eagerly, bombarding her with questions.

"What did you guys do?" Taliba asked, her eyes wide.

"What did Father do before this?" Hamza wondered aloud.

"Was the water cleaner back then?" Habi chimed in, her voice filled with hope.

Sara sighed deeply, her gaze dropping to the floor as her expression grew somber.

"Unfortunately, I cannot answer any of that," she whispered. After a brief pause, she added, "But no, the water was not cleaner back then."

Habi groaned in disappointment, sinking back slightly as the others chuckled softly at her reaction.

"There are things I cannot say, even to the next family after mine," Sara admitted, her voice low but firm. "We all made a promise to never speak of it. However, I can offer you a solution for your gald problem."

The children's curiosity about the secrecy surrounding Sara's old family only grew, but Rafi, ever focused on protecting his own, was determined to prioritize their immediate issue.

"I'm interested," Rafi said, his tone resolute.

"Very well," Sara said with a grin, sitting up straighter. "Hear me out on this: you'll need to donate your gald to charity."

The children's faces twisted with confusion, clearly baffled as to how that could possibly solve their predicament.

"I can see the confusion in all your faces," Sara giggled. "But do you remember the rule of 'taking care of those around you'? Well, isn't the rest of the hive part of those around you too?"

The children exchanged uncertain glances, still trying to grasp her reasoning.

"Saif spent his entire life taking care of the lower hive," Sara continued, her tone softening. "But now, he's far too old to be of much use to them anymore." She sighed, a wistful look crossing her face. "If only I could tell you everything, then maybe you'd see Saif in a different light. But believe me when I say this—back when we gave gald to others, Father actually smiled a bit."

The children sat in stunned silence, processing her words.

"But why would he be happier with strangers having gald than his own children?" Naji asked, his brows furrowed in confusion.

"That's the thing, Naji," Sara replied, surprising the group with how well she had already remembered his name. "You're all under Father's protection now. He worries about you—every single one of you. He doesn't have the time or power to help others like he used to. That little act of kindness, giving to others, fills a void he can no longer address himself."

"Then why did he decide to adopt us?" Tariq asked, his tone tinged with curiosity and doubt.

"Saif has a reason for everything he does," Sara said cryptically. "You'll find out yours soon enough."

She paused before adding, "Don't leave tonight. But as soon as the sun rises, consult with Saif. He will grant you freedom when the time comes."

"Can we at least get a hint of what Father did before?" Rafi pressed, his curiosity refusing to relent.

Sara considered Rafi's question for a moment, her smirk growing as if she were amused by a private thought. Instead of answering, she raised her free hand to her lips, her index finger hovering just above them—a clear gesture for silence.

The shed grew quiet, the air heavy with unspoken words and lingering curiosity.

—

Sara finally decided it was time to leave her old home. Standing at the doorway, she kissed her child gently on the forehead and turned to take one last glance at the children gathered behind her.

"May we see each other again in this little big town we call home," Sara said with a warm smile.

The children waved as she stepped outside, and the door closed softly behind her, leaving the shed quiet once more.

"She's weird," Hamza said, breaking the silence. "Should we even do what she suggested? She couldn't even tell us anything about the old family."

"She had her reasons," Taliba replied calmly.

"And what if her suggestion *did* work, though?" Rafi interjected. "It's my fault Father found out about the gald. Now I have to fix it. Her reasoning seemed viable."

"But what about the yummy foods and the chance to move out?" Hamza asked, his voice tinged with worry.

"We can always make more and hide it better, Hamza," Rafi said firmly. "We just need to make use of the gald we have in hand right now. I say we do it."

"I agree!" Habi chimed in excitedly. "It's like the stories Father used to tell about the wolf who stole from the bigger packs to feed his pups! It's exciting."

"Well, if Rafi and Habi are in on it, then it's already settled," Taliba said with a shrug, her tone resigned but supportive.

"Then we'll tell him when he comes back," Rafi concluded, a determined edge in his voice.

As the children finalized their agreement to donate the gald to charity, Naji could be seen quietly rummaging through Father's workspace. He opened jars, rifled through drawers, and flipped through the pages of Father's books with an intensity that made the others uneasy.

"Naji, what are you doing? Have you gone mad!?" Taliba hissed, her eyes darting toward the door as if expecting Father to return at any moment.

"It's no problem," Naji said dismissively, barely glancing up. "My curiosity is getting the better of me. I want to know what happened to the old family and the lore behind Father."

The others exchanged wary glances, unsure whether to stop him or let him continue.

While Taliba was the reasonable bookworm, Naji was the cynical truth-seeker. Both shared a thirst for knowledge, but Naji's curiosity often pushed him beyond reasonable boundaries—like rummaging through Father's belongings without permission.

"Come on, Naji," Rafi said, stepping closer. "I'm just as curious as you are, but this is going way too far. Why would Father even leave something as secretive as what Sara mentioned sitting out on his desk?"

"Maybe it's to remember," Naji mused, his hands pausing over a drawer. His tone was distant, as if already lost in thought. "Sometimes people leave things in plain sight—not to share, but to keep the memory alive for themselves."

Rafi frowned, unsure whether to accept the reasoning or to pull Naji back before Father returned.

Habi, the youngest and most curious, decided to join in on the scavenger hunt, finding the whole ordeal exciting. She gravitated toward Father's large book filled with the mysterious language. Carefully, she turned its pages, her small hands delicately flipping through them, even though she understood absolutely nothing.

"Habi, you should know better!" Taliba scolded, crossing her arms in disapproval.

But Habi didn't respond. Instead, her hand froze on a particular page, her eyes fixed on it with intense focus. Her demeanor shifted, and the room seemed to hold its breath.

Without saying a word, she slowly lifted her hand and pressed a finger to her lips, mimicking the gesture Sara had made earlier.

Taliba and Rafi, baffled by Habi's strange reaction, stepped closer to see what had captured her attention.

Habi had stopped on the inside of the back cover, which at first appeared blank. But with careful observation, faint markings began to emerge. The ink had faded over time, but with patience and focus, the image slowly came into view.

At the center of the cover was a delicate, black-inked hand, segmented at the joints, with its fingers bent downward. Only one finger stood upright, pointing skyward. Beside the hand was a small ink blot that seemed to represent a thumb. The gesture was unmistakable—it silently whispered, *hush*.

"She wasn't telling us to be quiet," Taliba gasped, realization dawning on her. "She was giving us a hint."

The children crowded around Habi, all mimicking the mysterious hush gesture they had just discovered. For a moment, they shared a sense of intrigue and wonder—until Rafi broke the mood.

"This doesn't matter anyway. We can't even read it," Rafi said with a sigh, crossing his arms.

"I don't even think there's a way to learn this language," Naji added cynically. "Not unless Father decides we deserve to know this squiggly-lined mess."

Habi tilted her head, still clutching the book. "Do you think big sister Sara knows?" she asked softly, her curiosity shining through her uncertainty.

The group pondered Habi's question briefly but ultimately shrugged it off, realizing they might never see Sara again—the last link to Father's old family.

"Maybe Father was a thief like us," Hamza speculated.

"Who isn't a thief down here?" Tariq countered. "He had to be something bigger, like a famous mercenary or something. Why else would Sara say he helped people all the time?"

"Okay, you guys can stop with your conspiracy theories," Taliba groaned, pinching the bridge of her nose. "We should focus on the matter at hand—the gald."

"All of my hard work, gone to waste," Rafi muttered, frowning deeply. Habi, noticing his mood, stood on her toes and patted his head, offering a comforting gesture.

"Is our pact still going to continue after this, Taliba?" Rafi asked.

"This is just a lesson," Taliba reassured. "Of course we'll still join you on future assignments. But first, we need to handle this one properly. We'll wait for Father to return and propose our offer to him."

"I wonder what he does when he's out all the time," Hamza said, his curiosity resurfacing.

"Work. That's all I know," Rafi replied with a shrug. "Now put all the stuff back where you found it, and let's get back to our beds."

Naji sighed as he carefully returned the objects he had rearranged, his natural inclination for organization evident even in mischief.

Habi gently closed the book with the inked hush symbol and placed it back in its rightful spot on Father's desk. Before stepping away, she turned to Rafi, raised her finger to her lips, and mimicked the hush gesture once more. Her playful expression silently conveyed, *You didn't see anything.*

Rafi smirked but said nothing, letting her have her moment.

Once everything was back in place, the children hurried to their bedrolls, anticipating Father's sudden arrival. They slipped into their respective rolls but stayed huddled close together, their breaths quiet as they waited.

"So here's the plan," Rafi began in a hushed tone, causing everyone to wiggle closer, resembling a cocoon of conspirators. "We speak with Father. We donate the gald. Then we begin our heists. We keep the gald on lockdown and stay under the radar. No drawing attention to ourselves. Got it?"

"Aye," the children whispered in unison, their resolve firm.

Just as their agreement settled, the shed door creaked open, and Father stepped inside, his presence filling the room.

Chapter Six

"*Papa wolf hunted the rabbits today,*
   the eldest pup joined to learn the way.
   The second pup gathered to help the third,
   who cried from hunger but said not a word.
"*But the fourth pup fell, so still, so cold,*
   the second carried their coffin of old.
   The eldest dug while Papa stood by,
   And together they buried the fourth with a sigh.
"*Beneath the dunes, where the whispers play,*
   A tiny tombstone now marks the way.
   A pup who wandered to lands unknown,
   Left the third to grieve alone.
"*The third cried out, her heart torn in two,*
   'Why did the fourth leave without a clue?'
   With tears in her eyes, her sorrow grew,
   'They left so fast, no goodbye to pursue.'
"*Papa wolf hunted the rabbits once more,*
   The third pup followed where none had before.
   But soon the eldest would suddenly fall,
   Leaving the third to answer the call.
"*Papa carried him, heavy with loss,*
   The third dug deep through the sand and moss.
   Together they buried the eldest with care,
   As silence lingered on the desert air."

Father stood at the center of the room, the warm glow of the ceiling lantern he held casting soft shadows as he told one of his stories. The children, snug in their bedrolls, listened intently, their usual worries momentarily forgotten.

"I love your stories, Father," Habi said with a smile, her voice full of genuine warmth.

"I'm glad you do, Habi," Father replied, his tone softer than usual.

As the story concluded, Rafi decided it was time to address the matter they had been preparing for. "Father, I have a request," he began, sitting up slightly.

Father looked at him, his expression neutral but attentive.

"When you came home, we had been discussing the idea of—donating the gald we have to charity," Rafi said, his voice steady despite the weight of the words.

Father paused, the hesitation clear in his stance. "Sara suggested that, didn't she?"

The children stiffened, caught red-handed once again.

"Perhaps," Rafi replied, doing his best to sound nonchalant.

Father sighed, a mixture of exasperation and understanding crossing his face. He was well aware of Sara's tendencies, but the offer satisfied him. It served as an appropriate punishment, as well as aligning with the wisdom Sara had shared.

"You may donate the gald," Father said, his tone firm, "but only under my supervision. Is that understood?"

"Yes, Father," the children replied in unison, their voices steady with acceptance.

Father stood and moved away from the children, his hand reaching to extinguish the candle within the lantern's shell.

"At first light, we will depart. Good night, my children," he said, his voice calm yet final. With a gentle puff, the lantern's glow disappeared, plunging the shed into darkness. Father then returned to his workspace, the faint sound of his quill scratching against paper soon filling the quiet room.

Habi, nestled between Rafi and Hamza, inched closer to Rafi in her bedroll. From beneath her clothing, she pulled out the kissed coin Rafi had given her earlier and held it up for him to see, its faint outline barely visible in the dimness.

"I'm keeping this," she whispered, her voice soft but resolute.

"Good," Rafi replied just as softly, a small smile forming on his face.

—

The children drifted into a peaceful slumber, their exhaustion finally overtaking them. In her dreams, Habi found herself in a lush green oasis surrounded by crystal-clear shallow ponds. The oppressive desert heat seemed far away as her family laughed and played together in the cool waters.

Father was there, leading them into the pool, his usual stern demeanor softened into warmth. Rafi took Habi's hand, gently pulling her from the dunes to the soft, sandy shores. She hesitated for a moment, her toes just brushing the water, before everyone jumped in at once, sending sparkling droplets into the air as they laughed and splashed together.

In the midst of the joy, Habi found a moment of courage and told Rafi, "I like you," her voice shy but sincere. Rafi simply smiled, splashing water her way in playful response.

Father called out, his voice kind and inviting, asking the children to gather around him. One by one, they swam toward him, their laughter filling the oasis.

Habi lingered waist-deep in the water, watching from a distance with a smile. But as she took a step forward to join them, she stumbled—and fell.

Habi plunged deeper into the depths of the pool, far beyond where she had thought it was shallow and safe. She tried to cry out, but no sound escaped her lips. Instead, water rushed in, and she began to choke, her limbs flailing as panic set in. She didn't know how to swim, and the more she struggled, the darker and colder the water became.

Above her, the silhouettes of her family faded into obscurity, dissolving into the void as she sank further. The abyss surrounded her, unrelenting and infinite.

Finally, she hit the bottom, her descent slowing until she landed gently on unseen ground. No light pierced the gloom, and the oppressive weight of the water vanished. She stood, her breathing normal despite the impossibility of it all.

Around her, the emptiness shifted and warped. From behind, a hand reached toward her shoulder. She turned quickly, her heart pounding, and froze in terror.

Three figures stood before her—two men and one woman. Their faces were unfamiliar, yet their gazes locked with hers, cold, unblinking, and unyielding.

Terror coursed through her as the figures didn't move, only stared. Then, as one, they raised their hands, and a tremor shook through her very bones.

They lifted a single finger to their lips and hushed.

And just as the figures hushed, the ground beneath Habi gave way, crumbling into nothingness. She fell again, deeper into the unending void. The cold wrapped around her like a vice, the silence now deafening.

Her body spiraled as she descended, weightless yet unable to stop. The abyss seemed infinite, an endless chasm that swallowed her whole. The three figures above faded into the distance, their unyielding gazes lingering in her mind even as their forms disappeared into the darkness.

Deeper and deeper she plunged, the void pressing closer with each second, until there was nothing but the sensation of falling—forever.

—

Habi jolted awake from the nightmare, drenched in sweat and tears, surrounded by the oppressive darkness of the shed. She scrambled out of bed, crawling to each child, checking to make sure they were still there, confirming they hadn't vanished to some distant oasis. Even Hamza's familiar snores were present. Her eyes darted to Father's workspace, only to find it swallowed by the same pitch-black void. He was probably asleep at his desk, lost within the absence of light.

The nightmare had shaken her so deeply that she hurried to the restroom. The trip to the restroom at least wasn't a strenuous task. It was strategically placed behind the shed.

Habi wobbled carefully, watching each step as she made her way to the shed door. With quiet caution, she unlatched the knob and slipped outside, bathed in the dim glow of lanterns from the street. Passersby and vagrants caught fleeting glimpses of her—a small figure clinging to the shed wall, moving like a mouse, skirting through the shadows.

At last, she reached the bucket, topped with a wooden board for a seat. She was about to settle onto it when something suddenly caught her off guard.

She heard it—a whisper. The sound seemed to come from nowhere, and she couldn't make out the words or even the direction it originated from, but it was unmistakable. Fear gripped her, and now, even the simple task of using the potty felt impossible.

The whisper grew into two, and Habi began to wonder if she was still trapped in a dream. To be sure, she pinched herself, and the sharp pain confirmed it—this was no dream. The fear that had already settled in her chest deepened.

Overcome with fear, Habi couldn't bear to stay outside any longer, where the cold desert breeze grazed the hairs on her arms. She rushed back toward the shed, causing a small ruckus as she fumbled with the door, and dove into her bedroll, seeking the safety of its warmth.

Rafi groaned, his eyes barely open and still heavy with sleep.

"Habi—what are you doing?" he mumbled, his voice rough with fatigue as he yawned.

"There's ghosts in the back!" Habi whispered urgently, her voice trembling with a mix of fear and desperation. "They tried talking to me! Can you please come with me so I can use the restroom?"

"Are you for real?" Rafi chuckled, his amusement cutting through his tiredness.

"Yes! Please come with me," Habi insisted, her wide eyes pleading as she tugged lightly on his arm.

Rafi sighed, rolling out of bed with a weary motion. He knew what needed to be done and prepared to escort Habi to the back. Habi followed closely behind him, her steps hesitant as he led the way out the door.

Once again, Habi found herself on the bucket, but this time she wasn't alone. Her favorite Rafi was there, standing guard as she took care of herself. He kept his gaze averted, his attention focused on the night around them, listening for the whispers Habi had claimed to hear. But all that reached his ears were the faint trickles from the bucket, nothing more.

"It must've been your imagination, Habi," Rafi said, his tone still groggy but laced with reason. "It might've even been the people walking about."

Habi hopped off the makeshift seat and walked toward him, her expression firm despite her small stature.

"I swore I heard it," she insisted, her voice unwavering.

"Okay," Rafi said, finally giving in as he straightened himself. "Then which way did it come from?"

Habi pouted as she looked around, unable to pinpoint the exact direction of the whispers. That was mostly because she heard it surround her.

"Let's just get back to sleep, alright?" Rafi yawned, rubbing the back of his neck.

"Okay," Habi agreed quietly, trailing behind him as they returned to the shed.

Once they were nestled back into their bedrolls, the stillness of the room seemed to amplify every thought in Habi's mind. She lay awake, her eyes staring into the darkness above, unable to shake the whispers or the memory of those haunting figures. Her mind wandered restlessly, trying to make sense of what she had seen and felt.

"Do you believe in ghosts?" Habi whispered softly toward Rafi, who was already turning over in his bedroll, clearly annoyed.

"No. We have a long day tomorrow. Now go to bed," Rafi mumbled, his voice thick with exhaustion as he drifted back toward sleep.

"How about djinn? Monsters? Aliens, even?" Habi continued, her voice trembling slightly with a mix of fear and wonder.

Her mind raced as she recalled the whispers and her recent nightmare, which felt different from any she had experienced before. This wasn't just her usual fears manifesting in her sleep. It felt real, as though something—or someone—had been trying to reach out to her, their presence lingering in a way she couldn't fully comprehend.

"*Habi*," Rafi warned, his voice low and firm, clearly bothered by her antics.

Habi heard the irritation in his tone and decided to stay quiet. Instead, she let her gaze linger on his sleeping face, peaceful despite the short distance between them. With a soft sigh, she closed her eyes, her thoughts spiraling into vivid imaginings of the paranormal and supernatural.

Scenarios of djinn, ghosts, and eerie whispers swirled in her mind, filling the quiet darkness around her. The unease clung to her for what felt like an eternity, but eventually, exhaustion took over, and she drifted into a restless sleep.

—

Dawn broke, and the first rays of light crept into the shed. Father was the first to wake, lifting himself from his desk. He stood, took a drink from his canteen, and lit his pipe, filling the air with the sharp scent of tobacco.

Strangely enough, there was an unusual sense of excitement in his demeanor as he prepared for the day ahead.

As he glanced back at the children, he saw they were all sound asleep. Hamza had sprawled out of his bedroll, his belly exposed to the cool air. Naji and Tariq were tangled together, invading each other's personal space. Taliba lay gracefully, like a queen in her sleep. And Habi—Habi was curled up tightly around Rafi, clinging to him like a baby monkey to its mother.

Father walked over to them, his steps careful as he gently nudged each child awake. One by one, they stirred—yawning, rubbing their eyes, and slowly becoming aware of the towering figure before them.

"Is it morning already?" Taliba yawned, stretching lazily as she sat up in her bedroll.

Hamza groaned as he stirred, only to be met with a sharp ray of sunlight piercing directly into his open eye. He hissed in discomfort, his face twisting into a pained grimace.

"Ugh, stupid sun," he muttered, cursing under his breath as he turned over, attempting to shield his face from the intrusive light.

When Rafi awoke, he quickly realized he couldn't move much. Habi had pressed herself close, applying her weight onto him as she slept soundly, unaware of his discomfort.

"Habi," Rafi groaned, his voice drawn out with little effort to restrain it. "Get up." He hadn't gotten much sleep himself, his rest disturbed by the events of the past night, leaving him with little patience.

When Habi gently opened her eyes, the first thing she saw was Rafi's face, a sight that brought her a sense of bliss. But as she turned over to look at what stood between the children, her eyes suddenly snapped wide open. Her vision, still adjusting from the remnants of sleep and the dim light, made the large figure appear dark and hazy, as if it were something just out of reach of her understanding.

"It's the ghost!" Habi exclaimed, pointing dramatically at Father, her eyes wide with terror.

Father, unfazed by her antics, simply shrugged off the implication, clearly too tired—or too accustomed—to entertain her early morning shenanigans.

The rest of the children, however, burst into laughter, their groggy moods instantly lightened by Habi's unexpected outburst. Even Taliba cracked a smile, shaking her head at the little one's imagination.

"Wash up and prepare your pouches. We leave as soon as everyone is ready," Father instructed, his tone brisk and commanding.

The children immediately set to work, retrieving their coin pouches, which had been safely tucked beneath the pillow sides of their bedrolls. They had been preparing for this moment, but while the others seemed eager to follow through, Rafi hesitated.

In his mind, the wealth they held was something he had technically earned. A small sense of pride tugged at him, making it difficult to part with the gald. Quickly, he lifted his bedroll and peered through the cracks in the wooden boards beneath it. To his relief, the small vault he had hidden there was still secure, untouched and concealed.

Satisfied, he straightened up, masking his hesitation, and joined the others as they got ready.

The children's morning routine was simple but steady. They would wake, wash at the pond, and then gather to share whatever meal Father had prepared for breakfast. The children were disciplined enough to make their way to the pond on their own, while Father stayed behind to prepare the bowls. Of course, Rafi was entrusted with the full responsibility of leading the group and ensuring they returned safely.

As soon as Father walked out, the children followed—but instead of heading in his direction, they turned toward a different path that led to the pond.

The mornings in the lower hive were no different from any other time of day. The same soulless folk lingered in their shelters, while the same merchants hawked their wares to anyone willing to listen. The only saving grace of Koura's mornings was the absence of heat. The desert was most temperate during the shift from dawn to high noon, offering a brief respite before the sun's relentless blaze took hold.

When the children finally made it to the pond, they were always relieved to find that the water remained warm, offering a small comfort against the otherwise harsh differences of the desert. It was a popular spot among locals, serving as a place to cool down, even if it wasn't the cleanest of ponds. The water also served as the district's primary drinking supply, prized for being the most 'pure'—though, in truth, its purity was a relative term.

The children exchanged a few words as they washed and drank their morning beverage, each moving quickly to dry off before the chill could settle into their bones and leave them vulnerable to illness.

"I miss the middle hive," Habi said with a small frown, her voice wistful.

"Be careful with what you say, Habi," Rafi warned, his tone low but firm. He shared her sentiment but knew the danger of speaking it aloud. "We don't want anyone down here to hear that."

"Okay," Habi replied with a pout, her small frame sagging slightly as she nodded in understanding.

The children began their trek back to the shed, not much time having passed since their wash. As expected, they arrived home just in time, the comforting scent of freshly cooked stew and beans wafting through the air. It was a clear sign that Father had already returned and started preparing their meal.

Rafi opened the door, and they found Father reading at his workspace. Six wooden bowls filled with stew sat in the center of the shed, waiting for the children. Each meal was accompanied by a slice of bread and a wooden cup of cold water—a rare luxury. But Father had his ways of securing such things.

"Welcome home," Father said, as he did every morning, his voice warm yet routine.

The children filed in one by one, settling next to the bowls with practiced ease. Almost ritualistically, they chanted in unison, "Thank you for the food, Father." The moment the last word was spoken, they eagerly dug into their meals, savoring each bite with hunger-fueled haste.

The meal consisted of the usual—slices of red beef mixed with black beans, the broth bubbling as it cooked. The children used their bread slices to either dip into the stew as a spoon or to soak up the flavorful liquid, making the most of every morsel. The cold water was a welcome relief, its crispness a rare treat. They drank slowly, careful not to gulp it too quickly and risk choking. But more than anything, they relished the rarity of fresh, cold water. To Habi, it was a refreshing change, though it couldn't quite compare to the taste of the water from the middle hive.

They chatted and laughed together as if they were a normal family sitting at a proper wooden table, feasting at a buffet. For the children, mealtime became a moment of connection, a chance to bond despite the circumstances. They realized that, even in the lower hives, sharing a meal was one of the greatest ways to feel like a family.

Once they finished their meal, the children hurried to the pond as a group, washing their bowls and cups with swift efficiency. They returned home immediately afterward, where Father would store the woodenware next to his desk. This routine was a precautionary measure against disease and infestations, given how rampant plague was in the slums.

The meal wasn't filling, but it provided just enough energy to get the children through the morning. Father knew better than to overfeed them; he wouldn't tolerate six lethargic children sprawled about the shed. A light meal kept them active and ready for the day ahead.

"Now that we're all satisfied," Father announced, his voice cutting through the room, "it is time to fetch the gald. We are leaving."

The children sprang into action, scattering to their bedrolls to retrieve their pouches. Taliba hesitated for a moment, her frown betraying her reluctance. The gald had been her motivation for creating the pouches in the first place, and now it was about to be given away.

Noticing her unease, Rafi stepped up beside her, giving her a reassuring pat on the back and a playful wink. It was his silent way of saying, *We'll make it through this.*

After this dog and pony show is where the real adventure begins, Rafi thought to himself, already imagining the challenges and excitement waiting in the next chapter of their lives.

The children fastened their pouches securely around their necks, tucking them carefully under their shirts once more. Each of them stood in a quiet line as Father inspected them one by one, ensuring the pouches were properly concealed and they were ready to leave.

Satisfied with their preparedness, Father gave a simple gesture toward the door, his movements deliberate yet calm.

"Let us depart," he announced, opening the shed door and stepping aside to lead them into the cool morning air.

—

At first glance, it looked almost comical—an elderly, tall man herding his children like sheep, playing the role of a shepherd. Onlookers would catch sight of the children, easy prey to any passerby, before their gaze shifted to the cloaked, hooded figure known as 'Father', leading them with quiet authority.

Their task was simple enough: visit the main hub of homeless shelters in the main square, then donate their gald. But the journey to the hub was another matter. The group had to navigate through dark, winding alleys and dangerous territory, an area teeming with gangs, courtesans, and sellswords. The region was known as *The Sleeping Complex,* a name that reflected the lack of enforcement and order in the area. It was a place where the most heinous crimes were committed, and the children knew all too well the stories that came from its shadowed corners.

Whenever they found themselves in areas where crime thrived, the children would huddle close to Father, seeking the safety of his presence. Rafi and Hamza, always vigilant, would take the rear flanks as an extra precaution, relying on their exceptional strength to protect the group. Father led the way, taking point, his every step calculated as he steered them through the dangerous streets.

As they traveled through the chaotic streets, the children witnessed countless muggings, illegal trades, and even acts of public indecency. But they had grown up here, in the heart of the lower hive. They were almost immune to the madness around them, numb to the violence and desperation. They understood the harsh reality—they could be the next body left in the gutter, lifeless, with flies swarming and maggots feeding on them. Father understood this too, his sharp eyes constantly scanning the surroundings, ever aware of the dangers lurking just beyond their path.

The air in the Sleeping Complex reeked of rot and decay, the stench of neglect hanging heavy in the streets. But the children knew that once they reached the main square, they would be free of its dangers, the chaos and violence left behind as they moved toward safer ground. It was a short, yet perilous journey, but the promise of a reprieve kept them moving forward.

"Hey, Pops, you sellin' 'em?" a man with a crooked grin and several missing teeth called out as the group passed too close to a crumbling, derelict building.

Father and his children didn't so much as glance in his direction. They had been taught to ignore distractions like this—a survival skill essential in their world.

With their heads down and their steps steady, they moved with purpose, avoiding eye contact and any unnecessary interaction, as if the man's taunts were nothing more than the wind.

The man snickered, his laughter raspy and mocking, before retreating back into the shadowy confines of his pitiful excuse for a shelter.

Just before they reached the main square, a brawl erupted in front of them, spilling out from a nearby alleyway. Several assailants were viciously beating a single man, his cries and yelps of pain filling the air. The group walked past them without a second glance, as they had been taught, but they could still hear one of the attackers unsheathing a knife, the blade scraping against its scabbard. Then, suddenly, the man's cries ceased. All that followed were the chilling, gurgling sounds of someone choking on their own blood.

Despite the mentally taxing journey through the heart of the Sleeping Complex, the group finally arrived at one of the main squares, a relative haven nestled within the innermost part of the outer ring. The chaotic and dangerous streets they had braved were now behind them, replaced by the bustling activity of the square.

Though the square was far from tranquil, its constant hum of life and commerce offered a sense of security. Here, among the merchants, vendors, and workers, the group could catch their breath, knowing they had momentarily escaped the perils of their journey.

"Is it over?" Habi asked, her voice trembling as she clung to Taliba, having shielded her eyes behind her older sister for most of the harrowing trip.

"It's okay. We're out," Taliba reassured her, gently patting Habi's head.

"Never thought I'd see that place again," Tariq muttered, glancing back toward the path they'd taken.

"Likewise," Rafi added, his tone firm but distant as he tried to shake off the lingering tension.

Before them stood one of the main squares of the lower hive, its grounds crowded with numerous stalls and booths, resembling a bustling flea market. The chaotic scene of merchants and customers was framed by sandstone buildings, which, though worn, were still in relatively good condition—but far from the pristine homes of the middle hive. As the group entered the square, they immediately noticed an oddity: several patrols of Ghazi soldiers moving through the crowd. Some were stationed at specific stalls and buildings, their presence too deliberate to be mere coincidence. The children could sense something was amiss, though they couldn't pinpoint what it was. Habi and Rafi exchanged a quiet glance, a silent understanding passing between them. They knew that the Ghazi's presence likely had something to do with a certain matter the duo was all too familiar with.

"There are many Ghazi today. Stay well-behaved," Father instructed, his tone firm as he stepped further into the square.

The children exchanged brief, uncertain glances, hesitating for only a moment before falling back into their practiced rhythm. They knew better than to question Father's warning.

This time, Habi stuck close to Rafi, clutching the edge of his sleeve as they weaved through the crowd. The square teemed with activity, but the increased presence of Ghazi patrols created an undercurrent of tension. The group moved carefully, each step calculated to keep them unnoticed amid the watchful eyes of the enforcers.

"Rafi, are they here for us?" Habi whispered, her voice trembling just enough to betray her fear. She kept her tone soft, ensuring Father wouldn't hear.

"There's no way," Rafi whispered back, his voice calm but firm. "They wouldn't send this many just for a couple of kids. Let's not think about it."

Habi nodded quietly, agreeing without a word, her hand gripping his sleeve just a little tighter.

After weaving through the maze of stalls and pedestrians, the group finally reached the main building that housed the endless stream of homeless. Some of the individuals spilled out of the building itself, setting up makeshift tents around the property, seeking what little shelter they could. The caretakers and volunteers were working tirelessly, rushing between stations to serve food, provide water, and offer whatever aid they could. Each day brought a new mouth to feed, and another slot in the building was quickly taken up, the cycle of need never seeming to end.

HABI

Two Ghazi soldiers stood at the entrance, their faces unamused by the chaotic, almost animalistic display of the lower hive citizens. Armed with scimitars, these soldiers also carried long bronze spears with steel tips, a red cloth hanging loosely beneath the blades. It was clear from their stance that their duty today didn't involve managing the throngs of the undesirable. They allowed the people to move freely in and out of the building without interference. It wasn't their problem—at least not today.

Father motioned for his children to stay close, forming a tight formation around him. The square grew more crowded as they approached the open entrance, the flow of people threatening to overwhelm anyone who strayed too far. The children obeyed without question, their movements synchronized, ensuring they neither got lost nor trampled.

At the entrance, Father caught the attention of a nearby Ghazi. Without hesitation, he nodded toward the armored figure and said firmly, "The Sultan is Great."

"Aye," the Ghazi replied.

The other Ghazi sneaked an eye on Father, only to be exposed to a dark hood. He was about to pay no more attention to him until he saw the little ones grasping onto him. One of the children specifically caught his eye, but he also paid no heed to it. The crowd was too wild to care too much about a single child walking into a homeless shelter.

Habi sweltered as she immediately looked away from the Ghazi's gaze.

Inside the building, there was barely any space to stand or walk. The floor was crowded with bodies, some sleeping, others begging. The group had to tread carefully, inching their way between heads and limbs. A pathway only opened when a nurse or caretaker passed through, and even then, it was narrow and fleeting.

One of the caretakers approached the group, saving them a little bit of time.

"Excuse me, ma'am," Father called, raising a hand to catch the caretaker's attention.

The woman paused, breathing heavily and wiping sweat from her brow as she noticed his gesture. Her exhaustion was evident, but she straightened herself and responded.

"Yes?" she said, her tone polite but weary.

"I'd like to lend a helping hand," Father said. He remained vigilant, even within the supposed safety of the shelter. The mere utterance of words like 'gald' and 'donate' could instantly spark a storm amongst the sea.

The caretaker smiled and her eyes widened, knowing exactly what Father had meant.

"Please, follow me," she said, gesturing toward a wooden counter where other volunteers were busy assisting patrons.

Father turned to his children and gave a silent gesture, instructing them to follow. Without hesitation, they fell into formation, walking close behind him as they made their way through the tight space.

The walk to the counter was almost effortless, as the caretaker led the way, parting the sprawled limbs.

Thankfully, within moments, they reached the counter. The air grew thicker, making it harder to breathe as carbon dioxide levels rose steadily.

The helpful caretaker waved the group over to the volunteers before swiftly departing in another direction. She was insanely busy today.

"How may I help you?" The young volunteer woman asked at the counter.

"Children, take them out and hand them to her," Father instructed. The children knew the assignment, aware that his words had to be as meek as possible. Following his instructions, the children dug into their shirts and lifted the pouch off from their necks. Father then took each pouch individually before setting them on the countertop.

"I understand," the volunteer said with a warm smile, bowing her head slightly. "Thank you, oh so very much! The Sultan is Great!"

"The Sultan is Great," Father echoed.

Rafi couldn't help but let out a quiet snicker as he watched his hard-earned gald vanish in the blink of an eye. The frustration of losing it lingered, but a small smirk tugged at his lips. At least he still had the wooden box safely hidden and the unanimous agreement from the others to join him in future heists. That thought alone was enough to keep his spirits high.

The volunteer carefully collected the pouches and inspected their contents. After giving them a nod of approval, she turned and disappeared around a corner into the back rooms, whose interiors were hidden from view.

After a brief wait, she returned to the counter with the empty pouches and handed them back to Father.

"That was a lot. We thank you so much for your help," the caretaker said, her gratitude evident in her tone.

"No problem," Father replied with a slight grin.

The sight of it sent a ripple of unease through the children—it was rare, almost unheard of, for Father to grin. He hardly ever smiled, even around them, and seeing it now around a stranger made them more uneasy than reassured.

"May you help lead us out?" Father asked, his voice calm but firm.

"Of course," she agreed, gesturing for them to follow as she led the way toward the exit.

The children wondered why he had asked for help in the first place. The sea of bodies was no longer an issue. It took a moment before they realized that the escort wasn't meant for the countless homeless. It was to dispel any suspicion the Ghazi might have had. Seeing an escort would confirm that Father's presence was legitimate, a business matter and nothing more.

Once again, the volunteer parted the crowd and safely escorted the group back to the entrance, where the two Ghazi soldiers stood guard. This time, Habi didn't glance around. The Ghazi paid them no attention either.

"I can breathe again," Naji whined, taking a deep breath of lovely lower hive air.

Even with Naji's quiet complaints, Father pressed on, leading the group to the edge of the square where foot traffic thinned and the noise faded into a distant hum.

"You've all done well today. Be proud of yourselves," Father said, his tone carrying an uncharacteristic warmth.

Commendations from Father were so rare that the children paused, savoring the unexpected praise. Even those still uncertain about the morning's events allowed themselves a small moment of pride.

"I suppose we can treat ourselves today," Father added, his voice lighter than usual.

"Curry?" Habi blurted out, her eyes lighting up as she hopped in place, her excitement palpable.

"No," Father said with a small smirk. "Something even better. Come along now."

Curiosity piqued, the children exchanged eager glances before falling in line behind him.

The children stayed close behind Father as he continued along the path skirting the edge of the square. They wove through a few narrow alleyways, their anticipation growing with each turn. Restlessness set in as they speculated about what the treat could be, unable to resist the urge to whisper their guesses.

"I don't even know the other types of food there are besides some meat and bread!" Hamza exclaimed, throwing his hands up in exaggerated disbelief.

"I don't think we've ever had fish before," Taliba mused, her voice thoughtful. "Seafood is pretty exquisite, or so I've heard."

The others exchanged curious glances, their imaginations running wild at the thought of trying something entirely new.

Father simply let the children's minds wander with imagination, interested in their theories.

Suddenly, Father came to an abrupt halt, causing the children to stumble into one another like a row of falling dominoes.

Father's gaze fixed on the figure ahead, identifiable by the deep purple garb beneath a polished steel chest plate etched with an eight-pointed star. A golden bar embedded in the armor denoted rank, while a dagger rested at the small of their back. At their hip hung a longsword, a stark emblem of authority. Though he shared the appearance of the two Ghazi soldiers flanking him, this man stood apart—a Ghazi officer, a leader attuned to the directives of the Kouran army's high command.

Ghazi officers were renowned for their inquisitive nature and sharp intellect. They maintained personal informants in nearly every corner of the city. A bit of gald was all it took to sway the thoughts of the desperate and needy.

Father understood that altering his course would draw unwanted attention, so he subtly signaled to the children behind him to keep moving forward.

The Ghazi trio scanned the area as Father's group advanced at a measured pace. The officer, sharper than his counterparts, demanded silent eye contact from each of them—not just Father, but every child—as they passed.

"You lot, stop there," he commanded, his voice roughened by years of tobacco.

Father and the children halted at once.

The officer signaled to his men, who moved swiftly to flank the ragtag group, one covering the front and the other the rear. His sharp eyes remained fixed on the children, studying their faces with an intensity that met their fearless expressions.

All of the children returned his gaze, but one girl in particular was not as eager for a fight.

"There's been a report of two lower hive children intruding into the middle hive," the officer declared. "They attacked a child citizen. One of them—" he extended a knife-like hand toward Habi, "had golden eyes. I've lived in this city my whole life, and I've never seen a child with golden eyes—until now."

Rafi stepped in front of Habi, a shield between her and the officer. The other children closed ranks instinctively, forming a tight, protective circle around them.

The officer took a step back from the children and turned to face Father, whose hood still obscured his eyes.

"Unveil yourself, and tell me—why do you have a criminal—maybe two, under your wing?" The officer snarled, but Father did not respond. "Are these even your children? Perhaps you're just another trafficker?"

Father remained silent, refusing to yield to the officer's subtle taunts.

The officer waited for a response, but when silence lingered, his patience snapped. In a swift motion, he unsheathed the dagger from his back, pressing its sharp point against Father's throat. His longsword remained untouched—too cumbersome for the narrow alley, where even a misstep could scar the walls. The other two Ghazi soldiers drew their scimitars in unison, the curved blades now leveled at the children.

"Take the golden-eyed child," the officer commanded coldly.

The children erupted in protest, their voices sharp with defiance as they tightened their formation around Habi. They shielded her with their bodies, a human barricade against the Ghazi's advance.

"I'll cut you all if you don't move!" one of the Ghazi bellowed, his voice laced with threat.

The officer chuckled at the sight of his soldiers struggling to push past the children, but the amusement was short-lived. A sudden, sharp pain shot through his left cheekbone, catching him off guard.

Father's open palm landed a forceful right hook, sending the officer sprawling to the ground. The dagger slipped from his grasp, clattering onto the alley floor.

The blow threw back the veil of Father's hood. The two Ghazi soldiers froze, stunned by the sight of the man bold enough to strike one of the Sultan's men. Their shock was palpable.

"Do not touch my children," Father growled, his fists clenched and his one eye burning with fury.

The officer on the ground spat a mix of blood and saliva, then slowly turned his gaze toward Father. The confidence in his expression evaporated instantly, replaced by the unmistakable look of a man torn between fight and flight.

As recognition struck, due to past reports, the officer's eyes widened. With a desperate roar, he shouted at the top of his lungs, "It's Saif Sabbah! Kill him!"

Chapter Seven

"Rally on me! It's Saif Sabbah!" the Ghazi officer yelled, his voice rising in urgency, hoping to draw the attention of any nearby Ghazi reinforcements.

As the officer's desperate call for help echoed, Father was already two steps ahead, formulating a strategy and plotting his escape from this predicament.

Father drove his foot forward in a powerful front kick, sending the nearest Ghazi crashing to the ground, winded. In a fluid motion, he crouched, spun, and hurled a handful of sand into the eyes of the rear Ghazi, temporarily blinding him and buying time for the children. The group scattered like ants, seeking whatever cover they could find in the crumbling alleyway. Rafi, Hamza, and Tariq, quick to react, charged at the disoriented Ghazi, tackling him to the ground. A violent struggle ensued as they fought to wrest the scimitar from his grasp.

Still crouched, Father snatched up the dagger the officer had dropped, his movements swift and precise. He rose to his feet, immediately facing the officer, who had already scrambled upright. The officer brandished his longsword, eyes filled with desperation as he prepared to eliminate this fearless foe.

"Your head will earn me the Sultan's highest blessings," the officer taunted, his voice strained as he struggled for breath.

The officer swung his blade toward Father, but Father, calculating the limited space in the narrow alleyway, easily dodged the attack. The officer lunged again, unleashing a flurry of strikes, but Father danced around him, expertly dodging and even guiding the officer's sword toward the stone walls. As soon as the blade clanged against the wall, Father seized the moment, closing the distance in a heartbeat. With a swift motion, he locked the officer's sword arm under his armpit and, using the force of a charging bull, drove him into the sandstone wall. Without hesitation, Father headbutted him, the impact ringing through the alley.

Just as Father prepared to deliver a fatal blow, the first Ghazi had already regained his footing. With a fierce war cry, he charged toward Father, his scimitar raised and ready to deliver a downward slash.

Father tightened his grip on the pinned officer and dropped to a knee, using the officer's body as a shield. The Ghazi's blade struck with force, slicing into the officer's shoulder instead of Father.

The officer's pained cry echoed, but Father showed no mercy for the man with a gold tongue. Without hesitation, he shoved the officer toward the charging Ghazi, sending him stumbling into the path of the blade, causing the Ghazi to recoil in surprise.

As Father regained his footing, the Ghazi aimed another strike at his neck. With inhuman speed, Father intercepted the blow, meeting the scimitar with the blade of his dagger. The clash of steel rang out in the tight space, a screech of metal on metal. In a single, fluid motion, Father rode the length of the scimitar, closing the distance, and then swiped the dagger across the Ghazi's throat. With a final upward slash, he drove the dagger under the man's jaw. He held the gaze of the man's eyes as blood poured from his wounds, the light in his pupils fading as life slipped away. The dagger had proven to be a devastatingly effective weapon in the confined alleyway.

As the bloodied body collapsed to the ground, Father swiftly pried the scimitar from the man's weakening grip, his own hands now tightly clutching the weapon.

The officer, now on his feet once more, quickly shifted to a defensive stance, blocking and deflecting the strikes from Father's scimitar with desperate precision.

To Father, the officer's resistance was nothing more than a futile show, meant to waste both his energy and resolve. As the clash of blades continued, Father deliberately spat in the officer's face, creating a brief window of vulnerability. With precise speed, he hooked the dagger into the officer's armpit, causing him to cry out in pain and terror. Seizing the moment, Father drove the tip of the scimitar into the officer's open mouth, the blade slicing through to the back of his neck. The officer's scream was cut short as his body went limp, motionless and lifeless.

Meanwhile, the rearmost Ghazi finally overpowered the three children, though not without consequence—he had lost his scimitar in the struggle. Rafi, now holding the weapon, prepared to strike, but before he could act, Father walked over and delivered a brutal kick to the Ghazi's face, knocking him back down. Without hesitation, Father stomped on his face again, then raised and angled his leg for another crushing blow. When the next stomp landed, the Ghazi's head snapped violently, his neck cracking before his body went completely limp.

"Give me the blade," Father demanded, his voice steady despite the labored rise and fall of his chest.

For the first time in his life, Rafi felt a deep, unwavering respect for Father, though it was tempered by a surge of fear after witnessing the carnage left in his wake. Without a word, he immediately handed Father the scimitar, his hands trembling.

Father grabbed the blade with a sharp motion, aggressively sheathing it into the belt hidden beneath his cloak, his actions swift and deliberate.

"We must leave. Quickly now," Father ordered.

The trio who had fought the Ghazi were panting, exhausted from the struggle. Meanwhile, Taliba, Naji, and Habi, who had been hiding in the shadows, emerged and quietly tailed the rest of the group.

As the conflict unfolded, a crowd of lower hive onlookers had gathered, watching intently. At the time, none of the group noticed them, their focus consumed by the fight. Despite the growing number of spectators, none of them called for help or tried to intervene. In fact, most of them were smiling, some even cheering, as if they were witnessing a spectacle rather than a violent clash.

As Father and the children sprinted deeper into the alleyway, the sounds of armor clanging and steel rattling grew louder behind them. The rally had worked—reinforcements were on their way.

A quick glance toward the back, and they soon found out that they were exposed to a large squad of Ghazi soldiers chasing them, yet they had the advantage of distance.

But as Father had expected, he remained confident they would be fine. The chaos and danger only fueled his certainty that they could navigate whatever came next.

The masses from earlier swiftly filled the alleyway, blocking it to the point where even a mouse couldn't slip through. The citizens of the lower hive harbored a deep hatred for the Ghazi and their authority. They loathed the privileges and wealth that separated them from the upper classes. To them, those from the higher hives weren't simply doing their jobs—they were symbols of a life far better than their own. The crowd was fueled by envy and resentment, and it was this very animosity that kept so few Ghazi from patrolling the lower hive.

"Move out of the way!" the soldiers shouted, their voices sharp with authority, but their words fell on deaf ears. The crowd only pressed closer, a wall of defiance that refused to yield.

The moment the order was given, chaos erupted. Screams of terror and cries filled the air as the crowd surged forward, hurling curses and garbage at the Ghazis. Makeshift knives flashed, and some even resorted to biting their attackers. The poor, fueled by rage and desperation, gouged out eyes and clawed at throats, tearing at their victims with primal fury. The mob, now a feral force, ripped the squad to shreds, driven by the resentment sparked by Father's actions. It was a violent reckoning, one that echoed the deep hatred and desperation simmering beneath the surface.

As the chaos subsided, Father pulled his hood back into place and motioned for the children to stay close. Small stains of blood marred his cloak, but they barely registered to him—such marks were inconsequential. In the lower hive, a splash of red was nothing unusual. After all, everything here bled.

—

After a long walk, the sounds of screams and shouts faded into the distance, and they finally reached a familiar, quiet area where they could rest. The weight of the day's events hung heavy in the air, but for now, there was a brief moment of respite.

None of the children spoke a word after the altercation, each of them lost in their own thoughts, still processing the intensity of both the attack and Father's violent retaliation. Some of them wondered in silence: *Were they still considered safe, if the very thing that saved them was deemed scarier than those who had attacked them?* The question lingered in the air, unspoken, but heavy in their minds.

When the group finally found refuge in the hollowed remains of an abandoned building, its only notable feature a crumbling stairway, Habi began to whimper. The weight of it all—fear, violence, and uncertainty—pressed down on her until she broke into tears, her quiet sobs filling the desolate space.

Taliba was the first to embrace her, pulling her close in comfort.

"I was so scared," Habi cried. "They were going to take me—and hurt you."

Rafi gently wiped the tears from her cheek and joined the hug, his voice steady and reassuring.

"They're not taking you, Habi," he murmured. "They're not taking anyone. I won't let that happen. Father won't let that happen. You saw him!"

After a moment of silence, Rafi's thoughts began to drift. *Just who is Father?* he wondered. Sara and the Ghazi always called him Saif Sabbah—a name that felt heavy with significance. It was a name worth remembering, especially since even an officer seemed to recognize it. The uneasy feeling gnawed at him, a sense that Father was hiding far more than he revealed.

Father approached Habi, his expression softening as he gently patted her head. Her sniffles continued, but the small gesture seemed to ease her trembling.

"I won't let any harm come to anyone," Father said firmly. Yet, as the words left his mouth, a frown crept across his face, his eyes darkening. A rare sadness settled in his expression. "But I must ask, my little Habi—why do the Ghazi know you? What did you do?" His voice wavered, the weight of the question pressing on him.

The children froze, startled by the uncharacteristic tremor in his tone. They had never seen this side of Father before—a vulnerability that unsettled them. The idea that one of them might be on a 'be on the lookout' list left the air heavy with unease, tension thickening in the silence.

Rafi stepped forward, determination in his posture as he decided to take responsibility now that Habi was compromised.

"It was my fault, Father," he admitted. "I brought Habi with me to the middle hive. A kid figured us out and threatened to call the Ghazi. He even came at me and tried to fight."

Father sighed, the realization of his fears settling over him.

"Does that explain the gald you had?" Father asked, his tone even but probing.

"Yes," Rafi replied, carefully avoiding the details of how he had obtained it.

"Did the boy deserve the beating?"

"I believe he did," Rafi answered without hesitation.

Father huffed sharply through his nose, a sound that carried both frustration and concern. He stood silent for a moment, as though wrestling with his thoughts, before his gaze softened slightly.

"Very well then," he said finally.

"Father, can you teach me how to fight like that?" Hamza blurted out, excitement lighting up his face. "That was so cool!"

"No," Father replied firmly, immediately shutting down the idea.

Hamza cursed under his breath, causing a few of the children to stifle chuckles. It was a small, unintentional attempt to lighten the mood, and though it didn't erase the tension, it offered a brief moment of relief, a reminder of their shared bond in the midst of everything that had transpired.

"I should be handing out a severe punishment for yet another undisciplined act to each and every one of you," Father growled, his tone sharp. The children flinched, bracing for the reprimand. "But all that matters now is that you're all safe, and the gald is in better hands now."

The children exhaled in relief, but Habi's face remained clouded with worry.

"Father, will they still send the bad people to come grab me?" she asked, her voice small as she frowned.

Father shook his head, a quiet sigh escaping him, and gently lifted Habi into his arms. He carried her as if she were a small princess, cradling her with an unexpected tenderness that contrasted with the harshness of their world. The gesture, though simple, spoke volumes about the care he held for his children.

"There's two outcomes," Father started to explain. "Either the Ghazi will realize that a single child isn't worth the amount of troops they've already lost, or they will send the entire army down on the hive. The latter is more unrealistic. The lower hive outnumbers the army alone, and the people here are out for blood. You will be fine, Habi."

Habi then sniffled and smiled as she embraced the warmth of Father's touch.

Father then gently returned Habi to the ground where she could be reunited with the others.

"Now then, since we are closer to our destination now, let us continue," Father suggested, walking away with a purpose as if nothing had happened.

As the children trailed behind, Naji couldn't help but share his worries "Father is scary," Naji whispered.

"I know," Rafi agreed.

—

It didn't take long for the group to reach a large building, its vibrancy starkly contrasting with the dilapidated surroundings. While most of the lower hive's buildings were crumbling sandstone or gutted shells, this one was wooden, full of life, and brimming with energy. Red and purple silky curtains hung over glass windows, with a soft, dim light spilling through. The sounds of cheers and singing echoed from within, mingling with the raucous laughter of those outside, some of whom were drunkenly vomiting alcohol. Two guards, each twice the size of Father, stood at the main entrance. They wore the same tattered rags as everyone else, but their clothes were far better maintained. Bladed dirks were tucked into their waistbands, eyes scanning the crowd, alert for any trouble.

As Father guided the children toward the entrance, the guards immediately noticed a breach of their regulations.

"No kids allowed," one of them said flatly.

In response, Father wordlessly lifted his hood just enough to reveal his face. The shift in the guards' demeanor was instant.

"Welcome back," the other guard said, stepping aside to let Father and the children pass into the building.

Upon entering the building, the group was immediately immersed in a large, bustling setting. An endless expanse of tables and chairs filled the space, with guests scattered throughout, enjoying their time. At the far end of the room, a wide stage stood, its dark curtains drawn tightly together, hiding whatever was behind them. To the right, a round counter was packed with patrons, each absorbed in their own revelry as they drank freely from bottles of imported liquor that gleamed from the shelves. On the left side of the room, the recreational area beckoned, a lively mix of drinking games, a dance floor pulsing with movement, a gambling section where coins clinked, and even an arm wrestling table where competitors tested their strength. The air was thick with laughter, music, and the raucous energy of a crowd indulging in all the excess the hive could offer.

But, just like any other well-paid establishment, there was a sign. However, this one was different. It wasn't posted at the entrance, but rather hung prominently inside the building, suspended over the tables where it was the first thing anyone would see upon entering.

The Tavern, the sign read.

The children stood mesmerized, their eyes glued to the dazzling colors and the vibrant sounds of joy that filled the air. It felt as though they had stepped into a completely different world, one far removed from the gritty realities of the lower hive. Barmaids rushed from table to table, their movements swift and practiced, delivering drinks and meals with grace. Meanwhile, the bartenders behind the counter displayed their professionalism and skill, flipping bottles and pouring drinks with a dexterity that left the guests in awe. The atmosphere was alive with energy, a stark contrast to the tension they'd left outside.

"Is that my friend Saif?" a man called out, wandering out from a crowd who parted a way for him.

The man who caught their attention was light-skinned and middle-aged, with a noticeable pot belly that hinted at a life of indulgence. His accent was unmistakably foreign, a clear sign he hailed from the western regions—a common occurrence in Koura, given the city's allure to foreigners. He wore a simple gray garb, but the red overcoat that draped just below his waist gave him a sense of distinction. What most intrigued the children, however, was his meticulously groomed brown mustache, a fine specimen of prestige that seemed to match his piercing green eyes. atop his head sat a black, worn-out top hat, slightly tilted as though it were his crown. He carried himself with an air of importance, as though he were the star of the show, though not the protagonist. His presence alone marked him as someone impossible to ignore, a figure of undeniable significance in the turmoil of the city.

"Oh, you even brought the kids!" the man exclaimed in a jolly tone.

"Gunther," Father said, addressing him by name. "These are my children." He gestured to them in order from tallest to shortest, introducing each one: "Rafi, Hamza, Tariq, Taliba, Naji, and Habi. Children, this is Gunther Blythe, the owner of this establishment."

The children, having been taught well enough by Father, responded in unison with a polite, "Hello," whenever greeted by someone of importance. It was a small but meaningful gesture of respect, something they'd learned to do in the presence of those who held sway. The warmth and liveliness of The Tavern helped ease the tension, its jovial atmosphere offering a temporary escape from the terror of recent events. The sounds of laughter, clinking glasses, and the cheerful chaos around them gradually faded the haunting memories, allowing them a brief moment of normalcy amid the storm.

"All of them are adorable. You've taught them well," Gunther said with a warm smile. "So, how may I assist the great Saif Sabbah today?"

"The children deserve a special treat," Father replied. "We are here to dine."

"And dine you shall. Follow me," Gunther said, his voice cutting through the chatter as he personally guided the group into the bustling crowd. The children stayed close to Father, their eyes darting warily at the unfamiliar faces surrounding them. Yet, navigating the throng was no challenge. Gunther moved with an almost effortless authority, his mere presence creating a clear path as the crowd instinctively parted for him. No one obstructed their way, and the group passed through without incident.

A few steps beyond the lively main floor, Gunther guided them to a quiet corner where a large,well-appointed table awaited. Set apart from the crowd, the spot exuded an air of exclusivity, clearly reserved for distinguished guests. Plush chairs encircled the table, and its elevated position provided a clear view of the entire floor while maintaining a sense of privacy amidst the surrounding activity.

"Go ahead and make yourselves at home, children," Gunther said with a warm smile, gesturing for them to take their seats.

The children rushed over to the chairs in a rush, filled to the brim with excitement and curiosity. Their eyes couldn't stop darting around at the interior's festivities. As soon as they were seated, Father nodded toward Gunther, silently asking him away momentarily to privately speak.

"One of the barmaids will be with you shortly. Order whatever you like—it's on the house today," Gunther said with a smirk before walking off with Father, the two disappearing around a corner.

"This is so cool!" Hamza cheered, running his hands over the smooth table surface. "An actual table!"

"I don't think I've ever sat in a chair like this before," Taliba added, lightly rocking the legs of her chair as she rubbed the armrests. Her wide eyes gleamed with fascination. "Who knew a place like this even existed in the lower hive?"

Habi's eyes lit up as she discovered something beneath the table. "There's food under the table!" she exclaimed with a wide smile, her small fingers tugging at a sticky substance wedged underneath the tabletop. Without hesitation, she sniffed it, then took a small taste. Her face scrunched up in confusion. "I don't know what it is," she said, still holding the sticky substance in her hand, her curiosity clearly outweighing any caution.

"You probably shouldn't be eating it then," Rafi said with a laugh, patting her back.

Out of curiosity, Tariq and Naji tried out the 'food' from below as well. They were not impressed.

Suddenly, a young barmaid dressed in rags and an apron arrived at the table. Her long, silky black hair hung over her light olive skinned shoulders.

"This is an odd experience," the maid mentioned playfully as she noticed that all the guests at the table were underage. She then handed them wooden boards with papers pinned on them, identifying it as the menu. "What are we having to drink today?"

"We'll all have water, please," Rafi said, deciding against testing any of the other drinks. It was the safer choice, especially as he became acutely aware of how dehydrated he was after the fight.

"Alright, take your time with the menu. I'll be back with your drinks," the maid replied, heading off toward the bar.

"She's hot," Hamza said, practically drooling.

"She's out of your league," Taliba retorted, shaking her head.

The two locked eyes, silently bickering as if they could argue telepathically. Meanwhile, Habi picked up a menu, glanced at the unfamiliar words, and set it back down. Frustrated, she scooted closer to Rafi and shared his menu instead.

"What's this?" Habi asked, pointing at a word she didn't recognize.

Rafi glanced at it, momentarily surprised she didn't know, though it made sense—she'd likely never encountered it before.

"Steak and eggs," he said.

"I want that," Habi declared.

"Me too," Hamza chimed in.

One by one, the other children echoed the decision, all agreeing on steak and eggs.

"Guess I'll get that too, then," Rafi said with a chuckle.

Once their decision was made, it didn't take long for the barmaid to return with six glasses of water. Hamza kept his eyes glued to her, but otherwise, they managed to successfully order six dishes of steak and eggs. When the maid took the menus and wandered off again, the children resumed their usual chatter.

As the children sat at the table, two men, clearly intoxicated, staggered by, supporting each other as they laughed and joked. Their mirth faded when they glanced at the group of children. One of the men's eyes went wide.

The children quickly noticed the strange men, preparing themselves for a brawl, but miraculously, it never came.

"Do me eyes deceive me?!" the drunken man exclaimed, his eyes wide with disbelief. "Thems stories were true! Look at the golden-eyed lass!"

Another man leaned over his shoulder, both of them staring at Habi with wide, unsteady gazes. Habi glanced up at them, clearly puzzled by their strange attention.

"Oi there, I know thems stories too!" the second man slurred. "Oi, lass, you see them dead folk, yeah?"

Habi sat still like a block of ice, referring back to her last night's experience, wondering if that's what the men meant.

"If ya see mum, tell 'er I love 'er! Birthed me well into the lower hive she did!" the man gagged and laughed, slapping his knee.

The man over him pulled him back and laughed along, "Oi, you're scaring the kids man! Thems belong to Gunther! Look! Tis' the guests of honor table!"

The forward man cursed and apologized, "Ah snap! Sorry! Sorry! Just lemme know of what the dead speak, ya? Many stories to tell indeed!"

Both of the men laughed and stumbled away from the children's table.

"What was that?" Taliba asked, raising a brow.

"Drunks," Rafi replied flatly.

"What if I *do* see dead people?" Habi pouted, glancing around at everyone. "I had a dream last night where you all disappeared, and I fell into a pond. Then I saw two people I've never seen before. I even heard whispers in the potty!"

"Sounds like you had a bad time," Hamza said with a chuckle, sipping his glass of water. Taliba immediately elbowed him in the side, making him spill a few drops.

"Okay, I'm sorry! Ow—" Hamza yelped. "Still, I've never heard of any golden-eyed stories. Not even Father mentioned them."

"Could be an urban legend," Naji suggested.

"Or it could just be Habi being little and having a wild imagination," Tariq added, laughing.

"But it's true!" Habi protested, her small voice rising like an indignant pup.

"Let's stop teasing her," Rafi said firmly. "We've dealt with enough for one day."

"Our plates aren't even here yet. I'm starving!" Hamza groaned, patting his belly.

As the children continued to banter, Father finally re-emerged from the corner.

"Oh, we forgot to order—" Rafi began, realizing they hadn't considered Father's meal, but he stopped mid-sentence as Father interrupted.

"No need. Gunther is providing a meal for me," Father reassured them. "Well then, what did you all order?"

"Steak and eggs," the children replied in unison.

"Good choice," Father said with a nod of approval. He took the nearest available seat, settling between Rafi and Tariq. "Now—it's time to address some issues."

The children swallowed nervously, some placing their glasses of water down before giving themselves a chance to enjoy the cold, refreshing taste.

"There's a reason I've forbidden any of you from venturing toward the upper hives," Father began, his tone firm. "I made this rule for a reason, yet you constantly break it."

Rafi opened his mouth to apologize again, but Father held up a hand and continued.

"But I can also do nothing to stop it. I know you kids well—some seeking a life of adventure and some for riches," Father sighed, sipping his glass of water. "The ones who came before you were the same. I even promoted the idea back then. But now—I only wish for all of your safety. So now, as the fourth rule, if you venture out, please return safely. You're all now unchained. You're all still children. Be responsible."

The children pouted, realizing that the combination of the donation and the fight had made Father more lenient. He understood that, despite their good hearts, his children were caught in the fire. He knew it wasn't right to physically restrain them in a crumbling home, so the most he could offer now was clarity. Clarity in knowing that as long as they were together, they could take care of themselves and return home.

"Do not raise suspicion, and do not let me hear of any more wrongdoings, is that understood?" Father said, narrowing his eyes at the children.

They nodded silently, avoiding his gaze.

"You all did well today," Father acknowledged. "From giving the gald to showing courage in protecting Habi. I raised you well—even if you are all a bunch of *deviants*."

The children giggled, appreciating the newly discovered side of Father, even if his last words were laced with scorn.

"Food's here!" Hamza cheered, his eyes fixed on the barmaid as she effortlessly balanced two platters of their meals.

The barmaid waltzed over to their table, placing the two platters down and handing each child their respective steak and cutlery. Father's order was a small bowl of hot tofu soup, steaming with chili spices. She then scanned the table, noting the glasses of water that were the most empty. After everyone was served, she retrieved the empty platters and bowed. "Enjoy your meal, esteemed guests," she said before walking away.

The children made sure everyone had their dish, as it had become a habit to start eating only once everyone was served. The brief observation didn't take long, and they immediately chorused, "Thank you for the food!" before eagerly diving into their rewards.

Almost all of the children ignored the cutlery. Hamza, Tariq, and Habi were guilty of picking up their steak with their hands, devouring the meat like wild animals. The juices dripped down their fingers as they eagerly savored the flavor. Taliba, the most well-mannered at the table, excluding Father, who gently slurped his soup, used a fork and knife with proper precision. Rafi and Naji, on the other hand, stabbed their steak with the fork as if attempting to slay it. Father observed them all, amused by their hunger, excitement, and habits. He never bothered teaching them table manners, considering it one of the least important lessons in the lower hive. Taliba had learned proper etiquette on her own, through books and practical experience.

"It's so good!" Tariq exclaimed, grinning through a mouthful of food.

Habi, with grubby hands, focused on her fried eggs. Curious, she poked a finger into the yolk and brought it to her mouth, sucking on it thoughtfully.

"What is that?" Habi asked, as yolk dripped from her lips.

"That's egg yolk, silly," Rafi said, shaking his head with a chuckle.

Habi widened her eyes in surprise at the revelation, then eagerly devoured the entire egg in one swoop. Taliba, seeing the chaos, patiently took the time to show everyone how to properly hold their utensils and cut the steak. However, despite her efforts, the others were more interested in their own way of eating. Still, they had the spirit, even if they didn't quite follow the rules.

Halfway through the feast, the children began to slow down, their stomachs filling with the rich, savory food. Habi, her curiosity piqued, finally decided to let it take the better of her. She looked around the table, eyeing Father as he sipped his soup quietly.

"Habi?" Father's soft voice broke the silence, sensing her hesitation.

She tilted her head, her fingers still covered in steak juice, but now focused on him. "Father, I have a question," Habi asked.

"Ask away, little Habi," Father leaned back in his chair, finished with his small meal.

"Do you know what 'golden-eyed' means?" Habi continued, pointing at her eyes. "I'm curious."

Father huffed air out of his nostrils and said, "It's nothing but an urban legend. No reason to dwell on it."

"But I wanna hear it," Habi begged, her voice insistent.

"Yeah, I wanna hear it too! Some folks passed by and joked about how she can see dead people!" Hamza chimed in, his curiosity piqued.

Father pressed his lips together momentarily before exhaling a long sigh.

"Very well," he relented. "I shall tell you the tale of the 'Necromantia'. It's a story that dates back long before my time. I'm surprised it's still remembered today—it's ancient."

"Say it!" Habi urged, her excitement bubbling over.

"Calm down, Habi," Rafi chuckled, patting her head lightly.

Father smirked slightly, a rare expression that caught some of the children off guard. He took a deep breath, leaning forward to command their full attention, even as their half-finished meals sat forgotten.

"Alright then," he began, his voice low and steady. "Here is the legend of the golden-eyed summoner of the dead."

Chapter Eight

"Before the fall of the Heaven's Roots—massive veins of branches that stretched into the sky and anchored into the world—sorcery was at its peak. Dragons soared, djinns roamed freely, and the fae caused mischief. It was during this time that a golden-eyed child was born. She grew into a woman of unparalleled beauty, but she was cursed with constant nightmares—visions that haunted her both in her dreams and in waking life. She was terrified at first, but eventually, she grew immune to the fear.

"Her ability to see and communicate with the dead turned her into a formidable force. The dead spoke secrets, exploited weaknesses, and wove lies. No one wanted to be near her, and so she fled to the caves, seeking solitude to hone her powers. She even attempted to end her own life, but death refused her. She grew more isolated, withering away in the darkness of the cave, despising those who lived, and hating the dead for tormenting her since birth.

"Then, she made a decision. She would return the torment to the dead. What greater way to torture those who were either restless or at peace than by bringing them back to life to suffer again? She mastered the power to resurrect the dead—harvesting souls from graveyards, battlefields, and places of worship. Her vengeance was not only against the living, but against humanity itself.

She sowed chaos wherever she went. No matter how many times she was slain, she would always return.

"In the end, the only thing that could destroy her was time itself. She aged, and eventually, she succumbed to the natural passage of life. But even in death, her legacy remained. Her actions left behind a world forever marked by her scorn, and it is said that the dead will always wander as a reminder of her curse. Another soul, another human, will suffer as she once did. And so the cycle continues, until none are left. For where the gods gave life, she delivered death."

Father finished his story.

The children stared at him in silence, their bodies frozen in place. The story had sent a chill down their spines.

"And that's a *minor* story?!" Naji blurted, his shock evident.

"He did say it's a very old story—an urban legend at that," Taliba added, trying to sound calm.

But among them all, Habi was the most visibly shaken, her superstitious nature amplifying the fear sparked by the tale.

"I can see the dead! What if you're all not real? What if I become a bad girl?!" Habi whimpered, her voice trembling. She usually loved Father's stories, but this one felt far too personal.

"It's just a tale, Habi. Don't worry about it," Rafi said with a light chuckle.

Hamza gently pinched her cheek and asked, "Is this real?"

"But the dream I had! The whispers I heard during potty time! They were real!" Habi insisted, her eyes wide with fear.

The children laughed, trying to ease the tension, but her words didn't go unnoticed by Father. His gaze lingered on her for a moment, thoughtful and cautious.

"Care to tell us about your dream, little one?" Father asked, leaning forward and resting his elbows on the table. His fingers intertwined as he propped his chin on them, his eyes fixed on Habi.

Habi, always the excitable one, eagerly nodded. "Yes! Yes!" she exclaimed.

Then she began to share her experience.

"Last night, I had a dream where you all were in it," Habi began, her voice quick with excitement. "We went for a swim in a pool, and then I fell deep, deep into the water. Down below, three people I've never seen before reached out for me, but then I fell again." She paused to take a quick breath and a sip of water. "Then I woke up because I was scared and had to use the potty. When I went to the back, I heard whispers, so I ran back inside to find Rafi."

"I didn't hear anything, by the way," Rafi added, shrugging.

Father's brow lifted with curiosity. "What did the three people look like? And what did the whispers say?" he asked, his tone steady but clearly intrigued.

"I—I don't know," Habi admitted, her voice uncertain. "I think it was two men and one woman. I don't really remember."

"I see," Father said with a nod, his expression thoughtful as he glanced down at his empty bowl. "Strange indeed."

The children watched Father, noticing how he seemed lost in thought. He lingered on the tale longer than they had anticipated.

"Do you believe her story, Father?" Taliba asked, her tone curious.

"There's not much to go off of," Father replied thoughtfully. "Although the story seems a bit far-fetched, I believe in her, at least. Some say that dreams are a reality of their own."

Habi, content with Father's answer, smiled and eagerly finished the rest of her half-eaten steak.

As their time together continued, Gunther appeared, clasping his hands with satisfaction as he admired the lively scene of his guests enjoying themselves.

"My friend Saif," Gunther called out. "How is the dine?"

"Good as always, Gunther. The children love it," Father replied. "Thank you for treating us today."

"No problem," Gunther said with a warm smile. "After all you've done for me, I only wish I could do more. Feeding the bellies of these children is the least I can do."

As they conversed, Father's attention drifted to the main entrance behind Gunther, where a familiar pair of individuals entered. Both were Ghazi. His gaze sharpened as he observed them, all the while feigning interest in Gunther's ramblings about his business's success.

The two Ghazi scanned the room, their eyes methodically sweeping over the patrons, until one of them raised an arm and gestured toward the door. Moments later, several more Ghazi entered, some clearly officers by their distinctive attire.

Gunther, noticing the shift in Father's focus, turned to look—and immediately froze, his expression stricken with shock.

"Why are they here?" Father asked, pulling his hood low over his face. The children noticed the shift in his demeanor and instinctively slouched down in their seats, peeking cautiously over the top of the table.

"I don't know. They don't come here that often, especially in troves," Gunther wondered. "Perhaps they're hungry? I will go assist them. You do what you have to do, my friend."

With Gunther's parting words, he walked over to the Ghazi with open arms, welcoming them inside The Tavern. The other guests fell silent, their eyes narrowing as they glared at the platoon like a pack of wolves closing in on prey.

"Greetings, Sire!" Gunther said, addressing the lead officer at the head of the formation. "How may I help you today?"

"We are hungry," the officer replied curtly. "Fill the bellies of the men so we can carry on."

"Of course, Sire! On the house as always for our military! The Sultan is Great!" Gunther proclaimed, his tone full of enthusiasm as he gestured toward a group of empty tables near the bar, positioned well away from Father and the children.

"The Sultan is Great," the officer said.

Most of the patrons in The Tavern were regulars, well aware that even in the presence of gold tongues, they should not let the atmosphere sour. If any suspicion or violence marred the peace, the Sultan's men would be swift to destroy the establishment. So, the crowd quickly resumed their singing, chatting, and laughter, quietly acknowledging the presence of the Sultan's enforcers but refusing to let it ruin their night.

As the guests continued with their activities, Gunther personally led the Ghazi soldiers to a private corner, distancing them from the drunken revelers and rowdy patrons. A few of the Ghazi remained standing, keeping a vigilant watch to ensure no one encroached on their space.

"I will fetch a barmaid for you, Sire," Gunther said with a practiced smile. "Might I ask what business brings so many of the Sultan's will to my establishment today?"

"I shan't speak," the officer replied, pulling out a heavy pouch of gald and placing it on the table with a dull thud. The faint clinking of coins inside punctuated his words. "Unless, of course, you know of the one-eyed man and the golden-eyed child."

"Ah," Gunther said, his eyes flickering to the pouch as he assessed its weight. "Interesting."

—

Father seized the opportunity while Gunther was distracted, quickly gathering the children and signaling for a barmaid.

"But I haven't finished my steak!" Tariq whined.

"Should've ate faster then," Hamza said with a teasing elbow to his side.

The barmaid quickly approached, recognizing Father immediately. Everyone in The Tavern was familiar with him, and they knew better than to hesitate if he ever needed assistance. Meanwhile, Gunther continued his act, engaging the Ghazi with small talk, trying to keep up the appearance of hospitality.

"Let us access the backdoor," Father instructed the maid, his tone calm but firm. "Children, stay low and let the patrons shield your exit."

The children nodded in unison, obeying without question.

"Of course," the barmaid replied quietly. "Follow me."

The group moved seamlessly through the crowd, blending into the lively disarray of The Tavern. Skirting around the stage, they slipped through a discreet side door tucked near its edge, entering the dimly lit backrooms.

The barmaid led them down a narrow hallway, her steps swift and purposeful. At the far end, she stopped at a sturdy door, turning the knob cautiously. She peered outside, scanning for any signs of prying eyes, before easing the door open with deliberate care.

The group stayed concealed in the shadows, tense and silent, awaiting her signal as she stepped outside to confirm the coast was clear.

The barmaid froze as two Ghazi came into view, their backs turned to the doorway. Their imposing figures cast long shadows in the dim light. The Tavern's usual lively atmosphere felt distant now, replaced by the tense stillness of a cordoned-off building. Their hands rested lightly on the hilts of their weapons, a silent warning to any who might disturb their vigil.

"Oh my, you scared me!" the barmaid exclaimed, feigning surprise with a touch of genuine nervousness.

"Ma'am," one of the Ghazi said, his tone formal but wary. "What brings you out here?"

The barmaid began fanning herself, exuding a casual air as she unbuttoned the top of her blouse. Her movements were calculated, a distraction meant to draw the guards' attention and buy time. Smiling flirtatiously, she tried to disarm their suspicion, though her sharp, alert eyes betrayed her underlying caution.

"It's so hot in there," she whined, stepping forward slightly before turning to face the doorway again, keeping the Ghazi within her sight. "I just needed some fresh air."

Meanwhile, the Ghazi had their attention on another pair of eyes.

Father seized the moment as the Ghazi's attention remained fixed on the barmaid. He moved quietly, his steps measured and purposeful, positioning himself just behind the door frame. The guards were distracted, their eyes locked on the barmaid's feigned allure, oblivious to the danger lurking so close.

Before the Ghazi could react, Father delivered a swift, open-palmed strike to the left guard's nose, the impact sending the back of his head crashing into the wall, rendering him unconscious. Without hesitation, Father followed up with a precise palm strike to the right guard's temple, sending him staggering and then collapsing to the ground. He paused briefly, scanning the fallen bodies to ensure they were truly incapacitated, taking advantage of their lowered guard. The children who lurked in the shadows couldn't even comprehend the speed and precision of his actions.

"Thank you," Father said to the maid.

"No problem," she replied with a light giggle, buttoning up her blouse. "For a moment, I thought I'd have to pull a few more strings." She winked playfully. "Until next time." With that, she slipped back into the building.

The children emerged cautiously, stepping around the unconscious bodies scattered near the doorway. They glanced at the scene in silence, their expressions a mix of awe and unease.

"Let us return home," Father said, his voice calm yet resolute.

Though the building's perimeter was compromised, the labyrinth of the lower hive provided them an advantage: countless alleyways and hidden shortcuts. The children instinctively gathered close as Father guided them into a narrow, shadowed alleyway. It was a longer route back home, but for now, it was the safest.

—

The familiar knob of the shed door turned and creaked open.

"Man, it feels so good to be home! Didn't know Father was such a badass!" Hamza exclaimed, stretching his arms wide as he flopped onto the comfort of his rolled-up bed.

"That was indeed an interesting trip," Naji added, settling into his own spot with a thoughtful nod.

Despite the violence directed at both the group and the Ghazi, the children seemed almost unfazed. Their resilience, forged by growing up in the harsh realities of the lower hive, made them accustomed to such dangers. Father's teachings had shaped them too, instilling in them the strength to endure and adapt to the world around them.

By this time, the sun had already set, and the lanterns flickered to life, casting a warm glow over the streets. One by one, the children entered the building, Father carefully accounting for each of them. Once everyone was inside and safe, it wouldn't be long before Father would have to part from them again, preparing for his late-night activities.

""I will be leaving again," Father said, his tone firm. "Remain hidden for the day and do not cause any trouble. Is that understood?"

"Aye," the children replied in unison, fully grasping the gravity of the situation. They knew better than to be mischievous, especially with the Ghazi actively searching for them—particularly for Habi, the most distinct and easiest to recognize among them.

Once again, Father shut the door behind him, his footsteps gradually fading into the night.

"Man, I am gassed out," Tariq yawned. "Lost our gald. Father wrecked some folks. Habi is the most wanted criminal in all of Koura. Ate some good food. I'm surprised we're still breathing!"

"I'm not the most wanted!" Habi cried out indignantly, drawing laughter from Tariq.

Rafi was the first to step in, gently patting her head to comfort her.

"It was a crazy day," Rafi agreed. "But we should all rest up and get ready for tomorrow. The deal is still up, isn't it?"

"So even after we almost got killed and Father gave us a lecture, you still want to go through with the plan?" Taliba asked, scowling.

"Well, we didn't get killed, and Father basically said he doesn't care anymore as long as we come back with all our limbs. Am I wrong?" Rafi shrugged.

"He didn't *exactly* say that, but—"

"Then there's no problem," Rafi interrupted. "We rest now, and tomorrow, we continue with our plan to get out of this dump!"

Taliba placed a hand on her forehead, shaking her head. "You're going to get us all killed one day," she said, rolling her eyes but smirking despite herself.

"Not if we stick together and have Father beating the crap out of those Ghazi," Rafi grinned. "Sounds like a good time, doesn't it, Habi?"

"But they're still looking for me," Habi said, her voice tinged with worry.

"They'll forget about you when the sun rises again," Hamza interjected confidently. "Don't worry about it. They've got better things to do!"

"Right then!" Rafi declared, standing tall and raising his voice like a military commander rallying his troops. "Let us rest! Tomorrow morning, we'll plan everything and head out for some riches!"

Habi gently applauded in awe and admiration.

Taliba on the other hand threw a dirty rag at Rafi and shouted, "Oh, go to bed already!"

The children laughed together before crawling into their bedrolls and extinguishing the ceiling lantern.

"Good night," Habi wished to the others as she laid in her bedroll, bundled up.

"Good night," the rest repeated.

—

The moon was at its peak, casting a soft glow through the shed. The only sounds that broke the silence were the occasional murmur of passersby and the distant chirps of nocturnal creatures. As Hamza's snores filled the air, little Habi suddenly awoke from her sleep—she needed to use the restroom again.

"No ghosts. No ghosts. No ghosts," Habi whispered to herself, her small voice barely audible as she waddled out the shed door, heading toward the back with cautious steps.

She quietly made her way to the bucket, managing to trinkle away without disturbance, though she half-expected some sort of encounter in the stillness of the night. She savored the endless expanse of stars above, breathing in the crisp night air of Koura, even if it carried a hint of dust.

Once she had finished, Habi jogged toward the front of the shed. Her heart stopped for a second, and her skin crawled. She was momentarily horrified by the sudden appearance of a young man, just as terrified as she was, standing before her.

"You scared me, little one!" the man said, raising his hands up as if Habi were a rabid dog. "What are you doing up so late?"

Habi's horror slowly gave way to doubt. She had no idea who this man was. *Father told us not to talk to strangers,* she reminded herself.

The man examined Habi for a bit, noticing a major feature.

"You're the golden-eyed child I heard about!" the man said in awe. "You and I have much to talk about. Care to join me on a nightly stroll?" He offered his hand, but Habi hesitated. Her instincts screamed for her to run from the stranger, and a flood of questions raced through her mind. *This was a bad idea.*

What if he hurts me? And *What if he turned me into the Ghazi?* Crossed her mind. She was prepared to make a run for it.

"I mean no harm, if that's what you're thinking," the man reassured, his voice soft. He then reached into his ragged pants pocket and pulled out a small toy. It was a tiny, handmade doll, crafted from wood and strings. Its face was adorned with a small, blushing smile, and its limbs were able to move around.

Habi, being as impulsive as she was, couldn't help but take an interest in the doll. She hesitated for a moment before accepting the offer, her eyes wide with curiosity. It was her first doll, and something about it felt special, even though she couldn't explain why.

"So it's a trip then!" The man smiled as he watched Habi mess around with the doll's limbs. "Follow me if you're interested. It'll be fun, I promise."

The man slowly walked away, and Habi, torn between caution and curiosity, glanced back at the shed. She knew she should be sleeping, preparing for the plan she had with the others tomorrow. But something in her stirred, a desire for adventure. Without thinking too much, she waddled behind the man, stepping away from the safety of home.

—

HABI

The duo wandered through the quiet corners of the lower hive, moving through the maze of dark alleys where little stirred. The distant hum of the city was muffled, leaving only the sound of their footsteps echoing off the crumbling stone walls.

"It seems you've taken a liking to the toy," the man said with a smirk, watching Habi play with it. "Given it a name yet?"

"Not yet," Habi replied, her focus still on the toy.

"That's fine," the man chuckled. "A friend gave it to me when I was younger, and I've kept it ever since. But I think I've outgrown it now."

"You have a good friend," Habi said with a small smile.

"And so do you, little one," the man replied warmly. "I've seen how your siblings look out for you."

Habi's eyes widened as she looked up at the man while continuing to walk.

"You know Rafi and the rest?" she asked curiously.

"Not really," the man replied with a faint smile. "I've only seen them with you. You all seem so happy together."

A brief moment of silence fell in between them as they rounded a corner in the alleys.

"Where are we going?" Habi asked, her voice filled with innocent curiosity.

The man took a deep breath, looking up at the sky with a serene smile. "A beautiful place with answers, little one. That is all. It's been great to finally meet you," he said.

"Oh! Father always says I should introduce myself when making a friend. I'm Habi. What's your name?" Habi asked.

The man's smile widened as he replied, "My name is Assad."

As the two exchanged quiet words, they finally reached an open patch of land, nestled behind several crumbling ruins on the outer rim of the hive. The sand here was soft and undisturbed, as if untouched by time. In the center of this small square of sand stood a lone tree, its jagged branches reaching out like twisted arms, with only a few leaves clinging to its brittle limbs.

The duo walked over to the tree and finally stopped in their tracks.

"Please, sit with me," Assad said, settling himself against the trunk of a tree.

Habi nodded and mimicked his actions, clutching the doll tightly to her chest as she sat down beside him.

"We're in the darkest corner of the lower hive. Look up," Assad suggested, his tone calm but purposeful.

Both of them looked up at the sky, and the city's lights seemed almost absent, allowing the stars to shine brighter than Habi had ever seen. Her jaw dropped as she took in the vastness of it all, seeing more stars than she ever imagined, scattered across the heavens and nestled between one another. Some of the brighter ones even formed shapes in the sky, though Habi had no idea what those constellations represented. She marveled at their beauty, feeling as if she'd discovered a whole new world above her.

"Beautiful, isn't it?" Assad said with a gentle smile, leaning back against the tree and resting his head on the trunk. "My friends and I used to come here every night to gaze at the stars."

"It is beautiful," Habi replied, her smile mirroring his as she mimicked his relaxed posture. "Thank you for the toy and for showing me this spot."

"No problem, little one," Assad said warmly.

The two lay in silence, their gazes lost in the endless sea of stars above. An ocean of lights stretched out, unbothered by the world below. It wasn't until that moment that Assad finally broke the quiet.

"Habi, do you know who your Father is?" Assad asked, his gaze still fixed on the sky.

"Yes, he's my Papa. He takes care of me and gives me and the others a home," Habi replied, absently fiddling with the doll in her hands.

"I see. But you also know him as Saif Sabbah, don't you?"

Habi grunted and nodded in affirmation.

"I see," Assad said again, his tone thoughtful. "It seems none of you truly know who he is. Perhaps I can shed some light on it?"

"Story time?" Habi asked eagerly, her face lighting up.

Assad laughed softly, mimicking her earlier nod and grunt. "Yes, yes, yes," he chuckled. "Here's the story."

And so Assad spoke:

"Long ago, when the current Sultan inherited the throne, Saif Sabbah was still young. You weren't born yet. But when the new Sultan took power, he immediately seized control of the city and shifted the tides of rights and equality. The walls that separate us now once welcomed new districts back then, until the Sultan, in a move that made no sense, claimed the city was running low on resources, despite all the trade flowing in. So, he separated the higher and lower hives, redirecting the goods to everywhere but here, to the lower hive. Everyone here had to work for a living—if it was even possible. Those who were stuck in a hive when the segregation happened were trapped. The walls became borders, not entrances.

"You see, when someone gains power, there's no longer any concept of good or evil. There's only power—and that's exactly what he took. The middle and higher hives appreciated the new order, but the lower hive, just as populous as the others, was left to suffer.

"Little did they know, everyone would suffer. The lower hive was abandoned, forced to fight for survival. The middle hive lived relatively normal lives, but under the Sultan's rule, they were taxed heavily, their children and adults conscripted at the Sultan's whim. The people of the higher hive remained isolated, unaware of the lives of those below them. The Sultan loved those folk, keeping them blissfully ignorant. And the nobles, well, they were the only ones who truly lived in wealth and prosperity.

"Your father, Saif Sabbah, was a rebel at heart. He was just like you all when he was younger—adventurous, daring, and rebellious. But most of all, he fought back against the Sultan's tyranny.

"Saif Sabbah would network with people all over the city, influencing them with the power of gald, wisdom, or pure charisma. He amassed an army, marching to the Sultan's gates, wiping out his loyal men. His greatest achievement, though, wasn't just rallying the people—it was forming a personal group of elites.

"They were known as *Hassazi*, or Assassins, in the old tongue. Saif and his trusted group kept their identity a secret. That's where the 'hush' gesture comes from—their motto was '*Silence is strength*'. They went on to eliminate many important figures serving the Sultan, right up until they reached the gates of the tower. But that's where it ended. No one knows for sure, but it's claimed that the Sultan possessed powerful abilities, not just for himself but for those closest to him. His army crushed Saif's forces easily, recruiting more with little effort, while Saif lost his friends, his family, and an eye.

"After that, Saif retired to the lower hive, where he had grown up. He helped those who refused to fight, caring for the youth and elderly. He even tried to adopt orphans, training them to be Hassazi, but they were too immature, too naive, and they paid the price. Now, he lives as a scholar, teaching those who seek knowledge. That's how he found you, Habi."

Assad finished.

He then turned over to see Habi's expression, but he ended up flabbergasted instead.

Habi was fast asleep, holding the doll tight to her chest.

Assad would then chuckle and stand up.

"Well played, little one," he said as he walked away from the tree, letting the little one rest under the night sky.

—

Much later, in the early morning, when the sun still hid behind the dunes, Habi woke again—not because she needed to go to the restroom, but because someone was shaking her. Too tired to react, her vision was blurry, and a tall figure slowly emerged before her.

"Habi, what are you doing here?" Father said, his voice laced with concern. "Are you out here by yourself? Habi, wake up."

Habi groggily mumbled a few incoherent words in response, her eyelids barely lifting.

"What did you say?" Father asked, his worry deepening.

"Assad brought me here," Habi groaned sleepily, turning over and drifting off again.

Father's eyes widened, and had the children seen his expression, they would have been even more appalled. He took a cautious step back, then glanced over at where Habi was lying. Beside her head, an iron slate was embedded into the tree, bearing an inscription that read:

Here lies Assad Sabbah. May he rest. Never forgotten.

Chapter Nine

The sun rose gently over the horizon, casting its warm light on the people of Koura. The children awoke, stretching and yawning as they began their morning routine. However, something was amiss.

"Guys, where's Habi?" Rafi asked, his voice sharp with concern as he noticed her usual spot next to him was empty.

The children glanced at her vacant bedroll, then scanned the shed, realizing she was nowhere to be found.

"Uh oh," Hamza gasped, his alarm growing.

"We are so in trouble," Tariq groaned, placing both hands on top of his head.

"Did she wander outside by herself last night? What if someone took her?" Taliba asked, her worry evident.

"We were all asleep. We wouldn't have known," Rafi muttered, frustration creeping into his voice. He cursed under his breath. "And today of all days! I'm going to go find her!"

Rafi burst toward the shed door, flinging it open, only to be met by a familiar figure.

"Oh, hello, Father," Rafi stuttered, relief washing over him as he noticed another familiar face cradled in Father's arms. "Oh, thank the heavens, you found her."

Habi was still asleep, cradled in Father's arms. Without a word, Father walked inside and gently placed Habi on top of her bedroll. An object fell from her tiny paws, which worried Father even further. It was the doll that Assad had given her.

The children, oblivious to Father's mood, gathered around him, showering him with questions.

"Where did you find her, Father?" Naji asked, stepping closer.

"Is she okay?" Taliba added, her voice tinged with worry.

Amid the flurry of questions, Father chose to answer Hamza's, who pointed to the doll that had fallen to the floor and asked, "Where did that doll come from?"

Father took a deep breath and stared at both the doll and Habi's resting face.

"Sara made that doll for a friend," Father revealed, a deep frown settling on his face. "It was a long time ago."

"So Sara gave a toy to Habi when she was out and about? Not fair," Hamza grumbled, crossing his arms.

"No, the doll—" Father paused, his expression darkening, "the doll was buried along with the friend."

"Oh," Hamza murmured, his bravado fading as he sucked in a breath. "Sorry."

"It's a mystery indeed," Father continued, his voice steady but grim. "But we know nothing until she awakens. Tend to her, and I will fetch breakfast. Do not let her out of your sight if she stirs."

The children grunted and nodded in agreement as Father hurriedly left. They couldn't help but wonder what had stirred him so early in the morning. But of all things to wake Habi, it was the sound of the shed door slamming shut.

"Where am I?" Habi mumbled groggily, smacking her lips and blinking slowly.

"You're home," Rafi replied gently. "You weren't in your bed when we woke up. You had us worried."

Habi slowly sat up, her eyes falling on the doll lying on the floor beside her. She picked it up carefully and cradled it in her hands, whispering, "Good morning, little one."

"Where did you get that doll, Habi?" Taliba asked, her voice still laced with confusion over the chaotic morning.

"Oh, I made a friend last night," Habi said brightly. "His name was Assad, and he took me to places where we could watch the pretty stars together. It was exciting."

"You did *what*!?" Taliba's jaw dropped. "Habi, that is dangerous! Father taught you better!"

Habi flinched a bit from Taliba's sudden rise of volume.

"But he gave me a toy, and I'm fine, aren't I?" Habi pouted, clutching the doll tightly.

"Wait," Naji interrupted, his tone suddenly serious. "Did you say his name was Assad?"

Habi nodded quickly. "Yes, his name was Assad."

Naji's eyes narrowed as the memory clicked. "Back when Sara was here, she mentioned that name. She mentioned *Assad*."

Rafi's brow rose in agreement. "You're right. She did."

Naji leaned closer, his curiosity intensifying. "Did your friend say anything, Habi? Did he mention anything at all?" His questions came quickly, his instincts sharp. Whether it was about Father's past, the fall of Heaven's Roots, or something supernatural, Naji's desire to piece together the truth was evident.

Habi furrowed her brow, thinking carefully as her gaze shifted between her siblings and the doll in her hands.

"I don't remember much, but I do think he said words like, 'Saif' and 'Has-ah-see.'"

"Has-what-see?" Rafi echoed, voicing the same confusion the others shared.

"Has-ah-see," Habi repeated slowly. "He said Father was one of them, but I forgot what they do."

Naji muttered the word to himself, "Has-ah-see... Has-ah-see," over and over, hoping the repetition might jog some memory from the books he had read. But nothing came to mind.

"I don't know. I've never heard of it," Naji admitted with a sigh, finally surrendering to the mystery.

"Rafi," Habi suddenly said, drawing his attention.

"Yes?" Rafi replied, turning his head toward her.

"His name is Rafi too," Habi announced with a bright smile, practically shoving the doll into his face.

Rafi blinked, caught between pride and unease, unsure how to respond. Despite his confusion, he couldn't help but feel a strange sense of joy at her excitement. To humor her, he stammered, "Ah, hello, little Rafi." Saying his own name felt odd, but he played along, embracing the playful absurdity of the moment.

As the children gathered and played, neglecting their morning bath, Father returned, carrying a basket of freshly baked potatoes. Simple, yet hearty, the meal was perfect for the children, offering both comfort and sustenance to start their day.

"Father, can Rafi have one too?" Habi asked, holding up her doll for emphasis.

Father opened his mouth to say, *Rafi is already getting one*, but stopped himself, realizing she was talking about the doll.

"There are only enough shares for each of us," Father replied, a faint smirk tugging at his lips. "Perhaps you could halve yours with him?" he added, playing along.

Habi was content with that answer.

He handed out the baked potatoes to the children before taking one for himself. The children savored every bite, relishing the soft, steaming insides as the warmth filled their senses. They imagined how much better it could have been with cheese, a rare but delightful treat they'd had before.

"Father, I have a question," Naji said, his tone cautious but curious.

"Ask away," Father replied, taking a bite of his potato.

"What's a *has-ah-see*?"

Father froze mid-chew, his body stiffening. Slowly, he lowered the potato, holding it just under his chin as his sharp gaze bore into Naji's eyes.

"Where did you hear that word?" Father demanded, his voice cold and scowling.

"Habi," Naji admitted without hesitation. "She said her friend Assad mentioned it."

Father's gaze shifted to Habi, who was innocently chewing on her potato. A pang of pain struck his heart as the weight of the situation settled in, but despite it, he decided to ask anyway.

"Habi, what did Assad say to you?" Father asked, his tone measured but firm.

Habi paused, gulping down her bite before responding. "Assad said that you were a has-ah-see and that you did good things for everyone." She looked at Father with wide, innocent eyes, unaware of the tension her words had sparked.

Habi smiled, thinking it was a revelation worth sharing, but Father's expression remained unchanged. Without a word, he quickly walked to the shed door and locked it, causing the children to exchange worried glances. He then knelt beside Habi, his shoulders heavy with a sigh.

"Little one, do not ever say that word ever again. Do not say it around strangers," Father warned in whispers. "That word carries a weight that predates your births, and the Sultan will smite you if you ever so speak it in his presence."

Habi froze, her expression shifting from joy to sorrow as she realized her mistake. She knew, in that moment, that she had done something wrong.

"None of you were ever supposed to know," Father said, frowning as his gaze lingered on Habi's golden eyes. "But it seems the universe had other plans." He paused, his voice growing heavier. "Do not let the word 'Hassazi' leave your mouths outside these doors. It stays here, within our home. Do I make myself clear?"

The children slowly nodded, frightened by Father's morbid emotions.

"Habi, your friend Assad," Father began, his voice heavy with emotion as he sighed and hesitated. "He is no longer with us. He passed away many years ago." He paused, his gaze softening as he looked at her. "He was a child of mine."

Habi held her breath, the weight of the realization settling in. She now understood that she might have interacted with a spirit, just as the stories had foretold.

"But—but he was real," Habi said, her voice trembling as tears welled up in her eyes. "He even gave me his toy. He showed me where the stars were brightest." She clutched the doll tightly, her small frame shaking as she struggled to process Father's words.

Father remained silent and looked down at the floor, knowing that this day would come, specifically for the revelation of his past. He was a Hassazi, an assassin, the founder of the sect.

"Father, are you saying I saw a ghost?" Habi cried, her voice trembling as she struggled to keep her composure. "I—I just wanted to be normal, and I thought—" Her words faltered, and tears spilled down her cheeks. The truth was too much to bear. She had spoken to a dead man, someone who not only unearthed fragments of her father's past but also tethered her to the legacy of the old family. The legend of the golden-eyed lady now felt all too real—a destiny she desperately wished to escape.

"Habi—" Rafi murmured softly, pulling her into a comforting hug and gently patting her head. "Let's not think about it. Maybe if you don't believe it, it won't happen."

Rafi understood exactly why Habi was crying. She adored Father's stories, always taking them deeply to heart. Now, the parallels she saw between herself and the Necromantia filled her with fear, making the legend feel uncomfortably close to reality.

Father sighed deeply and stood, pulling his hood over his head.

"I must depart now. Please take care of her—and each other," he instructed, his voice firm but edged with concern. "Heed my lessons, children." Unlocking the door, he gave them a final glance before stepping outside, leaving the shed behind—and the children alone with a sobbing Habi.

"Habi, I'm sorry," Naji said softly, guilt weighing heavily on his tone. He felt responsible for putting her on the spot and triggering her tears.

Taliba reached over and took control of the doll in Habi's hands, holding it up in front of her face.

"Habi! Don't cry!" she said, attempting a poor imitation of Rafi's voice by lowering her pitch. "We are here for you, and we love you!" Taliba then made the doll tap Habi's forehead lightly, adding a playful *mwah* sound as if the doll had kissed her.

Rafi shot her a flat, unimpressed look, while Taliba grinned mischievously, clearly amused with herself.

"Think about it this way, Habi," Hamza said, jumping in with his usual enthusiasm. "You just gained a bunch of cool kid points!"

Habi continued to sob, but her tears gradually slowed, replaced by curious, wide-eyed glances as she looked at the doll.

Do it, Taliba mouthed at Rafi, pointing a finger at her lips with a teasing grin.

Really? Rafi mouthed back, his expression a mix of reluctance and disbelief.

Taliba nodded firmly, her expression encouraging.

With a resigned sigh, Rafi leaned closer to Habi, pulling her gently into a hug. He pressed a soft kiss to her cheek and tenderly wiped away the last of her tears. Habi sniffled, her sobs quieting as she leaned into the comforting gesture.

As her tears subsided, Habi gazed into Rafi's eyes, her expression soft and unguarded. The silence stretched between them, growing heavier with each passing moment. Finally, unable to take the tension any longer, Rafi spoke.

"Please don't make this awkward," he begged, his voice a mix of exasperation and quiet humor.

Habi quickly latched onto Rafi, burying her head into his chest and wiping the last of her tears on him.

"Thank you, everyone," she said, her voice muffled but full of sincerity.

She pulled away gently and sat back, her small hands reaching for the half-eaten potato. She took another bite, her expression distant, yet somehow calmer.

"I'm tired of crying," Habi pouted, her voice tinged with frustration.

This time, it was Taliba who reached out to gently pat her head. "And that's how you know you're normal," Taliba said reassuringly. "You cry and feel, just like anyone else. You know Father's only worried about all of us."

The others nodded in agreement, including Habi, who managed a small, hesitant smile.

Rafi sighed, relief washing over him, before breaking into a smile himself. He stood up, stretching his arms.

"Well then, Habi, let's stop worrying about that stuff!" Rafi declared, his voice rising with enthusiasm as he raised his fist like a commander rallying his troops for a grand charge. "Aren't you ready for adventure today? The day has finally come! Take my hand if you deem yourself worthy!"

He extended his hand dramatically toward her, a playful grin spreading across his face, as if daring her to rise to the occasion.

As Habi slowly reached for Rafi's hand, Hamza quickly grabbed it instead. Rafi swatted his hand away, his focus never wavering from Habi. Once her hand was safely clasped in his, he helped her to her feet, offering a steady support as she stood.

"So it is done," Rafi said with a warm smile, patting Habi's back. "You'll always be Habi to me!"

That small, playful gesture brought a bright grin to Habi's face. It was time to set aside the worries of conspiracy theories and focus on the present, working toward the future they all envisioned. The children gathered around, their expressions united, before all eyes turned to Rafi.

"Right then, what's the plan?" Taliba asked.

—

Rafi spread an old, torn piece of paper in front of the children and, with quick movements, scrambled over to Father's desk. He grabbed the jar of ink and a quill, then dipped it in the ink before starting to sketch. His lines were rough, childlike, but purposeful. He drew jagged shapes, marking out the shed with a simple box. The sewage tunnel was represented by two parallel lines, and the border gate was a large, bold circle. With whatever fragments he could recall from the other side of the middle hive, he scribbled hastily—the larger homes, the merchant stalls selling luxuries, all rendered in a crude, almost frantic scrawl.

Rafi pointed at the shed, and then he shifted it over to the sewage tunnel off to the side of the paper.

"I'm not going in there," Taliba said, shaking her head firmly.

"I can't even fit in there," Hamza added with a shrug.

"None of us are going in there," Rafi said with a chuckle. "This needs to be a team effort. That's why we're planning to take another route."

He then sketched a large circle over the drawing of the border wall on the far right of the paper, tapping his finger on it for emphasis.

"We're going through the wall," Rafi declared.

The children sat around dumbfounded, wondering what he meant by that. They knew going through the border gate wasn't an option, so that meant there had to be an exploit somewhere.

"When we were walking with Father to donate the gald, I noticed a pattern in this area near the wall," Rafi explained, pointing to the circled section on the paper. "There's a decent number of sandstone buildings we can climb, and they lead toward a small gap in the wall. But the problem here is—"

"It's in the Sleeping Complex, isn't it?" Taliba interrupted. Rafi nodded in confirmation. "Makes sense. That area's the darkest part of the lower hive, and no one really maintains it because it's dangerous."

"Wait, so let me get this straight," Hamza said, drawing Rafi's full attention. "You want us to climb buildings, avoid bad guys, and crawl through a hole in the wall? What if we don't all fit? And even if we do, how do we know what's waiting for us on the other side?"

Rafi smiled to himself as he added a line through the wall, marking the hole he'd mentioned earlier. His hand moved quickly, drawing more rough squares beyond the line, symbolizing the unknown spaces beyond the tunnel. His eyes twinkled with a quiet determination, the sketch becoming a map of both the known and the imagined, a roadmap of the future they would soon walk together.

"We'll all fit," Rafi reassured, his tone confident. "It looked much bigger than the drain tunnel—trust me on that. As for the other side, from what I remember, there should be buildings close to the hole."

"The only way to find out is to get there, yeah?" Tariq chimed in.

"Exactly," Rafi said with a nod, appreciating Tariq's support.

Habi looked at the drawing, trying to understand everything, but instead, she could only understand that they must go on top of a box, pass a line, and go onto another box.

"And that's just the route," Rafi continued, his tone shifting to a more serious one. "Now we need to figure out what to bring with us. Hoods, pouches, weapons—even that's worth considering."

"Why would we need weapons?" Naji asked, his brow furrowing.

"It's the Sleeping Complex, Naji," Rafi replied. "Who knows what they'd wanna do if they saw six kids wandering around."

"How about a bag for the goods?" Hamza suggested.

"You know what? Just because you came up with a good idea, you're now carrying the bag if we find one," Rafi said with a grin.

Hamza cursed as the children laughed.

"Good news for us is that I made a friend who lives down in the complex some time back. Gotta network around here," Rafi said, clearly proud of himself, convinced everything would go smoothly. "He's already in on it, and he should be able to help us out with what we need."

"How long have you known him?" Taliba asked, raising a skeptical brow.

"About a week," Rafi replied casually.

"Amazing," Taliba sighed, rubbing her temples.

—

By noon, the children were ready, each one donning their ragged hoods and wearing the handmade pouches around their necks. Though the pouches were intended for carrying gald, Habi took advantage of hers to place her new little friend inside, ensuring it would be with her wherever she went. They checked each other for proper fit, their movements efficient and practiced. Satisfied, they stepped out of the shed, the door creaking shut behind them, and began their journey toward the Sleeping Complex.

As they walked, the children discussed further preparations for their journey. Suggestions flew between them—canteens for water, rations to stave off hunger, and even blankets for warmth when the night grew cold. Despite the plans being thorough, none of them anticipated an overnight adventure; their goal was to complete the task at hand and return before the day was done.

HABI

The children moved through the cluttered streets, huddled together as they navigated the rubble and the crowd of aimless citizens, all drifting through the lower hive in search of a better life. The air was thick with sand and dust, kicked up by the bustling crowd, making each step more difficult. Rafi led the way, familiar with the route and the person they needed to meet. Hamza, ever cautious, took the rear, convinced his position made him the best shield against any surprise attacks. The rest of the children walked in between, with Habi at the center, protected by the circle of bodies around her. It wasn't just her fragility that placed her there—it was the shared understanding that the Ghazi might still be watching. They all knew the danger of being the golden-eyed child, and none of them took it lightly.

As they walked, Habi's thoughts drifted in an endless tide. The heat clung to her, sinking into her skin despite the shade of her hood. The past few days had been overwhelming, each moment more impossible than the last. First, she had been hunted by the authorities, just because she happened to be at the wrong place at the wrong time with Rafi. Then, she had unwittingly exposed Father's past as a Hassazi. And as if that weren't enough, she had discovered that she could speak with the dead. It felt as though fate had cast a heavy hand on her, pushing her to the center of a story she never asked to be part of. The weight of it all sat on her chest, and she couldn't shake the feeling that the universe had spun her into a role she didn't want to play.

To calm herself, she reached into the pouch and softly rubbed the doll, a small comfort in the midst of the chaos. Taliba, walking beside her, noticed the worry etched on Habi's face.

"You okay, Habi?" Taliba whispered, glancing at her younger sister.

"I am okay," Habi groaned, fanning herself weakly. "It's hot."

"I know," Taliba agreed, wiping her brow as the heat bore down on them. Everyone felt it. "We should've brought some valuables to trade for water or something."

Rafi could feel Taliba's eyes glare daggers at his back, overhearing the conversation.

"You're right, okay?" Rafi sighed, trying to keep his composure. "I'm just a little excited. Let that fuel you for now. We're almost there. It'll be colder once we're in the complex."

Hamza attempted to spit to emphasize his frustration, but nothing came out—his mouth was too dry, and his lips were cracked.

"Are we there yet?" Hamza whined, his voice hoarse.

—

The children finally found respite from the direct sunlight, though the heat still clung to the air as they ventured deeper into the Sleeping Complex. The place, situated in the lower hive, was shielded from the sun's harsh rays, thanks to the tall walls and the Sultan's imposing tower. As the sun rose and set, the angle of the structures ensured that the area stayed in shadow throughout the day. The giant platform that extended from the tower only added to the darkness, casting an ever-present, looming shadow over the complex.

However, the shade did little to ease the suffocating atmosphere. The air was thick with the stench of rot and blood, an odor that seemed to seep from every corner of the decaying complex. Rats scurried across the cracked stone and rotting wood, darting between buildings made of crumbling sandstone. The complex was a place where survival was the only thing that mattered, and the children knew better than to draw attention to themselves. Every step was measured, every glance careful, for even the smallest notice from the residents here could spell trouble.

Rafi motioned for the group to be silent as they maneuvered through the maze of narrow alleyways, winding paths, and steep, crumbling stairs. The children moved as quietly as they could, sticking close together. Most of the complex's inhabitants were too absorbed in their own illegal dealings to notice the young intruders. The air was thick with the hustle of the underworld—whispers of trade, muffled arguments, and the occasional clang of metal from shady deals. The children pressed on, knowing their path was dangerous but determined to continue.

"Where's your contact?" Taliba whispered sharply to Rafi, her tone tense.

"I don't know. That's what we're looking for," Rafi whispered back, glancing around.

"Are you *serious*?!" Taliba hissed, her frustration boiling over. "You don't have a plan to meet up with them? We're screwed if we keep mucking about!" Her voice, though still hushed, trembled with barely contained anger as she glared at Rafi.

Rafi quickly hushed Taliba, raising his arm to signal the others to stop. Ahead of them, a trio of kids, around their age, were huddled in the middle of the alley, laughing and chatting as they played some sort of game.

"Oi!" Rafi called out to them as he walked forward. Taliba kept switching her gaze between Rafi and the kids with worry, but soon followed along with the rest.

All three of the kids turned their heads and looked directly at them, pausing their laughter for a moment in case it was an assailant.

"Ah hell, you actually came!" one of the boys laughed, locking eyes with Rafi. His grin was wide and mischievous as he stood up, brushing off his clothes. "Hey, hey, want in?" he asked, gesturing for the group to join the small circle where two other boys were engrossed in their game.

The boy who called out to them was caked in dirt, his features hard to make out. Dark circles under his eyes made his hazel-colored gaze stand out more than usual. When he spoke, his jagged, yellowed teeth showed, some of them missing entirely.

As the group approached the trio, their fear grew. A closer inspection revealed unsettling details that made their hearts race.

The boys were not playing a game, but instead, were playing with a dead dog. They were skinning and gutting it out, causing Taliba to hurl inside her mouth.

"Found this guy walkin' about and thought we could snatch it for food," the boy said with a grin. "Want some? The meat's pretty soft when it's cooked."

"No thanks," Rafi replied curtly, speaking on behalf of the group.

"Sucks for you if your tummy starts growlin' later," the boy teased. "So, what, you still up to cross the wall?"

"That's all we're here for, Faruq," Rafi said firmly. "Maybe some water and proper rations as well, if possible."

Faruq then stood up and wiped his hands on his clothes in order to remove some of the dog's blood on him.

"Sure, I can hook you up. Just make sure you keep your promise about my share," Faruq said with a smirk.

"Of course," Rafi replied, his tone firm, sealing the agreement.

The boys around the dog began filling their bags with the dog's meat and organs. Faruq did the same before leading the group to the point of entry. Their bags leaked with blood as they left the remains picked clean on the ground. Flies were already starting to return and gather around the carcass.

"Come on then," Faruq instructed, tossing the bag over his shoulder as it gushed against his back. The trio then began to wander off down the alleyway with the group trailing them.

The walk was short, and soon they arrived at Faruq's small, makeshift tent nestled beside a weathered wooden building. The trio dropped their bags onto the ground with a casual thud. Two of them, after exchanging a few words, wandered off deeper into the alley, leaving Faruq and the group standing in silence.

"We'll be back with wood. We eatin' good tonight!" one of the boys chanted as he walked away with another, leaving Faruq to focus fully on his clients.

"Right then, what do y'all need before the climb?" Faruq asked, ducking into his tent.

Rafi didn't hesitate to list their requests. "Canteens or flasks for water. Some rations for the trip. A backpack for the goods. And weapons would be nice."

"Damn, boy, I ain't your mama," Faruq quipped with a wide grin. "But I can get you all of that right now. Hol' up."

Faruq dove into his tent and tossed a few sets of small canteens, a leather backpack, a shiv, and a knuckle duster behind him. He then brings out a small bag of food, shaking it as he presented it to them.

"Where'd you get all of this stuff?" Tariq asked, his curiosity getting the better of him.

"I'm a smuggler, buddy," Faruq replied with a casual shrug. "Middle folk have friends down here, and vice versa. They'll trade good stuff for someone to fetch high-class tobacco or hashwabi—stuff like that." He pointed toward a small, dark gap in the wall above them. "I own that hole up there."

Rafi handed out the canteens to everyone, keeping his promise by giving Hamza the backpack. He kept the knuckle dusters for himself and gave the shiv to Tariq, knowing he was the fastest among them for hit-and-run tactics. Afterward, he accepted the bag of food from Faruq and shook it, listening to the rattling and chittering of its contents.

"What's in here?" Rafi asked, holding up the small bag.

"Live scorpions," Faruq said with a smirk. "Bite 'em down and save the tail. Easy treat."

Rafi widened his eyes in surprise as he opened the bag. Inside, several bite-sized living scorpions crawled around, some trying to escape the moment they saw the opening. He carefully reached in, snagging the one furthest from the clutter by its tail. He held it up to the rest of the group, the scorpion dangling helplessly from his fingers.

"Habi, you wanna try?" Rafi teased, wiggling the unfortunate scorpion between his fingers.

Habi, excited by the sight of food dangling from Rafi's hand, eagerly waddled over. Her wide eyes fixed on the strange critter, her curiosity outweighing her hesitation.

"Grab it by the tail and have at it," Rafi instructed, holding it out to her. "But don't eat the tail, unless you want the stinger to hit your tongue."

She grabbed the scorpion by the tail, holding it above her head as its pincers flailed in an attempt to pinch her. Without hesitation, likely driven by hunger, she bit down. The crunch echoed in her jaw as she separated the tail with her teeth, tossing it aside. She paused for a moment, considering the taste. It was strange—like chicken dipped into a pond—and she couldn't quite describe it, but she liked it.

"That one's a keeper," Faruq said with a grin, nodding approvingly at Habi.

Not wanting to be outdone, Rafi grabbed another scorpion from the bag and bit into it. To his surprise, he liked it too.

"You gotta be kidding me," Taliba sighed, pinching the bridge of her nose in disbelief.

Shortly after, everyone took their share of scorpions, slowly adjusting to the unusual snack. As they munched, Faruq disappeared into his tent and reemerged with a jar of liquid, the contents sloshing as he carried it. He removed the plug at the top, a faint scent of freshness wafting out, and nodded toward their canteens.

"Fresh water from the upper hives," Faruq said, holding up the jar with a satisfied grin. "A fine trade I got recently. Take some."

The children lined up eagerly, waiting their turn to fill their canteens. Faruq handed out slim ropes, demonstrating how to tie the canteens securely around their waists for easy access during the journey. He moved with practiced efficiency, his sharp eyes watching them closely, the hint of a smirk tugging at his lips.

The promise of earnings hung in the air, fueling his interest in their mission. Faruq knew the way of the world: you either worked toward your own dreams or helped someone else fulfill theirs. For him, it was as simple as that.

Once the children were fully equipped, Faruq did a final inspection of their gear. He checked their canteens, tested the knots securing the ropes around their waists, and examined their provisions. Nodding in approval, he stepped back, his grin rough and toothy but laced with a spark of pride and mischief.

"I hope none of y'all are afraid of heights now!" Faruq teased, his eyes glinting as he scanned the group.

Chapter Ten

Faruq guided the aspiring thieves through the dark, winding paths of the Sleeping Complex, deftly avoiding traps and skirting the more perilous zones where crime thrived. As they neared the towering wall dividing the hives, its immense silhouette rose above them, casting deep, jagged shadows across the ground. The silence of the desolate corner was broken only by the distant echoes of heated voices and the crisp crunch of scorpions as Habi chewed absently, her thoughts elsewhere.

The group soon came to a stop. The wall stood just a few dozen feet ahead, its towering expanse cutting off their path, mute and forbidding.

"Right then, y'all see these houses to our right?" Faruq said, his voice low but steady as he gestured toward the cluster of tightly packed sandstone buildings. "We're gonna start climbin' from there." He pointed to a small wooden shed nestled beside them. "And end up all the way up there," he added, stretching his arm toward the tallest sandstone structure, its four stories looming against the dim sky.

"What was that building used for?" Naji asked, curiosity flickering in his tone.

"Mortuary. Dead folk," Faruq replied with a shrug. "They shut it down when the bodies kept pilin' up. Four floors couldn't hold it all. That's why they built it way out here—keep the smell away from the homes."

The building stood tall, but the children quickly noticed some cracks that confirmed Rafi and Faruq's assessment. If viewed from the right angle, a small hole could be seen, exposing the bright blue sky beyond, a rare sight through the polluted air of the lower hive. It was small enough to be easily overlooked by both the lower and middle hive's citizens.

Faruq stepped onto a wooden crate, using it to hoist himself up onto the roof of the shed. He moved cautiously, staying near the edges where the foundation was most stable.

"Do what I did and stick to the edge. I made a hole in the shed once by steppin' in the center," Faruq advised, laughing to himself and shaking his head. "Once we're on thems stone houses, we should be fine."

The children watched in awe as Faruq stepped onto the protruding stones of the nearby sandstone building. With the ease of an acrobat, he scaled the wall, pulling himself up with practiced precision, each movement fluid and calculated.

"Are we goin' or what?" Faruq shouted from above with his arms spread out.

After watching Faruq's impressive climb, Rafi turned to assess the rest of the group. He quickly noted who was eager and who was hesitant, simply by reading their faces and body language. Habi, unsurprisingly, was the most excited. She bounced on the balls of her feet, her eyes fixed on Faruq as if imagining herself up there already. However, she would need a little boost to reach the higher spots.

The rest of the children seemed ready for the challenge, but one stood out. Rafi couldn't miss the way Taliba's legs trembled. Her wide eyes fixed on the heights above, the daunting void beyond the shade. It was clear she was struggling to mask her fear.

Rafi snapped his fingers at Taliba, pulling her back to the present.

"Taliba, you good?" he asked, concern lacing his tone.

"Oh yeah, I'm fine," Taliba replied with the ease of a seasoned liar.

"Okay, you want to go first then?"

"No," she answered without hesitation.

Rafi squinted, a wide grin spreading across his face. "Very well then, I'll go."

The children waited their turn, careful not to crowd the unstable wooden shed, which seemed to groan with every movement. Rafi took the lead, following Faruq's motions as he swiftly ascended the sandstone building. Habi, eager to stay close, followed right behind him. Due to her smaller stature, she wasn't quite as fast, but she pushed forward with determination. Hamza stood behind her, ready to offer a hand if needed. With enough willpower and effort, Habi managed to scramble up the wooden shed, and with Rafi's help, she steadily climbed the stone wall. After a few determined steps, she finally joined the others on top of the building.

Hamza and Naji followed suit, barely breaking a sweat as they scaled the climb with ease. Tariq was ready to go next, but before he could start, Taliba had to face the challenge. Her hesitation was palpable.

"Why are you going last, Tariq?" Taliba asked, her tone sharp.

Tariq grinned mischievously, his voice laced with teasing mockery. "I don't know, maybe you need a boost? Or maybe you'll fall? Who's to say?"

Taliba's eyes narrowed, her irritation flaring. "Shut up," she snapped, stepping onto the crate without another word.

Taliba's heart skipped a beat as she pulled herself up onto the shed. She stuck to the edge, her fingers gripping the wood tightly as she slowly moved upward. Just as she found her footing, a sudden, sharp crack rang out beneath her feet. Her body froze, and she yelped, certain she was about to plummet. But fortune favored her, as the crack had come from one of the loose wooden planks in the center of the shed, not the edge she was clinging to.

"You're fat!" Tariq insulted, laughing as he pointed at her. He meant no harm at least. "Just don't look down!"

Taliba was too afraid to bite back at Tariq's bark. His words distracted her as she subconsciously made it to the stone wall, eager to get off the shed. She carefully climbed the wall, occasionally slipping and missing her grip. But soon enough, she reached the top of the stable sandstone building, reuniting with the rest of the group. Tariq was already there, and she hadn't even noticed him pass. Now the others had something to tease her about.

The path to the hole resembled a long staircase for giants, with a mix of flat tops and slanted roofs offering various routes. However, Faruq knew the safest and most efficient way. The next obstacle was a flat, grainy wall with no footholds. Faruq took a few steps back and sprinted toward it. The ledge he needed to grab was normally just out of reach, but he was prepared. Using the bottom of his shoes as a temporary anchor against the wall, he kicked off with his other foot. Keeping his body weight forward, he maintained his sprint's momentum, and with one final leap, his hands grabbed the ledge. It was a clean performance, one he took pride in. After regaining his footing on the next building, he spread his arms and called out to the others.

"Just like that!" Faruq shouted from above. "Run into it, stay close, and keep thems feet movin' until you latch!"

"Learn something new everyday, right guys?" Rafi smirked, facing his family. "See you guys up there."

Rafi took a deep breath, focusing on his route. He dug the balls of his shoes into the ground, feeling the momentary resistance. That was the key, and he hoped the others would catch on. The trick to the wall kick was all about friction and momentum working in sync.

Rafi sprinted toward the wall, kicking his feet up and slamming against it. He grabbed the ledge with one arm, barely holding on, but Faruq was quick to help him up.

Habi, eager to stay close to Rafi, rushed toward the wall before the others could react. She jumped to climb it but fell just short of reaching the ledge. Her forearm scraped against the wall, but it was a minor injury.

"Alright, you're too short," Rafi chuckled. He then kneeled and offered an arm out for her. "Try it again. I got you this time."

Habi, frustrated by her near miss, returned to the group and tried again. This time, she grabbed onto Rafi's arm, who was more than happy to help her up. Once she regained her footing on top, Rafi patted the dust off her.

"Why are we doing all of this when we could just lift each other up from down here?" Taliba shouted from below, placing her hands on her hips.

"Who else is gonna teach ya if you don't do it yourself and learn!?" Faruq yelled from above. "Ain't supposed to be easy, princess!" He snorted and laughed after talking back to her. Rafi nodded and shrugged, gesturing toward her.

All Taliba did was roll her eyes and sighed as a response.

Hamza and Naji executed the task with little incident. Hamza smacked into the wall a couple of times, while Naji scraped his fingertips by missing the ledge. Once again, Tariq stood ready as the anchor, in case Taliba wasn't up for it.

Taliba took a deep breath, closing her eyes for a moment before reopening them with razor-sharp focus. Once locked in, she sprinted toward the wall and followed the motions. Thanks to her height advantage, she smoothly latched onto the ledge. The rest helped her up, saving her energy for the tasks ahead.

Tariq, on the other hand, moved with ease. His nimbleness as he scaled the wall even caught Faruq's attention.

"Done this before?" Faruq asked, watching him with a hint of approval.

"Oh yeah," Tariq replied, flashing a confident grin.

Faruq smiled back as he led the group over the rooftop toward the next obstacle. The sandstone roof ahead sloped on both ends: one side was a climb, while the other acted as a downward ramp. Between this building and the mortuary tower was a small gap. Though the gap appeared narrow, the drop on the other side could easily injure them—if not worse.

"Right then," Faruq said, drawing a steady breath. "This one? We can't afford a single mistake. If you mess up, you're going down. Plain and simple. Land on your feet if you miss—at least you might live through it. Had a buddy try this jump with me once. He missed. Bled out before I even made it down."

Faruq's story not only struck fear into the children, but also taught them to be vigilant.

"Follow me and stop at the crest," Faruq instructed, hopping onto the worn out stoned roof. His foot slipped a bit by the landing, but he was easily able to crawl up otherwise. "Stay low and hold on to what you can. We'd usually just run up this thing and leap for it. Ain't doin' that with y'all now."

The roof was stable enough to support the weight of all seven children, even as some of them slipped, loosening dirt and sand. When they reached the crest of the roof, they all latched onto the slanted edge and peeked over to scout the area ahead. Just down the smooth slope, a small landing could be seen on the next building. Below it, a dark gap yawned wide, almost as if dark tendrils were beckoning them to drop.

"Watch what I do and do it right," Faruq told them. He pulled himself over the crest and slid down the slope with a steady drag. One hand stayed behind him, the other in front for balance. His feet were planted, but he skidded down the ramp at an alarming speed. The children held their breath as he neared the edge of the roof, but with his experience, he jumped at the perfect moment, landing effortlessly on the platform with both feet.

In order to get the task done and over with, Rafi slid down the slanted roof and nailed his landing, proving his resilience and dexterity.

At this point, Taliba was shaking up the entire roof, and the others knew its source. Tariq and Naji were the first to comfort her.

"You don't have to do this," Naji whispered, his voice barely audible.

"I'm doing it," Taliba said, her voice trembling. "We're going to see the middle hive together."

Just like before, Habi went next. However, as she began to slide, she lost her footing, immediately worrying the others. Rafi cursed and leaned forward, ready in case she fell. Habi slid on her bum, her hands skidding through the falling sand. She may have been silent, but she wasn't afraid. In fact, she was having fun.

As she closed the distance to the platform, she made a leap that skipped the heartbeat of every child. It was a low jump, but she landed. She skidded on the landing, then stood up, unscathed.

"Woo!" Habi cheered, raising her arms up in victory.

"Oh, sweet roots of the heavens and gods of Skania, so help me," Rafi muttered, clutching his chest dramatically as if on the verge of a heart attack. After regaining his composure, he gave Habi a quick pat-down and offered her a grin. "Good job," he praised, nodding approvingly.

The rest of the children made it over to the landing as well, while Tariq continued rubbing Taliba's back at the crest.

"You can do this, Taliba. I believe in you," Tariq said firmly.

"What if I fall? What then?" Taliba asked, her eyes darting nervously between the landing and the gap.

"Keep thinking like that and maybe you will," Tariq said with a sly grin. "You gonna let little Habi outshine you like that?"

"She doesn't know better. I, on the other hand, know exactly what happens if I mess up."

"Then don't mess up," Tariq smirked, giving her back a reassuring pat.

Taliba focused all of her energy before breaking the crest. As soon as she felt ready, she took a deep breath and crawled over.

She maintained her balance as she slid down the slope, everything going according to plan as she stared straight ahead at where the others stood. But with a quick glance at the dark gap, she froze. Terror spread through her body as she began to hyperventilate. She was closing in on the edge of the ramp, and Faruq was the first to notice something was wrong. He saw how Taliba remained in the sliding position, unprepared for the leap that was soon to come.

"Jump, you buffoon!" Faruq barked, his voice cutting through the tense air.

It didn't take long for the others to notice the unusual hesitation. One by one, they began shouting, their voices rising in urgency.

"Taliba! Jump! Jump, damn it!" Rafi yelled, his desperation echoing louder than the rest.

By the time Taliba snapped out of her trance, she had slipped off the edge of the roof. Miraculously, guided by pure instinct, she threw her arms above her, grabbing onto a protruding stone brick just below the landing platform. The impact left her dazed as she looked up at the others, who quickly extended their hands to help. Her breathing became erratic, and her grip was slipping with the sweat pooling in her palms, but the dirt and sand clinging to her hands were enough to keep her from falling.

"Eyes on us, Taliba," Rafi called out as he reached for her. "Just don't look down!"

Of course, Taliba looked down.

Below her, the opening faded into an endless darkness. She couldn't see the bottom, leaving her with no sense of how far the drop was. The uncertainty made her feel sick.

After countless attempts to pull herself up, kicking against the wall with her feet, Taliba finally mustered enough strength to leap and grab onto one of the children's arms. Luckily, it was Hamza's arm, and his weight provided a solid counterbalance to hers. The others quickly helped her up, either by pulling on her clothes or holding onto Hamza to prevent him from being dragged forward. After a brief struggle, Taliba was lifted onto the platform, away from the gap. They positioned themselves as far from the ledge as possible, just in time to see Tariq flying through the obstacle without breaking a sweat. Once he landed on solid footing, he helped pat down Taliba, brushing off the dust and sand.

"Thought it was over for you for a second there," Tariq said with a smirk.

"That was cool!" Habi exclaimed, patting Taliba's scraped hands enthusiastically. The sharp sting made Taliba wince, drawing her attention to the damage.

"Oh, that's not cool," Habi added, her excitement fading into concern.

Faruq forced his way to Taliba and inspected her condition. He kneeled down, checking each limb for any injuries that might stop her from moving forward. He nodded at some parts and grimaced at others, lightly tapping the scrapes and wounds to gauge her reaction. Aside from a few cuts on her fingers and some bruises on her knees and shins, Faruq deemed her relatively safe to continue, giving his approval with a nod.

"A lil' bit chapped up, but she's fine," Faruq said, inspecting her hands with a raised brow. "Never seen somethin' like that. Shoulda been dead, maybe. The heavens like you today!"

"Thanks, I guess," Taliba muttered, her fingers trembling from a mix of pain and adrenaline. "What's next?"

Faruq snorted and signaled the group to look up with a nod of his head. The mortuary building they stood on was made of several sandstone bricks stacked on top of each other. Most of these bricks were the size of two children lying side by side, and the structure appeared hastily constructed, with uneven architecture. This created a steep pathway, functioning like a ladder, but with bricks instead of wooden sticks locked between two poles. The children had to spread out and wait for those ahead to advance. Following Faruq's instructions, this method would ensure proper coordination and enough space to avoid any hindrance.

"Take yer time on this one," Faruq advised, his tone steady. "Make sure you got two points of contact at all times!"

To demonstrate, he climbed onto a brick, gripping the ledge with one hand while bracing a foot against the flat surface. His other foot dangled freely in the air. "Three's safer. Four's for when you're just muckin' about. Don't want y'all fallin' now, like lil' princess over there."

He meant Taliba, and she blushed from embarrassment. The children wanted to join in the banter, but they held back, knowing it was too soon, given how she had nearly fallen from the roof. Once Faruq climbed a bit further up, Rafi followed, and the sequence of events continued. The height of each stone brick was the size of Habi, so she had to exert more effort than the others. Thankfully, each brick they climbed provided a solid resting platform, allowing them to prepare for the next step.

Taliba was content with the obstacle, as long as she didn't turn her head to look behind her. The children had reached a point where no one was safe to drop from where they stood. They all felt the arid heat carried by the wind as they continued to climb toward the summit of the mortuary. Rafi seized the opportunity to glance down and around from where he hung on the building. From his vantage point, he could clearly see parts of the Sultan's tower in the center of the city, and the wall that cast a shadow over the entire Sleeping Complex. The dwellers below appeared no larger than ants. Beyond the lower hive, a vast, endless ocean of sand stretched across the horizon, the atmosphere blurring from the heat. It was a beautiful sight, and he had to share it with the nearest climber.

"Habi! Check that out!" Rafi called out, nodding his head toward the open space behind Habi.

Although Habi's heart sank into her stomach, she admired the scenery. Part of her was afraid, realizing just how high she truly was, but the other half was filled with pure thrill. After a brief moment of gazing, she pushed forward, continuing to climb to shake off the uneasy feeling in her gut. At least she was having fun.

"There will be a flat top when we reach it," Faruq advised anyone below who could hear him. " We can rest there and wait for the others."

The steep climb wasn't as heart-racing and horrific as the others, but it was definitely the longest. The children were only halfway up the mortuary when the sun began to shift. But with persistence, they reached the top of the building by afternoon. Not a single child encountered any major issues. The flat rooftop was narrow but lengthy. At the far end, a hole could be seen, weathered by the harsh environment and time itself, never maintained due to its unfortunate position. Some small debris lingered in the opening, but it was mostly cleared out from Faruq's past smuggling trips. The mortuary hugged the border wall but wasn't sealed tight against it, leaving a gap. However, the pathway to the hole wasn't much of an obstacle—just a small hop. This is where Faruq's practical guidance would end, as he had no business in the upper hives that day.

"Right then," Faruq said, walking toward the hole. "I ain't going with y'all today. Too many of us. Ain't much of a problem for any one of youse anyway. Maybe for the princess, I don't know."

Taliba remained quiet. She would never hear the end of this.

"When you climb through this hole, there'll be a building right below you," Faruq explained, his tone firm. "From there, you're gonna have to jump, tuck, and roll straight ahead down the rooftops. If you don't make your legs go limp before landing, you will get hurt. If you don't soften the landing with your shoulder and roll, you will get hurt. If you do neither and land on your belly or back, you will *definitely* get hurt. And if you die, it ain't my fault."

"We know, Faruq," Rafi replied, a touch of gratitude in his voice. "Thanks for getting us this far."

Faruq smiled, already beginning his descent back down into the complex. "When y'all are ready to come back, just remember this spot and climb the roofs back to this hole here. I'll let y'all figure out the how on your own. Now go get me some gald."

Rafi nodded as Faruq moved to clap and shake hands with each of them in farewell. When he reached Habi, he leaned in and whispered with a grin, "You stay good now, you hear me? Youse a crazy one."

Habi wasn't sure how to take that as she waved him goodbye. Shortly after, Faruq began sliding down the mortuary bricks on his bum without turning back.

"Well, we all made it," Rafi announced, spreading his arms wide in triumph before the group. "Never knew you had a fear of heights, Taliba."

"I'm not sure if I have one anymore after all of that," Taliba muttered, rubbing her scraped fingers with a sigh. "Is this really the only viable route for all of us?"

"No one ever looks up here," Rafi explained. "The sewer's unbearable, and the main gate wouldn't work unless you somehow hitchhike on one of those ever-so-rare merchant wagons. And guess what? We don't get wagons down here, Taliba. Enjoy the scenery at least!"

"I'm not looking down," Taliba whined, clutching at her sides.

"If not down, then look straight ahead," Rafi encouraged, a grin spreading across his face. "Take it in—look how high up we are! Don't think anyone else ever gets to experience this!"

Rafi's joy was contagious, lifting the spirits of the others. Their motivation soared to an all-time high, as if they could rule the entire city just by standing atop this abandoned building.

"It was fun! Little Rafi thinks so too!" Habi added, pulling out her pouch that contained the doll.

The children laughed and took a moment to catch their breath before deciding to cross the boundary. Rafi leaned in close to inspect the hole, glancing back at the others as he did so. It seemed large enough for everyone to pass through without issue. With a determined nod, Rafi took the first leap, gripping the ledge and hoisting himself up. For a brief moment, he dangled over the narrow gap below, then swung himself over and into the crawl space. Crouched low, he scanned the area ahead, eyes sharp for any sign of danger or obstacles.

"There's a rooftop not too far below this," Rafi said, pointing down. "It's an easy drop, but after that, there's a line of homes. Lots of people are walking around, but they're far enough away. See you all down there!"

With that, Rafi dropped through the hole. The children held their breath until they heard the faint, reassuring thud of his landing.

"I'm fine! Come on out!" Rafi's voice echoed faintly from below, carrying just enough confidence to ease their nerves.

One by one in previous order, the children clambered their way through the hole and made the small drop onto the other side of the wall.

Rafi and Habi beamed with wide smiles as they reunited with the middle hive, greeted by the fresh air and clear skies. The sense of accomplishment washed over them, invigorating their spirits as they took in the open expanse.

The others stood in stunned silence, their jaws dropped as they took in their surroundings. It was the first time any of them had set foot in the middle hive, and it felt like stepping into an entirely different world. This was where their heists would begin—their ticket to a better life.

Chapter Eleven

The children took a moment as they embraced the unfamiliar breeze of the middle hive. Off in the distance, they could hear the joyous voices of merchants, citizens, and children. The part of the hive they stood in was also covered in shadows, due to the sun's angle against the Sultan's towers, the ominous platform overhead, and the walls. It provided a temperate atmosphere with valuable reprieve for them. The skies weren't as dusty and polluted as the lower hive, and all of the buildings were intact. The middle hive was a place of stories only heard from Father. They didn't even know what to expect from the higher hive and noble layer—but that's if they ever made it that far.

Rafi stepped to the edge of the rooftop, planning a route down for the children to safely reach the streets. As Faruq had warned, the only way down involved more rooftops and careful leaps. At least the buildings ahead appeared more stable.

"All right, the only way down is here," Rafi said, motioning toward a line of buildings with flat roofs that descended in a staggered pattern. Some rooftops were strung with wires hung with clothes, while others displayed bird cages or tables set for outdoor dining. To the children, it was an unfamiliar and striking scene. "Remember what Faruq told us: leap, tuck, limp, shoulder impact, and roll. Got it?"

The group remained silent, their gazes darting between Rafi and the rooftops in the distance.

"Okay, I'll show you," Rafi offered, stepping forward with a steadying breath.

Rafi never had to perform a break roll in his life. He never thought that one of his modes of transportation one day would be standing over fifty feet high. It was a mixture of pure excitement and fear that ran through his veins, and he was ready to tackle it.

The building had a gap in between them. The gap was wide enough to bolster a narrow alleyway for those below, deep enough to injure their legs. The pattern remained the same as far as their eyes could see. Some of the buildings even had little wooden planks connected to each other for ease of travel, but there were very few in between. The majority of the obstacles involved spring jumps. The children could only imagine what they would have to do to get back to this hole.

Without any more thought, Rafi took a few steps back and prepared his rear foot for launch. As soon as he felt ready, he sprinted toward the edge of the roof and leaped into the air, pointing his feet downward and spreading his arms out. The children quickly ran to the edge after he leapt, just to bear witness to his landing. It didn't take long for Rafi to reach the next building. As soon as he felt the ground closing in, he turned off the feelings in his legs and softened the landing by immediately bracing with his shoulder by rolling forward. Once he fully spun, he gracefully bounced back on to his feet and came to a halt, resisting the inertia with it.

"Woo!" Rafi cheered, throwing his arms up triumphantly.

"That was awesome!" Hamza roared, his voice filled with excitement as the group broke into applause.

Their cheers merged seamlessly with the constant buzz of noise around them, drawing no unwanted attention.

"Do it like that, and you'll be fine!" Rafi called out from a few feet below, his confidence infectious.

Rafi stepped aside to make room for the others, positioning himself safely out of the way.

Habi, grinning with excitement, followed the motions and made the leap. Her landing and roll were so fluid it almost seemed instinctive, earning impressed looks from the others.

Hamza, however, decided to experiment with the short drop. Instead of tucking and rolling, he attempted to land squarely on his feet. The impact, though from only about five feet, sent sharp vibrations up his legs. He stumbled forward, grimacing as he joined Rafi and Habi, who looked just as startled as he felt.

"Okay, yeah, that kinda hurt," Hamza admitted, rubbing his shins and knees with a wince.

"Thanks for showing everyone what *not* to do, Hamza," Rafi said, laughing.

Soon after, Naji landed perfectly. Taliba decided to analyze the drop before plummeting down. Her fear of heights had lessened, but she had only conquered the fear of climbing higher, not falling.

"Easy drop, Taliba! You got this!" Hamza cheered. The other children joined in with encouragement, while Tariq patted her on the back for good luck.

Taliba shook her head, took a few steps back, and took a deep breath. She then followed the motions that were performed before her and landed on the platform gracefully.

"See? Wasn't that fun?" Hamza laughed, his voice full of energy.

Taliba's blood surged with a blend of fear and exhilaration. She had overcome the daunting leap, though she knew greater challenges still lay ahead. Tariq landed shortly after, steady and composed.

"It wasn't that bad, I guess," Taliba said with a soft sigh.

The next obstacle was a wooden plank laid across the gap between their building and the next. The children crossed it with ease, facing no further issues.

The next building down posed more of a problem. It was about a ten-foot drop, and landing could be tricky. The children knew the return trip wouldn't be as easy as they'd thought. Rafi peeked over the edge to scout the landing, and Habi joined him out of curiosity, wanting to be with him.

"That's pretty far down," Rafi said, eyeing the building with the wooden dining table and the dark gap below. "I don't know how we'll get back up."

"Can we use the table?" Habi suggested, glancing at it thoughtfully.

"We could," Rafi replied, frowning. "But it probably won't be there tomorrow if the owner notices it's been moved."

Habi frowned as well.

"Unless there's another way up, and we just don't know about it," Rafi mused, scanning the area for possibilities.

Habi, lying on her belly with her arms dangling over the gap, peered into the shadowy depths below. Her eyes narrowed as something unusual caught her attention. She traced a faint pattern on the wall beneath her, her expression shifting to one of discovery.

"Rafi, there're bricks missing," Habi said, her voice laced with excitement. She pointed eagerly at the wall beneath her. "Look, look!"

Rafi kneeled next to her and followed her gaze. Though the building was stable, part of its structure was missing—specifically, a few layers of bricks in the wall. Rafi whistled and patted her on the head.

"Good catch, Habi," Rafi said, nodding with approval.

Habi smiled and treasured his touch.

Rafi stood up and turned to face the others, "Alright, we found a way back up. There's holes in the wall below us to climb. We should be fine. Let's go!"

Once the revelation was shared, Rafi took a few steps back, sprinted, and leaped to the next building. He landed safely and rolled, but he could definitely feel the impact on his shoulder from the higher drop.

"Careful with this one," Rafi advised, making room for the others once more.

One by one, the children crossed the gap and landed safely, until it was Taliba's turn again. She peeked over the edge, glancing at the others with hesitation.

Without a word, Taliba lowered herself from the ledge and hung there for a moment. She then kicked off the wall and landed on her feet below, softening the impact with a crouch. Rafi and the others said nothing as they watched her make a risky move that could have sent her into the gap or broken her legs.

"Yep, I felt that one," Taliba admitted with a wince, though she remained unscathed.

This time, Rafi shrugged and rolled his eyes.

Afterwards, Tariq safely rolled and landed. The next task was the last. It was time to reach the streets of the middle hive.

Rafi scouted over the ledge again. He was able to spot a dark gravel path below, shaded by the next building across from them. There was little to no foot traffic in this path, assumed to be a part of the residential property. Right under the ledge was a small square shed they could safely drop on. From the shed, they could touch the streets safely.

Rafi led the way down, with Tariq remaining the last to follow. As they reached the shed, they could hear the thin metal creaking beneath their weight. Rafi raised his hand, signaling the others to wait as he dropped with

Habi, who happened to be with him. Once the duo scooted off the shed, the children followed quietly in a line.

A few moments later, they finally reached the ground. The pebbles from the gravel scrunched beneath their feet.

The children remained silent, ensuring that their hoods were up and their gear intact and accounted for. They didn't know who roamed in the area, so the children took precautions as they followed the sounds of the larger audience. On their way there, they happened to stumble upon a water well that was placed at an open intersection between all the homes.

"Yes!" Hamza hissed, his whisper sharp and eager.

"Fill up your canteens and drink up. We're gonna need it," Rafi whispered along, retrieving his canteen and popping the plug open. The children did the same.

Rafi fetched water with the nearby available bucket and pulled it back out. Almost like a ferocious pack of animals, the children surrounded the bucket and dipped their canteens in. The surface of the water was filled with air bubbles as the canteens engulfed its contents.

Once satisfied, they would all chug down their respective canteens until they couldn't breathe. Everyone's eyes lit up as the fresh, cold feeling, and taste of the water was never thought to have existed. Rafi and Habi welcomed it back into their gullets, while the others not only drank their fill, but poured some over their dirtied bodies. All of them were too excited to even speak, as the only thing coming out of their mouths were trails of water streaming down their chins.

"That's amazing!" Naji gasped loudly.

Habi took the initiative to follow Rafi's advice, pressing a finger to her lips to hush Naji. Naji reactively pursed his lips, his eyes wandering off.

Abruptly, footsteps echoed from a short distance along the gravel path. The children quickly topped off their canteens as Rafi waved them toward the sounds of the market area. With one last sip of the precious water, they ran away from the scene, leaving a puddle behind them that surrounded the well.

A residential woman later spotted the strange puddle as she prepared to fetch water, two buckets in hand.

She simply giggled and shook her head as she dipped a bucket into the well.

"Kids will be kids," she said.

—

After a refreshing respite and run, the children finally reached the source of commotion. There was a vast ocean of merchants, citizens, and children that laid before them. Despite the crowd, it was done in a more organized fashion in comparison to the lower hive, which was more of organized chaos. The smiles of merchants enchanted those around them, and the children held the hands of their parents, laughing away. Some of the middle hive children even had a small playground that included toys and obstacles they could play with. Aside from the joyous community, there was an unfortunate addition to the crowd that was unfavorable to the group. Whereas the lower hive had minimal Ghazi or none, the middle hive was more enforced with them. Ragged hoods were a common form of dress wear, but the children knew to remain cautious.

The children huddled safely on the outer rim of the square, developing yet another scheme.

"All right, guys, we're gonna have to split up," Rafi suggested, glancing around at the group. "Six of us is way too many—it'll draw attention. If we split into pairs, we'll save time too. Good?"

The children nodded, discussing among themselves who would go with whom. Habi's decision was already set in stone as she stood right next to Rafi. He was fine with this outcome.

It didn't take long for them to decide. Taliba suggested teaming up with Hamza to be the brains of the group, while Tariq and Naji, who were very close, decided to pair up as well.

"Right then," Rafi started again. "Meet back up at the water well we were at as soon as the sun sets behind the Sultan's tower. We'll get home before nightfall."

The children nodded and immediately separated, as half of the sunlight had already faded. Taliba and Hamza ran toward the far end of the market, while Tariq and Naji headed to the other end. Rafi and Habi decided to test their luck in the center.

Though the market was a large square that spanned much of the middle hive, it wasn't the main one. A paved road ran through the center, directing traffic toward the border gate and up to the higher hive.

Rafi took Habi's hand and guided her through the sea of people, weaving between families and stalls. Most were polite enough to give the children the right of way, but a few shot them disapproving glances.

The plan was to 'acquire' as many valuables as they could, but there was no point in doing so on an empty stomach. Some of the scorpions were shared, but Habi hogged most of the snack to herself. Things took another unfortunate turn when Rafi remembered his mistake.

"Taliba was right. I should've brought some goods to trade," Rafi muttered, cursing under his breath. "Dammit, I just made this a lot harder!"

"We could put on an act again, like you did last time," Habi suggested, patting his back in a small gesture of comfort.

"We can, but I'm not sure how stingy those food stalls are," Rafi replied, his gaze darting to the bustling market ahead. "Too many eyes to steal."

Habi thought for a second and came up with an idea that might just work.

"What if we use those many eyes to help us?" she asked, a sly edge to her voice.

Rafi stared at her, his face blank. "How so?"

This time, Habi took Rafi's hand and dragged him to the nearest food stall with a crowd. They followed the irresistible smell of freshly cooked kebabs, filled with lamb and vegetables. It must've been popular, given the long line of people waiting for their turn.

"Oh, I'm so hungry—mother forgot to pack us our gald!" Habi cried out suddenly.

Rafi was confused at first, but then he caught on to her tactic.

"I'm sorry, sister, it's my fault that we rushed out to see the market!" Rafi cried along.

Both of them made sure to speak loudly enough for everyone nearby to hear, and it worked. Curious onlookers spotted the duo, who clutched their stomachs in a dramatic manner. They could feel the eyes on them, the pity, and the guilt directed their way.

"Brother, I just wanted to try this food here!" Habi pointed at the kebab stall, which caught one of the worker's attention. "Mother always told us that their food was delicious, but how can we buy it if we have no gald!?"

"It was foolish of me!" Rafi acted. "We barely get enough food at home in the first place!"

The guests began to mutter among each other, mentioning how they would feel bad if they didn't help two children who were hungry. Finally, a guest at the front of the line sighed, carrying a single kebab.

"Can I have another of the same order?" the guest said to the merchants, shaking his head. "I can't stand irresponsible parents who let their children roam without gald."

The merchants agreed to the order as the guest walked over to Habi and Rafi, offering his kebab.

"I know it's only one, but maybe you two siblings can share it?" the guest offered, holding out the kebab.

"Are you sure, sir? You waited so long for your food," Rafi asked, hesitating.

"It's fine. I don't have to be at work for a while. Please, help yourselves."

Rafi accepted the kebab with a grateful bow. Habi followed suit, bowing deeply.

"Thank you, sir! I hope this doesn't happen again!" Habi called out, her voice filled with gratitude.

The man smiled warmly as the two retreated into the crowd.

"He was so nice," Habi said, smiling up at Rafi.

"You're evil," Rafi chuckled, shaking his head.

Habi's smile faltered, her brows furrowing as she glanced at him. "I'm evil?" she asked, her tone unsure.

"In a good way, dork," Rafi laughed, ruffling her hair. "I have to be careful with you. My talents have been rubbing off on you."

Once there was clarity between them, Habi laughed as well. Rafi tore the kebab in half and offered it to her. It didn't take long for them to devour their meal as they made their way to the next stop.

—

The duo had yet to find a proper stall to steal from, mostly because they were too busy having fun in the middle hive. They took the time to play at the playground and spectate street performers who could juggle objects and play music. They were living the life they never had, and they didn't regret a single moment of it.

"Do my eyes deceive me?" a raspy voice called out, catching the duo's attention as they wandered.

Beside them sat an old woman surrounded by trinkets and jewelry spread out on a faded cloth, shaded beneath a worn tent. Her long gray hair cascaded to the ground, and her wrinkled arms and gnarled fingers were exposed, dressed in rags not unlike the children.

"Come, come, my children," she hissed, beckoning them with a crooked finger. "Do you ever seek to know your destiny?"

"We don't have any gald, ma'am," Rafi replied cautiously.

"Oh, no matter!" she crooned. "The fortunes of children are free. Curious though, are you not?"

The two hesitated for a moment, but in the end, they agreed to her offer. They followed her welcoming gestures as they seated in front of her.

"What are your names, little ones?" she asked, her voice low and creaky.

"I'm Rafi. This is Habi," Rafi introduced, gesturing to his companion.

"Ah yes, I have foretold this meeting since days began," the woman said with a crooked smile, revealing her rotten and missing teeth. "My name is Arwah. Let us begin, then."

The two quickly realized that the free fortune-telling wasn't entirely altruistic—it was also a ploy to draw in more customers. As soon as they sat down, a pair of curious onlookers gathered behind them, quietly observing the scene.

"Little Rafi, please hand me your right hand," Arwah instructed, her bony fingers reaching out expectantly.

Rafi offered his hand as Habi looked in awe, wondering what his fortune would be.

Arwah turned Rafi's palm upward and began to examine it. She pricked her fingers into his skin before, to both Rafi and Habi's disgust, licking it. She then closed her eyes and held his hand with both of hers.

"I see—" Arwah whispered, her voice trembling with mystery. "I see it all, young Rafi."

"What is it?" Rafi asked hesitantly, shifting uncomfortably as he felt the dampness of her touch on his palm.

Arwah took a deep, deliberate breath and exhaled slowly. "Your future—great fortunes lie ahead of you. You will become very powerful, young man. A name to remember, indeed."

Rafi smiled at Habi, and she smiled along. Arwah released his hand and gestured for Habi's next. Once again, Habi and Arwah followed the motions until Arwah closed her eyes.

When Arwah opened her eyes, they were wide with surprise. She tried to speak, but no words came out. Her jaw trembled as she struggled to find the right words.

This immediately concerned Habi and Rafi, until she finally nodded and spoke.

"Little Habi—" Arwah said at last, her voice taking on a solemn tone. "You should be careful, little one. You are reckless."

Habi frowned, her expression clouding at the words.

"However," Arwah continued, her tone softening, "you are very loving, and you will be loved by many. A symbol of change, yes, yes. Another name to remember, indeed." She smiled, her wrinkled face creasing further as her eyes gleamed.

Habi blushed, believing that she would finally have her chance with Rafi in the far future.

Arwah released Habi's hand and presented each of them with a trinket. Rafi received a golden-chained necklace, while Habi was given a silver ring adorned with a small ruby jewel.

"What's this?" Rafi asked, examining the necklace in his palm.

"Yours to keep for my services, little ones," Arwah said with a sly smirk. "I know what you seek."

The duo stood and bowed politely before her.

"Thank you for the fortune and the jewelry, ma'am," Rafi said earnestly.

Arwah said nothing as another guest expressed their interest with her services. Afterwards, the duo walked away, jarred by the strange event.

As the two returned to the busy streets, they inspected the jewelry and spoke to each other about their fortunes.

"You hear that, Habi? I'm going to be rich!" Rafi cheered, holding up his golden necklace with a grin.

"Maybe this will work after all," Habi smirked, glancing at her ring. "Many people will love me!"

"I already love you, though, Habi," Rafi said casually.

Habi froze mid-step, her body stiffening as the words sank in. Rafi stopped beside her, confused by her sudden reaction.

"You love me?" Habi whispered, her voice just loud enough for him to hear.

"Uh, yeah?" Rafi replied with a shrug. "I love the others too. I'm not so sure about Taliba, though."

Habi's disappointment was written all over her face.

"Okay, you a little more," Rafi said with a laugh, trying to lighten the mood.

Like night and day, Habi's expression transformed into a wide smile. She hopped over to him and wrapped her arms around him in a tight hug.

"That's good," Habi mumbled into his chest.

"It is," Rafi replied, patting her back. "Come on now, we need to gather more before the sun goes behind the tower."

"Yes, yes," Habi agreed, letting go and nodding eagerly.

The duo returned to their activities as the crowd grew ever more livelier.

—

HABI

With a pinch of luck, the duo finally spotted a jewelry stall that met their expectations. It was crowded and minimally manned, making it the perfect opportunity to slip in with some sticky fingers.

They made their way through the crowd, trying to catch sight of what was displayed on the tabletop. The items weren't exactly jewelry, but rather gemstones—sapphires, jades, emeralds, and almost every color of the rainbow. It explained the large number of buyers, as the stones were cheaper than actual jewelry, even if they were cut. There were no cases protecting the gems, making it an easy grab. After a brief discussion, they decided only one of them should attempt it. Habi volunteered, as she was the smallest.

She skittered through the crowd while Rafi remained posted at a short distance. Pushed around by eager buyers, Habi managed to find a spot where she could huddle beneath the arms of adults waving their gald. Three merchants worked the stall, each busy with transactions. Every now and then, one of them would glance back at the display, scanning for hands that didn't belong.

Habi waited for the moment when the merchant looked away, and when he did, she swiftly grabbed as many stones as she could with one hand. It didn't matter which kinds or how many, just as long as they were taken. She slipped the stones into her pouch, the little Rafi doll safely tucked inside to guard them. Quickly, she moved to the other side of the stall, positioning herself next to more adults. She waited for the merchant's attention to shift to a customer, and soon enough, she snatched more stones.

Just as Habi was about to secure the stones into her pouch, a hand suddenly shot out from the crowd and grabbed her forearm. It was small compared to the adults' hands, but still larger than her own.

"Yeah right, you golden-eyed brat!" the boy growled.

It was the same merchant boy who had worked at the previous jewelry stall some days ago—the same boy who had informed the Ghazi about her existence.

Chapter Twelve

Habi froze as the boy's hand tightened around hers. A faint bruise marked his cheek and brow, a lingering reminder of Rafi's attack. He tugged at her, trying to drag her away. Despite her resistance, it was no use—he was stronger than she was.

"Thief! Thief!" the boy shouted.

No one paid attention. The crowd drowned out his soft voice, which worked to Habi's advantage. *What would Rafi do in this situation*? she thought. The answer came to her quickly. Without hesitation, she swung her free hand and slapped him square across the nose just as he called for adult supervision. The boy winced in pain, his eyes welling with tears, but despite the sting to his already bruised nose, he was quick to pursue her.

Habi sprinted toward Rafi, narrowly avoiding several adults as she rushed past them. In one swift motion, she shoved the stones into her pouch, securing it tightly to free her other hand. A few adults noticed the chase, but they mistook it for just another round of children playing. They didn't spare a glance at Habi's distress or the boy's fury.

Just as the boy's hands reached for Habi's shoulder, a forearm shot toward his face. Rafi had spotted the danger from a distance, and he was ready. The boy crumpled, falling hard onto his back, and Rafi stood over him, locking eyes with him.

"It's *you*," Rafi spat.

The boy cursed at him and returned to his feet. By the time he stood up, Rafi and Habi had already taken off.

The chase continued as the duo weaved through the crowd, trying to lose the boy in the masses. Both sides were breathing hard, driven by nothing but pure instinct. It was a hunt—predator and prey locked in a relentless pursuit.

"Make way for the Sultan's men! Make way!" a man's voice bellowed above the crowd.

"Make way! Make way!" echoed more voices, the urgency spreading like ripples through the streets.

The duo didn't realize it at first, but they were running parallel to the paved road that cut through the heart of the market. Ahead of them, the crowd parted as tall golden banners came into view. The sound of hooves and clanging steel echoed from that direction, and the crowd began to mutter and applaud. Without hesitation, Rafi yanked Habi toward the edge of the crowd just as the boy closed in on them, still on the road. In that instant, an adult seized the boy and pulled him to the other side, leaving him looking up, puzzled.

"You wanna die, boy? Make way!" the adult hissed at the boy, his tone sharp. They didn't know each other; it was simply a concerned citizen trying to avoid trouble.

Once the crowd made a path, the battalion of the Sultan's men was finally observed.

Rafi and Habi pressed into the crowd, their gazes fixed on the men clad in steel armor riding toward the higher hive on horseback. Chainmail glinted beneath their plates, and at their hips hung shortswords, while their hands gripped polearms and reins. The eight-pointed star of the Sultan was finely engraved on their chests. Their helmets, shaped like an eagle's beak with steel wings on either side, featured narrow slits for their eyes. Some soldiers bore decorated pauldrons, adorned with gold medals or red cords tied around them.

"What is that?" Habi asked, her wide eyes glued to the procession.

"Those aren't Ghazi," Rafi explained, his voice hushed. "Those are Mamluks. The Sultan's vanguard and personal security. They're knights—the first to face violence. The Ghazi are more like a police force. While the Ghazi go on raids or support the city from behind the walls or the knights, the Mamluks go to war. I've only read about them in books. I never thought I'd see one. Or this many."

"They look scary," Habi whined, shrinking behind Rafi.

"They are," Rafi confirmed quietly.

As the Mamluks rode down the road, bystanders were often knocked aside for failing to clear the way. Not one of the knights paused. If someone stumbled beneath the hooves of a horse, they simply kept riding forward.

"Come on, let's get out of here," Rafi suggested, grabbing onto Habi's hand.

Habi kept her eyes on the Mamluk, both admiring and fearing them. Just as she was about to turn with

Rafi, a strange man was positioned in the center of the formation.

The man wore an olive-green long coat, decorated with several medals and ribbons on his chest. Steel greaves and gauntlets covered his limbs. His black hair was slicked back, and his mustache was neatly groomed. His face seemed locked in a permanent scowl, and his bright blue eyes locked onto Habi's with a piercing gaze.

Habi's heart raced as she turned and ran with Rafi. She knew fear well, and the look in that man's eyes had been its purest form. Thankfully, no further problems arose, and it seemed the march had been long enough to keep the boy at bay. By the time they made their way back to the meetup point, the sun was dipping behind the Sultan's tower.

While the citizens of the middle hive gathered for the spectacle of Mamluks, the young duo retreated into the residential area where several home dwellers responded to the celebratory uproar. As they passed through the homes and greeted the gravel path again, Rafi noticed a door that was left half opened, leading into someone's domain. This sparked a rather sinister, yet harmless idea in his mind.

"Hey, Habi, over here," Rafi called out, weaving his way toward an open wooden door. His eyes gleamed with curiosity. "Imagine the things they might have in here!"

"But isn't it bad to walk into someone's home?" Habi asked, her tone filled with worry.

Rafi shrugged off her concern and waved her over. "Come on, Habi, do we really need to pity those with better lives than ours?"

Before Habi could make a decision, Rafi had already invited himself into the home of another. She hesitated, scanning the area for any onlookers. Once she was certain they were unseen, she made the decision to follow him, trespassing onto another's property.

Inside the modest home, the duo was greeted by a large room with carpeted floors. Tapestries adorned the walls, and a wooden table stood at the center, surrounded by four stools. At the back of the room, a small hallway led to a dead end, where a glass window let in light; two doorways flanked the hall. Behind the table, large pouches of grain, seeds, and non-perishable foods—canned goods and nuts—were neatly stacked along the back wall.

"This must be where they dine. I'll check the room on the left, and you check the right," Rafi suggested, silently jogging toward the left room.

Habi waddled right behind him, still trying to understand and take in her newly discovered surroundings.

"Find the good stuff quick before they come back," Rafi whispered, rustling through wooden wardrobes and drawers in the other room.

As soon as Habi stepped into the right room, the scent of incense hit her. On top of a long wooden dresser, a recently lit sand pot with incense sticks stuck in it emitted a soft, curling smoke. Across from it, a large, soft bed lay on the floor. She longed to explore more of the room, but she had to follow Rafi's lead—time was uncertain, and the owner's return could come at any moment.

She yanked open drawer after drawer, only finding dresses and undergarments fit for a woman. She even dug her hands beneath the clothes, searching for anything of value hidden away. With persistence, she finally pulled open another drawer, revealing a chaotic spread of jewelry—rings, necklaces, bracelets, and cut gemstones, all scattered haphazardly. The sight of the valuables made her heart race. Without hesitation, she grabbed a handful of items and stuffed them into her pouch, filling it to the brim.

"Habi, let's go!" Rafi demanded as he stuffed items into his pouch as well in the hallway.

Out of urgency, Habi didn't even spend the time to secure the drawers. She immediately ran out the room and down the hallway with Rafi. Both of them snatched a can of food from the large bag as they exited the building.

When they returned to the gravel path, a few residents were making their way home, likely assuming that the march of Mamluks had come to an end. Without a word to each other, the pair veered toward the water well, their footsteps quickening. Their hearts pounded in their chests, adrenaline surging through their veins; they'd never stolen from someone else's home before.

—

As Rafi and Habi ran down the gravel path toward the well, they could spot two familiar figures sitting next to it.

"Whoa there you two, why the running?" Tariq said and stood up, worrying if there was someone following them.

The duo slowed their pace, taking a brief moment to catch their breath. Rafi chuckled with every exhale.

"Boy, did me and Habi get a haul," Rafi grinned, his excitement barely contained. "We grabbed some from the market, and we took a lot more from someone's home."

Tariq and Naji stared at him, their expressions a mix of disbelief and concern.

"Don't tell Taliba that," Naji cautioned. "She'd lose it if she found out you two trespassed."

"Aren't we technically trespassing right now?" Rafi shrugged with a sly smile. Leaning in, he whispered, "We don't belong here."

"Good point," Naji admitted with a nod. "Me and Tariq scored some goods from the market too. Our best tactic so far has been pickpocketing. With so many people bumping into each other, no one's paying attention."

Tariq and Naji bumped each other's fists and patted their hard earned pouches on their chest.

Habi took a quick look around her and spoke about her worries.

"Where's Taliba and Hamza?" Habi asked, glancing around.

"Don't know," Tariq replied with a shrug. "Haven't seen them since we got here."

Speaking of the missing children, they could hear the light skitter of gravel approaching them from a path.

And behold, Taliba and Hamza arrived in last place. Both of them looked exhausted as the valuables jingled from their pouches. Hamza's backpack seemed half filled.

"You two look like you had a good time," Rafi joked, a sly grin on his face.

Taliba scowled at him while Hamza chugged from his canteen and refilled it at a nearby well.

"We got stuck behind the Sultan's men," Taliba revealed, her frustration still evident. "There had to be hundreds of them, and the crowd wouldn't stop shoving us around."

"Got anything good at least?" Tariq asked, raising an eyebrow.

"Half food, half coin," Hamza replied. "Taliba wouldn't stop complaining about how much we were walking."

"And rightfully so," Taliba shot back. "You do realize we had to climb those buildings *and* walk miles in a circle, right?"

"It wasn't that bad," Hamza said with a laugh.

"It *was*!" Taliba whined, throwing her hands up in exasperation.

The children laughed as they were reunited once again. The sun, slowly sinking behind the Sultan's tower in the heart of the hive city, signaled it was time for them to return home. Before departing, they carefully counted their items and stowed them in Hamza's backpack to avoid losing any assets. Afterward, they refilled their canteens and made their way through the residential area, eventually finding the shed where they had once stood.

"This is going to suck," Hamza muttered with a heavy sigh.

"Yeah, I know," Rafi agreed, exhaling just as deeply.

All of them were tired from the result of constantly moving and being outside the entire day. Some of them would even suggest camping out in the current district, but that option was immediately vaulted over for the fact that Father would be worried. They could only imagine how Father would feel if he returned home and none of his children were there.

They pooled the last of their energy and helped one another up onto the shed. Tariq was the first to scale the obstacle with ease, reaching the top and offering a hand to the others. This time, Hamza took on the role of anchor. If he hadn't felt heavy before, he certainly did now, weighed down by the heavy pack slung over his shoulders. One by one, Tariq pulled each child up and over, creating a sort of chain effect. Rafi, waiting at the next ledge, was the next to offer a hand. Each child groaned with exhaustion as they made their way over the obstacles. Lifting Hamza required a collective effort, with the others working together to heave him up.

When they reached the wall with missing bricks, they followed the same order as before, with Tariq climbing first. None of them looked back unless it was to help someone else up. Habi, however, was distracted, taking in her surroundings—glancing up, down, and side to side. Below, a child appeared from the house beneath her, watching with curiosity. The child waved at Habi, and she smiled and waved back.

After the short interaction, the children continued to scale up the building. The child below would run back inside the house, telling someone with joy, "Mother, can I join the kids on the roof?"

The children heard the faint words and immediately quickened their pace. By the time the mother and child reached the gravel path, the children were already traversing the wooden plank back up. They boosted each other onto the next building, finally reaching the hole in the wall.

There was minimal conversation between the children, as they all focused on going home and keeping each other safe. Once they all reached the top, they hopped through the hole and accounted for one another.

"I hate to say it, but I can't wait to be back in that shed of a home," Taliba grumbled.

"Same," Tariq added, gasping for air.

One obstacle at a time, they climbed down the mortuary and landed on the platform. The next obstacle was deemed to be an honest trial, as it was the slanted roof they all slid down on.

"We have to make a run for it and grab onto that crest," Rafi instructed. "Mess this up, and we'll all end up like Taliba."

Taliba shot him a glare and elbowed his side, earning laughter from the others at his expense.

After a brief moment of respite, the children systematically ran and leaped across the gap, scrambling up to the crest. One by one, they made it, waiting for Hamza to make his jump. They lay down and reached out their arms to help him. If he grabbed hold of one, the others would pull him up.

Finally, Hamza made the leap but fell short of the crest, struggling to reach it unlike the others. He scrambled up as best as he could, but the weight of the backpack was dragging him down. When they saw him losing his grip, Rafi leaped over the crest, trying to anchor his feet to the edge. The others worked together to stabilize him as Rafi reached down and grabbed Hamza's hand.

"Not today, buddy. Get up here!" Rafi shouted, pulling Hamza up with his remaining strength.

Hamza pulled himself up as best as he could, inching forward with whatever limb he could move. With one final effort, he made it to the top of the crest—but there was a problem. Due to his weight and the downward slope of the roof, he suddenly lost his footing, barreling down the side and taking Rafi, Tariq, and Habi with him. It wasn't a long drop, but the impact was still jarring.

Rafi managed to catch himself when he landed, only scraping his knee. Tariq fell onto his back but broke his fall by spreading his arms wide, softening the blow. Hamza was sprawled on his side, covered in sand and bruises. Habi, unfortunately, tumbled headfirst but managed to protect herself by raising her arms toward the ground. She stumbled to her feet, blood trickling down her forehead. As her hand touched the wound, she winced in pain and gasped at the sight of her own blood dripping onto the floor. Without thinking, she let out a loud wail and burst into tears.

Naji and Taliba slid down the slope to assess the situation. They quickly determined that Rafi and Tariq were unharmed, as they were the ones helping the others. Tariq rolled Hamza onto his other side to check his injuries, while Rafi immediately rushed to Habi's side.

Rafi cursed as Habi's blood stained his hands when he lifted her bangs, "I'm here, Habi!" He took off his shirt and slapped it on top of Habi's head, applying pressure.

"Keep your hands on this and you'll be fine," Rafi assured, keeping one hand on the rag and the other on her cheek. "Hey, hey, look at me. I know it hurts. Please don't cry."

In another miraculous moment for Habi, Rafi kissed her cheek and guided her hands to the rag. Her cries of pain slowly turned into sniffles. She unintentionally scored another smooch.

"Am I going to die?" Habi fretted, her voice trembling as snot dripped from her nose.

"You'll be fine, don't worry," Rafi reassured her.

"Hey, guys, Hamza's messed up," Tariq interjected, his words sharp with urgency.

When Hamza was rolled over, the entire left side of his body was scratched in red. On the bright side, he was still conscious. Tariq and Naji quickly helped remove the backpack and supported him as he struggled to his feet. Hamza wobbled as he stood, his body unevenly weighted from the injuries he had sustained.

"Woo, yeah, good to know to never do that again," Hamza laughed, though he winced as he tried to walk it off.

"We'll help the both of you down. I can take the backpack," Rafi offered, stepping forward.

"Thanks," Hamza said with a grateful grin.

Rafi picked up the backpack from the ground and slung it over his shoulders, immediately feeling the weight settle heavily on his back. Taliba stayed close to Habi, noticing how unsteady she had become on her feet. She gently used her canteen to rinse the blood from Habi's forehead, offering her a few sips of water as well.

The group carefully made their way down, sitting on their bums and sliding off each ledge. Rafi occasionally tossed the backpack to the next level, following Hamza's earlier demonstration to avoid injuring himself. The others helped lower Habi down, making sure to catch her when she landed.

"How do you feel right now, Habi?" Taliba asked, letting Habi hook an arm around hers.

"I'm okay. It just hurts here and there," Habi replied softly.

"You're lucky to have a thick skull then," Taliba teased with a giggle.

Slowly but surely, the children finally made it back onto the streets of the lower hive, right into the Sleeping Complex.

The sunlight began to fade as the dark encroached across the horizon. It was nearly a prime time for dangerous activities to occur in the complex, and the children knew it as well. Quietly, they started making their way toward home, carefully avoiding the silhouettes and groups of people scattered about. In the distance, they could already hear the faint echoes of screams rising from the ruins.

As they walked down the loneliest choices of alleyways, they spotted a group of four other kids hanging out at the steps of a wooden shack. None of them seemed familiar. They were laughing and chatting until they noticed Rafi's group approaching. The other children's eyes flicked over the ragged, exhausted faces of Rafi and his friends, and then to the sizable bag strapped to Rafi's back.

As Rafi's group was about to come to a pass, Rafi made eye contact with all four of the kids, and he knew they had ill intent. Rafi saw how the kids would dart their eyes at the damaged ones, sizing themselves up with Hamza. Their clenched fingers became a dead give away.

But before Rafi could act, the four ruffians already took initiative. One of them swung his arm straight into Naji's face, knocking him onto the ground. Taliba let out a yelp as she witnessed the strike. Tariq got tackled by another while the tallest rascal of the bunch threw fists at Hamza. Rafi was dealing with the last child who attempted to push him down onto his back and incapacitate him with the added weight. As Rafi was defending himself from blows, Habi was trying her best to pull the child off of him, giving him her strongest slaps on the back of his head. It wasn't effective, but it gave Rafi enough time to reach into his pocket and brandish the knuckle duster. Once the weapon was set up, he swung a right hook straight into the kid's jaw, knocking him off.

One of the other ruffian's cursed among the chaos and shouted, "He stabbed me! He stabbed me!" The children recoiled back, grabbing onto his belly as blood leaked from it. Tariq had utilized the shiv he had.

The child who clotheslined Naji had tricks in his pocket as well, brandishing a shiv of his own. The closest one to him at the time was Taliba, and her heart immediately jumped out of her chest as soon as she realized she was the next target.

Hamza was essentially grappling on the ground with his opponent. The taller kid had an arm around Hamza's neck, attempting to choke the air out of him. Within a few seconds, that same kid that had an advantage soon found a knuckle duster in his face, releasing his grip on Hamza.

Habi and Tariq went on to help Taliba, hoping that Rafi was able to tag along. However, Rafi became immobile as soon as the first kid he knocked out recovered and threw him on the floor. The thug smeared his face full of blood into Rafi's eyes as he held down the arm with the duster.

Taliba dodged the shiv strikes to the best of her ability, but she still cried out whenever the boy's shiv made a cut on her arms. Tariq saved the day for her as he stabbed the boy in the back, sweeping his legs in the process. The boy dropped his shiv, which flew over to Habi. With adrenaline only keeping the children moving, Habi picked up the shiv as soon as she discovered that Rafi was pinned down on the ground. And without any further hesitation, Habi ran over to the fight and lunged the shiv into the boy's back. She would repeat the motions again and again until the boy finally cried out and rolled away from Rafi. As soon she went to help Rafi up, she noticed the red stains on her hands when she dropped the shiv. She was shaking, tainted with another's blood.

"Get Naji up! We're moving!" Rafi shouted to everyone.

Hamza tried to slap Naji awake, which didn't work, but it at least confirmed that he was still breathing. Tariq joined in on the help to stabilize Naji, which finally made them able to limp away with him.

Taliba even gave one of the groaning kids on the ground a parting gift as she ran her foot into one's face during departure. If the children weren't exhausted before, then they definitely were now as soon as their blood ceased to boil.

—

By the time the children reached the perimeter of the shed, night had settled in. They kept their distance from any other residents of the lower hive, even though they were no longer within the Sleeping Complex. They were battered, every step a struggle, especially after draining their canteens dry on the way. The adrenaline had pushed them forward, but it had long since worn off, leaving them feeling more broken than before. No words were exchanged throughout the entire journey, except for the occasional check on each other's condition.

Tariq was mostly unharmed, having dealt the most damage to the cockroaches, second only to Rafi, who had only suffered another's blood in his eyes. Taliba sobbed softly, clutching the cuts on her arm, while Naji's nose bore a fresh bruise. Hamza's side was streaked with blood as the scrapes began to worsen. Habi, too, was unharmed—she had managed to evade much of the fighting—but she was no longer the same. Her eyes were empty, drained of energy, and her face wore an emotionless expression that was unfamiliar, even to herself. The adventurous spark that usually lit her up was gone, swallowed whole by the exhaustion and the brutal brawl. She wanted to cry, but there was nothing left in her.

"I'll check for Father," Rafi said as he gestured to the others to hide within the shadows of the alleyway before the shed.

He glanced around the shed before slowly easing the front door open. Inside, only darkness greeted him, thick and oppressive. The only sounds were the scuttling of critters in the corners and the soft creak of his footsteps on the worn wooden floor. He moved cautiously toward Father's workspace, checking to see if perhaps he had simply fallen asleep at his desk, lost to the dark. But when he patted the seat, he found it cold and empty.

After his quick check, he signaled for the others to come inside. They filed in obediently, and Taliba lit the lantern, its flickering glow casting long shadows across the dim interior. The others collapsed onto the familiar wooden floor, weary and battered. Rafi moved quickly to his bedroll, lifting the loose plank beneath it to hide the bag of stolen goods among his stash. Once it was tucked away and the plank secured, he glanced over at the others. The soft light of the lantern revealed just how filthy they were—grime and blood streaked across their clothes and faces. It was the kind of mess that would make Father ask too many questions.

"We did a good job today and made it back home in one piece. Cheer up!" Rafi said, trying to lighten the mood.

"We almost died at least three times," Taliba sighed. "I don't know if we're going to make another trip anytime soon if we're still hurt like this. Your plans are ruined."

"No, they're not," Rafi countered. "I've always planned to play the long game. We got riches, had fun, and made it back home. We can wait as long as we need to—it's just the sooner, the better. Now you've all had a taste of the middle hive. It just makes me want to move out even more!"

"It was nice and fun for sure," Hamza added, sprawled out on the floor as if he hadn't just been fighting for his life. "I'm down for it again. Whatever it takes, right?"

"Whatever it takes," Rafi echoed. "I'm done being poor and surrounded by those roaches."

"We may be poor," Taliba said, her voice softening, "but at least we're happy together."

She had a point. The ambition to leave the lower hive and live off gald was a dream shared by all of them, especially Rafi. But none of them had ever stopped to consider whether their happiness would be the same outside the only life they had ever known—whether it would feel as whole as it did now, when they were together as a family. Rafi sighed, letting Taliba take the win. He had no argument to offer, no clever retort. The truth was hard to swallow, but it was the truth nonetheless. Yet, even so, the pull to strive for something better—a chance at a happier life—was something none of them could ignore.

"Let's go wash off before Father gets back," Rafi said, changing the topic.

The children helped each other to their feet and made their way toward the local pond. Their empty canteens slapped against their hips with each step, the sound dull and rhythmic as they trudged down the worn path through the slums. When they finally reached the water, they plunged in without hesitation, emerging moments later, soaked and gasping. The coolness of the pond offered a brief relief, but as they rinsed off, some of them winced, hissing in pain as the water stung and reactivated their wounds.

"How are we going to hide this from Father?" Taliba asked, absently rubbing the scabs on her arm.

"Just tell the truth," Rafi suggested. "Say some kids tried to jump us, and leave it at that. He'd believe it, considering the riffraff around here. I doubt he'd want to hear about how we climbed buildings and crawled through a hole."

"I mean, that works, I guess," Taliba replied with a shrug, letting the idea settle.

As the children prepared to walk back home, Rafi noticed that Habi was still sitting at the pond and feeling the wound on her head. The small injury clogged after enough pressure had been applied to it, but she still had sorrow written all over her face. While the others turned to leave, Rafi hesitated. He couldn't bring himself to walk away just yet. Slowly, he sat down beside her, the weight of the silence between them settling in.

"Hey Habi, you good?" Rafi asked, splashing at the dirty pond water, his tone lighter than the moment warranted.

Habi stayed silent for a few seconds, her expression distant, before finally speaking.

"I stabbed a boy in the back today," she whimpered, her voice barely above a whisper. "I feel bad." She ran her fingers through the murky water, though her hands were already clean of blood. "His blood got on my hands, and my head hurts."

Rafi grinned and leaned in closer to her, wrapping an arm around her. She enjoyed the gesture, but it wasn't strong enough to pull her out of her temporary mental pitfall.

"That's what I like about you, Habi," Rafi said, his voice calm but full of conviction. "You're the nicest person I know. The most human, even. But considering where we are, we have to know how to balance being both a caretaker and a protector. Be loving one moment, and ruthless the next. I don't think you did anything wrong, Habi. If anything, you protected me, and I thank you for that."

Habi smiled softly and leaned her head on Rafi's shoulder.

"So am I still a good person?" she asked quietly.

"Of course you are, silly," Rafi laughed. "Sometimes, when the bad guys show up, you have to be even worse than them. When it gets tough, you better get tough, right? Be ruthless. Be ruthless to anyone who wants to harm us."

"Be ruthless?" Habi repeated, testing the words.

"Be ruthless!" Rafi exclaimed, standing up and helping Habi to her feet.

"Be ruthless!" Habi echoed, her voice gaining strength.

"Let it all out, Habi! Let your worries and anger go, and don't let anything drag you down! Be ruthless!" Rafi encouraged with a wide grin.

"Be ruthless!!!" Habi roared, her voice ringing out.

"Shut up, you stupid kids!" a homeless man yelled from across the street behind them.

Rafi and Habi shared a brief, quiet chuckle, their laughter cutting through the tension of the moment. It was a small release, a fleeting moment of comfort amidst everything they had endured. Afterward, they fell into a peaceful silence as they made their way back home. By the time they returned, the others were already stretched out on their bedrolls, their bodies worn and quiet. Rafi and Habi settled into their own, each one adjusting to the familiar weight of exhaustion. Taliba, who was sitting up, reached for the lantern and gently began to extinguish the flame, casting the room into a soft, flickering darkness.

"What took you two so long?" Taliba asked, stifling a yawn.

"Small talk, nothing big," Rafi replied with a shrug, already closing his eyes.

Habi suddenly let out a playful roar, more like a small cat than anything else, startling the others. At least her spirits seemed to have lifted.

"Yep, it's bedtime, all right," Taliba giggled, shaking her head as she blew out the candlelight.

Much later, Father returned home, his steps soft as he settled at his desk. Glancing over at the sleeping children, he smiled, a sense of peace washing over him. They were safe and sound under his roof.

Chapter Thirteen

Habi was the first to awaken, though she found herself standing on a dark, surreal plane of existence. Her toes sank into the black grains of sand beneath her feet, coarse and unfamiliar. The children were nowhere to be seen, and the roof of the shed was far from her mind. This time, she felt it—something was different. She knew this was a dream, yet it carried an unusual significance, as if she were fully lucid and aware of her surroundings.

As she looked around into the abyss, the familiar whispers that had once terrified her during a simple trip to the restroom began to fill the air. This time, though, she could hear their words clearly, but they made no sense to her.

Oye, leet ano

Galdi opta ki-le

Spoka o cha cadeave

She heard the words, unsure of what to make of them. The whispers echoed through the void, growing louder before finally fading into complete silence.

Suddenly, the dreamscape warped and shifted into a familiar environment. Habi found herself standing on soft sand in the streets of the lower hive. Yet, everything felt different. The skies were brighter, and the people around her appeared healthier, their faces less worn and more vibrant.

"*Oiye,* Habi" a girl greeted, scaring Habi.

The girl appeared to be about Habi's age—young and spirited, with an inch or so of height over her. They shared the same olive skin, but the girl had sharp, hazel eyes that seemed to glimmer with curiosity. Her dark hair was bobbed into neat, straight cuts around the edges. Though she wore rags too, they were much more neatly kept than Habi's.

"Who are you?" Habi asked, her eyes scanning the girl from head to toe.

"I'm Talia," the girl replied simply, offering no further explanation.

Habi glanced around again, realizing that the faces and buildings were beginning to blur, the details slipping away like smoke. The clarity she had felt moments ago faded, leaving everything distorted and hazy.

Habi hesitated for a moment before finally asking, "Where am I?"

"*Muto o cha Cadeave*, the Land of the Dead," Talia revealed, her tone calm but cryptic.

Habi gasped, clutching her hands to her head. "I'm dead!?" she cried out in alarm.

Talia laughed softly and shook her head. "No, no, *galdi opta ki-le*, golden-eyed child. This is all but in your head—and yet, it is not."

"Please don't riddle me things, I'm bad at them," Habi begged, her voice pleading before her thoughts took a sudden turn. "Does that mean—you're not alive?"

"I am not," Talia said, her voice steady. "But I also am."

Time began to slow around them, and the people who once bustled with life now moved like sloths, their motions sluggish and drawn out. It was a strange sensation, but Habi didn't feel any danger. Instead, she felt strangely at ease in the surreal stillness of the moment.

"Okay, why am I here?" Habi asked again, sticking to the basics, her confusion growing.

"You have always been here. It is us who visit," Talia replied. "It seems you've endured enough trauma for us to finally speak, even when the night awakens."

Habi instinctively rubbed the spot on her head where she had fallen, the memory of the sharp pain from crashing headfirst down the slope still fresh in her mind. The sensation of the wound was faint, but she could almost feel the remnants of the impact.

"But how? And are you sure you're a kid like me? You sound way too smart," Habi said, scowling suspiciously at Talia.

Talia giggled softly and reached out to hold Habi's hands, her gaze locking with Habi's.

"Papa loved to teach me. He did well," Talia said with a bittersweet smirk. "Everyone in this world has mana flowing in their veins. But it remains dormant, because the Heaven's Roots once helped activate our inner abilities. There was a time when magic thrived, but that world is gone now. Humans chose to deny the gods' gift, fearing its chaotic nature."

She paused, her tone shifting to something more deliberate. "But you, Habi—you have a *kataliz*. It's small, but a *kataliz* nonetheless. Small enough to give you the ability to speak with us. To find answers."

Habi was intrigued by the story, but still unsure if she should believe it or not. This could've just been a crazy dream after all.

"Why do you keep saying those weird words? I don't understand them," Habi frowned, her frustration evident.

"A language of the old tongue, *Koumaic*," Talia explained, her smile soft. "Papa taught me that too. I can help you learn it if you'd like."

"I don't think I can learn a new language just like that. It took Father years to teach me the common tongue," Habi sighed, her shoulders slumping.

"Anything can happen with a little bit of mana and the tales from the dead," Talia replied with a mischievous grin.

After their conversation, Talia suddenly grabbed Habi's face and headbutted her square in the forehead. There was no pain, only a rush of unexplainable energy that surged through Habi's body, making the hairs on her arms stand on end. She felt a chill for a moment, but it faded just as quickly, leaving her feeling normal again. When she looked up, Talia was gone.

"Talia? Where'd you go?" Habi wondered, scanning around her.

As Habi looked around, the scenery warped once again. She found herself standing in the rain, the wet sand squelching beneath her feet. A figure appeared before her—a man cloaked in shadow, his face hidden beneath a hood. In his hand, he held a flickering lantern, its light casting an eerie glow on the scene. Beneath him, a toddler lay crying loudly, curled up in the cold, muddy earth, completely alone.

"Another one?" the man said, his voice shaking. "Why do people court, only to leave their young to rot like this? But—you're still alive."

The man gently cradled the cold child, lifting them from the ground. As the toddler's eyes fluttered open, a bright, innocent laugh erupted from their tiny mouth. The child reached up, grabbing at the man's beard with playful curiosity, tugging at it as if it were the most amusing thing in the world. The man smiled beneath his hood, his expression unreadable but softening in the glow of the lantern.

"Golden eyes. You're a special little one, aren't you?" the man said with a grin that didn't quite reach his eyes. "I'll take care of you. You'll have a roof over your head and plenty of friends to play with."

Habi watched as Father walked away, holding her younger self in his arms, the echoes of the past fading in her mind. She barely remembered how it all started, the warmth of those moments now distant and clouded by time.

The dreamscape began to flicker, shifting erratically as scenarios warped before her eyes.

The next vision showed how Father found younger forms of Tariq and Naji, both fighting over a piece of bread. The next one showed Father lending a hand out to Hamza who stood and cried next to another boy who lay dead. After Hamza, it was Taliba.

Younger Taliba ran from Father, hiding in the wreckage of a burnt building, her small body trembling. Father walked over two dead bodies, stepping over them with quiet apology, but Taliba, still scared, refused his reach.

"Little one, I'm just trying to help," Father pleaded softly.

Curled into a fetal position, little Taliba shivered, her small frame trembling until Father draped a worn-out blanket over her. The threadbare fabric brought a faint sense of warmth and comfort.

"I'm here to help, little one," Father murmured gently. "Your parents won't be coming back, but I'll be here."

He reached into his pocket and handed her a few slices of potatoes, their simple offering easing her fear just enough to make her feel a bit safer.

"What's your name, little one?" Father asked, his voice kind and patient.

Taliba didn't speak, only looked at him in confusion. It was then that Father realized she didn't know the common tongue.

"I see—I'll give you one, then," Father said with a faint smirk. "I'll give you a name close to my first daughter's, the one I lost many years ago. Your name will be Taliba."

After speaking the name, he gently handed her another slice of potato, the gesture carrying both warmth and quiet sorrow.

The scene warped once more as Habi's eyes widened at the sight of a younger Rafi.

Compared to the others' pasts, Habi recognized the area where Father found Rafi. It was the Sleeping Complex, and Rafi stood there, threatening Father with a broken bottle.

"I mean no harm, little one," Father said gently, raising his hands in a gesture of peace. "I just want to offer you a better chance. You seem alone out here, are you not?"

"I'll shtab ya, youse ole foo!" Rafi's childlike voice rang out, his thick accent making the threat strangely amusing despite the tension of the moment.

Father didn't react, instead, he pulled out some bread and water in front of younger Rafi. Rafi's eyes lit up at the sight of the rare luxury, reaching for it eagerly. But Father pulled it away just before he could touch any of it.

"Drop the bottle, and you can have it," Father said. "I don't have much of a home, but if you help me take care of it, I'll give you food, water, and a place to sleep. Deal?"

"Fuh youse!" Rafi spat defiantly.

"Language!" Father growled, his tone sharp enough to make little Rafi flinch.

Ultimately, Rafi couldn't resist the temptation. Starving and desperate, he dropped the broken bottle and grabbed the food and water. As he devoured it, he kept a wary eye on Father, unsure of what to expect next.

"Good. Follow me if you want more, then," Father said, turning and walking away, leaving Rafi with an important decision to make.

He hesitated for a moment, uncertainty flickering across his face as he considered whether to trust Father. But the sharp growl of his stomach pushed him forward. With a reluctant step, little Rafi waddled after Father, his small frame moving tentatively. As he did, the dreamscape began to dissolve, melting into an endless dark void.

Silence enveloped her, heavy and cold, pressing in from all sides. Habi's voice echoed in the emptiness, yet no answer came. She stood alone, her words fading into the still air. "Talia?" she called again, her voice quivering slightly. But there was no response.

"Anyone there? Talia?" Habi called out once more, her voice trembling with unease.

As if answering her call, whispers surrounded her again. This time, she could understand what they said.

Sulso cha yulha o highteni
Anye et manate ishta
Dana wakanye anye slitan
Sultani ye gupta
Hassazi fitot
Vet ala iz dey kaye
Hoosh, hoosh
Since the birth of Heaven
To its magical roots

Where people once slain
The Sultan had grew
Hassazi fought
But only if they knew
Hush, hush

Habi didn't know how, but the words in Koumaic translated perfectly into her mind. The small phrase by itself told an entire story that she couldn't even begin to comprehend and put together. She knew the dead were trying to tell her something, but their riddles only made her conjure more questions.

Then there was fire.

She didn't burn from it, but flames engulfed the void, lighting up the darkness. Within the flames, a man's silhouette appeared, holding a sword. Habi could feel his menacing eyes glaring at her, even though she couldn't fully see them.

Ola-te kati
Tread carefully

The whispers warned.

After the warning, the flames grew hotter, and the silhouette suddenly ran toward Habi. She wanted to scream, but she froze instead. The end of his sword pierced her chest.

—

Habi woke up sweating and screaming, startling every child around her just before sunrise. Father reacted immediately, believing there was a hostile presence in the shed.

"Habi? Are you okay!?" Rafi shouted, holding onto her as she shook in terror.

Habi didn't respond. She only began to sprout gibberish in Koumaic, which the children didn't understand. However, Father could.

"*Meeta scuro! Cha cadeave spoko moite! Meeta hona tiniye jahat dey antya!*" Habi cried, hanging onto Rafi as if her life depended on it.

Rafi looked over at the others, and they all shrugged. Hamza pointed to his head, quietly indicating that she might be having an episode from her head injury.

"Habi! Hey, I'm right here!" Rafi comforted, hugging her and kissing her cheek.

From the kiss, she calmed down, but not fully. She turned to look at Rafi's face, only to be even more terrified.

Behind Rafi, a dark silhouette loomed, holding the same sword that had stabbed her in the dream. She yelped in fear, pushing Rafi away, then bolted for the shed door, racing out onto the streets.

Father cursed and immediately followed in pursuit, with the children right behind him. The shock of Habi's erratic behavior had shaken off their drowsiness.

Although Habi ran as fast as she could, she couldn't outrun Father's long strides. Before she could get any further, he swooped her up and cradled her, just like when he had picked her up in the rain as a baby.

"Habi, are you okay?" Father asked. "*Po-toito hamadsha moite*?" Father whispered in Koumaic.

Do you understand me? Is what he said, and Habi absolutely did.

"Father, what is happening to me?" Habi whimpered. "My head hurts. I don't know why I know these strange words. I don't know what I saw. Talia did something to me!"

Father's eyes widened at the name. Habi had never seen it before, but it almost seemed as if he were about to tear up along with her.

"Whose name did you just say?" Father asked, his voice unsteady, a hint of something unreadable in his expression.

"Talia," Habi replied, frowning. "She was young like me and visited me while I was dreaming!"

Father wanted to speak, but no words came out. He was saddened, knowing exactly who Talia was to him. After a brief moment, a small smile appeared on his face. He didn't know whether Habi's experiences were a gift or a curse, but he knew that his first blood child was still watching over him. He also knew that Talia was watching over the children. The same went for Assad, his disciple from the old family. If both of them were trying to reach out to Habi, he wondered if his other friends—perhaps even his enemies—might try to reach her as well.

Father gripped Habi tight to his chest as the children finally caught up to the duo.

"Father?" Habi sobbed, her voice trembling. She wasn't just sad—she was overwhelmed by the sight of something she had never witnessed before: Father crying.

"What happened?" Rafi asked, panting as he hurried over, his face etched with concern.

The children watched in silence, their voices stilled, as Father quietly wept into Habi's shoulder. Habi, overcome, let her own tears flow freely, sharing in the raw emotion of the moment.

—

After the chase, Father and the children returned home. Habi held Father's hand as they entered, scanning the shed for any lingering phantoms. This time, there were no eerie silhouettes.

Some of the children returned to their rolls, tending to their tired bodies, while others—Rafi and Taliba in particular—stayed with Father. He had Habi sit in his lap at the desk, and they watched with curiosity, eager to learn what Father had planned for her. Father paid them no mind.

Father pulled out his logbook, the one he wrote in daily, and opened it to the most recent page. He let Habi examine it, pointing to the words written in Koumaic.

"Do you understand this?" Father asked Habi. "If you do, do not speak it."

Habi nodded, afraid to breathe a single word out her mouth. She was able to read the writing, but she couldn't understand its purpose due to the lack of context.

"Interesting," Father sighed, his gaze distant. "It's strange how the universe aligns to create such coincidences within this home. I once spoke of the tale of Necromantia, and now you claim to have seen those who have passed, even claiming their knowledge."

Habi could feel Father's eyes judging her, as if she could hear the theories running through his mind.

Is this the Sultan's doing? Was Habi a spy all along?

Is this all in her head? Is she taking the story of Necromantia to heart and recreating it?

But how does she know Koumaic in such a short time?

Habi loved stories, and her mind began to wander, imagining the possibilities of what Father thought about her. She also wondered whether he was a superstitious person.

Rafi and Taliba only stared at the two on the desk, believing that the head trauma Habi received finally made her go crazy.

Speaking of the head injury, the small scab on Habi's head caught Father's eye since she was directly under him. He raised her bangs and ran his fingers gently over the scab.

"What is this?" Father asked, his expression darkening into a scowl.

"Uh—I fell on my head," Habi replied nervously.

She told the truth but left out the details. It was easy enough for Father to believe the injury was from a simple fall—he didn't need to know it was because she had slid down a roof from forty feet up.

Father examined the wound one last time and said, "You should be more careful, little one."

Habi responded by placing her hands on her head and making a face that screamed *oopsie*.

Father finally turned his attention to Rafi and Taliba who seemed worried about their sister.

"None of you wish to rest?" Father asked, his gaze sweeping over the group.

"We're just worried about Habi," Rafi replied. "She *did* just scream and run off suddenly."

"The matter is settled for now," Father said, gently placing a hand on Habi's shoulder before releasing her back to the others. "But if it happens again, little one, do not run. I did not sense a hostile presence when we awakened. We are all here for you."

"Okay," Habi murmured, pouting as she lowered her head in shame.

Maybe it was all in her head after all, but not entirely. Habi thought her nightmares were so vivid that they manifested in the darkness before her. However, both she and Father agreed that this was no mere coincidence. Assad and Talia had both been very close to Father, and she had spoken to them. The most shocking discovery was her sudden knowledge of Koumaic. Even Habi was scared of herself at times, now, more than ever.

Father resumed his activities at his workspace, while the trio returned to their beds. Rafi gave Habi a thumbs up, and Habi copied it back.

"Strange times we live in, indeed," Taliba said with a yawn, stretching her arms lazily.

Chapter Fourteen

A week had passed since the children's first climb. Most of their injuries had healed, though some were not fully recovered. During this time, the children spent their days at home, playing in the shed or within the immediate area. They kept to their daily routine with Father, staying on his good side. The stash under the floorboards remained safe for now, as there was no reason for suspicion.

Habi hadn't received any dreams or talked with the 'dead' recently, which made her question her own sanity. On the topic of sanity, Rafi was struck with boredom, feeling his band of thieves was falling back into complacency. It had only been a week since they tasted the wondrous water of the middle hive, but to him, it felt like ages had passed. Rafi was ready to get back to business, especially since everyone's injuries had finally healed to an extent. He just hoped their spirits hadn't faded away with the pain. After Father left for his activities again, Rafi decided to break the ice.

"Hey Habi, how are you holding up?" Rafi asked, settling down beside her in the shed.

Habi lay on her back, staring at the ceiling. Her finger was busy picking her nose when the question came. She responded with nothing more than a short groan.

"That's good to hear," Rafi chuckled, shaking his head.

After the talk, Habi crawled over to Rafi and hugged his waist from the floor, sluggishly laying her head on his lap.

"Am I crazy?" Habi asked, her voice soft and uncertain.

"Aren't we all a little crazy?" Rafi replied with a shrug. "I'm ready for another round, but I don't know about the others."

When the two looked around the room, they spotted Hamza napping, Taliba reading a book, and Tariq drawing on pieces of paper with Naji. This pattern hadn't changed much over the past week, and it began to irritate Rafi.

Taliba caught Rafi's gaze and immediately returned to her book, covering her face. The cuts on her arm were healed and scarred over, leaving a grim reminder of the past week's brawl.

"Hey guys," Rafi called out to the others. All of them stopped what they were doing and paid attention, with the exception of Hamza, who he had to kick awake. "Don't ya think it's time to get the work started again? We did good last time."

Rafi sort of expected it, but the kids remained silent. Habi, on the other hand, was up to the task, knowing the dangers of the trek. It didn't really matter to her, since she was going to be with Rafi regardless. The other children were still scared from both the climb, the descent, and the fight in the Sleeping Complex. He would've thought they would be over it by now, considering that they were attuned to life in the lower hive, but the looks on their faces told a different story. It was always believed that people remembered the negative experiences more than their achievements, and they were living proof of it.

"Do we have to take the complex again?" Taliba asked, her voice tinged with lingering fear as she tried to muster her courage.

"It's the best path we know, Taliba," Rafi replied. "It's not like we get attacked every day of our lives! Plus, we need to uphold our end of the deal with Faruq. He helped us get up and over."

"You mean *you* need to uphold the end of *your* deal," Taliba shot back, her scowl deepening.

"Taliba, don't start this," Rafi snapped, his irritation matching hers.

"Hey now, guys, let's not fight," Hamza interrupted, stepping between them with his arms raised in a calming gesture.

"Both of you have a point," Naji interjected, his tone measured as he joined the conversation. "The longer we stay down here, the more likely we are to end up on the streets with the rest—and probably fighting again, even with Father around. Father isn't going to be alive forever."

He paused, glancing at Taliba and Rafi in turn. "But we also need to be more careful about how and where we move. We let Faruq lead us on a dangerous climb without any practice or experience, and we got careless in the complex. I'm just as mad as Taliba about getting jumped—I mean, I got smacked in the face and passed out!"

Naji sighed, his frustration evident. "Fighting here doesn't help anyone. It's simple: either we do, or we don't."

Even Naji had enough of the constant bickering between the children. His explanation silenced the entire shed. Rafi and Taliba even nodded at each other, setting aside their differences and coming to a silent agreement to finish the job they had started.

"My boy Naji hit the spot," Tariq said, stepping in. "We either stay here forever, fighting for scraps and our lives, or we do something about it."

Ambition began to grow in each child, slowly dragging them out of their complacency. Being comfortable was nice, but the longer they stayed at home, the less they desired to leave that safety. Except for Rafi—he was always hungry for more adventure.

"The sun's still high. Now we know what to expect!" Hamza said with a smile, stepping into the circle the children were forming.

"Be ruthless!" Habi suddenly shouted, bursting into the center with a small war cry. Her voice rang out with determination, though her head began to swim, caught between the oppressive heat and her lingering insecurities about her powers.

The children laughed, while Rafi rubbed the back of his head, looking away slightly. He knew he was the one responsible who had taught her to be relentless in her actions.

"So, are you all up for it again?" Rafi asked, a glimmer of excitement in his eyes. "I've got a better plan this time for how we can acquire things."

His statement raised internal questions among them all, but the idea of something better was too enticing to ignore. So, none of the children questioned him, instead relying on his prowess as their leader.

"Then it's settled! Let's make the trip!" Rafi cheered, his excitement breaking free as he shook off the boredom that had been weighing on him.

—

The children carefully organized the equipment given to them by Faruq. Hamza carried the backpack, its contents safely stashed under the shed, while Rafi and Tariq kept their weapons close. Rafi also tucked a few valuables into the bag, preparing for the possibility of meeting Faruq again, who was promised a share of their spoils for his assistance.

Habi double-checked her pouch, ensuring that little Rafi, her cherished doll, was nestled securely inside alongside the kissed gald coin from many nights ago. With everything in place and their preparations complete, the group donned their hoods, masking their faces, and began their trek back toward the complex.

As the children made their way to the complex under the scorching heat, the merchants and citizens they usually passed began to take notice of their little train. They could feel eyes following them, but they paid it no mind, continuing to act as any child would, living a normal life. A normal life for a child in the lower hive didn't include school, as that was a luxury not afforded here. Instead, the norm consisted of chores and horseplay, which wasn't far from what they were up to. Meanwhile, children from the Sleeping Complex mingled in gang activities, believing they could do whatever they wanted, dismissing normal human morals.

"Aye, you kids off for a walk again?" a homeless man called out, his voice rough as he sat slouched to the side of the dusty path. "They learn quick nowadays, ya?"

Most of the children abided by the rule of not talking to strangers, but Habi on the other hand smiled and waved at him. The man smiled back, acknowledging the good in her heart.

As they hiked to the edge of the complex, they suddenly recognized a familiar face who was speaking with a group of men with daggers at their hips. This time, her child was absent from her arms.

"Sara?" Rafi called out, taking a sip from his canteen. The rest of the children stumbled slightly, bumping into each other as he came to an abrupt stop.

Sara turned toward them, her sharp eyes softening in recognition. She waved the men around her away, and they departed without a word of protest.

"Oh, well, if it isn't Saif's children," Sara said with a smirk, her soft voice carrying a soothing warmth that seemed to ease the tension in the group. "A little too close to danger, no?"

"But you're here too, no?" Rafi shot back, raising an eyebrow.

Sara giggled and walked to them, kneeling down to meet their eyes.

"Oh, Rafi," Sara said with a sly smile. "I was raised in the Sleeping Complex. I believe I can handle myself here. But may I ask, why are all of you here?"

Rafi sucked in his lips, knowing that speaking either the truth or spouting lies could get them in trouble. Sara was part of the old family, close to Father, and he didn't know whether to trust her secrecy. In the end, it turned out that he didn't have to say anything.

"We're going on an adventure to the middle hive!" Habi beamed, her enthusiasm unfazed, despite the heat and lingering turmoil clouding her thoughts.

The other children, except Rafi, facepalmed in perfect unison, turning their heads away from her as if to disassociate from the bold statement.

"Is that so?" Sara said, her tone curious yet skeptical. "And how do you all plan to do that?" Her eyes narrowed as she focused on Rafi, standing confidently at the front of the group.

Rafi decided to come clean, saving everyone the trouble.

"There's a path in the Sleeping Complex that leads to a hole in the border wall," Rafi explained. "We climb up and then descend into the middle hive that way."

Sara stood up, her gaze sweeping over each of the children as she nodded thoughtfully.

"Is it scary?" she asked, her tone probing.

Rafi hesitated for a moment, unsure if she was asking about the climb or the dangers of the Sleeping Complex itself.

"Be honest. Is the entire trip scary?" Sara repeated, her voice steady.

"It is," Rafi admitted, meeting her gaze. "But it doesn't bother us."

"It must bother you, if you and the one in the back are carrying weapons," Sara said, her sharp eyes narrowing. "I can see them in your pockets." She paused, then added with a soft smile, "But that's okay, little ones. I have some free time while my husband takes care of our child at home. Perhaps I can help escort you all through the complex?"

"You don't have to," Rafi said, shaking his head.

"I insist," Sara replied firmly. "I know the roads and the people here. I wouldn't be able to sleep at night knowing something might happen to Saif's children—or to my own child someday, when I'm not there."

"Does that mean you won't tell Father?" Rafi asked cautiously.

Sara laughed, covering her smile with her hand. "You think I wouldn't have done the same when I was your age?" she smirked. "Come, come, let us go now."

After the exchange, Sara gestured for the children to follow her, leading them into the depths of the Sleeping Complex like a teacher guiding her class. Rafi directed her toward the hole in the wall, and Sara skillfully navigated the paths, avoiding any potential confrontation. The group passed a few complex dwellers, but most were either absorbed in their own activities or offered a simple nod of acknowledgment.

"So, why did you *really* want to come along, Sara?" Rafi whispered, keeping his voice low as he walked beside her, away from the others.

Sara smiled faintly, her eyes scanning the path ahead with care. "You know how you jump over the gaps between buildings to get to the next one? Scary, isn't it?"

Rafi nodded, unsure where she was going with her question.

"When it feels scary to jump, that's exactly when you should take the jump," Sara continued, her voice calm yet laced with a quiet sadness. "Otherwise, you'll stay in the same place your whole life. Don't end up like me, Rafi." She smiled, but the gloom in her eyes betrayed her.

"I see," Rafi murmured, his lips forming a small pout as he absorbed her words.

During their conversation, Sara came to a halt, noticing a strange pattern. The complex consisted of tiny buildings and tents, scattered among narrow alleyways. As they walked, she pointed out a man who was walking parallel to them from a distant alleyway. She couldn't help but notice how quiet the complex had become in the immediate vicinity, with not even the usual screams of pain echoing through the halls of blood, crime, and disease.

"Why'd we stop?" Hamza asked, glancing around nervously from the middle of the line.

"We're being watched," Sara said, her voice low and serious. "Gather around me."

The children huddled around Sara, careful not to stand in front of her so as not to hinder her movements. Rafi and Tariq had their weapons drawn, while the others braced for any sudden impact.

During the tense standoff, Habi looked away toward another alleyway that intersected with theirs. A child with wide, sunken eyes stood at the center of the path, staring directly into Habi's eyes. Slowly, the boy pointed behind him, revealing a group of individuals hiding behind crates and piles of trash. Each of them armed with a small blade or shiv.

"There's someone there," Habi muttered, pointing in the direction of the child.

The children turned toward the direction Habi had noticed and immediately spotted two men approaching them, their postures low and ready. The man who had been walking parallel moved ahead, coming from another exit to approach them from the front. They were surrounded by three malnourished men, each armed with a weapon. Taliba shot a knowing look toward the others, as if to say, *I told you so.*

"We are just passing by, gentlemen. Please don't do anything rash," Sara said, her tone calm but firm.

"Ya know where you are, sweet cheeks?" the man in front growled, flicking the sharp edge of his blade menacingly. "You just brought us some good supply. You'll find a place too, if you're a good girl and come with us."

With that single statement, Sara knew they were child traffickers. The slums and the upper hives would pay a large sum for their labor and other illicit activities, and she was no stranger to that world. Over the span of her life, Sara had learned that even the Sultan's men were often complicit, turning a blind eye to these horrors.

"I'll tell you what, girl," the man said, spreading his arms wide, a smug grin plastered across his face. "You give us all them kids, and you walk out free. No problem at all, ya?"

"I'm afraid I can't do that," Sara replied, her tone unwavering.

"Oh, so you wanna die? Is that it? What? Think you can beat us all up?" the man sneered. His companions erupted in laughter as they began closing the distance, their weapons glinting ominously.

One of the men got closer to Tariq, who was positioned further away from Sara's huddle. Tariq had his shiv pointed at the man, poised to strike.

"I know I won't beat you all up," Sara sighed, her voice steady as the man reached for her wrist.

"I'm going to *kill* you all," she said, her gaze cold and unwavering. "That's what I'm going to do."

In the blink of an eye, Sara seized the man's wrist holding the blade and trapped it under her armpit. She swung her leg out and snapped it back, striking the man's calf inward and causing him to stagger. In one swift motion, Sara shoved him backward, twisting the knife from his grip while retaining control of his arm. As he crashed to the floor, she stretched his arm out, pinning his hand to her hip, and drove her foot into his elbow. A sharp crack followed, and the man screamed as his elbow bent at an unnatural angle.

Rafi cursed and rushed to assist Tariq with the two men behind the group. Tariq, taking a cue from Sara, lunged at the nearest man with a stab, but the man dodged effortlessly. In a swift counter, the man kicked Tariq in the chest, sending him sprawling onto his back.

"Oi, don't hurt the product that much!" one of the men shouted, his voice tinged with urgency. "Get that small one!"

The towering height and weight of the men effortlessly shoved the children aside, causing them to stumble and fall. They fended off Rafi's attacks with ease, one of them landing a kick to his face that sent him reeling. One of the men seized Habi, who struggled desperately to free herself but was overpowered without effort. Meanwhile, the other man turned to confront the real threat: Sara.

As the man squared off with Sara to buy his accomplice time to subdue Habi, he froze, momentarily holding his breath at the sight before him.

Sara stood spattered with the blood of the man she had felled. Her knife had just been driven into his throat before she withdrew it. Crimson streaks stained the street and her clothes.

When Rafi looked at Sara, he could hardly recognize her. The motherly, carefree expression he knew was gone, replaced by a cold, violent glare.

Sara surged toward the man. He tried to swing his blade at her, but she drove her knife into his forearm with lightning speed. Before he could react, she wrenched the blade free and, in one fluid motion, reversed her grip and plunged it into his eye socket. The man's jaw dropped in silent agony as he struggled to scream, his remaining eye rolling back. Sara twisted the knife and pulled it out, sending him crumpling to the ground. His body convulsed briefly before going limp.

The last man had managed to carry Habi a fair distance away, but her relentless struggles, combined with the children's blows to his legs, turned it into a grueling effort. After seeing the ferocity with which Sara dispatched his comrades, he pressed his shiv to Habi's throat and pulled her into a chokehold. The children froze and stepped back, fearing for their sibling's safety.

"Get back! I'll kill her if you take one step closer!" the man threatened.

Habi was choking and on the verge of tears, but a spark of defiance remained. In a desperate bid to survive, she sank her teeth into the man's forearm, making him yelp and pull back. The moment he released her, Sara hurled her blade into his chest. The man groaned as he dropped to the ground, relieved it wasn't a fatal wound, but he winced, feeling the blade's edge graze the surface of his ribs.

Sara quickly ended his relief, delivering a powerful kick to the man's chest, driving the blade deeper. He collapsed to the ground, and she mounted him, her hands gripping the handle of the knife lodged in his chest.

"Mercy!" the man choked, his voice wet and gurgling, likely from his own blood. "I'll leave! I'll–"

Before the man could finish his plea, Sara twisted the blade's handle, driving it further into his chest. When she was satisfied, she leaned close to his face and whispered softly.

"You shall never know peace," Sara whispered coldly, her voice low and unforgiving.

After her whisper, Sara yanked the blade free and plunged it into his throat. She followed with quick, brutal stabs to his eyes, jaw, and scalp. Each strike was fueled by raw fury, as though these men had ruined her once-peaceful walk through the most dangerous part of the lower hive.

The children couldn't bear to watch the brutal scene, turning their eyes away. Eventually, Sara came to a halt, the man lying motionless at her feet. She took deep breaths, her hands steadying, before turning toward the children. They stood frozen, horrified by the blood that drenched her.

"May I borrow one of your canteens, please?" Sara asked calmly, her voice steady and composed.

—

Sara rinsed herself with Rafi's leftover canteen water, pouring it over her head. The blood washed away, streaming down her face, but her rags were beyond saving. Still, the soaked and stained clothing could serve as a deterrent to any criminals thinking of attacking.

"I think Sara is scarier than Father," Habi whispered into Rafi's ear.

"Oh yeah," Rafi murmured in quiet agreement.

The children emerged mostly unscathed, save for a few nosebleeds from being kicked and shoved like insects under the men's feet. They weren't as horrified by the attack as they had been in the past, but they were deeply shocked by Sara's actions. They had always thought of her as an innocent mother, raised by Father. But then it clicked for Habi. She was the only one who truly understood who Father really was. She began to wonder if Sara's skills and savagery had been learned from her connection to the Hassazi. The secrecy surrounding Sara, coupled with her past with the old family, led Habi to make the unsettling realization.

Sara saved some water for Rafi and handed his canteen back to him. Then, she smiled at the children, her expression calm and warm, as if she hadn't just mutilated three men moments before.

"Sorry you all had to see that," Sara said, her voice soft with regret.

The children now chose their words carefully, unsure if their choices could provoke Sara and turn her against them. While it seemed unlikely, their best defense was that they were Father's children. So, they opened their minds freely, relieved to have Sara on their side.

"It's okay, we've seen worse," Rafi replied.

It was half true and half false. The children had witnessed murders, stumbled across discarded bodies, and even breathed in the stench of rotting carcasses. But this encounter was the most grim. They had never anticipated such sheer brutality from Sara, a woman they had always seen as fair and composed.

"True lower hive dwellers then," Sara giggled, her voice light and unbothered. "Now, which way was the hole again?"

Rafi awkwardly chuckled and pointed toward the entrance to the middle hive, not far from where they stood. However, a small matter nagged at one of the children.

"There was a kid back there. He looked like he needed our help," Habi murmured, the thought surfacing now that the chaos had settled.

Sara and the other children exchanged curious glances, their eyebrows raised in question. Sara stepped closer and gently patted Habi's head—a gesture typically reserved for Rafi's comforting hands.

"There were no children back there, little one," Sara said softly. "I would've seen them."

Now Habi raised an eyebrow, questioning herself. She could've sworn she saw a child who helped locate the thugs in the alley. Unless she was losing her mind again, she wondered if it was just her imagination, or if the child had once been one of the victims.

As the group made their way toward the ascending buildings near the wall, the children couldn't help but ask more questions, trying to break the silence that had settled around them.

"Where'd you learn how to do all of that?" Rafi asked, his curiosity getting the better of him.

"Can you teach me those moves, please?" Hamza chimed in eagerly.

"I want to be like you when I grow up," Habi added, her voice filled with admiration.

Sara laughed at their questions, her light, airy chuckle only deepening the mystery. She didn't answer a single one. Instead, she turned to face them, raising a finger to her lips in a hush gesture, her eyes gleaming with a smile.

"Hush, hush," Sara whispered softly.

The children immediately fell silent, their imaginations running wild. None dared speak again, fearing that Sara's quiet warning might turn into something far more terrifying.

—

With no further conflict, the group reached the bottom of the climb. Sara scanned the buildings leading up to the hole, already mapping out the route they needed to take. The children gathered around her like an ant colony around their queen, waiting to see what she would do next.

"Quite the climb, is it not?" Sara said with a grin, glancing at the daunting path ahead.

"It is, but it can be done," Rafi nodded confidently. "Are you sure you don't want to come with us, Sara?"

Sara giggled softly. "I'm afraid I'm far too large for that opening." It was a lie—she was slender enough to fit through, and the children knew it. Yet, they chose not to challenge her words. "I also have a little one waiting for me at home. I wouldn't want to keep them waiting, would I?"

That, at least, was the truth.

The children understood her decision and thanked her for saving them, though the way she did it still haunted them. Before parting, she patted each of their shoulders, wishing them good luck on their travels. They reminded her of her younger self with the old family.

As she turned to walk away, she muttered a blessing in a strange language, the words carrying an air of mystery and weight.

"Vay cha ys sposhish ulta toito."

May the Gods watch over you.

Habi overheard and understood it. While Rafi climbed onto the crate that led to the top of the shed, Habi waved Sara farewell and shouted, *"Vita toito, yai mistra!"*

Thank you, big sister!

The children shrugged it off as gibberish, but Sara froze when she heard Habi's words. She didn't turn back, only offering a quiet smile before continuing on her way.

Chapter Fifteen

The children climbed once more, but this time, they worked smarter, not harder. They moved easily between the gaps, careful not to exert themselves fully. They helped each other up to each new ledge, their movements more coordinated. Hamza became the anchor, a steady platform for the others to step on while they assisted him upward. They had learned from their previous climb, especially with Faruq no longer watching over them. Even on the sloped roof, Taliba understood the lesson, avoiding the temptation to drop down and scrape herself again. The obstacles were no longer just easier—they were faster. Their past mistakes had become ingrained, and their teamwork flowed seamlessly. Before long, they reached the summit of the mortuary building, standing before the hole leading to the middle hive.

Rafi scouted ahead once more, making sure there were no changes or potential threats. When he deemed it clear, the children descended the familiar buildings and stepped back onto the middle hive streets. Almost immediately, they gathered at the neighboring well, refilling their canteens.

"Is it just me, or was that way easier?" Hamza asked with a smile, taking a long drink from his water canteen.

"Learn the hard way first, make it easier the next, ya?" Tariq chuckled, leaning against the wall.

Taliba was still shaking from the climb and descent, but not as much as before, since she came out unharmed. Sara's previous ferocious display didn't help her come to her senses either. She had to speak and get her mind out of the dark.

"All right, now that we're here, what's your plan for this run?" Taliba asked, watching Rafi as he helped Habi fetch water.

"Right then," Rafi said, straightening up. "Gather around me—we gotta keep it low."

The children followed his command, huddling next to the well, where wasted water pooled on the ground.

"We're going to walk into these homes and steal their stuff," Rafi declared, his tone unapologetic.

"You can't be serious," Taliba hissed, her surprise evident at Rafi's bluntness.

"Oh, I am," Rafi replied. "Listen, the market may be fun, and we could hit it sooner or later, but the real prizes are inside these folks' homes. They've got food, clothes, valuables—you name it! Nothing like the scraps in the lower hive."

"That just sounds wrong," Taliba shot back, her voice edged with frustration.

"You act like what we've been doing hasn't been wrong," Rafi countered, his eyes narrowing.

Taliba scowled at him, but she couldn't deny the truth in his words.

"Okay, but how are we going to get into the homes? What if the people are home? What if the doors are locked?" Naji asked, folding his arms.

"Well, it's easy to find out if someone's home. As for the locks, we'll just use the windows. Don't think there are locks for windows down here—I keep seeing people open them without any extra step," Rafi explained confidently.

"Hmm, you may be right about that," Naji admitted. "Now, what's the plan to see if someone's home?"

"Easy," Rafi said with a smirk. "Just knock, run away, and watch."

"There's no way all six of us are going to be able to hide if they answer," Taliba pointed out skeptically.

"That's why we split into groups again," Rafi said, already forming a plan. "You and Hamza can take one end of this hood. Tariq and Naji on another. Same goes for me and Habi." He stuck to the same lineup they had used during their last trip to the middle hive. "If they answer the door, just move on to the next. Simple as that."

"I guess it'll work," Taliba said reluctantly. "Let's get to it then. Meet back here the same as before? The sun behind the tower?"

"Good deal," Rafi agreed with a nod.

After the children patted each other's back for a safe trip, they then parted ways and took control of different segments of the neighborhood that hugged the wall. Without the regards of taking in the well-being of those that lived here, their plan was executed.

From the well, Rafi and Habi took the path furthest from the wall and market, deliberately avoiding as many citizens as they could. They often saw parents walking with their children, which they considered a good sign. Most pedestrians paid no attention to the two hooded figures moving through the neighborhood, as the middle hive was safer than the lower one, offering children more freedom. Instead, it was the children who took notice of Rafi and Habi, wondering if they were available to play games or sports. Even Habi found herself tempted by one child's offer when she saw a group of kids behind them, playing with toys.

"Later, Habi. Not now," Rafi reminded, his tone firm but gentle.

"Okay," Habi pouted, her disappointment clear as she waved farewell to the other children instead.

After carefully navigating the secluded areas of the neighborhood, the duo finally found a spot away from prying eyes. The buildings around them had solid foundations, with layers of sandstone at the bottom and wooden frames at the top. Some homes featured fenced-off patios and intricately carved sandstone stairs leading to their doorways. To Rafi and Habi, it was a mystical sight, unfamiliar yet strangely captivating.

"All right, Habi, I'm going for this one," Rafi said, pointing to the nearest home on his right. "You hide back over there, and I'll come join you soon. I don't hear anything from this house, so it might be good."

Habi nodded, waddling away and turning the corner to hide behind another building.

Rafi crept up to the front door, knocking loudly three times. The moment his knuckle left the wood, he darted away, sprinting toward Habi, who was already peeking around the corner, one eye fixed on the door.

"Let's give it ten seconds," Rafi whispered, crouching beside her.

About six seconds later, the door creaked open, revealing a young woman who cautiously glanced around the vicinity. Without uttering a word or curse, she rolled her eyes, shook her head, and closed the door behind her.

"Well, that one's a bust," Rafi whispered, clicking his tongue in mild annoyance. "I'll mark it with a rock or something so we don't try it again."

Rafi picked up the largest rock he could find in the gravel path and placed it gently at the corner of the house. Once the home was marked, the duo walked over to another.

Habi hid again as Rafi tried to eavesdrop on any indoor activity. To his amusement, he didn't hear a single footstep or creak of the floorboards. After confirming the silence, he knocked on the door again before quickly running back to Habi.

Ten seconds flew by, and no one answered the door.

"We may have a hit," Rafi said with a sly smile. "If we get in, remember—just take a small amount that can fit in our pouches. We don't need the whole Ghazi army coming down on us."

Habi nodded, her heart racing with excitement, knowing she was about to journey once again into the unknown.

Once the duo gathered their courage, they crept over to the door. Rafi tried the handle, and, unsurprisingly, found it locked.

Rafi cursed under his breath and nodded toward the nearest window. When they reached it, he placed his palms on the glass and effortlessly pulled it up. He was right—there was a lack of locks on the windows in the middle hive.

As the window slid up, Rafi peeked over the ledge and scanned the room. It looked ordinary—just a wardrobe and two floor beds, from what he could see. He took one last glance at the street to make sure no one was nearby, then climbed over the window's ledge. He crawled into the room and offered his hand to Habi, who was eager to follow. Habi planted her feet on the home's exterior and crawled through the opening to join him.

"I'll check the other rooms. You check this one," Rafi instructed quietly, his voice barely above a whisper.

"Okay," Habi agreed with a nod.

Rafi sneaked to the room's door and carefully stepped out, glancing around to see if anyone was nearby. Meanwhile, Habi went straight to the wardrobe. When she opened its fine wooden doors, she was greeted by rows of dresses and suits hanging neatly in front of her. At the bottom, small boxes were folded shut. Without hesitation, she opened them, revealing rings and necklaces piled on top of one another. She picked a few pieces, focusing on the rings that would easily fit into her pouch. Once satisfied, she closed the box, making it look exactly as it had been.

After her small plunder, her attention was drawn to a unique dress. It was a black gown, draped over one shoulder, with lower frills that gleamed majestically in the window's light. When she touched it, the fabric felt incredibly soft—silk, she thought, a luxurious material. As she admired the dress, she pulled it out and draped it over her body. It was far too large for her, but her imagination soared, imagining herself in its elegant form.

Suddenly, Rafi returned to her.

"I struck some gald and a watch," Rafi whispered, a quiet cheer in his tone. "How did it go in here?"

Habi turned to face him with a bright smile, the oversized dress draped over her small frame.

"Do I look good in this?" Habi asked, smirking gleefully.

She was expecting a grand compliment, but instead, Rafi said, "That doesn't even fit you."

"That's not what you're supposed to say!" Habi frowned, dropping the dress in frustration.

"What am I supposed to say?" Rafi frowned back, genuinely confused. "Okay, okay, you look beautiful in it. Now put it back, and let's get out of here."

Content with his answer, Habi blushed and carefully hung the dress back in the wardrobe, making sure to seal it shut. Once everything was back in place, the duo crawled back out through the same window they had entered.

Rafi closed the window quietly and marked the house with a small pebble to avoid returning by mistake. Then, he and Habi wandered off toward another home, ready to continue their search.

This time, Rafi hid as he let Habi take a turn knocking and running.

"Just do what I did, and you'll be fine," Rafi said with a grin, confidence radiating from him.

Habi aggressively nodded and jogged over to the door, her pouch jingling with every step. Her knocks weren't as loud as Rafi's, but they were efficient nonetheless. Once the deed was done, she ran back to Rafi and peeked around the corner with him.

Ten seconds passed, and no one answered.

When they tried the door this time, the handle turned fully, and it creaked open. Rafi paused, realizing that an unlocked front door likely meant the owners weren't far. Despite the risk, he decided to take the plunge. In the lower hive, leaving a door unlocked would have had drastic consequences—but this was the middle hive, and he was willing to gamble on the difference.

The duo raided the home with speed and silence, running in one second and out the next. They obtained more valuables, but not much to their liking.

As Rafi marked the home, he spotted a man walking toward the door from around the other corner of the house. The man must have made a trip to the well, as he was carrying two buckets of water in both hands.

The man saw the children but said nothing, assuming they were just playing with the sand and gravel.

A few seconds later, he walked inside and locked the door behind him.

"That was a close one," Habi whispered, her voice barely audible.

"Sure was," Rafi agreed, wiping a bead of sweat from his forehead. "One more house and we'll call it a day. My pouch is getting heavy. Did I say it was easy, or did I not?"

"You sure did!" Habi giggled, her eyes lighting up as she admired the determination in Rafi's gaze.

The duo walked further away, having been spotted by a resident, even though no suspicion seemed to weigh on them. They simply didn't want to be around if the man happened to realize some of his necklaces were missing.

Once they settled in a secluded area, Rafi and Habi decided to push for one final house. Rafi approached the door and knocked loudly, the sound echoing through the quiet surroundings. Meanwhile, Habi quickly ducked behind a nearby corner, finding a spot to hide and observe.

"What'cha doin'?" a soft, gentle voice suddenly asked, startling Habi from behind.

Habi spun around to see the source of the voice—a young girl dressed in a bright, colorful shirt and skirt. Her dimples deepened as she smiled, her pale skin flushing a warm red.

"Are you playing a game with that cute boy?" the girl giggled, stepping closer and peeking from behind Habi. "Can I play too?"

At first, Habi was about to accept the girl's request, but her enthusiasm quickly vanished when she heard the girl call Rafi 'cute', Habi didn't like that one bit.

"He's mine! Go play somewhere else!" Habi growled, her voice sharp and protective.

"Why are you so angry? I just want to play! The other kids always play with me!" the girl shot back, her tone growing defensive.

"Go away, boy stealer!" Habi snapped.

"Boy stealer!?" the girl exclaimed, her cheeks flushing as the verbal sparring intensified.

As the two argued, Rafi finished knocking on the door and quietly retreated to Habi's hiding spot.

"Hey, Habi, remember, this is our—who the hell is that?" Rafi asked, squinting at the nicely dressed girl.

Both girls turned to him, their faces lighting up with excitement at his presence.

"Hi!" the girl waved cheerfully, still crouched beside Habi. "Can I play with you two?"

"Don't trust her, Rafi! She's a demon!" Habi cried, scrambling away from the girl and latching onto Rafi's arm.

"Okay, it's time to go," Rafi said, clicking his tongue, clearly weirded out by the odd situation. He grabbed Habi's hand and started guiding her away, leaving behind the girl and the potential loot inside the house.

As they walked off, Habi stuck her tongue out at the girl, who simply stood there with her hands on her hips, squinting at them from afar.

Rafi kept an eye on the girl to make sure she didn't follow them, then turned his attention to finding another home to raid.

"Making friends?" Rafi chuckled, glancing at Habi with a smirk.

"Enemies," Habi corrected, her tone sharp.

"Right then," Rafi said, shaking his head. "Hide behind that building over there, and this time, make sure no one sneaks up on you."

Habi mocked the Ghazi salute with a playful gesture before jogging away from the scene. Once she was clear, Rafi sprinted to the house and knocked loudly on the door. After reuniting with Habi, he quietly counted to ten, watching and listening for any signs of movement inside. When there was no response, he nodded at Habi and led her to the house's steps.

He tried the door, but the handle wouldn't budge. With the front entrance blocked, the duo rerouted to a nearby window that was easy to reach. Rafi followed his usual routine, sliding the glass up and crawling inside. Once in, he turned back to pull Habi up after him.

"All right," Rafi whispered. "I'll check the starting room this time. You go ahead and look around. Grab what you can—we're done after this one."

Habi nodded and slipped out into the hallway, moving silently toward the door across from her. She gently turned the knob and opened it, slipping in between the small gap and closing it behind her without a sound. The scent of recently lit incense hit her immediately, the sticks sizzling in their pot, with smoke lingering in the air. She scanned the room from right to left, noting several displays of jewelry and stones arranged on tabletops. On the walls, there were multiple papers pinned with drawings and letters that she couldn't make sense of from where she stood.

To the left of the room, Habi froze. An elderly woman lay on a floor bed, her gaze either fixed on the ceiling or, possibly, asleep—Habi wasn't sure. To avoid drawing attention, she held her breath and tiptoed toward the tables where the jewelry was laid out, eager to snatch whatever she could.

"Dana—is that you?" the elderly woman said, her voice raspy and tired. "Come, my child—I wish to feel your touch. I love you."

The woman didn't turn her head or make any movements aside from the subtle rise and fall of her chest, her mouth barely moving. Habi assumed she must've been in pain or disabled in some way, and her little heart stirred with sympathy. Instead of reaching for the valuables, she walked over to the woman.

As she neared, the woman seemed to sense her approach, slowly extending her hand, palm up, as if waiting for Habi to offer hers. Habi hesitated for only a moment before gently laying her small hand in the woman's, who then slowly, carefully, clenched it with a faint, almost imperceptible smile.

"My sweet Dana—you're ever so soft—you're shaking," the woman murmured, her eyes remaining closed. "Always remember, Dana—" she coughed weakly, pausing to catch her breath. "I am your mother—I will always be here for you if you need someone to touch. Life will always put you in hard circumstances, and I want you to know—you are not alone."

Habi frowned, her heart sinking as the woman gently released her hand. The woman's expression softened, and she returned her hands to her chest, offering Habi a tender, almost wistful smile.

"You are a good girl—don't let anyone say otherwise," the woman wheezed, her voice faint. "May I hear your voice, sweetie?"

Habi was reluctant at first, but she played along with the woman's request in a soft tone.

"I love you, Mama," Habi whispered, the words feeling foreign but sincere as they left her lips. She realized, in that moment, that she had never said those words before.

The woman smiled and said nothing more.

At that point, Habi knew the woman had figured it out—that she wasn't speaking to her own child. Despite the realization, the elderly woman simply lay in bed, her smile never faltering, content with the moment and the connection she had made with a stranger.

After the strange event, Habi quietly left the room without stealing a single object.

She gently shut the door behind her and regrouped with Rafi, who was about done scouring the room. His pouch was nearly filled to the brim, jingling with various goods.

"Any luck?" Rafi asked, slipping the last ring into his pouch with a satisfied expression.

Habi shook her head and pouted.

"That's fine. We have more than enough," Rafi assured her. "Now let's get out of here and enjoy the time we have before the sun sets behind the tower."

"Okay," Habi agreed, nodding as she followed Rafi back out the window.

Rafi marked the last home with a pebble, even though their raids were done for the day. The markers were meant to last for their next outing in the coming days. Once they were in the clear, the duo jogged toward an open area filled with the sound of cheers and laughter, blending seamlessly into the crowd of children playing on a patch of grass. A few parents stood nearby, keeping watch over the scene.

"I'd say we have about an hour left," Rafi said, glancing at the sun's position. "What do you wanna do in the meantime?"

A red ball made of rubber material rolled over toward Habi's feet. She was unsure exactly what this object was, but it seemed harmless at least.

"Pass the ball!" a child yelled joyfully, waving eagerly at Habi. Behind him, several other children waited, their excitement palpable.

Habi spotted the ball nearby and knelt down to pick it up. With a determined toss, she lobbed the ball toward the boy, but it fell short, bouncing a few feet away from him.

"Oh, come on, you can do better than that!" the boy teased, laughing as he retrieved the ball. "Wanna join? We're playing ball-tag!"

Habi smiled and turned to face Rafi for permission. As if Rafi were her father, he shrugged and nodded.

"Hand me the pouch so you don't lose it, at least," Rafi said with a grin, holding out his hand.

Habi lifted her necklace pouch up and over her head, handing it to Rafi for safekeeping. While Habi ran to learn how to play ball-tag, Rafi sat on the sidelines with the parents, securing Habi's pouch around his neck.

The boy threw the ball and it tapped Habi's shoulder.

"You're it!" the boy laughed, darting away as the entire playground scattered, leaving Habi standing there with the ball in her hands, looking confused.

"Chase us and toss the ball, doodoo head!" a girl teased, sticking her tongue out at Habi before sprinting off.

The instructions were simple enough for Habi to follow. She ran toward the nearest child and tried to throw the ball at him, but missed. She quickly retrieved it and tried again, missing each time until one of the boys stood still, as if waiting for her to hit him. Seizing the chance, Habi threw the ball and struck him in the chest.

"You're it!" Habi laughed, her excitement bubbling over as she finally got to experience being chased.

The game continued as time seemed to fly by. Rafi watched with a sense of pride, seeing Habi enjoying herself among the unknowing children. The ball had been passed around several times, and now it was Habi's turn again to tag someone. Her breathing was heavy, but her blood raced with joy. She relished the fun, chasing the others with the ball. Then, out of the corner of her eye, she spotted a girl laughing quietly, standing apart from the main group. The girl readied herself to run, but Habi was already closing in. Habi had already thrown the ball at the retreating girl.

"You're it!" Habi laughed, her voice ringing out with joy as she tossed the ball.

The children around her stopped running as soon as they saw Habi throw the ball at an empty corner. Habi began to run, but turned back to see what the children were looking at. The red ball continued to bounce toward a neighbor's home, with not a single girl in sight toward that direction.

"What ya throwin' at, blindey!?" a child shouted, laughing as the ball missed its mark. The rest of the children joined in, their laughter echoing around the playground. "Go get the ball!"

Habi stood frozen for a moment, confused by the sudden disappearance of the child after she tossed the ball. Embarrassed by the awkwardness, she quickly shook it off and ran toward the ball. When she reached it, she inspected it carefully, looking for any sign of damage or, strangely enough, the lingering presence of the girl.

"You should leave," the girl giggled, suddenly appearing right next to Habi. Her voice was soft but carried an eerie weight. "It's not safe. Be careful on the way back."

Before Habi could respond, the girl faded away as quickly as she had appeared.

"Are we gonna play or what!?" a boy shouted from the playing area, breaking the strange moment.

Habi snapped out of her trance and quickly responded to the children's calls to continue playing. As she reached the grassy patch, the children laughed and scattered, as if nothing unusual had happened.

Habi jogged and prepared to toss the ball at a boy who was in arm's reach. But suddenly, the boy stopped in his tracks.

A strange aura of darkness began to shroud the boy, twisting and forming into a silhouette that Habi instantly recognized from her dreams. Terror gripped her as her gaze locked onto the blade in the figure's hand. Her instincts took over, and with tunnel vision, she swung the ball like a weapon, striking the shadowy figure square in the face.

The figure collapsed to the ground, but Habi didn't stop. Fueled by fear, she pummeled it relentlessly with the ball, each strike driven by pure panic. When the ball rolled out of her grasp, she tossed it aside and continued her assault with her fists, her breaths rapid and shallow as she attacked with everything she had. Her terror consumed her, her actions fueled by the memory of the nightmare made real before her.

"Habi! Stop! Stop!" Rafi yelled, grabbing her by the shoulders and pulling her away from the figure. "Habi, what the hell are you doing!?"

"It's the demon from my dreams!" Habi gasped, her chest heaving as she struggled to catch her breath. "It's the–"

As her vision cleared, Habi froze, holding her breath as the reality of what she had done sank in. Her heart plummeted to the bottom of her stomach.

The other children stared at her in horror, their expressions full of fear, as if she were some hideous monster. Parents rushed to secure their children, pulling them back protectively.

The parents of the boy she had beaten pushed through the crowd toward her. It was the same boy who had shown her kindness during the game of ball-tag. Now, he was crumpled on the ground, his face streaked with blood and tears as he whimpered, clutching his face in pain.

The father of the child grabbed Habi's wrist, pulling her toward him with force. His wife directed another parent to call for the Ghazi, while she hurriedly tended to her son's wounds.

"Where are your parents, you little brat!?" the father yelled, his voice booming with rage. "That's my son! He did nothing wrong! I should strike you where you stand!"

The father's free hand clenched into a fist, tempted to strike Habi in the face.

"Wait a second, isn't that the golden-eyed child from many nights ago!?" a mother shouted from the crowd, her voice rising above the chaos. She seemed to be someone who followed the city's news closely. "Those two are from the lower hive!"

"Rats! They're rats!" other parents began to chant, their voices filled with anger and disgust. The crowd's hostility grew louder, and the once playful atmosphere turned dark as more voices joined the outcry.

During the growing tension, Rafi had had enough. He quickly brandished his knuckle duster and struck the father who was gripping Habi's wrist, delivering a sharp blow to the man's groin. The father recoiled with a loud groan, loosening his grip on Habi.

Before the crowd could escalate, the duo bolted toward an alleyway, distancing themselves from the angry citizens. The commotion started to spread, with neighbors peeking out from their homes, curious about the ruckus. Some of the parents and children gave chase, shouting for justice as they followed the pair into the shadows.

"Stop those two!" the crowd shouted, their voices rising in desperation, hoping someone ahead would hear and block their escape.

"I'm sorry, Rafi! I'm sorry! What do we do!?" Habi cried, tears streaming down her face as she ran frantically behind him.

"I'll get us out of this! Just let me think!" Rafi said, his mind racing as he darted ahead, trying to come up with a plan to evade the angry mob.

He knew they wouldn't be able to retreat back to the climbing area, as that would've taken too much time. It would also reveal their secret path. The drain was closer, but they wouldn't have time to pull the manhole cover out before the crowd trampled them. So instead, he decided to make a risky move.

"We're going to the market!" Rafi decided, his voice firm as he made a sharp turn toward the bustling streets.

"Okay!" Habi whimpered, her tears still flowing as she followed closely behind him.

The duo took a sharp turn and sprinted toward the bright exit, where thousands of people stood. Rafi was betting on losing the crowd in the chaos.

As soon as the duo reached the market square, with the riot tailing behind them, they plunged into the bustling sea of people, weaving and shoving their way through. The cries of the angry parents were drowned out by the cheers and roars of the market. Chaos erupted as bystanders were pushed around by those in pursuit. Arguments and brawls broke out, and the two thieves found themselves trapped in the middle of it. At one point, the crowd separated Rafi from Habi, tearing them apart. Rafi cried out her name, but his voice was lost in the turmoil.

"Move! Move! Get out of the way, or I'll strike you down!" several men yelled, their voices cutting through the chaos as they brandished their scimitars, clearing a path.

Suddenly, Habi felt a heavy impact to her nose as a Ghazi soldier forced his way through the throng. The impact sent a sharp pain through her, but she barely had time to react before more Ghazi soldiers followed, pushing and shoving their way through the crowd. The citizens scattered, some trying to avoid the soldiers, others yelling at them to stop. The Ghazi moved with precision, creating an opening in the crowd as they surged forward, determined to regain control of the situation.

As a result, Habi fell to the ground, the worst possible position at that moment. Feet of all kinds stomped over her head and body, each step delivering sharp jolts of pain. She curled into a fetal position, her arms desperately shielding herself from the mayhem above.

The crowd was oblivious to her plight, every person too preoccupied with the unfolding disorder to notice the small girl beneath them. Pain surged through her with each kick and step, her breaths growing shallow and frantic.

"Rafi!" she cried out, her voice hoarse and cracking with desperation. Tears streamed down her face as her pleas dissolved into the overwhelming din of the riot, unheard and unanswered.

She cried and cried, even when she was being lifted and dragged away by Rafi who came back for her. Her face was stained with dirt, blood, tears, and bruises.

"Rafi! Rafi! It hurts!" Habi wailed, clutching onto Rafi with all her strength, tears streaming down her face.

"Can you walk!? We have to get out of here!" Rafi shouted, his voice urgent as he wrapped his arms tightly around her, shielding her from the relentless crowd.

Rafi didn't wait for a response. He kept Habi in his arms and took the brunt of everything ahead of him. He was just as bruised as her, but not as bad. They forced themselves through the horde whilst getting pummeled by swaying hands and rigged knees. After treading through the gauntlet, Rafi and Habi fell to the floor on the outskirts of the market, away from all troubles. When they turned to look back, there was a brawl between shoppers and furious parents. One party was unaware of the children who caused this mess, and the other became sidetracked by the former obstructing their way. To the duo's surprise, the chaos nearly stopped abruptly, solely due to the actions of the Ghazi.

There were many people in Koura's hive city, and while most of them worked to keep the economy running, the Ghazi showed no hesitation in cutting down those who disrupted the process. Scimitars swung through the air, blood splashing overhead. As the sight of Ghazi enforcement silenced the crowd, the fighting stopped. On the ground lay men, women, and even children, bleeding from their wounds, tended to by their relatives and partners. Some were dead, others clung to life. Some citizens mourned, while others apologized, begging for mercy.

"Move! Get back to work! All of you!" a Ghazi bellowed furiously, his voice cutting through the commotion. "This is what happens if you think this is all a game! By the Sultan's name!"

With a few pommel strikes to the head and the threatening swings of their scimitars, the Ghazi quickly restored order. The victims were mostly locals, those who opposed how the Sultan ran the city. Foreigners, on the other hand, knew better than to even make eye contact with the police or military and thrived by keeping to their own business.

"I got them killed—" Habi murmured, her voice breaking as she frowned. "I'm a bad person—"

Rafi scowled and stood up, pulling Habi gently to her feet. He pointed a firm finger at her face, his expression unyielding.

"You don't say that," Rafi said. "You are a good person. You and I both know that. The family knows that. Don't let the lives of these good folk taint you."

Without hesitation, he hugged her tightly and planted a kiss on her cheek. "I don't know what happened back at the playground, but you're still Habi to me. Now let's go before anyone recognizes us."

"I love you, Rafi," Habi sobbed, tears spilling freely as she clung to him.

"I love you too," Rafi replied, his voice steady and reassuring.

The duo rushed to the water well, where they had planned to meet up with the others. The sun had dipped behind the Sultan's tower, and they were late.

Returning to the gravel path, they pulled their hoods low and slipped past the wandering citizens, who paid them no mind. But the struggle had clearly taken a toll on Habi. Rafi noticed her uneven gait, her eyes darting nervously. She was hunched over, walking with a limp. Unbeknownst to Rafi, her vision was becoming blurry, and her breath shallow.

"Hey, hey, Habi! Drink water!" Rafi commanded, holding her steady as he retrieved his canteen and guided the open lid to her mouth.

The water helped calm her, but it wasn't a solution to all her problems. The trek to the well felt endless, every step a struggle as Rafi refused to let go or give up on Habi.

"By the gods, are you two okay!?" a familiar voice called out, filled with concern. It was the voice of a girl they both recognized.

Taliba and the rest of the crew were already at the well, waiting for them. She inspected Habi's face with a look of horror. Habi didn't realize it at the time, but she looked far worse than she thought. Her arms were scraped and bruised, her face bloodied, with a slight tinge of purple across her cheeks and eyes. Her eyes couldn't even focus directly into Taliba's.

"Rafi, what happened!? She needs help!" Taliba cried, her voice filled with panic.

"We're not going to ask for help here," Rafi said firmly, shaking his head.

"Well, she's in no shape to make the climb either, so what is it?" Tariq growled, frustration clear in his tone as he stepped closer.

HABI

As the children bickered over how to proceed, Habi's vision began to blur, her surroundings taking on an eerie, shadowy quality. Silhouettes started to form around them, gradually solidifying into the shapes of human figures. Each one bore a worried expression, their faces etched with concern as they seemed to gaze directly at her.

The world around her dimmed, the light fading as the silhouettes grew clearer. Habi's breath quickened, and the last thing she saw was Rafi shouting her name, his face full of alarm. Her sense of hearing dulled, his voice becoming a distant echo before everything went silent.

Chapter Sixteen

Habi woke to the laughter of children. As her vision cleared, the bright glow of ceiling lanterns filled her view. The soft, warm bed beneath her provided comfort as she rolled onto her side to take in her surroundings. The room was spacious and lavishly decorated, with silk curtains draped over glass windows and counters adorned with displays of jewelry. Beyond the room, the cheerful voices of children carried on, their lively chatter echoing through the air.

She gently pushed herself off the comfortable floor bed and crept toward the door, left ajar. Peeking through the small gap, she saw familiar faces sitting at a dining table, munching on freshly cooked meals. As soon as she opened the door, Rafi was the first to spot her, his eyes widening in relief as he quickly stood up from the table.

"She's awake!" Rafi exclaimed, his smile alight with relief. "Come join us, Habi! We've prepared some food for you!"

Habi wandered toward them, her gaze drifting over the paintings on the walls and the carefully arranged furniture. She settled into a fine wooden chair between Rafi and Hamza, who were cheerfully enjoying their cooked chicken breasts. Hamza, grinning, poured water from a jar into the cup before her. The fresh water shimmered in the light, its coolness mirrored in her eyes as she felt the soft breeze wafting from its icy surface.

"We made it, Habi! We've got a home, and we're out of the slums! This is unbelievable!" Rafi laughed, leaning in to kiss her lips instead of her cheek this time.

"There's so much food and water!" Taliba chimed in, her excitement bubbling over. "I can't wait to start school!"

"You're such a nerd, Taliba," Hamza teased with a grin. "The kids around here are actually cool. They even invited me to play ball-tag with them!"

Naji gestured toward Habi's untouched food.

"Are you gonna eat?" he asked. "Don't let it go to waste! I cooked it for all of us!"

Habi looked down at her plate and stretched her arms out, feeling the freedom of her body—no bruises, no scars, and no pain. She picked up the chicken breast and devoured it quickly, savoring the taste. Afterward, she drank the ice-cold water, the chill refreshing her from the inside.

"You look so cute when you eat," Rafi said with a playful smile.

Finally, Habi decided to voice her thoughts.

"Where are we?" she asked.

"We're in the middle hive, silly," Rafi explained, his tone light. "We sold enough jewelry to cross the border and still had plenty of gald left to get a place to call home!"

"How long was I out?"

"A couple of days. We kept an eye on you while we were trading. Relax a little, dork!"

The children laughed, and the warmth of the meal filled the air. Rafi gave Habi a grand tour of the home, pointing out its elegant textures and beautiful decor. Each room had its own charm, with rich tapestries, intricate carvings, and soft lighting that made it feel like a different world. Habi marveled at everything, feeling a sense of awe at the luxury she'd never experienced before.

After the dishes were cleaned and the laughter died down, the children trotted off to their soft floor beds, each tucked under warm blankets in a separate room from Habi's. Habi didn't notice at first, but the bed she had woken up in was right next to Rafi's, offering them a quiet closeness as the night settled in.

Without any more obligations, the children drifted into a deep slumber, but Habi couldn't sleep. She lay there, staring at the ceiling, her mind racing with disbelief. She could hear Rafi's peaceful breathing beside her, and, without thinking, she gently reached out to feel his back, registering the warmth of his presence.

"Rafi, I can't sleep," Habi murmured, her voice tinged with a soft whine.

Rafi didn't respond, and his breathing became more shallow.

Habi tried to fall asleep again, closing her eyes and emptying her mind, but none of her tactics worked. She rolled over to touch Rafi again, but this time, he wasn't there.

Immediately, she sprang up and looked around the room. There was no sign of him, and she could've sworn he was just lying in bed a couple of minutes ago. Instead of waiting for his return, she got out of bed and went to search for him.

She wondered if Rafi had forgotten something in another room or if he had unfinished business with one of the other children. With that thought in mind, she opened the door across from her room and saw her other four companions sleeping in a line against the wall, each on their own bed. Rafi wasn't in this room either, and the only sounds she could hear in the house were her own footsteps and breath.

She wondered if the others knew where Rafi might have wandered off to, feeling as though much more time had passed since she closed her eyes. From right to left, she attempted to wake Naji, who was fast asleep, his face covered by the blanket.

"Naji, wake up," Habi whispered, gently shaking his shoulder.

Since there was no response, she decided to uncover his face from the blanket, rolling him over to see him fully.

And just like that, Habi scrambled away, tumbling to the floor.

Naji's lower jaw was missing, his face mutilated with chunks of flesh hanging loose. A broken arrow shaft was embedded deep into the side of his skull.

"Naji!? Naji!?" Habi cried, panicking. She crawled over to the others, begging for help, but her terror only escalated.

Tariq had an arrow driven through his mouth, tearing through his cheek, his eyes rolled back into his head. Taliba's empty sockets gaped where her eyes had been, her tongue severed in two. Hamza's face was nearly unrecognizable, an arrow buried deep in the center of his skull.

Habi froze, unable to speak. Her mind raced, and all she could think of was escaping. She ran as fast as she could, searching for the door that would lead her out. The interior of the house seemed to warp around her, the walls twisting and turning as if distorting in her panic.

This was a nightmare, and she knew it. Her heart was about to force its way out of her chest, but she knew it.

After countless turns, she finally reached the door that led to the outside world. But when she opened it, all she saw was more darkness. She fell. Fell and fell, the ground beneath her vanishing as the home faded away into nothing. She screamed, but no one could hear her.

It all ended as soon as she felt the sharp blow to the back of her head.

—

"She's still breathing, but she's shaking," Rafi said, cradling Habi's unconscious form in his arms. Her head rested on his lap as the others gathered around her. Taliba quickly tore a strip from her tattered clothing, dampened it with water, and gently wiped the blood and sand from Habi's body.

"At this rate, we're going to be late and Father–" Taliba began, but Rafi interrupted sharply.

"None of that matters right now. We need to take care of her," he said, his scowl deepening.

"I know, I was just mentioning it—sorry," Taliba replied softly, understanding that all their attention had to remain on Habi's condition.

"What do we do? There's no way we can move her like this," Hamza said, concern etched on his face.

"If it stays like this, we might have to camp here for the night," Naji suggested, his tone grim.

Rafi tried to form a plan as he gently ran his thumb across Habi's wounded face. He had an idea in mind, but it would mean splitting the group up as dusk settled in. Unfortunately, it was the only viable option, unless he wanted to risk staying in the middle hive, where the Ghazi and nosy neighbors roamed.

"Tariq, you're coming with me to the slums. We need to find Faruq," Rafi said firmly. "We'll travel light and swift. Faruq might have medicine in his stash of contraband. He's our best chance."

"Aye," Tariq agreed without hesitation.

"Let me come with you," Hamza offered.

"No, I need you here with the others to care for Habi," Rafi insisted. "I trust you to protect them from danger. I don't know what the nightlife is like in the middle hive. Please, Hamza," he pleaded.

"Aye then," Hamza said, straightening up, proud to take on the role of protector.

"Taliba, Naji," Rafi continued, "find a safe, secluded spot far from anyone. Trust no one and do whatever it takes to keep Habi breathing. Tariq and I will return as soon as we can."

Taliba and Naji nodded, carrying the lightweight Habi away toward a dark corner. Hamza followed them, prepared to stand watch and put on the facade of a child enjoying the outdoors.

"Stay safe, you two," Hamza said, his voice steady.

"Likewise," Rafi replied, giving a brief wave before nodding to Tariq, who stood poised to leave. "Let's go."

The duo began their climb with speed, while the main group huddled together. Habi's head laid limp in Taliba's lap.

—

Exerting all their energy, Rafi and Tariq reached the streets of the Sleeping Complex without wasting any time. The real challenge now was finding Faruq, and they hoped he was resting near his tent.

"How are we supposed to find Faruq in this damn darkness?" Tariq muttered, frustration evident in his voice.

He was right. Their climb had been swift, but it lasted long enough for the sun to vanish completely. The only light now came from scattered street lanterns, and the complex offered little illumination.

"I remember where his tent is, or at least the general area of it. It's our best bet," Rafi said.

"The kid's a smuggler," Tariq pointed out. "There's a good chance he's not in the same spot."

"Well, if we can't find his tent," Rafi sighed, taking a swig from his canteen, "then we'll have to ask around with the locals."

The duo wandered toward the last known location of Faruq's tent, which was discovered about a week ago. As they walked, they braced themselves at every turn they took, knowing that a sudden ambush could occur at any moment. Their feet sloshed in slimy matter, but it was too dark to identify what it was. The rotten smell that followed answered their questions soon enough. They evaded several ongoing muggings and shady transactions, fully committing themselves toward the direction of Faruq's camp. But as soon as they reached the familiar opening, the tent was absent.

Rafi cursed and Tariq angrily let out a breath of air.

"Why don't we just steal from a doctor or pharmacy or something?" Tariq suggested.

"Too risky," Rafi replied. "And we wouldn't even know what medicine to grab. Faruq would know—he deals in specifics in his line of work."

"Where is that rat?" Tariq muttered, his eyes scanning the shadows.

"We can't stop. Keep moving," Rafi ordered, his tone firm.

Now that their search for Faruq's tent had yielded no results, the duo decided to wander deeper into the complex, keeping a sharp eye out for signs of trade or socializing. These activities were often tied to smuggling, making them a promising lead. It was a risky approach, but it was the only option they had. The alternative was hoping to stumble upon the black market by chance, which was well hidden from the average person. Though rumors suggested it was somewhere within the Sleeping Complex, it could really be anywhere in the lower hive. Only those well-connected knew its true location.

After several attempts to locate a reasonable group, while evading many other dangerous ones, the duo finally made a potential find.

It may have taken hours and half of their water supply, but the duo finally spotted a promising lead. A man in a suit emerged from a well-lit building, flanked by two beautiful women. His fingers were adorned with tattoos and rings, and several gold necklaces draped around his neck. He conversed briefly with another man, who handed him an item the duo couldn't make out. Then, the man was offered a woman who helped guide him into the building behind them.

"Excuse me, sir," Rafi said, startling the seemingly wealthy man. "May I ask you something?"

The man chuckled, casting a dismissive glance at the boys without bothering to meet their eyes.

"Aren't you kids a little young for this place?" he said with a sly grin. "Unless you're offering yourselves? I'm sure some older woman—or maybe a man—might take interest in that."

Tariq scowled at him, but Rafi held him back.

"We just want to know if you know a boy named Faruq. He's a friend of ours," Rafi said.

"I don't know, kid. Do I?" the man snickered, glancing at the woman beside him, who let out a soft giggle.

Rafi pouted, reaching under his shirt.

The woman immediately brandished a knife from beneath her clothing, pointing it at Rafi.

Rafi remained calm and slowly pulled out a necklace from his pouch of goods. The man's eyes lit up at the sight of the golden chains. Satisfied by the reaction, Rafi offered the necklace to him.

"Thought you were reaching for somethin' else there, kiddo," the man grinned, snatching the necklace from Rafi's hand. "Faruq's a supplier for plenty of folks. Gotta keep the roach's name under wraps. Must be serious if you're handing me this."

"Can you tell me where he is? Maybe where he likes to hang out?" Rafi pressed.

The man tilted his head toward the entrance of his building.

"Kid's sniffin' around in my den," he said with a smirk. "Consider yourselves lucky."

Once they confirmed Faruq's location, the man waved his hand toward the entrance, signaling them to walk inside. The woman who had brandished the knife motioned for them to follow.

The front of the house was brightly lit with lanterns, but as they moved further in, the light dimmed. A long, dark hallway stretched ahead, where only the glow of candles from nearby rooms provided a hint of ambience. Doors lined both sides of the hall, and behind many of them came the sounds of laughter and moans. The warmth and humidity outside were nothing compared to the stifling heat within.

The strong scent of incense invaded their nostrils, while their ears were filled with the pleasurable cries of men and women.

Finally, the woman stopped at a door and pushed it open without knocking. Inside, Faruq was lounging between two women, his arms draped around them casually. A group of men sat at a nearby table, where a white, powdery substance dusted its surface. The room burst with laughter as the group indulged in their revelry.

"Your friend," the woman said with a sly smile before walking away, leaving Rafi and Tariq at the threshold.

"Faruq!" Rafi called out from the hallway, his voice cutting through the noise.

Faruq cursed, staggered, and coughed all at once, his movements unsteady.

"Oi? Is that me boy, Rafi?" he said, his eyes widening in surprise. "Didn't know y'all were into this scene too."

"We're not," Rafi said, his voice urgent. "We need your help."

Faruq cursed, kissed one of the women on the cheek, and leapt from his seat. He stumbled toward the duo and shut the door behind him, his eyes dilated and unfocused.

"Better be big, man. Big boss ain't lettin' me chill all day," Faruq said, sniffing and rubbing his nose.

"Habi is hurt and unconscious in the middle hive," Rafi whispered.

"Oh yeah, that's big," Faruq grimaced, his demeanor shifting.

"Do you have anything—or know of anything—that could heal her? We're relying on you," Rafi pleaded.

"I don't know. What she got goin' on by the hurt?" Faruq asked, his voice low.

"She got trampled in a crowd. Her body's covered in bruises, and I think she got hit in the head a lot. She's out, but she's breathing," Rafi explained.

Faruq paused, his face scrunching in thought. Rafi could almost see the gears turning.

"Think she needs some ointment for the ouchies. But for her head? She's probably all goofed up. Hashwabi'll do the trick!" Faruq declared confidently.

"Hashwabi?" Rafi frowned. "You mean the drug that's mixed with a bunch of crap? No. There has to be another way."

"If you want her up, moving, healing, and living without pain, then I suggest you use hashwabi," Faruq said with a grin. "What? A mix of opioids, psychoactives, analgesics, and stimulants ain't gonna hurt nobody! Slum folk love it all the time! Ain't that bad, trust me. Just a lil' bite."

Rafi and Tariq exchanged glances, seeking mutual understanding in the moment. Fortunately for Faruq, it didn't take long for them to come to an agreement under these circumstances.

"Deal," Rafi agreed with a firm nod.

"Speakin' of deals—might as well take my share right now, along with a little extra for these fine medical services, if you will," Faruq said with a sly smile, extending his hands like a beggar expecting alms.

Rafi quickly pulled out his pouch and handed over some jewelry to Faruq. The sooner they satisfied him, the sooner they could reach Habi and heal her. Even Tariq contributed some of his share. Faruq's hands overflowed with gold and glitter, making him recoil from the two.

"Hey, hey, that's enough, man. Don't be flauntin' too much in these parts now. Not even I can save y'all," Faruq warned, quickly shoving the items into his pockets. "Right then. Follow me, and I'll get ya all set up."

"Thank you, Faruq," Rafi whispered.

"Too soon for thanks, no? Thank me when Habi's walkin' again," Faruq replied with a smirk, motioning for them to follow.

Faruq threw the door open and shouted, "See y'alls later!" The voices inside echoed their farewells as he pulled the door shut behind him. The trio moved carefully down the narrow hallway, weaving through the gathered adults without making contact, and stepped out into the cool night air. Their eyes blinked, struggling to adjust from the dim, warm glow of the interior to the oppressive darkness of the streets outside.

The group trotted toward the rear of the building, which, now that they scanned the perimeter, seemed much smaller on the outside than it appeared inside. Rafi wondered how such a modest shack could accommodate so many patrons, but he knew it was none of his business.

Directly behind the building, the two children who had been with Faruq during their first meeting stood guard beside a pile of trash. To any passerby, they might appear to be rummaging through the refuse, but in reality, a tent was pitched nearby, concealed in the shadows cast by the darkness enveloping the entire complex.

"So that's where you were," Tariq snickered.

"Hey, man, I gotta keep moving, or else these sticky-fingered folks'll snatch my stuff, ya?" Faruq shrugged nonchalantly. Turning to the two child guards nearby, he added, "Oi, these two are good. I'm grabbin' stuff for 'em."

Without a light, Faruq dove into the opening of his tent, rummaging and feeling for objects that seemed familiar and essential. He tossed a small object and a bag out behind him, then crawled out of the tent, securing the items before presenting them to the duo.

"This small guy is the ointment," Faruq said, presenting a small jar that was the size of his palm. "Made of a bunch of stuff. Doesn't taste good. Rub it into the ouchies and it'll be gone before you know it."

Tariq retrieved the ointment and secured it in his pouch.

Faruq presented a bag, pulling out three items from within, which were a pipe, a bag with flint, steel, and papers, and finally, the green hashwabi powder.

"Got the whole kit. Really good seller," Faruq grinned, clearly proud of his stash. "Pad the 'shwabi up, slap it in the pipe, light the paper with flint and steel, and puff puff! Don't eat it, though. Tastes awful and you'll probably die—not gonna lie. Give Habi this, and she'll be flying over walls like the gods themselves blessed her."

"You seem a little too excited about this," Rafi said, his concern evident.

"Of course I am. Hashwabi's good," Faruq sniffed, handing over a small bag of the substance and its paraphernalia.

"Are you using the product?" Rafi whispered cautiously.

"We don't talk 'bout that," Faruq hushed him with a pointed look. "Now get a move on. Don't y'all have a dying Habi? I wanna get back to my fun."

"Alright, alright. See you when we see you, Faruq," Rafi chuckled, waving as he turned to leave. Tariq followed closely behind.

"Yeah, yeah," Faruq muttered, waving them off before disappearing back into the building's entrance.

—

The middle hive neighborhood had begun to light their lanterns, brightening their homes. The streets glowed with the warmth from several houses, as some adults ventured into their nightlife activities. Yet, one corner of the winding gravel path remained shrouded in darkness, where Hamza still kept watch, sitting quietly. Habi, still unconscious, rested on Taliba's lap, who had dozed off unexpectedly. Naji passed the time by clicking his tongue in rhythm, mimicking the distant sound of drums and brass.

"Never thought I'd see the nightlife of the middle hive," Hamza said with a yawn, gazing at the dimly lit streets. "Almost looks like a fairy tale."

"Why are Rafi and Tariq taking so long?" Naji grumbled, tossing pebbles onto the gravel path. After a while, he grew bored of the game and tipped his water canteen upside down, draining the last drop. "Out of water again," he muttered, frustrated.

Hamza took a long swig from his canteen, draining it before handing it over to Naji.

"Your turn for the water run," Hamza said with a chuckle.

Naji sighed, rising to his feet and wobbling over to the water well several feet away, canteens in hand. He wasn't concerned about Taliba's supply, as she had last drunk from it a couple of hours before her nap.

A few moments passed as Naji finally reached the well and drew water with the bucket. He took a few swigs from his refilled canteen before dipping it back into the bucket.

"It's past curfew, child," a deep voice rumbled, startling Naji.

He turned sharply, finding himself face-to-face with the steel-plated eight-pointed star emblazoned on the soldier's chest.

"Where are your parents?" the Ghazi demanded, his tone unyielding.

Naji swallowed hard, his mind racing as he tried to come up with the right words to say.

"They're over there, sir," Naji said, pointing toward the shadowy corner where the others were waiting. "I was just getting water. I'll head back to them now."

"Very well. Take me to them," the Ghazi ordered, his piercing gaze fixed on Naji.

Naji hadn't expected that. While he had never witnessed how the Ghazi enforced curfew during the darkest hours, his curiosity about Koura's laws had driven him to read extensively on the subject. From what he remembered, the Ghazi upheld the Sultan's strict orders, ensuring children didn't wander the middle hive at night. The higher hives were exempt from this rule, while the lower hive had no regulations at all.

If a child was found during curfew, the Ghazi would escort them to their parents. But for those identified as runaways, undesirables, or homeless, the consequences were far graver—execution and disposal on the spot. It was the Sultan's brutal method of culling the working class, ensuring that only those who contributed to productivity and results had a place in society.

For someone from the middle hive to rise in status, they had to prove their value. Naji and the others, however, were far from meeting that standard.

"Take me to them, boy," the Ghazi growled, his voice low and threatening, repeating the command with unmistakable authority.

Naji remained silent as he led the Ghazi toward the others, his mind racing to concoct a plan to save not only himself but the others as well. Yet, no solution came to him. If he told the others to run, Habi would be a problem. If he pretended his parents had wandered off, the Ghazi would become suspicious. If he tried to flee on his own, the Ghazi would give chase until he was caught. He was out of options.

Hamza spotted the Ghazi following Naji from a distance and quickly shook Taliba awake. He tried to do the same with Habi, but she didn't budge.

"Why's a Ghazi following Naji?" Taliba hissed, suddenly jolted awake by the alarming sight.

"This is bad," Hamza muttered, his expression darkening. "If I had to guess, it's because we're not supposed to be here."

Unfortunately, before the group could come up with a plan, the Ghazi was already breathing down on them.

"Oh, this is my brother, and those are my sisters," Naji said, turning to gesture toward the group. He faced them with a forced smile. "Hey, guys, have you seen Mama or Papa?"

Taliba and Hamza seemed lost at first, but then Naji silently mouthed the words, *play along*.

"They said they forgot something in the house," Hamza improvised smoothly. "Our sister got sick while playing outside and fell into a deep slumber. We stayed here with her while my older sister went to call Mama for help. Mama forgot the medicine, but she should be back soon."

The Ghazi observed the group thoroughly. He saw how Taliba held an unconscious Habi in her lap, and how nervous both Naji and Hamza were.

"Why were you children out just before the highest moon?" the Ghazi demanded, his eyes narrowing as his hand tightened on the handle of his scimitar. "It shouldn't take all night for help to arrive."

The children froze, knowing that they had been caught.

"For the last time, where are your parents? I will ask no further," the Ghazi demanded, his voice cold as he drew part of the steel blade into view, its sharp edge gleaming in the dim light.

Before the children could plead their last words, a pebble struck the back of the Ghazi's head, catching his attention. The children's eyes widened with recognition, while the Ghazi's burned with rage.

"Oi, you stupid gold tongue! Screw yer Sultan!" Tariq shouted, pointing at the soldier with an underhanded finger—a gesture considered highly offensive to those in authority.

The soldier didn't hesitate to draw his blade and charge toward Tariq. Luckily, Tariq was quicker and perfect for the job of distraction. As soon as the Ghazi took a few steps forward, his pride wounded, Tariq had already lured him away from the others. With Tariq here, that also meant Rafi had to be nearby.

They expected Rafi to emerge from the shadows, and he did exactly that once the coast was clear. He quickly pulled out the hashwabi kit and the ointment that Tariq had given him before the chase.

"No way, you guys actually found Faruq," Hamza said with a relieved smile. "Wait, how long were you hiding there?"

"Been there for a bit," Rafi replied, handing a small jar of ointment to Taliba. "Needed the gold tongue to get closer to you guys, so Tariq could bait him away from the rear. Taliba, start rubbing that stuff on Habi's wounds."

"Is Tariq going to be fine?" Taliba asked, worry evident in her voice as she opened the jar. She dipped her fingers into the greenish substance, its texture clinging like melted wax. The strong menthol scent hit her immediately. As she spread it onto Habi's bruised skin, it glided on smoothly.

"He'll be fine," Rafi assured her. "He's quick on his feet. I gave him a long enough time frame to break off when it's clear." He dug into the kit, laying out the pipe, firestarter, and paper beside Taliba.

"Is that hashwabi?" Naji asked, his eyes narrowing as he studied the bag of green powder laced with specks of white in Rafi's hands. "Faruq recommended hashwabi?"

"The ointment is for healing," Rafi explained. "The hashwabi's for the pain and to get her moving. We need to leave as soon as she's up." He handed a pinch of the hashwabi to Naji. "Pack that up with your hands. I'll set up the flint, steel, and paper. Taliba, is Habi still breathing?"

Taliba laid her free hand on Habi's chest, feeling the rise and fall of her breath. She nodded to Rafi as she continued rubbing the ointment onto Habi's wounds.

Hamza helped Naji pack more hashwabi until it was rolled into a substantial size for the pipe. They rubbed it together between their hands until the substance formed clumps. The process didn't take long, as they quickly distributed the rolled hashwabi to Rafi, who then placed it into the mouth of the pipe.

"Hamza, take the pipe and keep it in Habi's mouth. I'll get the fire going," Rafi instructed, handing the prepared pipe to Hamza.

Rafi grabbed the flint and steel, positioning them above a piece of paper. He struck them together repeatedly until a spark caught, igniting the paper. Quickly dropping the tools, he lifted the burning paper to his mouth and blew gently, coaxing the flames to grow.

As Hamza steadied the pipe and carefully sealed Habi's lips around its opening, Rafi burned the hashwabi with the flame. A dense, lingering smoke billowed from the pipe's mouth, flowing into Habi's lungs as her body instinctively inhaled. The stench was a harsh mixture of chemicals and burning herbs, singeing the hairs in their nostrils and clinging to the air around them.

Habi breathed in and out as the chemicals entered her system. Her breaths quickened with each puff, until she suddenly woke, coughing uncontrollably.

"Oh, thank the gods!" Taliba exclaimed, a smile breaking across her face as she cradled Habi's head in relief.

The children watched as Habi's pupils constricted sharply upon awakening, only to dilate moments later from the hashwabi's effects. Her corneas reddened, and her expression twisted in confusion and discomfort.

"What—what is that!?" Habi coughed violently, her body wracked as if trying to expel the substance from her lungs.

Though concerned, Rafi leaned closer, his voice calm but firm. "Don't worry about it, Habi," he said, relieved by her awakening. "Keep breathing it in. It's supposed to help."

Habi took another breath of the hashwabi and coughed once more. Her vision grew hazy, and her mind felt light, but suddenly she was on her feet, ready to move. It was as if the pains and bruises that had covered her body no longer existed, just enough to push her and the others out of the middle hive.

"No more!" Habi coughed, her voice trembling. "Why's it so dark? I wanna go home. The dead people will chase me again!" she whimpered, stumbling toward Rafi in a clumsy, disoriented manner.

To calm her, Rafi pulled out Habi's pouch and handed it back to her, revealing the small doll inside. Her face lit up as she took the pouch, wrapped it around her neck, and kissed the doll.

"My husband. I love you, husband," Habi giggled, holding the doll tightly.

"That's right. You go ahead and kiss your husband," Rafi said, playing along as he steadied her, guiding her balance.

Taliba secured the ointment while the others cleaned up the hashwabi kit. Once all their belongings were packed into Hamza's bag, they began their journey home.

"I'm worried about Tariq," Taliba said with a pout.

"He'll catch up. Don't worry about it," Rafi reassured her.

When the children reached the climbing area, they helped each other over the shed and walls. Habi was a little wobbly, but her energy was through the roof. She waved and spoke to things that weren't there, leaving the others unsure if it was the hashwabi or if she was actually seeing dead people. Regardless, they made it over the wall without trouble. As they reached the dreaded sloped roof, Hamza jumped, bag in hand, and rolled it over the crest to the other child, who grabbed it as it fell. That decision made his climb much easier.

Soon enough, the children returned to the streets of the lower hive with zero mishaps.

They hid in the shadows, taking the most direct path toward their home. To the ears of slum dwellers, they were nothing more than rats scurrying through the streets. Given the late hour, it didn't take long for the children to reach the outskirts of their shed. Now, all they had to do was wait for Tariq, to avoid further questions from Father, who was likely home by now.

"Where is Tariq?" Naji whispered, his voice barely audible.

"I don't know," Rafi hissed, frustration creeping in as he cursed under his breath. "He's supposed to be here already."

It seemed Habi's hyperactive state came to an immediate stop as she suddenly grew tired, yawning and leaning onto Rafi's side. The combination of the ointment and hashwabi had clearly worked, as Habi didn't wince from her wounds once during their entire trip. Rafi could only imagine how hard she mentally and physically crashed as soon as they reached the perimeter of their home for a temporary rest.

"Come on, Habi, we're almost there," Rafi said with a smirk. "We just need to wait for Tariq."

"I miss Tariq," Habi murmured with a yawn.

"I miss him too," Rafi replied softly.

Chapter Seventeen

The cheers and excitement of the middle hive buzzed through the air as adult citizens indulged in Koura's lively nightlife. The scent of alcohol mingled with songs of glory and mystery, blending seamlessly with the rhythmic beat of drums echoing through the market. It could have been a perfect night—if the noise hadn't drifted away from Tariq's ears.

Tariq's breaths came in rapid gasps as he sprinted through the neighborhood bordering the market. He had a rough sense of where he was in the middle hive, but there was no time to pause and assess—his pursuer, a determined Ghazi, was still on his heels. Nearby patrols began to notice the commotion, quickly realizing why their ally was plowing through clusters of citizens. Though the chasing Ghazi was winded, his legs drove him relentlessly forward. Tariq was too fast for him, but reinforcements were closing in.

"Omar, what are you doing?" another soldier called out, noticing the exhausted Ghazi struggling to keep up.

"The boy—" Omar gasped, panting heavily as he jogged forward. He pointed at Tariq, who was now darting away, leaping over a short fence with ease. "Undesirable—he needs to be put down," Omar wheezed, refusing to admit the truth: his bruised pride from being struck by a mere pebble.

With that brief explanation, the soldiers surrounding Omar quickly resolved to enforce the law, their training compelling them to act without question—even against a lone deviant child. Unfortunately for Tariq, two of the soldiers were equipped with recurve bows and arrows. The moment Omar singled him out, they drew their weapons, locking onto their target, and joined the pursuit.

Tariq glanced over his shoulder and saw that the lone Ghazi chasing him had multiplied into four. His heart sank as he spotted bows in the hands of two of them. Staying in the quiet outskirts of the neighborhood would only make it easier for them to draw their arrows and take aim. Thinking fast, Tariq grabbed a lantern pole and used it to pivot sharply, redirecting himself toward the bustling market.

The fresh Ghazi, brimming with energy, were now directly behind Tariq—close enough to almost grab him. Adrenaline fueled his every step as he bolted through the narrow alley leading to the market. He shoved over crates and trash piles in an attempt to slow them down, following up with quick, sharp turns. But the Ghazi had the advantage—they knew these streets far better than he did.

The soldiers could see Tariq was nearing his limit, and the turn he'd just taken led into a desolate alley with no pedestrian access or nearby homes. It was the perfect spot. All one of them needed to do was steady themselves, notch an arrow, and take aim.

The arrow was a hasty decision, and it fell short—striking Tariq in the calf.

Tariq cursed as he hit the ground but quickly scrambled back to his feet, limping toward the nearby crowd. The pain hadn't registered yet—only the dull pressure of the arrow's impact—as his adrenaline surged to its peak.

"Dammit!" one of the Ghazi shouted in frustration. "He's running into the crowd!"

Before the group of Ghazi could get a clear look at Tariq's face, he had already vanished into the sea of bodies.

One of the Ghazi cursed and barked, "Cordon off the perimeter! By the Sultan's name, this rat will be taken down!"

Another Ghazi paired with an ally, shoving their way through the crowd as they followed the blood trail Tariq had left behind.

"Move! Move!" the Ghazi commanded, their voices sharp and authoritative, clearing the path as they pressed forward.

Tariq could hear the soldiers' shouts, but he had already gained significant ground, weaving through the crowd of citizens.

Tariq passed several merchant stalls until he spotted what he needed. In one swift motion, he snatched a folded outfit from under the noses of a few distracted individuals gathered around a tabletop. He quickly pulled the purple tunic over his ragged clothes and tore a strip from the pant leg. Scanning the area for any sign of the Ghazi, he took cover next to a stall surrounded by onlookers and sat down. It was a risk, but the arrow's tip was pressing deeper into his calf. He knew he shouldn't remove it, but he had no choice if he wanted to keep moving. His past experience with being stabbed reminded him that leaving a foreign object lodged in the skin could prevent more severe bleeding. That's exactly what the torn piece of pants cloth was for.

Amid the chaos, the Ghazi were setting up a cordon around the market, while a few patrolled within its confines. Tariq could spot their armor from a distance, but he kept a low profile, careful not to be seen.

Tariq placed the cloth in between his teeth and bit down, taking a few deep breaths before finally dislodging the arrow from his calf. He silently roared and winced, as the arrowhead tore more skin and muscle when it was pulled out. As blood began to leak out, he removed the cloth from his mouth and shoved as much as he could into the open wound, acting as a gauze. Once satisfied, he tore another piece from the pant's leg and bandaged himself. With all the tearing, the luxurious pants quickly became a pair of ripped shorts, but fashion was the least of Tariq's worries right now. He slipped himself into the purple shorts before the citizens began to grow suspicious, with some already worried as to why a child was out at night, bleeding. No citizen interacted with Tariq, only noting his presence. None of them wanted to bear the responsibility of being with a child who was not supposed to be out and about when a Ghazi came around.

Tariq slapped his makeshift bandage twice, then set off again, relieved that he wasn't running this time. He hoped the purple garment would provide enough disguise for now. At first, he didn't notice, but there wasn't a single child in the crowd. Surrounded by the blend of vibrant colors worn by the people, it would take the Ghazi some time to spot him as anything more than just another piece of fabric in the sea of bodies.

Tariq limped as he made his way toward the general direction of the climbing area, sipping from his canteen. Several adults glanced down at him, then quickly looked away. He was relieved that there weren't any die-hard citizens eager to enforce the curfew. Most of the adults seemed indifferent, especially when it wasn't their own child in trouble.

As Tariq focused on his path, he noticed the familiar eight-pointed armor not only approaching him from the crowd but also standing at the edges of the market. If he stepped even a foot beyond the gathering area, he would be caught and likely slain. Instinctively, he changed course, slipping into the crowd, blending in with the women's dresses and the fabrics of nearby stalls. He was effectively caged in, and he knew it.

As if the gods were watching his struggle, Tariq suddenly saw an opportunity—one that parted the crowd like a wave.

Two horses, their hooves clattering against the stone and sand, pulled a wagon laden with crates of goods. The rider snapped the reins, urging the animals forward through the bustling crowd. The crates were tightly packed, leaving no room for Tariq to climb inside—a bad idea even if there had been. However, the wagon's large wheels raised it high enough off the ground, creating a narrow gap that sparked a desperate, risky idea in Tariq's mind.

As the rider sat at the edge of the wagon closest to the horses, Tariq weaved through the crowd as quickly as he could, staying just behind the wagon. The people obstructing the wagon's movement allowed Tariq to match its pace, jogging parallel to it. He slipped between two citizens, then swiftly dropped to the ground, rolling under the wagon and grabbing onto the wooden bars beneath it, which served as its foundation. The wheels were dangerously close, but Tariq's nimbleness allowed him to avoid being run over, though his heels scraped the ground. In one fluid motion, he hugged the wooden bar tightly, lifting his legs to rest them on a lower bar. Now, all he had to do was wait.

The wagon shook and trembled as it rumbled over the paved road through the market. Tariq watched feet shuffle past, none of their owners aware that he was hidden just beneath them. He even spotted the edges of scabbards and military boots from the Ghazi as he hitched a ride. But none of the soldiers gave the merchant wagon a second glance. Tariq quietly slipped through the entire cordon undetected.

Tariq decided to hold on a little longer, just in case the Ghazi were still nearby, outside the market. The crowd had thinned, but his worries remained. All he could hear were the horses' hooves clattering against the sandstone road beneath him, accompanied by the casual chatter of residents nearby. He had no idea which direction the wagon was heading, but at that moment, it didn't matter. He was simply relieved to be out of sight, invisible to the eyes of the Sultan's soldiers.

When the sounds of conversation faded, leaving only the rhythmic clatter of hooves, Tariq decided to detach himself from the wagon's underside and dropped to the ground. He braced for impact, but the fall was still strong enough to knock the air from his lungs. As he rolled to his feet, he found himself in a quiet, dimly lit street, lantern poles lining each side of the road. The wagon disappeared into the distance, heading toward a wall cloaked in shadow. Only the light of the moon illuminated the wall's height, and to Tariq's dismay, he quickly realized this wasn't the border to the lower hive—it was the boundary to the higher hive.

Tariq hesitated, torn between turning back to the slums or giving in to his curiosity. He asked himself, *What if he stayed and scouted the rarity of the higher hive's walls? What if he uncovered something that could help the others?* The streets around him were unnervingly quiet, as if intentionally so, given their proximity to the wall that separated the sophisticated folk from the rest of the city. Tariq wanted to know more. He wanted to be *that kid* to return home with valuable information. He ignored the pain in his calf and the blood that had begun to seep out again. In the end, his impulsive desire won out, and he limped toward the wall that separated the rich from everyone else.

—

Tariq stayed off the main road, keeping a careful distance from the wall, listening to the quiet conversations of the guards posted at the gates. He considered that if the wall were shorter, a climb might be possible. However, that theory was quickly dashed when he noticed the mobile torches above him, signaling the presence of archers.

Tariq walked along the wall as far as he could, his eyes scanning for cracks or holes, his hands feeling for any imperfections in the stone. He wanted to believe there was a way through, but the walls seemed pristine and impenetrable. The sandstone was well-maintained, and for good reason.

Tariq's disappointment began to settle in, realizing that his scout might have been for nothing. He knew the others were likely already home, waiting for him, but he couldn't shake the feeling that this opportunity was too rare to ignore. Yet, as he pressed on a little further along the wall, something caught his eye—a strange sight.

Tariq noticed that the buildings maintained a decent distance from the wall, leaving a clear path for walking. However, to his surprise, there was one small building that broke this pattern—a dark, unlit wooden shack pressed tightly against the wall, disrupting the open walkway. Its position didn't seem to obstruct much, but it piqued Tariq's curiosity. He wondered if this mysterious shack might have a door leading directly into the higher hive. Without hesitation, he decided to investigate.

When Tariq approached the door, he saw a paper sign pinned to it, reading, *Foreclosed. Trespassers will be punished*, in bold black ink. But rules had never been something Tariq cared much about, so he shrugged off the warning and tried the door handle.

The door creaked open as Tariq tiptoed inside. The space was barren—no decorations, windows, or lights. He had expected to find a squatter or perhaps a guard sleeping on duty, but there was nothing. The shack was small enough that he could see all four walls from the doorway, and there wasn't another door in sight. However, one thing immediately caught his eye: a wooden trapdoor a few feet away from the entrance, standing out starkly in the otherwise empty room.

He hesitated at first, unsure of what lay beneath—a haunted basement or perhaps a secret hideout for criminals. But then he reminded himself, *Did I really come all this way just to chicken out*? With a deep breath to steady his nerves, Tariq grasped the handle of the trapdoor and lifted it open.

As Tariq lifted the trapdoor, he disturbed the dust and sand scattered across the shack. A blast of sand blew into his face, forcing him to spit and cover his mouth. Once the dust settled, he caught a whiff of a strong substance coming from below. It wasn't fecal matter, sewage, or rot—it was something different, yet oddly familiar.

That's when it hit him. Tariq recognized the smell immediately—it was the same substance Rafi had been carrying. The mix of hashwabi was unmistakable. He realized he had stumbled upon a narcotic tunnel. A thought struck him like a bolt of lightning: *If everyone in the lower and middle hive used drugs, why wouldn't the rich as well?*

After confirming the smell, Tariq noticed a man-made stairway leading further down into the tunnel. He carefully stepped down, testing each step to make sure it was secure. As he descended, his heart raced, and to his relief, he found that the tunnel stretched out before him—a dark abyss that seemed to howl in the silence, directed toward the wall.

Tariq quickly hopped out of the hole and secured the trapdoor, leaving the shack exactly as he had found it, with the door shut behind him. This discovery was a stroke of luck. Instead of scraping by, snatching coin by coin in the middle hive, he had found an opportunity for the children to take the coin by bulk. This pathway could lead to their success, potentially even elevating them to the status of middle hive citizens—or more.

With his findings in mind, Tariq made a mental note, sticking to the edge of the neighborhood as he walked toward the climbing area.

He made it to the climbing area, carefully avoiding the attention of partygoers and Ghazi as their faint voices drifted through the air. Now that he wasn't being chased, he felt a sense of relief, but he remained cautious.

Finally, after the long detour, Tariq refilled his canteen at the water well and began the climb, wincing with each step due to his wounded calf. With determination, he made his way back to the lower hive.

—

Back at the children's shed, Naji confirmed that Father was home by opening the door and chatting with him at his workspace. This gave the others the opportunity to hide the backpack and their pouches of goods in the backyard, using trash and debris to camouflage them. Once their treasure was secured, they reunited with Naji, who was confronting Father.

"Quite late, is it not?" Father growled, exhaling a cloud of smoke from his pipe.

The children stood before him, their heads bowed in submission. His sharp gaze quickly shifted to Habi, who was slumped on Rafi's back, her body battered and bruised, her face pale in slumber.

"What happened?" he demanded, his scowl deepening.

One of the children had to look Father in the eye and tell the story of how Habi got hurt once again. Rafi was the one who took that mantle.

"We went to play with some other kids," Rafi began, his tone steady despite the lie. "One of them picked a fight with Habi. She got beat up while we were trying to pull the rat off her. Don't worry—we taught the kid a lesson afterward."

Father was experienced in interrogating not only his children but many figures from the past as well. He knew the signs and patterns of each child when they lied, and Rafi's tell was when he gritted his teeth every time he stopped speaking. However, Father disregarded that notion as soon as he took a whiff of them.

"Now explain to me why Habi smells like hashwabi?" Father growled, his teeth clenched in barely restrained anger.

"The kids we were playing with smoked hashwabi," Rafi lied smoothly. "It got all over us."

Rafi believed that Father was buying into his tale, but Saif ultimately decided to simply play along, to see how twisted Rafi's story became.

After another look at the children, Father realized that someone was missing.

"Where is Tariq?" Father asked again, his tone colder this time.

The children exchanged uneasy glances, the silence broken only by Habi's faint snores.

"He'll be back soon. He forgot something at the play area," Rafi lied for the third time, forcing a confident tone.

Father let out a long sigh, his gaze sharp and unrelenting. "So what you're telling me," he began, "is that you all went to play with other kids. That you, seasoned little schemers, somehow allowed Habi to get injured for an extended period of time? That you were surrounded by hashwabi users, yet only Habi reeks of it? And now you expect me to believe that Tariq, who *never* forgets anything, left something behind at a playground—at this hour?"

Taliba lowered her head and slightly turned to Rafi, mouthing, *busted*.

"One more chance," Father warned, his voice low and dangerous as he retrieved a long, slim branch from his drawer. The sight of it made the children instinctively flinch, each of them fully aware of the sharp sting it delivered.

"Speak the truth, and I will spare you all," he continued, his gaze settling on Taliba. "This time, Taliba speaks."

Now the spotlight was on Taliba, who darted her eyes back and forth between Father and the branch. Rafi shut his eyes and took a deep breath, knowing that Taliba was about to fold and reveal their entire operation.

"We went to the middle hive. Habi got trampled by the crowd. A friend gave us hashwabi to ease her pain. I even put ointment on her bruises. Habi passed out, so we had to wait, and then the Ghazi showed up. Tariq distracted them to keep us safe," Taliba blurted out in a rapid rush, her words tumbling over each other.

She was terrified of the punishment looming over them and spoke the truth—at least half of it. The other children held their breath, silently relieved that Taliba hadn't mentioned anything about trespassing or burglary. They hoped the admission of crossing into the middle hive and the rest of her account would be enough to satisfy Father.

It was a believable story, one that seemed more realistic to Father's ears. However, even though Father lowered the branch, there was still a missing answer.

"Why did you all go there?" Father demanded, his scowl deepening.

"We wanted to see how fun it was," Taliba replied quickly, her voice trembling slightly as she forced a smile. "We love the water and the kids that play there," she lied, hoping it sounded convincing enough.

Father nodded at her confession, showing a hint of pity. He kneeled down and patted Taliba on the head, offering her a moment of comfort.

"Taliba, is that Tariq behind you?" Father asked, his voice calm but his sharp eyes narrowing as he focused on her reaction.

Not only did Taliba turn back to observe Tariq, but the others did as well. However—Tariq wasn't there.

Father whipped the branch straight into Taliba's bum, causing her to cry in pain and hop off toward her bed. She almost fooled him, but Father knew her pattern when she lied as soon as she spoke the last sentence. Taliba loved to play with the ends of her hair that draped down to her waist.

"Father! I'm sorry!" Taliba cried, holding onto her wounded butt.

Next, Father quickly whipped Naji and Hamza, who reacted accordingly to the pain. The entire shed was filled with their cries.

"Rafi, go put Habi down on her bed," Father instructed, his tone firm.

Rafi swallowed hard, sidestepping cautiously toward Habi's roll, instinctively keeping his backside angled away from Father.

"If I put her down, are you going to whip me too?" Rafi asked, trying to strike a bargain.

"Are you going to tell me the truth?" Father countered, his eyes narrowing.

"I will. Please spare me," Rafi pleaded, his voice breaking slightly. The other children, still rubbing their sore backsides, exchanged glances. It was rare for them to see Rafi, usually so composed, beg for mercy.

As Rafi gently laid Habi in her bedroll, Father's swift motion caught him off guard. The branch lashed across Rafi's thigh with a sharp crack, causing him to yelp in pain.

"*Ow*! We made a deal!" Rafi cried, clutching his leg as he turned to face Father, betrayal etched on his face.

"That was for the first mass punishment. I'm considering another," Father said, his glare piercing as he loomed over Rafi. "Now tell me—why did you all go to the middle hive?"

"Stealing! We were stealing!" Rafi blurted, raising his hands defensively as though to ward Father off. His voice cracked under the weight of his confession, and the room fell silent.

Father's expression shifted slightly, the confession apparently meeting his expectations. Rafi's words hung heavy in the air, and the tension in the room grew thicker.

Father huffed air through his nostrils and lowered the wooden torture device. He pinched the bridge of his nose and took a slow drag from his pipe.

"Not so hard to speak the truth, is it now?" Father said, his tone cold but measured. "I know I cannot keep you all contained, but lying to me is a grievous mistake. You were told your freedom wouldn't be obstructed, and yet you return home with Habi covered in bruises. And not from here—no, this happened in the middle hive."

His gaze darkened as he continued, "You even managed to catch the attention of the Ghazi again. Do you know what that means, little ones?"

The children were too occupied to answer, their bodies trembling from the lashes as tears dripped down their cheeks.

"That means you cannot go back anytime soon—maybe ever," Father growled, his voice heavy with anger and disappointment. "*First*, you let Habi become compromised, and *now*, it's all of you. Do you know how *horrible* that sounds?"

His words hung in the air like a storm cloud, but just as the tension threatened to break, Father let out a sigh of relief. The familiar sound of running footsteps echoed from outside the door, signaling an approaching figure.

Tariq finally made it home, but he was completely confused by the situation he walked into. However, he quickly understood the result, seeing his siblings crying and rubbing their bruised bums.

Upon his return, everyone noticed how dirty Tariq looked, despite the newly acquired purple clothing. The most striking detail was the blood that soaked the cloth around his calf. Tariq also seemed relieved to finally catch his breath after being constantly on the move.

"Tariq, are you okay, my child?" Father asked, his voice softening with genuine worry as he extended a shoulder to help stabilize him.

"Damn Ghazi shot an arrow in my leg," Tariq confessed without hesitation, wincing as he leaned on Father for support. "But I am fine, Father."

Father helped seat Tariq on the floor and began to unwrap the cloth around his calf. He nodded to Tariq, who returned the gesture, signaling each other to brace for the sudden surge of air exposure against the wound.

"Taliba, get me some rags from my drawer," Father instructed. Taliba obeyed without hesitation, carrying no resentment from earlier.

She quickly retrieved the rags and, remembering the jar of ointment tucked in her pocket, handed it over as well. Father's eyes narrowed slightly as he immediately recognized the product.

"Once I get the cloth off, use the ointment when I tell you to," Father said firmly. "Now, hand me your canteen."

Once Father received Taliba's canteen, the process to heal Tariq's calf had begun.

Father gently peeled the sticky cloth from Tariq's leg, tossing it aside with a wet slosh as it hit the floor. He then moved to remove the blood-soaked gauze, working carefully but deliberately. Tariq winced, his breath hitching as the shift in pressure sent a sharp sting through his calf.

Once the gauze was fully removed, the wound oozed slightly, though far less than before. The injury had begun to clot on its own, but Tariq's movements during his escape had repeatedly torn it open, delaying the healing process.

Father poured water from the canteen onto Tariq's calf, carefully cleansing the wound of dirt and potential infection. Once it was clean enough, he prepared the rags and gestured to Taliba, signaling her to apply the ointment.

"Rub the ointment around the entire calf," Father instructed. "Dab just a little at the edges of the wound, but don't put any inside."

Taliba applied the ointment carefully, and once she finished, Father wrapped up Tariq's calf, tying it securely. While ensuring the wrap was snug, Father turned to Hamza, who was closest to the desk. "Hamza, hand me my stool," he ordered.

Hamza delivered the stool, and Father placed it below Tariq's injured leg. He gently raised the boy's leg onto the stool's support beam, leaving it there as he finished his work.

"Keep your leg elevated for a while," Father said, adjusting Tariq's position. "It'll help reduce the bleeding."

Tariq looked over at Habi, who slept in the next bedroll, and then turned to Rafi, who gave him a thumbs-up. Tariq returned the gesture, signaling that he was fine. While Father continued tending to his wound, Tariq subtly gestured to Rafi. He pointed at himself, then to his mouth, and then at Rafi.

I need to speak with you.

Rafi interpreted.

Rafi acknowledged Tariq's request with a slight nod, before turning his attention to Father, who was preparing to make an announcement. All of the children could see how stressed Father looked. His eyes were sharp yet droopy, as if exhaustion had taken its toll. A vein throbbed at the corner of his forehead, a visible sign of his frustration.

"All of you are *grounded* until everyone is fully healed, is that understood?" Father declared. "Only two of you are allowed outside at a time, and you *will* keep each other company. You are limited to this shed, the yard, and the pond. That is all. If I find out that one of you breaks this rule, I will chain you to the floor myself."

The house arrest wasn't a huge blow to the children; in fact, they were somewhat relieved that Father seemed to have either forgotten about their act of thievery or simply chose to ignore it. They needed the rest, even though some were growing impatient—especially Rafi and Tariq. Rafi, frustrated by the situation, wanted nothing more than to leave the mess behind as soon as possible, while Tariq was bubbling with excitement over the valuable information he had uncovered.

"Yes, Father," the children replied in unison, their voices subdued as they bowed their heads in acknowledgment.

After such a long and exhausting day, the children finally agreed that it was time for it to end. Tariq, drained from all the physical exertion, had already fallen asleep. One by one, the others followed suit, surrendering to their fatigue, and soon the shed was filled with the quiet sounds of their collective slumber.

Father never truly enjoyed punishing his children, despite what his actions suggested. They reminded him of his younger self, of the old family he had left behind. Each one of them carried that same rebellious streak, a trait that ran deep in the veins of every lower hive dweller. He rescued them from the streets, giving them shelter and a chance at a better life, hoping to protect them from the harshness of the world. Yet, he understood the risks all too well. Like a hungry dog kept caged for too long, they would eventually lash out—no matter how much he tried to keep them contained.

Father finally extinguished the lantern and settled down to sleep. A small smirk tugged at the corner of his lips as he lay in the darkness, his mind turning over the events of the day.

He wanted to see them succeed.

Chapter Eighteen

The sun's rays gleamed high in the bright blue sky, casting a warm glow over a small gathering in a peaceful grassy plain. The only sounds that echoed through the tall leaves were the gentle gusts of wind and laughter from afar. There was no chaos, no death, no worries—only serenity, as Habi sat amidst the grass, surrounded by familiar faces.

Habi laughed as she sipped from her porcelain cup, filled with tea—though she had no idea what tea truly tasted like. Around her sat Talia, Saif's child, and Assad from the old family, each holding their own cups. Nearby, a few hashish plants stood, their pungent scent blending with the atmosphere, adding to the haze that softened the edges of their faces. Despite the faint fog surrounding them, the group was in high spirits, sharing in the peculiar yet oddly delightful moment.

"You're so funny, Habi!" Talia laughed, her cheeks glowing with amusement.

"I know I am. They laugh with me all the time!" Habi beamed, her grin wide and confident.

"Are you sure they're not laughing at *you*?" Assad teased, raising an eyebrow as he took a slow sip from his cup.

The trio continued laughing, as a tall wooden golem emerged from the hills near them.

"Little Rafi! Welcome back! Come! Join me!" Habi laughed, her voice bright and cheerful as she waved the golem over.

The doll that Habi had in her pouch was now standing ten feet tall, and able to move on its own. It never spoke, but Habi was able to understand how ecstatic it was to be invited.

"So, how's the husband?" Talia asked with a teasing grin.

"He loves me, and I love him! Life is good," Habi declared confidently, a proud smile on her face.

Suddenly, Rafi appeared from behind Habi and sat right next to her.

"Oh, Habi, I can't wait until we get a home together and live wonderfully!" Rafi laughed, leaning in to kiss her cheek.

"*Cute*," Assad chuckled, joining in the laughter.

The group had a great time together, until they ran out of tea. Habi volunteered to refill everyone's cup, retrieving the jug from the center of the group.

One by one, she happily poured tea into each empty cup. Even Rafi joined the party, offering his cup to be refilled as well.

It was right after Rafi that Habi stopped pouring and stared at the unexpected visitor sitting next to him.

"Oh? Who are you?" Habi asked, holding the jug to her chest.

The dark silhouette remained silent as it sat motionless, glaring at Habi's eyes.

With sheer fear, Habi backed away from the silhouette and placed the jug back in the center of the gathering.

"I need to go," Habi mumbled, her voice distant as she stood and began walking away from the group.

"Don't go!" Talia pleaded, her tone filled with concern.

"It's not safe! Don't go!" Assad added, his voice rising in alarm.

"Habi, don't go!" Rafi called out, desperation lacing his words.

None of the patrons stood up to stop Habi from leaving. Not even the golem or the silhouette moved; they simply stared at her, turning their heads like owls.

As soon as Habi descended the hill, out of the guest's view, the entire landscape collapsed into darkness, shattering like broken glass.

—

Ten days had passed since Father imposed house arrest on the children. Habi's bruises had faded, and Tariq's puncture wound had finally scarred over. The children followed the rules word for word, staying within the yard and by the pond to avoid the threat of being chained to the house. They managed to maintain their morning routine throughout the vacation, but soon ran out of ways to entertain themselves. Boredom set in so deeply that Habi even resorted to performing front and rear somersaults in the shed. Tariq mostly rested his leg, while the others took turns organizing their valuables and tidying up the place. Though their week had been uneventful, they appreciated the time it gave them to secure their goods in its proper hiding spot—the stash beneath the shed.

"Habi, how many times are you going to keep rolling?" Rafi asked, watching her execute yet another somersault.

"Until I can finally do a front and back flip," Habi replied, determination lighting up her face.

"Maybe you can, at this point. Try it out," Naji smirked, scratching his belly as he lounged lazily nearby.

Before Rafi could stop her from hurting herself, Habi had already taken up the challenge.

She leaped into the air and spun forward, tucking her head in. But instead of landing on her feet, she hit the ground on her back. Fortunately, she had practiced the flip a few days earlier, away from prying eyes, so she was prepared for the fall. Even so, she let out a harsh grunt as she landed.

The children laughed when Habi rolled back onto her feet.

Tariq, still confined to his bed, hadn't been able to move around like the others during the past week. Because of this, he hadn't found the right moment to tell Rafi about the discovery he had made. Either Rafi would leave the shed to do whatever Rafi did, or Father would be home. When Father was around, he could hear everything that happened in the shed, which would ruin the purpose of keeping the revelation within their circle. But now, Father was absent.

For the past week, Tariq had kept the location fresh in his memory, waiting for the day he could move without tearing his calf apart again. Today was that day.

While Taliba was immersed in a novel she had already read, Naji counted the bugs on the walls, and Hamza mimicked Habi's rolling, Tariq took the opportunity to slowly rise to his feet and gently walk toward Rafi, who was watching Habi's performance. He felt a surge of pride, knowing his leg was no longer in pain and that he could finally join the others once more. The thought of venturing into unknown lands filled him with excitement—he was eager to see what the world beyond these walls had to offer.

"Hey, Rafi. I know it's been a minute, and I've been bedridden—but I've got some news for you," Tariq whispered, settling down beside Rafi as they watched Habi and Hamza rolling around like maniacs.

"Oh yeah, you wanted to tell me something back then, huh?" Rafi said, his brow furrowing as he tried to recall the moment. "What's up?"

Tariq glanced around, noting how everyone was occupied, except for Taliba, who exchanged a brief glance with him before returning to her book.

"I found a path to the higher hive," Tariq whispered, his voice as soft as the moment demanded.

Rafi raised a brow, leaning in closer. "Explain," he whispered back.

"When I was distracting the Ghazi, I ended up near a shorter wall, which turned out to be part of the higher hive's boundary. I always thought the wall was impenetrable, but I found a shack connected to it. There's a narco tunnel underneath—it leads straight to the rich folk," Tariq explained, his tone hushed but confident.

"And you're sure?" Rafi asked, skepticism mingling with curiosity.

"Pretty sure. Rich folk need their drugs too. They've got the money for it. I can lead everyone there—whenever we're ready to set out again. Go big and go home, right?" Tariq said with a smirk.

"Might even ease the roaches off us in the middle hive while we play with the money bags," Rafi grinned. "But is it safe?"

"Don't know," Tariq admitted, shrugging. "But the area is pretty secluded, away from people and the Ghazi."

"How long do you think the trip will take?"

"We'll have to leave earlier than usual. It's a far walk," Tariq said, glancing at the ceiling as if calculating the time and distance in his head.

Rafi nodded, taking Tariq's word. "We'll set out tomorrow morning. Father should be able to clear us from being grounded today, since you're up and walking again—and Habi's back to trying to hurt herself," Rafi chuckled.

The duo briefly glanced at Habi, who was as energetic as ever. Since her recovery, she hadn't stopped moving, constantly attempting to learn new things while being confined to one area. She had already made decent progress on her leg splits, now able to stretch her legs further apart than before. She bounced between practicing beginner gymnastics and learning new words, often snuggling with Taliba and her books.

"Rafi, look!" Habi beamed as she attempted an intermediate split, her excitement radiating.

"Nice," Rafi said with a smile, nodding approvingly.

"I think she likes you," Tariq teased, nudging Rafi lightly.

"I know," Rafi smirked. "But my main concern right now is getting everyone out and living the best life we can. That's just how the world works, unfortunately. If you don't have gald, then how do you expect to progress?"

"I'm with you on that," Tariq agreed. "But we can always make money. The time we spend together, I believe, is more important."

"Don't give me that, Tariq," Rafi chuckled, shoving him playfully. "We literally see each other every day. How about we see each other every day with a proper meal?"

"Yeah, but we're just kids, man," Tariq said with a shrug. "We can get a job when we grow up."

"And do what, Tariq? I'm not gonna grow up here and see us become criminals for the rest of our lives. I don't want to end up like Faruq, and I don't want to see Taliba and Habi working the streets. This ain't it, Tariq. Come on, you're great at running. Don't you want to go to school, be an all-star on a sports team, and get paid for it? Doing what you love?"

"I mean, that sounds nice—" Tariq started.

"Then we're gonna make it happen," Rafi cut him off. "We're going to the higher hive and making it happen. You in? Why are you trying to back away now after telling me that?"

Tariq grinned and nodded. "I'm not backing away. I was just curious to see how you felt about it all—I'm in. You gonna tell the others?"

Rafi nodded, running his tongue between his teeth as he thought.

"Yeah, I'll tell 'em right now," he said, standing up. "Hey! Gather 'round me! I got some good news!"

The children paused their activities, turning their attention to Rafi and Tariq.

"I can hear you just fine. Just say it," Taliba sighed, barely looking up from her reading corner.

"Okay, Taliba, I'm not gonna yell the entire thing," Rafi snapped, scowling at her.

Taliba rolled her eyes but set her book aside, joining the others as they formed a small circle. Once everyone was present, Rafi took a deep breath and proposed the plan.

"We're going to the higher hive tomorrow morning," Rafi began, his voice steady and confident. "Tariq is leading the way. I don't know what it looks like beyond those walls, but something tells me we'll come back with enough to buy ourselves into the middle hive and call it home."

"We just had bad experiences in the middle hive *twice*, and now you want us to go to the higher hive?" Taliba asked, her tone filled with disbelief.

"We're all alive, aren't we?" Rafi shot back, using the same reasoning as always.

"This is the higher hive, Rafi. What if we don't come back alive? Not even *you* know what lies behind those walls," Taliba countered.

"I've heard tales about the higher folk," Hamza interjected excitedly. "Luxury pools, grass, daily parties, even gold shavings in their food! You know I'm down for this run, Rafi. If the middle hive is their norm, imagine what those goldies have!"

"I'm curious too," Naji added. "I've heard it looks completely different from anything we've seen so far."

"I heard they can have pet rabbits. I love rabbits!" Habi said gleefully, her eyes sparkling.

"Come on, Taliba," Rafi said, gesturing toward the others who seemed captivated. "It's like the gods themselves showed Tariq the way to fortune. This could literally be the last job we ever have to do. Think about it! One run, maybe another, and boom—no more Father, no more bad food, no more fights. Heck, we could get all the books in Koura, maybe even from all over Skania, just for you!"

"That's a little far-fetched, don't you think?" Taliba sighed, crossing her arms.

"I don't even know what that word means, and I'm going to ignore it. Are you in or not?"

"Okay, but how are we going to get the riches, exactly?"

"Easy," Rafi said with a smirk. "We'll break into their homes. Stay low, grab what we can, and get out, never to return. I don't think I want to test their security twice."

"*Break in*!?" Taliba exclaimed. "You want us to *break in*? This is the higher hive, Rafi. We don't even know what we're dealing with! And I know for a fact our rags won't blend in with the people up there."

"Then we'll just acquire some rich folk clothes," Rafi shrugged.

"You're missing the point," Taliba said, pinching the bridge of her nose in frustration.

Meanwhile, Habi tugged on Tariq's shirt, catching his attention.

"Is this what it feels like to have a mama and papa arguing?" Habi whispered, her wide eyes fixed on Rafi and Taliba.

Tariq, one of the few children who had known the presence of both parents, glanced at her and gave a small nod.

"Yep," he replied with full resolve, a hint of amusement tugging at the corner of his mouth.

Rafi and Taliba continued their quarrel, oblivious to the sound of footsteps approaching the door. Habi waddled over to the entrance and silently waited for Father to walk in. Tariq, Hamza, and Naji noticed her standing there, but Rafi and Taliba remained locked in their argument, neither willing to back down.

As soon as the door creaked open, the squabble fell silent as Father stepped into the shed with his trusty pipe and a bag of goods.

Habi didn't say a word. She simply lifted her arms, asking to be picked up. It was her way of showing she was healthy again—and because she loved being taller than everyone else.

"You seem well, little one," Father said softly, lifting Habi into his arms and cradling her gently. "All healed up?"

Habi nodded, extending her arms and brushing her short bangs aside to reveal her previously wounded forehead.

Father turned to face the other previously injured child, Tariq, who now stood with the rest of the children. All of them waited patiently, anticipating any sudden news or announcement that Father might bring. Tariq subtly shifted his weight between his legs, quietly demonstrating that he was fully recovered. They all hoped this would mean the end of their house arrest.

Still cradling Habi, Father walked over to the children and closely examined Tariq's calf, which appeared to have scarred over successfully.

"All is good then?" Father asked.

"Yes, Father," Tariq replied, nodding firmly.

Father gently set Habi back on the floor with the others and took a puff from his pipe, preparing to deliver the ultimatum regarding their arrest.

"Well, you all seem eager to hear what I have to say," Father chuckled softly, a plume of smoke curling from his lips.

He wasn't wrong. The children were brimming with anticipation, eager to return to what the world had to offer—some more than others.

"Did we all learn something during the time spent?" Father asked, his eyes scanning each of them.

The children nodded together, their expressions a mixture of sincerity and resolve.

"Good. Then each of you, tell me one thing you've learned," Father requested, his gaze settling on Rafi to start the cycle.

"Speak the truth," Rafi said firmly.

Father nodded in approval and turned to the next child.

"Be more careful," Taliba added.

"Don't take food and water for granted," Hamza said thoughtfully.

"Run faster, and don't look back," Tariq said with a smirk.

"Be humble," Naji said simply.

"Don't hit your head," Habi chimed in with a small grin.

Father took another puff from his pipe and silently seated himself at his workspace, logging his activities in the Koumaic-written logbook. The children gathered around him, like flies, patiently waiting for his judgment.

"Your house arrest is now lifted. You may all return to your desired activities, whatever they may be. Do not let those same events happen again unless you wish for a harsher punishment. Is that understood?" Father said, his tone firm but measured.

"Yes, Father," the children responded happily, their voices unified.

Father smirked, and the rare expression still managed to catch the children off guard.

"As it may seem now that the first two rules of this family are obsolete, do we all remember the remaining, most important rule? If so, please recite it," Father said, his sharp gaze sweeping over them.

Almost in unison, though some trailed slightly behind, the children recited, "Take care of those around you."

"Good," Father said with a nod of approval.

—

Moments later, Father left the shed once again, off to his unknown activities. The children were ecstatic, their ban finally lifted, and they celebrated with joy inside the shed. However, it was Rafi who chose to get right back to business, now armed with the new information Tariq had shared with him.

"Higher hive tomorrow, right guys?" Rafi mentioned casually.

"But I wanted to play ball with you all," Habi whined, her voice laced with disappointment.

Rafi patted her head with a warm smile. "Yes, but imagine all the time we'll have to enjoy once we finish this last trip, Habi. It's the higher hive. Just one valuable from there is worth all our earnings combined, if not more!" he said with a grin.

"I still don't like the idea of trespassing, especially since it's rich folk property, Rafi," Taliba said, her worry evident.

"That's fine," Rafi said confidently. "It's literally meant to be a hit-and-run situation anyway. Go in, get what we need, come out, and never return."

"And what if we fail?" Taliba pressed.

"We won't fail," Rafi replied firmly.

"Taliba did bring up a good point earlier," Naji interjected. "For starters, we should at least get proper clothes—better than what we have on right now. It'll help us blend in from the narco tunnel and up. She's also right about not knowing what to expect up there."

"One step at a time, guys. This is too much for my head," Hamza groaned.

"Then let's start by acquiring proper wear," Tariq suggested. "Get some clothes from the middle hive, sleep until the next dawn, and then take the narco tunnel. Simple as that."

"Okay—then who's going?" Taliba asked.

"Aren't we all?" Hamza said, looking around.

"No, she's right," Naji agreed, siding with Taliba. "Even though it's been a while, I don't think all of us should go. I know that Habi should stay, especially since she's always the one getting hurt, and a lot of citizens there know of the golden-eyed child."

349

"Hey, I'm not always hurt!" Habi growled, planting her hands on her hips indignantly.

The children burst into laughter, brushing off her protest as Naji continued.

"The Ghazi recently saw me and Hamza. And they literally chased Tariq—a whole lot of them. We're all compromised," Naji pointed out. "But Taliba stayed hidden in the dark during all of that, and Rafi—well, somehow, Rafi's always sneaking past their eyes and noses."

"I'm a good thief," Rafi said proudly, crossing his arms with a smug grin.

"Yeah, *okay*," Taliba snorted, rolling her eyes.

Naji coughed to regain their attention and continued, "So, that really only leaves the two who butt heads the most."

"You want *me* to go with *him*?" Taliba frowned, pointing at Rafi with obvious reluctance.

"It's better to travel in pairs from here to the climb, and you two are the only ones who can do it without raising any alarms," Naji shrugged.

"Hell, we'll get to it then," Rafi agreed, brushing off her annoyance. "Hamza, I'll be taking the pack, along with some rings and stones. Gonna sell them off and buy the clothes. No troubles, yeah?"

"Got it, boss," Hamza said with a grin, pulling his backpack out from under the floorboard and handing it over to Rafi.

Habi went to her bedroll and retrieved the doll she cherished deeply. Waddling over to Rafi, she extended it toward him with both hands.

"Little Rafi will help keep you safe. Do not let the wicked tongue of Taliba sway your heart," she said, her words flowing like poetry.

"Okay." Rafi smiled, clutching the doll tightly.

Taliba shot the pair a strange look, her face twisting at Habi's pointed words. She turned sharply to the others.

"And you're all just fine with this!?" she demanded.

"An extra day to relax before the big day? Hell yeah, I'm fine with this," Hamza said with a laugh.

"It's the only sensible option, Taliba. It's just a clothing run—you're all paying for it anyway," Naji added with a smirk.

Rafi was already stuffing a few valuables into his pack, while Taliba was still trying to face the reality of traveling with him, alone. Rafi slipped on his neck pouch and handed Taliba hers.

"Come on, let's go," Rafi said, slinging the pack over his shoulder.

Taliba let out a heavy sigh, taking the pouch and tucking it under her rags.

"Fine, let's go," she muttered, pouting.

Habi shot Taliba a sharp glare, pointing to her eyes and then to Taliba's.

"He's *mine*," Habi hissed through clenched teeth.

Taliba rolled her eyes as she and Rafi exited the shed, securing the door behind them.

"It's not fair that Taliba gets to go on a date with Rafi!" Habi protested, crossing her arms tightly.

"I mean, they kinda fight like a couple," Hamza quipped, grinning as he laughed.

Habi unleashed a flurry of slaps on Hamza's back, her swift strikes drawing laughter from everyone.

"Never speak of that again!" she warned, her assault showing no signs of stopping.

Still catching his breath from the laughter, Tariq stepped in. "Come on, Habi. Let's go find some folks to play ball with."

"Fine, but Hamza is not invited," Habi huffed, glaring at him.

The shed exploded with laughter as Hamza threw his hands up in mock surrender.

—

Rafi and Taliba moved effortlessly through the Sleeping Complex and over the climb, their practiced skills and deep familiarity with the terrain evident in their every step. With the sun high overhead, they reached the middle hive in good time.

Without delay, they refilled their water canteens, relishing the cool, clean taste of the middle hive water—a luxury they hadn't experienced in ten long days. Their words were few, limited to practical tips and quiet gestures as they helped one another during the ascent and descent.

Once refreshed, they set off toward the bustling market, where citizens and merchants gathered in a lively exchange of goods and chatter.

Rafi hoped none of the children or parents at the play area, where Habi played ball-tag, would recognize him if he happened to run into them. He shrugged off the thought, knocking a fist on his head three times to uncurse himself, convinced that trouble would manifest if he dwelled on it. However, their trip seemed to go smoothly without issue. No one paid them any mind, not even the Ghazi patrolling the area. To the masses, they were just two kids wandering around the square.

It was Taliba who first noticed a potential buyer near the center of the square. Determined not to risk separation, she avoided grabbing Rafi's hand and instead pointed through the bustling crowd before striding ahead.

Rafi hurried to keep up, his eyes fixed on Taliba's long hair and tall frame, which made her easy to track. After pushing his way through the dense throng, he finally caught up with her at a merchant's stall.

The stall wasn't as packed as the others, but the children still had to weave between other customers as Taliba examined the jewelry and assorted trinkets on display.

"Hey, we're selling, not buying," Rafi muttered, swinging the pack from his back to his side.

"Doesn't hurt to look," Taliba replied, her eyes still scanning the trinkets. "How much did you bring to sell?"

"A handful of stones and rings, that's about it. Should be enough for some proper clothes, yeah?"

"I hope so."

Before revealing his goods, Rafi called out to the merchant manning the stall. "Sir! I have an offer!" he shouted, drawing the man's attention.

A middle-aged man turned to Rafi, leaving the other attendants to handle the remaining customers.

"Oh, a little one?" the man teased, though Rafi was only a head or two shorter than him.

"I'm looking to sell these gemstones and rings. Our mother sent us out to do her bidding—trying to clear out the excess," Rafi said, spinning the story smoothly.

"Ah, I see," the man replied, pulling a topless wooden box from beneath the stall. "Go ahead and place the items in here. I'll appraise them, if you don't mind. I'm sure you know how this works if mama's fond of sending her kids for tasks like this, yeah?" he chuckled.

"Thank you, sir," Rafi said with a smile, carefully pouring the bag's contents into the wooden container.

The gemstones and rings tumbled into the container, scattering neatly enough to avoid overcrowding.

The man began appraising the goods, inspecting them closely, weighing each piece, and checking for authenticity. As he worked, Rafi's attention drifted to Taliba, whose gaze had been locked on a particular piece of jewelry since they arrived at the stall.

It was a bracelet adorned with charcoal beads, pearls, and sapphires. The vibrant interplay of colors seemed to captivate her, her focus unwavering.

"You want that?" Rafi teased with a chuckle.

"No," Taliba replied with a pout. "Besides, Habi would probably get mad if you got something for me anyway."

"Then what do you think Habi would like?"

"If you bit a piece of bread and gave it to her, she'd be happy just for that. Jewelry doesn't matter to her."

"But it does to you?"

"Not really," Taliba admitted, her frown deepening. "Just that specific one. From what I've read, the stone combination symbolizes protection and happiness—something I feel like I could really use right now."

Before Rafi could respond, the merchant returned, interrupting their conversation. "Appraisal is all done, young sir," he announced, pulling a pouch of gald from his belt. "All of this comes to six hundred gald. Is that an acceptable rate?"

"Yep," Rafi replied without hesitation.

As the transaction wrapped up, Rafi leaned closer to the man, lowering his voice to a whisper.

"How much is that black, white, and blue bracelet over there?"

The merchant glanced at the piece, then back at Rafi with a raised brow. "Ah, that one caught your eye? It's one fifty gald. Interested?"

Rafi quickly counted out gald pieces totaling one hundred and fifty and handed them to the merchant. The man accepted the payment with a nod and retrieved the bracelet, placing it in Rafi's outstretched hand. Taliba, her eyes wide, watched the entire exchange in silence.

"Thank you, little sir. Have a great day! The Sultan is great!" the merchant proclaimed with a cheerful grin.

"The Sultan is great," Rafi echoed, his tone light and playful.

Rafi stored the remaining gald in a smaller pocket on the pack and swung it onto his back. Then, he handed Taliba the bracelet she had so dearly desired.

"Why did you do that?" Taliba growled, her eyes fixed reluctantly on the bracelet Rafi held out.

"Because we're siblings, even if none of us are blood related. I still care about all of you," Rafi replied evenly. "Now, are you going to take it, or should I sell it back for a full refund?"

Taliba blushed and swiped the bracelet from Rafi's hands, wrapping it around her wrist. She took a long look at its gleam, the shine reflecting in her eye. She could already feel its innate power surging into her, while Rafi stood by, letting Taliba indulge in her superstitious thoughts.

"Thank you," Taliba mumbled, her fingers lightly brushing over the bracelet. "Habi is going to kill you for this."

"No, she won't," Rafi chuckled. "She's going to kill *you*."

Taliba rolled her eyes, turning away as she began scanning the market for a merchant selling clothes and fabrics.

"Hey, I'm joking!" Rafi called after her, breaking into a quick stride to catch up.

—

After weaving through more crowds and searching for a clothing stall that wasn't crowded with buyers, the duo finally stumbled upon a merchant worth their attention. Taliba was the first to spot the stall again, proving her keen eye for opportunity. Draped over wooden hangers and in open wardrobes, the stall displayed a variety of colors and materials, ranging from wool, cotton, fur, and even silk. It was organized well enough for the duo to easily distinguish between adult and child wear, and the pathways were wide enough for them both to walk through.

The merchant woman bowed with a warm smile, saying, "I hope you two little ones find what you're looking for."

Both Rafi and Taliba scoured through the child-sized tunics, gowns, garbs, and trousers. They flipped from one outfit to another, hoping to find a fit that called to them, before selecting sets for the others.

Rafi was a simple boy, picking out a burgundy wool vest bundled with a white button-up shirt and black slacks, all fitting his size.

"I'm gonna look spiffy with these on," Rafi smirked, holding up the bundle on a hanger for Taliba to see.

"Yeah, okay," Taliba replied with a roll of her eyes, her focus shifting to a gown that had caught her attention.

The gown she held up was a deep violet, paired with a crisp white blouse and a small corset designed to wrap snugly around her waist.

"I'm getting this one," Taliba declared confidently.

"Oh, come on, let's be more practical here," Rafi suggested, raising an eyebrow.

"I *am* being practical, stupid," Taliba shot back with a scowl, clearly committed to her choice. "This is perfect for a girl in the higher hive."

"Okay, but what about when we climb?" Rafi countered.

"We have a backpack, don't we?" Taliba mocked. "We can just change when we get to the other side to keep it pristine. Use your head for once."

Rafi snickered quietly to himself. "Should've never bought that bracelet for ya," he muttered under his breath before turning his attention back to the racks. He began picking out outfits for the other boys, each set resembling the one he had chosen for himself, with only slight differences in size to accommodate them.

Taliba even found a dark gray gown that seemed perfect for Habi. However, she quickly reconsidered, knowing Habi's youthful frame hadn't yet developed to suit such attire. Instead, she selected a white blouse and a pair of brown shorts, giving her the appearance of a schoolboy off to class.

"What, Habi doesn't get a gown like you?" Rafi asked, shaking his head in mock disapproval.

"Have you seen her? A gown would just slip right off," Taliba replied with a grimace.

"Whatever you say, *Miss Elegant*," Rafi mocked with a smirk. "So, are we done or not?"

"How about footwear?" Taliba suggested, glancing toward another section of the market.

Rafi cursed under his breath, but he agreed with the notion. Aside from clothing, footwear was another sign of wealth and status. The children never really cared about it, as they were always on the move and accustomed to their soles being worn thin. But without proper footwear, their lack of it could compromise them upon arrival.

"Hey, ma'am, do you happen to have six pairs of shoes or boots, fit for children about my height and size?" Rafi asked the merchant woman.

"Of course," she replied with a warm smile, leading the duo to another aisle in the stall, weaving past a few other buyers. She gestured toward the floor, where an impressive array of footwear was neatly displayed. The sheer variety left even Rafi momentarily stunned.

"Okay, can you hand-pick six pairs for me? We're all going to a fancy party," Rafi said with a confident grin.

"Buying for the whole group, are you?" the woman chuckled. "I'd recommend the leather shoes for the boys, and the matching variant for the girls."

The merchant pointed out the section of shoes she suggested, and, eager to move on, Rafi scooped up six pairs for the boys without even checking the sizes.

"Rafi, what if those don't fit?" Taliba hissed under her breath.

"Doesn't matter. We'll figure it out when we get there. People who care too much about this kind of stuff are weird," Rafi whispered back, his arms piled high with outfits and shoes.

"Well, at least let me help," Taliba offered, pulling a few shoes and clothing sets from his grasp to lighten the load.

"Are we all ready to order, little ones?" the lady asked, her pleasant smile never wavering.

—

Later that day, Habi and the others had already returned to the shed after playing with the other children in their neighborhood. Father occasionally popped in, checking on their health and feeding their bellies with snacks. But for the most part, the remaining four children in the shed were left alone. The sun was beginning to set.

Habi used the last of the natural light to draw a picture on a piece of paper, while the others laid on their rolls, counting the wrinkles in the wooden boards.

Over Hamza's snoring, Tariq leaned closer to Habi and asked, "Hey Habi, what are you drawing?"

"I'm drawing us," Habi replied, humming softly as she continued to scribble with focus.

Curious, Tariq crawled over to her and stole a glance at her artwork.

On the paper, Habi drew seven disfigured shapes of triangles, squares, and circles connected by lines. Each one had a face, and it was easy to tell who was who. All the figures were smiling and holding hands, with Father leading the pack from tallest to shortest. The only exception to Habi's perception of the height scale was that she squeezed herself in between Rafi and Taliba.

"Jealous?" Habi asked with a mischievous grin.

"Oh yeah, absolutely," Tariq replied, his voice dripping with sarcasm.

During her session, Habi caught the familiar pitter-patter of footsteps approaching the door. As soon as she looked up, Rafi and Taliba returned from their trip, a packed bag in hand.

The children cheered and gathered around, their laughter filling the space—everyone except Hamza, who remained fast asleep. Both groups eagerly shared their stories: tales of navigating the bustling market and the thrilling recount of winning the ball game's final point with an impossible goal. Amid the chatter, it became clear that all the remaining gald from the duo's sale had been spent.

Habi proudly displayed her drawing to the others. While Taliba quietly noted the off-scale heights in the sketch, Habi's sharp eyes caught sight of the bracelet glinting on Taliba's wrist.

"Where'd you get that?" Habi asked, pointing at the beautiful piece.

Chapter Nineteen

After Habi tortured Taliba and Rafi about how she didn't get special treatment from the shopping spree, the children later rested their aching bodies. They were finally able to experience the world again, suffering from the long arrest. Night would fall, and dawn would rise, where the children were committed to their departure for the higher hive. Or at least, one of the children was committed to such an early departure. Rafi was the first to be up, as he forced himself awake and scrambled to the others. Father had already left for his tasks, while the slumbering children were enjoying their long, healthy rest—until Rafi shook them awake.

Everyone groaned and whined, some burrowing deeper into their bedrolls in protest. Rafi, however, had barely slept, too excited about the life-changing trip ahead. Today was the day the children would finally get to explore the higher hive—but only if they managed to wake up in time.

"Hey! Hey! Wake up, you lot!" Rafi shouted, clapping his hands and hopping around.

Habi felt the early morning breeze brush against her face, now uncovered and exposed to the cool air. A small chill ran across her skin, prompting her to retreat back into the tattered warmth of her sheets.

But out of all the things that would get Habi to wake up, it was Rafi pulling down the ragged blanket from her head, and hovering his face over hers, whispering, "Habi. Habi. Habi."

It was bait, and Habi took it the moment she opened her eyes. She shot upright, her face flushing red as she reached for Rafi, who skillfully kept his distance while tending to the others. Rafi moved quickly, shaking several children awake, though Hamza required a firmer approach—a pinch to the nose that made him cough and stir. Groans filled the shed as the children realized the sun wasn't even fully up, with only faint blue light filtering through the gaps. It took a moment, but a shared understanding soon dawned on them all: today was the big day.

There was no time for their usual morning routine. They had all decided to skip Father's daily bread and their wash at the grimy pond. Today, they dreamed of eating and bathing like royalty, even if only for a fleeting moment. At the very least, they hoped to grab a proper meal in the middle hive before heading to the higher ring—though their stay would be brief, driven by the constant fear of being recognized.

Possibly for the last time, the children groggily pulled on their hoods, hooked their canteens, and secured their pouches. The clothes Rafi and Taliba had bought for everyone were already packed in Hamza's backpack, ready to be changed into once they made the crossing. Rafi had even brought along extra valuables to trade for food. The haul wasn't substantial enough to deplete his stash, but he still felt the sting of parting with it.

"Adventure! Adventure!" Habi cheered, hopping with excitement as her energy seemed to spark anew.

As Rafi secured his pouch around his neck, he noticed her doll still tucked inside. With a small smile, he retrieved it and handed it back to her. Habi clutched it tightly, beaming as she declared, "See? The doll kept you safe after all!"

"Where do you even get all that energy from?" Taliba yawned, running her fingers through her hair to fix a few stray strands.

"She keeps her mind empty—easy way to stay happy," Hamza joked, slinging his pack over his shoulders with a chuckle.

As the children suited up, Rafi went over the plan one last time, with Tariq standing beside him, ready to clarify for anyone who might have forgotten.

"We make the climb and head straight to the shack. Tariq will lead. After that, we'll just hope the tunnel is a simple walk," Rafi explained, scanning their faces for questions.

"What about food?" Naji asked, patting his stomach.

"I demand *sustenance*," Habi declared, crossing her arms dramatically.

"Where'd you learn a big word like that?" Rafi asked, raising an eyebrow.

"Taliba," Habi replied without hesitation, pointing a finger at her.

—

Some time later, the children finally set off for the climb. It had taken most of the morning to gather their spirits, but in the end, they managed. Joy filled the air as they shared stories about the mythical higher hive, speaking of its beautiful citizens, their riches, and their luxurious way of life. The children were especially excited to see the rumored glazing grasses and glittering pools—sights they had never imagined they would experience.

The children took their usual route, slipping through the undisturbed alleyways of the complex, careful to avoid any potential danger. By the time the sun began to rise, they had reached the climbing area, swiftly making their way up and over, landing in the middle hive before the day had fully begun.

Once everyone was accounted for, it was time for Tariq to take the lead. As usual, they refilled their canteens at the refreshing water well before heading toward the market. As promised, the children made a brief stop at a jewelry merchant, selling off all the goods in their bags. When they were handed a pile of gald, they went wild, eager to indulge in a food shopping spree.

As a group, they bought from several stalls—toasted sandwiches, fried fish on sticks, and, most importantly, cake and ice cream. None of the children had ever tasted such sweets before, and after devouring it all, they were left craving more. Their eyes gleamed with delight from the burst of flavors, smiles stretching from cheek to cheek. However, Rafi kept them in check, carefully moderating their intake to avoid overspending.

"The ice cream was so good! I want more!" Habi demanded, licking the remnants from her small bowl as she finished it last.

The children burst into laughter as they noticed Habi's face smeared with vanilla and chocolate. Rafi stepped in, taking the seam of his rag to gently wipe her face.

"If it's not past curfew, we can get more when we come back. But for now, we've got business to attend to, dork," Rafi teased, smirking as Habi's cheeks turned pink while he cleaned the last smudge from her lips.

"Okay, you two lovebirds," Tariq chimed in with a grin. "Are we gonna head out and walk all this food off, or what?"

With that, the children straightened up, stifling their giggles, and returned to the path Tariq had scouted earlier.

—

Avoiding the gaze of Ghazi like the plague, the children made their way toward the deeper parts of the surrounding neighborhoods, sticking to less-traveled paths. They occasionally passed a few adults tending to their property, but none of them paid the children any mind. The further they ventured from the heart of the hive, the fewer people they encountered. Most citizens were likely at the marketplaces or huddled inside their homes, avoiding the city's festivities. It made sense that some would choose to live on the outskirts of the neighborhood—unless, of course, they had no other option. In Koura, no home was left unfilled.

As time passed and the sun rose higher, Tariq finally led the children to the dreaded shack, which clearly stood out of place. It was dark, though not nearly as oppressive as the darkness of the Sleeping Complex. Not a single soul patrolled or passed through this area, and the children stood in silence, staring from one end of the alley to the other. It was eerily empty, even at this hour. The only sounds that filled the air were the distant murmurs from the market and the steady rhythm of their own breaths.

"This is it," Tariq said, resting a hand on the wooden shack. "It's a little dusty inside, but there's a trapdoor that leads to the tunnel."

"Nice. Let's get to it, then," Rafi replied with a smirk, already moving toward the door.

Tariq gestured for Rafi to take the lead. With a cautious nod, Rafi turned the knob and slowly eased the door open. A cloud of dust and sand burst outward, forcing him to shield his face. The faint light from outside seeped into the shack, barely illuminating the interior.

It was just enough for Rafi to notice something unusual. He crouched slightly, pointing to the floor. "Tariq, were these here when you found this?" he asked, indicating a clear adult-sized footprint in the thick layer of dust. The print was distinct and trailed toward the trapdoor a few steps ahead.

"No, they weren't," Tariq replied, frowning. "Don't even know how recent those prints are."

Naji stepped forward, crouching beside the footprint. He ran a finger through the edge of the imprint, gathering a thin layer of dust.

"I'd say they're at least a couple of days old, judging by how much dust I picked up," Naji guessed, studying his hand.

"Don't trust the sand," Taliba warned, her voice steady. "There are many storms."

As the children examined the footprints, Rafi moved ahead, gripping the edge of the trapdoor. With a swift motion, he lifted it open, the sudden noise startling everyone.

"See y'all down here," he said with a quick salute before disappearing down the stairs into the tunnel.

"Wait, Rafi! What if we run into someone in there?" Taliba called after him, her voice laced with concern.

From below, Rafi's faint voice echoed back, "It's a business tunnel. No one should be fighting here."

As the children listened to Rafi's footsteps descending the wooden steps, followed by the faint crunch of sand and dirt beneath his shoes, they exchanged glances before filing in behind him. Moving in a single line, they followed their usual tactic: keeping Hamza as the rear guard, ready to act if anything went wrong.

One by one, the children descended through the trapdoor, with Hamza securing it shut behind them, plunging them into pitch darkness. Unable to see their hands in front of them, they instinctively linked up, Rafi taking the lead and Hamza bringing up the rear.

Rafi felt the walls of the tunnel as he moved, gauging the space around them. The tunnel's height was sufficient for an adult to stand, while its width barely allowed him to spread both arms.

"It's kinda tight in here," Hamza grumbled, his voice echoing faintly from the rear of the line.

"There has to be a light source or something," Tariq said, squinting into the darkness ahead.

At those words, Rafi paused, a thought suddenly dawning on him.

"Hey Hamza, do you still have the hashwabi kit in the bag? We can use the flint, steel, and paper for temporary light," Rafi suggested, glancing back.

"I'll feel for it, boss," Hamza replied, dropping his bag and fumbling blindly through the first pouch he opened.

"Hey, who tickled me?" Taliba hissed, whipping her head around, unable to pinpoint the culprit.

"*Adventure*," Habi whispered mischievously, clinging to Taliba's waist. At least now, the culprit was identified.

As the children lingered at the bottom of the steps, Hamza rummaged through his bag with determination. A moment later, his voice echoed through the tunnel.

"Found it!"

"Light it up," Rafi instructed.

In the darkness, the screech and clatter of flint striking steel reverberated through the tunnel. After a few tries, Hamza managed to produce a spark that lit a small piece of paper. He quickly tucked the flint away and blew gently on the ember, coaxing the fragile flame to life. The paper caught fire but began to burn out rapidly, its flickering light casting fleeting shadows on the walls.

The brief illumination was enough for Naji to spot a stick nearby with a bundled mess at its tip.

"Think that's a torch?" Naji asked, squinting to make it out.

"Quick, Hamza, bring the fire here!" Tariq ordered, standing between Hamza and the potential torch, ready to act.

Hamza quickly handed the burning paper to Tariq, who passed it to Naji. Naji held the flame to the top of the torch, and within moments, the tinder caught fire, sending flickering light dancing across the tunnel walls. He unlatched the torch from its holder on the wall and passed it forward. Habi took it next, then handed it to Taliba, who finally passed it to Rafi.

The torch's light illuminated their immediate surroundings, casting faint, shifting shadows, though it wasn't strong enough to reveal the vast, shadowy pathways ahead. Still, it was better than the oppressive darkness they'd been navigating.

"Well, at least we can see our feet now," Rafi remarked, eyeing the carved scrapes of sand and dirt around him that made up the tunnel floor.

The smell of damp soil hung heavily in the air as the children pressed onward into the unknown. The flickering torchlight revealed old handprints smeared along the walls and horizontal scratches that didn't quite match the tunnel's natural curvature, adding an eerie sense of history to the space.

As they ventured deeper, the air thickened, heavy with moisture and an oppressive stillness. The fumes from the torch began to sting their lungs, making each breath feel shallower and more strained.

At a certain point, Rafi's chest tightened—not just from the air, but from the gnawing sensation in his gut. He couldn't shake the thought that the gods, if they existed, might be stacked against him.

The children came to an abrupt halt, colliding into each other as Rafi suddenly stopped in his tracks. Only he and Taliba, standing near the torch, could see the problem before them.

Rafi slowly waved the torch side to side, its flickering light casting uncertain shadows ahead. "We have a problem, guys," he muttered, cursing under his breath.

Before them stretched three separate paths, each one seemingly identical.

"Dammit, we're in a maze," Taliba sighed, her frustration cutting through the heavy air. "Point the light at the tunnel walls. Maybe others left signs."

As instructed, Rafi examined each tunnel path with the torch, noting several prints and scratches. Unfortunately, there was no discernible pattern, as all the paths had walls marked with random scribbles and gouged surfaces.

"They all look the same," Rafi coughed, the stale, smoke-laden air taking its toll on his lungs.

"Not a rope? Not an item? Not a body?" Tariq asked, scanning the walls with narrowing eyes.

"Nothing—dammit!" Rafi spat, his frustration echoing faintly through the tunnel.

In that instant, the children's morale dropped. They could have taken the risk of choosing a random tunnel, but the stakes were too high. Rafi knew that if he made that decision, someone could get lost, hurt, or worse.

As the children exchanged ideas, Habi's gaze remained fixed on the leftmost path.

Down that passage, a familiar face emerged from the shadows, waving at her. Without hesitation, Habi squeezed between Taliba and Rafi, pushing her way to the front for a clearer view.

"Assad!" Habi called out, waving eagerly at the man who had once delivered the doll she cherished.

The other children turned to look, their hearts pounding in sync with the eerie stillness of the tunnel. But to their shock, the path appeared empty—no one was there.

"Habi, there's no–" Taliba began, but before she could finish, Rafi raised a hand and shushed her, his expression tense.

Rafi turned to the others and pointed at Habi, who had her back turned to them. He then pointed at his eye, silently signaling, *her golden-eyed powers are going to help us.*

With a very soft whisper, Taliba said, "There's no way we can confirm this will work. It could be a trap, for all we know."

"She called the ghost by its name. She knows it. This is our best chance to get out of here before we all suffocate," Rafi whispered back, his voice steady. Then he turned his attention to Habi. "Hey Habi, see a friend?"

Habi nodded enthusiastically, her face lighting up as she pointed toward the empty air in the leftmost path.

"That's Assad! He's a good friend! I think he wants us to go that way," Habi explained with certainty.

"Then let's go. Maybe you can lead the way and welcome us to him?" Rafi said, offering a small, encouraging smile.

Habi nodded again and waddled down the leftmost path, catching the others off guard since she wasn't the torchbearer.

"Habi, slow down!" Taliba called out.

Rafi nodded to the others and took off after Habi, who had already disappeared into the shadows ahead. The faint light of the torch barely reached her, but they kept their distance, careful not to overwhelm or frighten whatever spirit she seemed to be following.

"Let's see how far she goes," Rafi whispered to the group, his eyes fixed on the path ahead as they moved cautiously behind her.

At first, Habi executed a small jog to catch up to Assad. However, it didn't take long for her to shift to a brief walk as she moved directly behind him. Assad turned his head and smiled at her, noticing how close she was.

"*Oiye pazi*, Habi," Assad greeted warmly, his voice echoing softly through the tunnel. "What brought you all here today?"

"We're going on an adventure to the higher hive! I'm excited!" Habi exclaimed, her joy radiating as she skipped closer. "How about you, Assad? What are you doing here?"

"I show up wherever I please, as long as I've left a memory there. You know that, little one," Assad replied with a hearty laugh. "But the higher hive, ah—it's a wonderful place, full of life and fun. May I ask, though, what business do you have there?"

As they walked, Assad took a right turn at another split in the tunnel, prompting Habi and the others to follow.

"Oh, Rafi wanted us to go and steal from the rich. He says it's our ticket out of the slums," Habi said matter-of-factly.

Assad came to a brief stop, his expression somber, before continuing forward.

"I advise against that, little one. But who am I to say what is right and wrong?" Assad said with a faint frown.

"What's wrong, Assad? You seem sad," Habi asked, her own face mirroring his expression.

"It is funny, *li ah-te*. I am against the way you all approach bettering yourselves and your lives, yet I am not against your passion and desire for change. Funny, is it not?" Assad said, his voice tinged with melancholy.

Habi stared blankly at Assad, her young mind unable to grasp the weight of his words. Assad chuckled softly, then continued to guide the group straight through another split in the tunnel.

"Perhaps now is a good time to tell you the reason why I am the way I am," Assad began, before abruptly adding, "Watch out to your left."

Habi instinctively hugged the right side of the tunnel, skirting past a cluster of brown, moldy debris jutting out of the ground. The others followed closely, their eyes catching the unmistakable sight of human bones—a half-rib cage protruding eerily from the dirt.

It was a dangerous trap for the inattentive, but Habi, unaware of the remains' grim nature, glanced at them with innocent curiosity.

The children in the back noticed Habi's sudden movement and, understanding the caution, mirrored her actions as they hugged the right side of the tunnel, carefully passing by the haunting remains.

"These tunnels have been here far too long, and with their age, they still serve their purpose," Assad continued, his voice echoing faintly in the narrow space. "Many have gotten lost within these walls, and many have smuggled their goods to the other side. Perhaps it was chance—or fate—that I met you here."

"You're just too nice, silly," Habi said, her cheerful tone bringing a soft laugh from Assad.

"I guess you're right, Habi," Assad chuckled. "Perhaps it's that same kindness that led to my demise."

"Oh? What happened?" Habi asked, her expression shifting to a pout, tinged with sadness.

Assad's smile faded slightly as he continued. "Sara may have not spoken of it, but she was there—with me and the others from the old family. It was me, Sara, Karim, and Lena. A strange event indeed," he said with a distant look, pausing to take a breath he did not need. "You know of the Hassazi, yes?"

"The has-ah-see? Yes," Habi replied, nodding eagerly.

"Then you know how Father formed the Hassazi—the assassins who vowed to dismantle the Sultan's tyrannical rule piece by piece," Assad began, his tone calm yet laced with a trace of sorrow. "When his ideology faltered, he withdrew from it all, becoming a hermit in the lower hive, where millions struggled to survive. That's when he began taking in children who had no direction, no future—I was one of them, of course. Back then, we were simply called 'the family', just as you are now."

He paused, his gaze steady but somber. "The difference, Habi, is that with your family, Father wants you all to live, to thrive, to find joy in life. He values those same ideals now as he did then. But we were different, little one."

Assad sighed, the weight of his words hanging heavy. "Father trained us to be Hassazi. We were his family, yes, but also his tools—his assassins."

Habi tried to piece everything together as she followed Assad, making a right turn down the shadowy tunnel.

"We murdered those of utmost importance," Assad continued. "Saif taught us to defend ourselves by giving us makeshift tools and throwing us into the Sleeping Complex to fend for our lives. Through that, we learned. Later, we followed his footsteps, taking out targets beloved by the Sultan and his gold tongues."

Assad glanced at Habi, his smirk faintly visible in the dim torchlight as he noticed the worry on her face. "The very reason I am like this, Habi? It's because all four of us—me, Sara, Karim, and Lena—attempted to take the life of the Kouran Army's Commandant, Hizan Al-Za'im. Only Sara survived. Three of us lost our lives saving her."

He paused, his expression darkening briefly before softening again. "Since then, Sara detached herself from the old family and vowed to live a life of peace. As for Saif, the weight of what he sent us to do broke him. He gave up on his mission and dreams. But Habi," Assad said, his voice gentle now, "he loves all of you, even if he doesn't show it well."

"I love Father too," Habi said quietly, her voice sincere and full of conviction.

Conversing with Assad made the time seem to pass much faster. After a short while, the group followed him through a left turn and came to a gradual stop. Before Habi stood another trapdoor, sealed above her.

"Is this the way out?" Habi asked, her gaze fixed on the wooden barrier.

"Yes," Assad replied with a nod. "It is the way to the higher hive. *Ola-te kati,* tread carefully, little one—both there and from."

"Thank you, Assad!" Habi said brightly, a wide smile on her face as she waved at him.

Assad smiled and waved back before deciding to fade and depart. Habi didn't catch it at the time, but Assad slowly changed his expression from a light grin into a devastated frown. With that, he disappeared into thin air, returning to the Land of the Dead.

"Habi, is your friend gone?" Rafi asked, catching up to her and noticing her waving into empty air.

"Yes! He found the way out for us!" Habi beamed, pointing to the trapdoor above. Excited, she reached for the latch, but Rafi quickly grabbed her arm, halting her.

"Let me do it, Habi. Don't want something falling down on you," Rafi said firmly, his tone protective as he moved to handle the task himself.

Rafi handed the torch to Taliba and squeezed past Habi, stepping up the wooden stairs to try the latch. There was little resistance, aside from a light dusting that fell as he moved. As soon as he slightly lifted it, he shoved the door open with full force and poked his head out of the hole, scanning for any danger.

Rafi deemed it safe and gestured for the others to extinguish the torch and follow his lead. Once all the children made it out of the tunnels and secured the trapdoor behind them, they were taken aback to find themselves in yet another dusty wooden shack.

While the children patted the dust and sand off themselves, Rafi creaked the front door open slightly and peered through the crack. All that followed was a string of curses.

"We sure this is the higher hive?" Rafi asked.

It was a redundant question, since neither child had ever experienced the view of the higher hive. All they knew was that the landscape in front of the shack resembled the barren path of the middle hive, and the sun had passed its highest point. The trek through the tunnel had taken longer than they expected.

"Keep your head up," Hamza said, smirking. "Don't think the rich folk would keep a crusty old shack next to all the good stuff, yeah?"

Hamza had a point. The children now believed they were beyond the walls, but only just barely. When Rafi revealed the exterior, the buildings around them resembled the layout of the middle hive. Even the shack was oddly placed, huddled against the wall. It was Taliba who concluded the likely length of the journey and their current position.

"The walls to the higher hive may be shorter in height, but with that walk—it must be extremely wide," Taliba observed, glancing upward.

"Would make sense, since the walls above us are guarded with archers and watchers," Naji added thoughtfully.

"Then how did we never get caught?" Taliba wondered aloud, her brow furrowing.

"Perhaps this area is of least importance to them," Naji suggested. "Or maybe they're all in on the secret of the narco tunnel and have pledged to turn a blind eye."

While the two were theorizing, Rafi was already digging into Hamza's pack, tossing the sets of sophisticated clothing to everyone. As planned, the boys received colorful vests and their matching buttoned-up shirts. Taliba got her personally chosen gown, while Habi was handed a pair of clothes meant for children attending entry-level classes. Finally, everyone was tossed a pair of shoes, though the sizes hadn't been determined beforehand.

"Why does Taliba get a dress?" Habi pouted, holding up her plain outfit with a hint of disappointment.

Taliba smirked and patted her hips, teasingly flaunting her developing figure. "You'll get there—just not anytime soon," she giggled, unwrapping her gown with a satisfied smile.

"Less talk, guys," Rafi interjected. "Change into the clothes so we can hurry and check out the hive. Time is ticking."

Realizing that lingering in the shack would only eat away at their precious time to explore, the children hastily shed their rags and changed into their new garments. Most of them beamed with excitement over their fresh attire, while a few were less than pleased.

"Ah, man, I look like a kid the rats wanna beat up around the block!" Hamza groaned, tugging at his outfit.

"These shorts are stupid! I want a dress like Taliba!" Habi whined.

The children laughed as they tried on their new shoes. Some were lucky to get a pair that fit perfectly, while others ended up with shoes that were either too large or too small. After a few swaps and trades, they finally completed their disguises, looking every bit the part of model child citizens.

Tariq adjusted his green vest and leaned down toward Habi, whispering, "Hey, Habi, be glad you don't have the gown. If Taliba needed to run, she'd be in trouble with that thing on."

"Haha! Stupid!" Habi laughed, pointing at Taliba with glee.

"What is *wrong* with you?" Taliba said, rolling her eyes but unable to suppress a small chuckle.

Naji helped Rafi secure the old rags into the pack, making sure everyone still had their neck pouches. Once everything was inventoried, Rafi walked up to each child, scanning them from head to toe, checking that everything that should be there, was.

"Right. It seems that we're all good to go," Rafi said, positioning himself by the door and gripping the latch. "Remember, stay close together. We don't know what to expect."

"Aye," the children responded in unison, their voices firm with acknowledgment.

Following everyone's affirmation, Rafi smiled and pulled the door open, revealing the bright rays of light above. He stepped out first, his feet sinking into the sand of unfamiliar lands.

—

For the most part, the higher hive was relatively simple, with buildings near the border no different from those in the lower hive. The children walked along the familiar gravel path, easily navigating the neighborhood. But as they ventured further, they began to notice more anomalies. The streets widened, empty of the usual crowd. The bustle and chatter that filled the markets were absent here. The higher hive was unnervingly quiet, and the children found it strange that they hadn't encountered a single citizen—or even one of the Sultan's men.

"Why don't we raid these homes right away?" Hamza whispered, glancing around at the modest-looking buildings.

"I'm not gonna waste time on a house that doesn't even scream luxury," Rafi replied, his eyes narrowing as he surveyed the area. "Plus, we still need to figure out if this is even what the higher hive has to offer. Go big and go home, right?"

"Where is everyone?" Taliba asked, her voice low as she scanned the eerily quiet surroundings.

"It's strange," Naji said, frowning. "We've been walking for this long, and we haven't even seen a single water well."

"The rich are odd," Tariq said. "Seems like they keep to themselves."

While the children conversed, Habi absorbed her surroundings. She glanced up at the high sandstone homes, then looked down at the cracks and pebbles beneath her, intrigued by everything around her. It wasn't until something unusually odd caught her eye as they continued along the gravel path.

Habi spotted a sliver of green jutting out of the path adjacent to them and she ran off to investigate it.

"Habi?" Taliba called, concern rising as everyone's attention shifted to the little one.

At first, they thought Habi was seeing dead people again, but it turned out she was jogging toward a patch of green that seemed out of place. As the children approached, they discovered more strands of greenery emerging from the sand. The closer they got, the more they noticed the earth beneath them transforming into soft, brown soil.

"Is that grass?" Taliba asked.

Before anyone could respond, Habi crouched, plucked a single blade of grass, sniffed it, and popped it into her mouth. She chewed briefly, then spat it out with a grimace.

"That's nasty," Habi said, wiping her mouth.

"Hold on—look at that," Rafi said, giving Habi's shoulder a quick pat.

Rafi pointed out how the sand gradually turned into dirt, and how the greenery spread out into glades. The gravel path before them shifted into paved stone roads, while the atmosphere around them seemed to change. All the children kept their eyes fixed on the beauty of the grass and the structure of the walkway. If they thought the surprises were over, they were mistaken. At the end of the path, a glossy, clean marble square stretched out, with a large fountain at its center. A few citizens dressed in fine clothes stood and sat around the magnificent architecture. Nearby, the long-awaited water well stood next to the fountain, its design clearly made by different methods. It was a completely new experience for everyone—one of luxury.

"Holy sh—" Rafi began, his jaw dropping in astonishment, but Taliba cut him off.

"I never thought we'd see anything like this," she said, her eyes glistening.

It was such an eye-catching sight that Rafi had to hold Habi back, certain she was tempted to jump into the crystal-clear fountain.

"Can't believe we made it," Tariq said, his eyes lingering on the grass tracing the stone foundation.

"Even the buildings look rich. These folks are living years ahead of us!" Naji added.

In contrast to the middle hive's use of sandstone for its buildings, the higher hive favored granite. While the homes in the middle hive stood about eight to ten feet high, those in the higher hive reached at least twenty feet, with some towering even higher.

"Oh my, you're such an adorable little one!" a woman exclaimed, her gaze locked on Habi.

The children quickly turned their attention to the sudden visitor, a woman who towered over them. She appeared young, with long, wavy auburn hair cascading over her shoulder. Her pale skin and emerald eyes nearly convinced Rafi they were made of actual gems. She wore a green gown embroidered with golden patterns, and a leather corset cinched tightly around her waist, accentuating her figure. A leather satchel hung from her shoulder, resting at her hips. The children knew immediately she was a foreigner—though one of wealth.

"Are you all siblings? Where are your parents?" the woman asked.

"Our parents told us not to talk to strangers," Rafi replied.

"Quite strict, even for living in this ring, no?" the woman said with a giggle. "Here, maybe these will cheer you up."

The woman cheerfully reached into her satchel and pulled out a handful of items. The children immediately dropped into a defensive stance, as they had been conditioned to do, but relaxed when they realized she had only retrieved a bunch of brown wrappers shaped like slim bars.

"Here, here, take it," the woman urged, waving six bars in front of the children.

"What is that?" Naji whispered.

"I don't know. Maybe it's–" Tariq began, but before he could finish, Habi snatched a bar and unwrapped it without hesitation.

Underneath the wrap, there was a solid, yet slightly creamy brown substance that revealed itself to her. As expected, Habi sniffed it and immediately took a bite.

Her eyes widened and she continued to devour the rest of the bar, leaving a brown mess across her lips.

"Have you never had chocolate before? What kind of parents are you living with?" the woman laughed.

"*More*," Habi demanded, holding out her hand.

"No, no, little one. As much as I'd love to fatten you up, chocolate isn't the healthiest way to do it!" the woman replied with a smile. "So, what's your name, young sir?"

The lady mistook Habi for a boy, which meant their disguises were working to some extent. However, Habi took offense to that.

"I'm a gi–" Habi began, but Rafi quickly interrupted.

"This is my brother, Habo. He's the youngest of us all," Rafi said smoothly. He then introduced the rest of the group, ensuring Habi's role was adjusted to match the woman's evident fondness for her. Once the introductions were complete, Rafi leaned close to Habi and whispered, "Play along."

"*Habo*," the woman repeated, her voice lilting. "Such a sweet young boy with beautiful golden eyes. Tell me, since I'm still learning about Kouran culture, does the name have a meaning?"

"It means 'handsome,'" Rafi answered with a confident smile.

"My, you do seem to speak a lot for your little brother. Are you perhaps the eldest?"

"That I do be, ma'am," Rafi replied with a polite nod.

It was strange, but Rafi was beginning to realize how different the cultures were between the hives. In the slums, a stranger suddenly approaching you would be seen as an attack. In the middle hive, it was more likely a form of solicitation or interrogation. But here, it seemed entirely normal—albeit in a much friendlier manner. Even so, Rafi refused to fully let his guard down, all while maintaining their facade.

"May I ask, ma'am, what is your name?" Rafi inquired politely.

"My name is Gwendyl, but you can all just call me Gwen," she said with a warm smile. "Please, if you're not busy with school or chores, let me invite you to my home."

With that, the children immediately grew suspicious. It was an odd request, but so far, Gwen had been nothing but delightful to them. They didn't even know what the consequences might be for refusing her offer.

"It's fine if you don't want to," Gwen said with a playful lilt. "However—you'll all be missing out on my roast chicken, garlic bread, and ice cream," she teased, her words almost sung.

"You can take me," Habi chimed in, her stomach clearly overruling her brain.

Rafi was about to stop Habi and her antics again when a devious plan began to form in his mind. It was as if the gods were handing him a free ticket to the heavens. He realized that if the higher hive looked like a paradise, the security must be just as strict. This invitation was a golden opportunity—not just for him, but for every child with him. Not only were they being offered a free meal, but a gateway to a treasure trove. This was how they would steal their way in and announce their citizenship in the middle hive, and Rafi was all for it.

"Don't worry, Habo. We're all coming too. I just hope our parents don't mind us being gone a little longer," Rafi said.

"That's splendid! Everyone who's visited my stead has only had good things to say about my cooking. I hope you all will too!" Gwen beamed.

"Wait, you're serious?" Taliba whispered to Rafi.

"Oh yeah," Rafi whispered back.

"Little Habo, care to take my hand?" Gwen asked, extending her hand to Habi with a gentle smile.

Habi eagerly took her hand, and the two marched toward the fountain square.

"Come along now, children!" Gwen called out, waving cheerfully to the others trailing behind her.

Though hesitant at first, the rest of the group eventually gave in, drawn by the promise of food and the opportunity to see more of what the higher hive had to offer. Excitement buzzed beneath their cautious steps.

But amidst the anticipation, only one of them harbored a deeper plan. They weren't just here to enjoy the comforts of the upper ring—they were here to take what they could.

HABI

What's yours, is mine, is what Rafi sang in his mind.

Chapter Twenty

Habi swiped her hand through the pool of water in the marble fountain, watching her clear reflection in its crystal clarity as she licked her fingers, still cold from the water's touch. She wasn't amused by its taste, but at least she enjoyed the view. Gwen stood close by, making sure Habi didn't fall in. Just moments earlier, Gwen had treated the children to a taste of luxury, offering them a place to feast for the day. Now, at Habi's behest, she guided the children toward the square, acting as though she were their own mother.

"Little Habo, have you not seen this fountain before?" Gwen asked, her curiosity piqued.

"No–" Habi began, but Rafi quickly cut her off, seamlessly keeping up their charade as higher hive children.

"We have," Rafi said smoothly, "but Mother always told us not to get too close. She said there's a monster in the water that drags children under."

He delivered the lie with practiced ease, weaving the tale on the spot.

Gwen laughed and shook her head. "There are no such monsters up here, little one. Oh, the tales parents tell, just out of worry for their children."

She pinched Habi's cheek affectionately but quickly pulled her hand back, surprised at the grime that transferred onto her pristine fingers.

"Oh my, when was the last time you bathed, boy?" Gwen asked, her tone tinged with concern.

"Oh, we bathe in the–" Habi began, but Rafi swiftly cut in, as always.

"A rough patch of sand kicked up while we were wandering the grounds. It was quite unfortunate," Rafi said with a practiced frown.

Gwen didn't say anything. Instead, she raised her brows and nodded, as if picturing a cloud of dust swirling around the children.

Feeling like the star of the show with Gwen fawning over her, Habi skipped away from the fountain and ran toward the strange device—a luxurious version of a water well. It was a large, curved pipe protruding from the ground, with a lever angled upward and away from the user. While Gwen hurried to catch up, Habi toyed with the lever, causing the faucet to pour water down at her feet.

"Whoa!" Habi exclaimed, eyes wide with wonder.

"That's adorable. Have you not used a water faucet before, little one?" Gwen asked with a gentle smile.

Habi was about to speak of tales from the lower hive, but caught herself, fearing Rafi would cut her off again. It had taken her a while to catch on to the facade, but at least now she was aware of it.

"Mother wouldn't let me use it," Habi lied, retrieving her canteen. She opened the lid and refilled it with water from another world. As she filled it, she even doused her head under the faucet, soaking herself halfway.

Gwen was immediately shocked and quickly lifted Habi's hand away from the lever.

"Habo! You're all wet now!" Gwen scolded, her voice a mix of exasperation and amusement.

Rafi and the other children feared their cover had been blown, as showering under a faucet didn't seem like something rich folk would do. However, that thought never crossed Gwen's mind. She was more inclined to believe that Habi was simply young and reckless.

"The dirt is gone," Habi said, wiping her soaked face with a satisfied grin.

Gwen sighed, shaking her head. "Your parents must have their hands full."

Rafi let out a large grin, since Gwen was technically correct. The children indeed, were a handful for Father.

Suddenly, Taliba nudged Rafi with her elbow while Gwen was occupied with Habi.

"What's the plan here?" Taliba whispered, keeping her gaze forward.

"We play along," Rafi whispered back. "She's clearly taken a liking to Habi, and I'm not about to test the security of the higher hive when she's handing us a golden opportunity. Think about it—she takes us into her home, and we can grab what we want. Just enough that she won't notice. Rich folks won't miss an item or two."

"That's a decent plan," Taliba admitted, "but have you thought about why she's so insistent on bringing us there? What if it's a trap? What if she knows something about Habi and her golden eyes?"

"If it's a trap, then we'll walk right into it," Rafi replied calmly. "And if it's not, then we're all good, no?"

Taliba gave Rafi a worried look, preparing to inform the others about his risky plan.

"We'll need to bet on the good heart of the rich folk, then," Taliba whispered to Rafi one last time before turning to quietly brief the other children.

As Rafi's attention turned back to Gwen and Habi, he saw Gwen drying Habi's hair and face with a clean white towel she pulled from her satchel. Once she deemed Habi decently clean, she folded the towel and returned it to its place.

"There, all better," Gwen said with a warm smile. "Is there anything else you'd like to see before we leave? It seems your parents are quite strict about keeping you kids under their roof."

Habi quickly glanced at Rafi, who made a gesture by slicing his hand across his neck, pointing his thumb behind him, and then pointing at the sky.

No more. Let's go. Little time left, is what Habi interpreted.

And Rafi was right—the longer they stayed exploring with Gwen, the longer it would take to accomplish what they'd originally come for. She also had to consider the time it would take to return home, knowing she'd have to sacrifice her fun.

Habi patted her stomach and said, "I'm hungry."

That single statement was all Gwen needed to know Habi was ready. Her face lit up with a bright smile as she extended her hand to Habi.

"Then let us feast!" Gwen declared cheerfully.

Habi took her hand without hesitation, and Gwen gestured for the others to follow.

"Come now, children. It's time to eat!" she called, leading them toward the gently sloping hills of paved stone.

—

It was a long, yet majestic walk. Compared to the middle hive, this ring was in a league of its own. While the market squares in the middle hive were crowded with citizens and rows of stalls, the higher hive had businesses housed in buildings, where locals could order their items in an organized fashion. The streets were well-kept, and though there were still alleys, they weren't as dark or mysterious as those in the lower hive. Several families lived in the granite buildings alongside the uphill path, smiling and laughing with their children as they returned from class. While the slums smelled of rot and the middle hive of sweat, the higher hive was fragrant with spices and perfume. It was almost as if this ring were a utopia, but Rafi knew that even if he sold all his goods, it wouldn't be enough to secure a residency here.

Just like the children in the middle hive, some of the locals happily waved at Gwen and her entourage. The only one who truly welcomed them back was Habi, leading the group alongside Gwen. The others merely nodded and stared, uneasy, wondering if one of the locals might suddenly jump out and lash at them.

"You children are so tense," Gwen remarked with a light giggle. "Have your parents punished you that much?"

The children didn't want to, but they knew they had to relax. The way they'd been raised had taught them to always be on guard, ready to fight or run at a moment's notice. However, there didn't seem to be any conflict here, making them stick out like sore thumbs—so much so that even Gwen had taken notice. Reluctantly, the children mimicked the posture of the other locals, dropping their shoulders and uncurling their fingers.

"Wow, Gwen, your house is very far. Do you make this walk often?" Taliba asked, her tone polite as she tried to fill the silence and exude a noble demeanor.

"Oh, this walk is nothing," Gwen replied. "It's a normal routine for me, gathering groceries and necessities for myself and my husband. I'm just a housewife, after all."

"Oh, you're married?" Taliba feigned surprise.

"I am," Gwen said, a faint blush dusting her cheeks. "But he's away most of the time, as he's in the military. I still love him with all my heart, though."

She paused, glancing at the group with a sheepish look. "I do apologize if this walk feels too long for you all—I live quite near the top. May I ask, though, what business do your parents partake in to have you all roaming so freely?"

"Father is in the military, and Mother is away on a trip right now. She works in sanitation," Rafi said smoothly, crafting a quick lie.

"Oh? Perhaps your father and my husband know each other? Although unlikely, given the Sultan's army houses millions of men. Still, who knows?" Gwen giggled. "And a mother who works as a cleaner? Please, do tell her I give her my graces for keeping the streets so beautifully clean!"

Well, at least Rafi now knew that sanitation was an acceptable word to use.

"I will let her know," Rafi said with a smirk.

As they conversed, the group finally reached the summit of the hill, where they could see the final wall that separated the nobles from the rest, along with the Sultan's tower in the distance. This was the closest the children had ever been to the tower, now able to make out its details and architecture. However, the walk to it would still take a few more hours.

Immediately, the children were introduced to a flat garden, full of vibrant flowers and lush greenery. Paved paths ran along the edges of the garden, allowing citizens to move with ease and enjoy the scent of the blooms as they passed. From this vantage point, the granite homes were more spread out, giving their owners larger plots of land and more property. Even more astonishingly, the homes here had three to four stories, and the air smelled clean—free of dust, as they were situated farther from the dunes that surrounded the city.

Gwen guided the children through one of many gardens, keeping Habi close and gesturing for the others to stay tight, as the height of the plants obscured their view.

"What's that?" Habi asked, pointing not at one specific flower but at all the vibrant blooms surrounding her.

"Have you never seen a flower either, little one?" Gwen said, her voice soft with curiosity. "Roses, hydrangeas, tulips, dahlias, and so much more grow in these gardens, brought here from all over the world of Skania."

She paused, leaning toward the nearest white gardenia. Taking in its scent, she smiled. "This one is my favorite. I love gardenias—they smell wonderful and look so mystical with their white petals."

"Can you eat them?" Habi asked, her tone entirely serious.

Gwen laughed and shook her head.

"I would advise against that, Habo," Gwen said with a soft giggle. "Now, this one here is a red rose, a universal symbol of love. Pluck one of these and give it to the person you hold dearest—they'll remember it forever, just as I did when my husband gave one to me."

Habi, captivated by Gwen's charm and words, immediately plucked a rose and handed it to Rafi. He took it with a grin, playing along with her gesture.

"You must be a really good brother, Rafi," Gwen remarked, her tone warm and approving.

"I guess I am," Rafi replied, his expression unreadable.

Habi plucked another rose, peeling the red petals from its stem and handing them out to each of the other children to show her admiration for them. That was until Habi let out a small yelp, as her thumb began to bleed slightly, causing her to drop the stem.

"Oh! Be careful of the rose's thorns, little one!" Gwen exclaimed, her warning coming just a moment too late. "Here, wrap your thumb with this."

Gwen retrieved the white towel from her satchel and wrapped it around Habi's thumb, putting pressure into her small wound.

"You can keep the towel, Habo. Just keep it on the wound, and you'll be good as new," Gwen said gently.

"Thank you," Habi replied with a small whimper.

"You're welcome," Gwen said with a smile. "Come now, let us continue. We're almost there."

With that, the children followed along. Unbeknownst to Gwen, Habi kept a petal to herself, curious to taste it. As they walked, she slipped the petal into her mouth, only to immediately spit it out.

—

The children had no words to describe what they were experiencing. Granite stairs led up to a large double wooden door, attached to a four-story mansion. There was even a raised patio with an awning where they could rest in reprieve. They could only imagine what might lurk inside this monster of a building.

"This is my home. Follow me now," Gwen instructed, climbing the stairs and unlocking the door with a key retrieved from her satchel.

Rafi was occupied with scanning the exterior, his eyes examining the windows and the white balcony above them. It was a small detail, but Rafi spotted gadgets with levers attached to the bottom of the window sills, identifying them as locks. This house was highly secured, and he let out a breath of relief, knowing that Gwen had just granted access to a band of thieves.

Once they were inside, they were immediately greeted by marble floor tiles and an expansive room. There were openings and hallways leading to even more rooms, causing the children to wonder what a man and woman could possibly do with so much space. And this was only the first floor.

"Beautiful, isn't it?" Gwen said as she led the children past the stairs and into a spacious dining area, far larger than the cramped shed they called home. The room was dominated by a long wooden table surrounded by ten chairs, with a basket of fresh fruit placed neatly at its center.

"I feel like we don't deserve to be here," Hamza whispered to the others.

"Yep," Tariq murmured in agreement.

Gwen gestured for the children to halt, then volunteered to pull the seats out from under the table, signaling each child to choose one. Without a word, the children settled into chairs with comfortable backs, finally relaxing into the luxury of their surroundings.

"Okay, I'll be right back. I need to retrieve items from the pantry so I can start cooking for all of you!" Gwen said, winking and walking away, turning a corner.

Along the walls, there were several decorations the children had never seen before. Beautiful fabrics and paintings lined the space, each one more intricate than the last. One painting caught their eye—Gwen and her husband standing next to each other in a noble pose. Beside it hung a glass frame full of military medals and ribbons, stacked above a golden-embroidered name in red fabric that the children couldn't quite read. These people were well off, far beyond anything the children had ever known.

"What now, Rafi?" Naji whispered sharply.

"Now, we wait. Don't want to start running around on an empty stomach," Rafi murmured back.

"Hey, *Habo*, you havin' fun?" Hamza teased, a smirk creeping onto his face.

"If my name has to be Habo to live here, then so be it," Habi declared with conviction.

"Okay, but what's all that on the table?" Tariq asked, his eyes fixed on the basket of colorful fruit.

"I don't know, so let's not tou–" Taliba started, cutting herself off as Habi reached for the basket and snatched an orange without hesitation.

Following her actions, Hamza, Tariq, Naji, and even Rafi jumped at the chance, grabbing different fruits for themselves. To Taliba, it was as if she had just witnessed a pack of wild dogs pouncing on a weakened rabbit.

Once all the fruit had suddenly disappeared, Habi sniffed her orange and bit into it. Right away, she spat it out, but remained curious, tasting the citric juices hidden within its peel. Hamza grabbed a banana and made the same mistake, biting into it with the peel still on. Rafi enjoyed his apple, while Naji savored his pear. Tariq fumbled with the vine of grapes, popping a bite of each juicy fruit from its stems.

"Hey, give me some of that," Taliba said to Tariq.

Instead of waiting, she snatched a few grapes from his hand and popped them into her mouth.

"These are good!" she exclaimed, her words muffled by the food.

"Mye, thuese are whally goof," Hamza mumbled through a mouthful, his newfound discovery of a banana peel evident.

"I just noticed something," Naji said, biting into his pear. "If Gwen is married and has all these fancy paintings and stuff—shouldn't they have kids of their own? And if they do, why aren't they around?"

"Maybe she hates them," Tariq suggested, casually spitting a grape seed onto the floor.

"Or maybe they just don't have any yet," Taliba added thoughtfully.

"Oh, it seems you've all helped yourselves to the fruit. That's good!" Gwen said, suddenly reappearing with a handful of raw chicken, a bag of flour, and some potatoes. Her smile was as bright as ever.

The children immediately stopped chewing as they watched Gwen slowly make her way through the kitchen, unfazed by their animalistic behavior.

"Oh, keep enjoying yourselves! I'll get to cooking," Gwen said cheerfully, setting her ingredients near the stove. She then walked to the corner of the room, retrieved some firewood, and carefully placed it into the stove's mouth.

As she worked, a shadow of sadness crossed her face. "I'm sorry if I worried you by bringing you here, or if the absence of children on the wall raised questions," she began, clearly having overheard their earlier conversation. Her hands paused for a moment as she continued, "It's just that... well, I'm unable to provide a child for my husband."

Her voice softened, heavy with emotion. "I don't want to go into too much detail, but sometimes I ask other parents if I can invite them and their children to my home, just to experience the feeling of a complete family. It's a strange habit, I know, but it's something I've been doing for a while. My husband and I have made many wonderful friends this way."

She glanced at the group, her eyes gentle. "When I met you all, I just... fell in love with your little group. And Habo—he's so unique, with those golden eyes. I've never seen anything like it before. I just wanted to put smiles on your faces, as if you were my own children."

Her gaze dropped slightly, and she sighed. "I apologize for being selfish."

After hearing Gwen's story, the children couldn't help but feel guilty for marking her as a suspicious woman. She was just a wife who wanted a family, almost in the same way the children yearned to thrive together. However, even though the story was heard through Rafi's ears, he refused to feel a sliver of pity for her. He had an objective, and he did not want a simple sob story to distract him from it.

The reality of their situation hit him—kindness could be a tool, but it was also a liability. Gwen had opened the door to opportunities—an opportunity that he intended to seize. So, despite the growing discomfort in his chest, Rafi steeled himself. He couldn't afford to feel sorry for her. They were here for more than just food. They were here to make their way in a world that would never accept them unless they took what they needed.

"Hopefully we've been good children for you, Gwen," Taliba said softly, her tone tinged with somber understanding. "I'm sorry if we've made you feel bad."

"No need for apologies, Taliba," Gwen replied, a faint smile crossing her lips as she recalled her name. "This is the fault of no one but mine alone."

It was the first time the children witnessed a different facial expression from Gwen, one other than her usual smile, ever since they'd met her. Some of the children believed her to be heartbroken, while others thought she was ill. Her face, usually warm and welcoming, now carried a trace of sorrow or fatigue, and it made the children exchange uneasy glances. It was a stark contrast to the image of the generous hostess they had come to know.

Gwen took one last sniff before fixing her composure, forcing another smile.

"Alas, there's no need to dwell on things beyond your control. It's best to accept it and move on, no?" Gwen said with a soft resolve, retrieving flint, steel, and some tinder from a nearby drawer. Her tone brightened as she added, "Let's have a good meal then!"

The children nodded and smiled at Gwen as she returned to her activities at the stove, lighting the tinder and adding it to the fire. While she was occupied, they leaned in closer to the table to consult with each other.

"Now I'll feel bad for stealing from her," Taliba whispered, her voice low and conflicted.

"Don't tell me you all fell for that story," Rafi whispered back sharply. "Whether it's true or not doesn't matter—she's still a rich lady, and we still need to earn ourselves a living."

"Come on, Rafi, she's still human. She can't even have kids, for heaven's sake," Naji argued, his voice tinged with guilt.

"Yeah, that's what she *said*," Tariq added. "Happy or not, we came here to do one thing, and Rafi's right. Her personal life is none of our business—only what we can snatch and grab."

The arguing children turned to face Hamza, who innocently raised his hands in submission.

"I don't care about what y'all are talkin' about. I just want the food and to get home safely," Hamza stated flatly.

"How about we ask her for gald?" Habi suggested innocently.

"That's a no," Rafi cut in immediately. "She thinks we're from the higher hive. Rich folk asking other rich folk for money doesn't add up."

"Isn't that how businesses work?" Taliba chimed in.

"We're not a business. We're damn kids!" Rafi shot back, his voice low but sharp.

"I mean, she seems nice enough to at least give us *some*," Naji theorized.

"No," Rafi growled, his tone final as he pointed a finger at each of them, his eyes like daggers. "This opportunity will never come again. Right now, we have the chance to go big and go home. Sure, we might run into Gwen again someday, but do you really think she'll keep providing for us? Especially when she's convinced we already have parents?"

He paused, his words deliberate and heavy. "This act won't hold forever. Sooner or later, she's gonna want to meet our 'parents', and when she catches on, we'll pay for it. And don't forget—her husband's *military*. If he finds out who we are, we're *done*. Understand?"

The children sighed and stopped debating, ultimately agreeing that their personal lives must come first. It was a test of morals versus survival, and in this case, being slum rats meant that morality couldn't take precedence. It was a shame, but even Habi frowned, realizing how important wealth and class were in this city—and perhaps in the entire world.

"Now that we're back on the same page," Rafi continued, "the longer we stay here, the more time we waste. Listen—we eat, scope out the house, and then get out before she catches on. Yeah?"

"Aye," the children murmured in agreement.

"Aye?" Gwen playfully mimicked, glancing at them with an amused smile.

The only reason Gwen was able to catch on to their agreement was because they essentially whispered it in unison.

"Aye!" Habi echoed joyfully.

"Aye!" Gwen laughed, turning her attention back to the stove as she tended to the chicken, washing the potatoes with practiced ease.

Rafi hopped out of his seat and glanced out the nearest window, observing how low the sun was. It was slowly getting dark, and they were running out of time. The children had largely underestimated the time of travel, as well as the time spent with Gwen.

"Maybe after the feast and some time to rest our bellies, we'll have to return home soon," Rafi warned Gwen.

"Oh, of course, that's fine," Gwen replied, retrieving the cooked chicken from the stove and placing it onto a large platter. She moved swiftly, dumping the washed potatoes into a bowl and setting out dishes on the countertop. Noticing the children's impatience, she opted to skip the flour for bread, prioritizing their meal instead.

Once everything was neatly arranged, she sprinkled salt and spices over the chicken and potatoes before serving the meal to the waiting children.

Gwen placed the fragrant chicken and bowl of potatoes at the center of the table before swiftly returning to the cabinets. She retrieved a stack of ceramic plates and several pieces of silverware, her movements fluid and precise. The children watched in quiet awe as she worked with almost inhuman speed, as if she had done this countless times before.

One by one, she set a plate and utensils before each child, including herself, her efficiency almost mesmerizing. Then, she fetched a stack of glass cups and uncovered a bucket of fresh water. Dunking two cups at a time, she handed them to the children in pairs, her motions seamless.

It was fascinating to watch. Every step she took was light, her shoes tapping softly against the marble tiles, and she moved with a peculiar grace, keeping her hands close to her chest like a cautious little mouse.

Finally, Gwen retrieved a stack of paper napkins, providing one to each child and herself, then placing the rest in the center.

"You're really good at this," Taliba remarked appreciatively.

"Not my first time," Gwen replied with a warm smile, reaching into the bowl and handing each child their own potato.

Once everything was set, Gwen picked up a fork and knife, preparing to carve into the juicy chicken she had so carefully prepared. Across the table, the children stared at the dish with hungry eyes, as if mere moments from drooling. Some had already started nibbling on their potatoes, savoring the soft, seasoned bites, while the rest sat in eager anticipation for the chicken—its tender white meat calling to them.

With careful precision, Gwen sliced the chicken into portions, ensuring each child received a fair share. The moment the meat landed on their plates, they wasted no time, devouring it hungrily, pausing only to take bites of their potatoes in between.

Though Gwen was accustomed to starting and ending meals together, she didn't mind their impatience. Watching them enjoy her food brought her a quiet satisfaction, their eager appetites a simple but meaningful reward.

"Any takers for the legs and wings?" Gwen offered, her knife poised over a chicken leg.

Everyone's hands shot up toward the ceiling, creating a huge dilemma for Gwen. So, instead, she cut some parts of the wings and legs into equal portions, handing them out to the children, keeping the smaller pieces for herself.

As Rafi ate, his senses remained sharp, his instincts never fully relaxing. Amid the sounds of chewing and murmurs of satisfaction, a strange rattling caught his attention. His eyes flicked toward the source, his ears tuning out the background noise.

The sound was coming from the front door.

His grip on his fork tightened as he watched the knob turn. A moment later, the door eased open, and a man stepped inside. Keys dangled from his fingers, the quiet jingle unmistakable. He didn't hesitate, didn't knock—he belonged here.

It was Gwen's husband.

Gwen stopped what she was doing and gently placed the utensils onto the table, acknowledging the sudden return of her husband.

"Be right back, little ones," Gwen whispered to the children before skipping toward the door.

"Is that gonna be a problem?" Hamza murmured, keeping his voice low.

"Don't know. Keep the act up," Rafi muttered back, barely pausing between bites.

Habi suddenly lunged across the table, her hands grabbing at the chicken, and with a firm yank, tore a leg clean off its body.

"Hey! Share that!" Hamza hissed, glaring at her.

"This is Habo's food!" Habi declared, clutching the leg possessively as she dug in.

Rafi chuckled at the sight as he returned his focus to Gwen and her husband. They were engaged in conversation, exchanging a kiss on the lips. The man glanced between his wife and the table full of children he didn't recognize. The look on his face said it all—he didn't react with surprise. Rafi assumed he was used to his wife's antics.

A few moments later, Gwen returned to the dining area with her husband.

"Hello, little ones, this is my husband, Hizan. He doesn't come home often, so today must be my lucky day!" Gwen beamed, pressing a kiss to his cheek.

"Please, dear, have a seat and rest. I'll cut some chicken for you and get you all set," she added, already turning back toward the table.

All the children waved at Hizan, but Habi was the only one who stopped chewing. She could've sworn she had seen this man before, but she couldn't place where or when. She was uncertain at first, until Hizan met her gaze—that's when she remembered who he was.

The man wore the same olive green long coat, decorated with ribbons and military medals. He was light-skinned and tall, dressed in a black button-up shirt and dark slacks. This time, Habi noticed the sheathed longsword at the left side of his hip. If his inky, slicked-back hair and pristine mustache didn't give it away, then it was definitely his sky-blue eyes that pierced into Habi's soul—the same eyes that seemed to have seen a thousand battles. This was the man who had led the Mamluks' march in the middle hive.

Habi held her breath for a moment, a new realization dawning on her. This one, however, she couldn't quite place. She had heard his name, 'Hizan', before, but the questions kept repeating in her mind: *Where*? *When*?

If this was the same man from the middle hive—and it most likely was—then Habi realized she might be in danger.

"It seems that you children are enjoying your stay," Hizan said, his deep voice laced with age and the faint rasp of tobacco. "Does the food satisfy you?"

"Yes, sir," the children replied awkwardly, their voices uneven as they chewed, all the while keeping a careful eye on him.

"That's good," Hizan nodded, his face unreadable, his expression as still as stone.

Not many of the Sultan's men could strike fear into the hearts of the children, but this one certainly did.

Hizan moved with unwavering confidence and walked with a silent gait that could unsettle even a seasoned fighter. The children couldn't help but wonder how a woman like Gwen could marry a man as terrifying as him. Several possibilities crossed their minds—perhaps Gwen sought wealth, power, safety—or maybe it was simply love. Regardless, Gwen was never the one to worry about. It was the man in the room, who surveyed each child with the sharp gaze of an eagle, that commanded their fear.

Hizan made his way to the end of the table, away from the children and closest to the stove. Gwen cut him a few pieces of chicken and served the rest of the meal alongside it. With the chicken nearly stripped to the bone, Gwen finally sat down to rest and dine, taking her seat to Hizan's left. It was a widely known cultural practice in Skania for a wife to sit beside her husband's scabbard.

Ever since Hizan took his seat, the table had fallen silent, with only the sounds of quiet munching and gulps of water breaking the stillness. Gwen glanced worriedly at the children, sensing that her husband's presence was frightening them—and she wasn't wrong.

"So—why have the gods gifted me your arrival this early, dear?" Gwen asked, breaking the quiet.

"It was a simple expedition," Hizan replied, taking a slow sip from his glass of water. "The Sultan ordered us to quell the southern advances into the desert. Their gear was primitive compared to ours. They were short work."

"Oh, any news from the west and north?" Gwen inquired, her curiosity piqued.

"The west and the north still depend on us for trade and exotics. We remain in good standing, though the west disapproves of our expanding politics and respected traditions. They're a land of piety and zealots—it's only a matter of time before their crusades start moving east. The north doesn't care; they're too consumed with their brewing civil war. Our real concern is the south and the growing threat of insurgency within our own borders."

"I thought the rebellions were finished. I thought they died off with Saif Sabbah," Gwen said, pouting slightly.

"I believed the same," Hizan admitted, setting down his cup. "But it seems his influence lingers. As long as there is power, there will always be those who seek to defy it. Hate spreads regardless of who sits on the throne."

He sighed, cutting into his chicken, but his eyes flicked up, catching sight of Habi. She was staring at him, unblinking, watching him in a way that made him pause mid-bite.

Habi was too busy piecing things together again. The mention of Saif and Hizan sent a chill down her spine as she recalled the full name and title of Gwen's husband that Assad had previously mentioned. He was Hizan Al'Za'im, Commandant of the Kouran Army, and Slayer of Hassazi.

"That little one is quite odd," Hizan murmured to Gwen, his gaze locked onto Habi's, unmoving.

When Habi heard that remark, she shied away and focused on her plate. She was relieved that Hizan didn't seem to recognize her from the middle hive. Then again, she doubted that a high-ranking general would bother remembering someone beneath his notice. Perhaps news of a troublesome golden-eyed child wreaking havoc hadn't traveled far enough up the chain of command.

"Oh, that's Habo. He's such a wonderful little boy," Gwen said with a smile, gently biting into a piece of chicken. After introducing Habi to her husband, she went on to acknowledge the other children, greeting them each in turn.

Hizan raised a brow, his gaze shifting between his wife and Habi, studying the child with quiet scrutiny.

"Interesting," he muttered.

—

The rest of the dinner was filled with long pauses in between small talk, as Gwen and Hizan shared their experiences during their time apart. The children mostly stayed quiet, occasionally making faces at each other while finishing their meals. As Gwen began gathering the empty dishes, Rafi glanced out the window and noticed how dark it had gotten. If it hadn't been for Gwen lighting the lanterns around the house, he might have missed the shift entirely.

"So, when do you return, dear?" Gwen asked, balancing the clattering plates in her arms.

"I rest for the night," Hizan replied. "Tomorrow, I must return to the noble ring, where I will oversee the training of future Mamluks."

"Oh, how honorable," Gwen grinned, pressing a kiss to his cheek.

"Officers and staff in command will handle the actual training. I'm only overseeing it—nothing glamorous," Hizan clarified.

While the two lovebirds continued their conversation, the children gathered once more at their end of the table.

"We need to make a move, now," Rafi whispered urgently.

"But how? Now they have two pairs of eyes hovering over us," Taliba murmured.

"We'll have to split them up," Rafi said. "Two of us need to lead them into different areas, giving the rest of us a chance to look around and grab what we can."

"And what excuse do we have to get them to separate?" Naji asked skeptically.

"I need to potty," Habi interrupted, bouncing in her seat.

Rafi smirked and nodded at Habi.

"That's one," Rafi approved. "Maybe Gwen will take Habi to the restroom."

"Then what about Hizan?" Tariq asked, his eyes flicking toward the man.

It seemed they didn't have to worry about Hizan, as he had already stood up from his seat, removing his coat and draping it over his arm.

"I will be heading to my quarters, darling. I must take an early reprieve and adjust my documents for tomorrow," Hizan said, pressing a brief kiss to Gwen's lips before stepping away. Just before ascending the stairs, he turned toward the children.

"Behave now, little ones."

With that, he retreated upstairs, his footsteps fading into the quiet.

"That might be a problem," Taliba murmured. "Now we don't know which room he's in."

"And so we proceed with caution," Rafi said, eyes sharp. "We'll be lucky to finish before Father returns home."

He turned to Habi. "You ready to make your move?"

"I'm dying," Habi whined, bouncing in place.

"Very well then," Rafi smirked. "Once she leads Gwen away, we move. Quiet, nimble steps. Slow tries on the doors—check every corner—get in, get out. If you run into Hizan, play it off as a mistake."

"This sounds scary," Taliba admitted, her voice hushed.

"That's because it is." Rafi's gaze flicked over the group. "We leave on your cue, Habi. If you come back and we're not here, ask Gwen if you can look for us. If that doesn't work, leave without us. Got it?"

"Why do *I* have to do it?" Habi pouted.

"Because you have a valid excuse," Rafi smirked, patting her head. "Don't worry, you'll see us again."

As she had before, Habi reached into her pouch for the little doll and handed it to Rafi, offering it for good luck and safe travels.

"I love you," Habi whimpered, her voice a mix of worry and the urgent need to relieve herself.

"I love you too," Rafi replied, pressing a quick kiss to her cheek.

Once the children shared their temporary farewell, Habi waddled over to Gwen, who was busy washing the dishes with a cloth and a water bucket atop the counter, where an open sink was built in.

"Excuse me, Miss Gwen," Habi said.

Gwen paused her scrubbing, turning to give Habi her full attention.

"Yes, Habo?" she asked warmly.

"I need to potty," Habi requested, bouncing on her toes.

Gwen smiled at Habi, then shifted her gaze toward the rest of the children. She observed how they were huddled together, conversing among themselves, deliberately looking away from her. She didn't pay much attention to their small gathering, but little did she know, the children were pretending to have a sophisticated conversation, with Rafi keeping a side eye on Gwen, carefully calculating her reactions to everything.

"I'll be more than happy to escort you to the restroom, little one. Please, right this way," Gwen said, extending her hand with a gentle smile.

HABI

Habi took Gwen's elegant hand once more, letting herself be guided across the kitchen, through the living room, and toward the farthest corner of the house. Just before they disappeared from sight, Gwen called back over her shoulder, "I'll return soon, children. If anyone else needs the restroom, please come this way."

With that, she turned the corner, Habi trailing beside her. Just before vanishing, Habi gave a small wave to the others.

"Quick, let's move. Silent and nimble, guys," Rafi whispered, already slipping into motion.

As instructed, the children scattered like ants, some scavenging the ground floor while others climbed the stairs. Silent and nimble, that's what they were.

Chapter Twenty-one

Taliba, Hamza, and Naji remained on the first floor, leaving the small group that consisted of Rafi and Tariq to scour the floors above. For Taliba and Naji, it was a convenient excuse to remain in the safe zone and avoid any chance of encountering Hizan in his quarters. Hamza, on the other hand, simply didn't want to deal with the stairs.

Valuables were displayed across the walls and tabletops throughout the first floor of the home. Unfortunately, none of the easily accessible items could be stored discreetly or hidden from view. Worse, every piece seemed significant enough that the Al'Za'ims would immediately notice if it went missing. There were no small trinkets—no rings, bracelets, or necklaces—anywhere on the ground floor.

The trio had already searched most of the rooms, deliberately avoiding the far corner, which apparently housed the restroom. The extra rooms they did find were eerily empty, devoid of furniture or decoration. This absence could mean only one thing—a grim realization that sent a chill through them.

"There's nothing we can take down here," Hamza sighed, regrouping with Taliba and Naji in the dining area.

"If they don't keep their trinkets down here," Taliba mused, "then that means they're all upstairs—probably in their personal rooms."

Hamza cursed, realizing that all their effort and meticulous planning was all in vain.

"Should one of us go up there?" Naji asked, glancing toward the staircase.

The trio thought about it momentarily, until Taliba offered herself as tribute.

"I'll go see if I can find them—maybe even help. I can also be a voice of reason if things go south. You two, stay here," Taliba instructed before swiftly making her way up the stairs.

"We're running out of time, man," Hamza whispered to Naji.

Naji nodded. "It's getting darker, and it's only a matter of time before Gwen comes back with Habi. This is bad."

—

As the trickling sounds faded, Habi swung her legs idly, perched atop the grandest toilet she had ever seen. The seat was padded, the ceramic structure sturdy and smooth—far beyond anything she was used to. Beside her sat a bucket of water, which Gwen had instructed her to pour down to flush once she was finished.

After tidying herself up and completing the task, she opened the door and stepped out, where Gwen stood waiting patiently.

"Did you wash your hands, Habo?" Gwen asked with a gentle smile.

Habi pouted, her cheeks flushed with embarrassment, as she returned to the bucket and rinsed her paws in its contents.

"There we go," Gwen giggled. "Come now, the others must be dying to go home."

"Okay," Habi agreed, falling in step behind Gwen as they rounded the corner.

As the two entered the dining area, Gwen immediately grew concerned, noticing that three of the children were missing. Habi's eyes widened, a sinking feeling confirming that something was wrong.

"Oh, hello, Hamza and Naji—where are the others?" Gwen asked, her eyes scanning the room, unease creeping into her expression.

"Oh, they went to follow you to the restroom, but I think they made a wrong turn," Naji lied smoothly. "They're probably still wandering around the first floor somewhere. It's quite a huge home, after all."

Gwen frowned as Habi approached her brothers, mouthing, *What happened?*

Hamza simply darted his eyes toward the ceiling a couple times, which told her, *They're still upstairs.*

Gwen, unaware of the situation at hand, sighed and shook her head with a grin.

"At least they're not the first children to get lost in my home," Gwen chuckled, shaking her head. "I'll go look around for them. Stay here, just in case they return without me, okay?"

The children nodded, their eyes tracking Gwen as she cautiously moved away, careful not to stumble in the dimly lit house, where lanterns flickered softly in every room.

From the next room, her voice rang out, steady but curious. "Rafi! Tariq! Taliba! Follow my voice!"

Her call echoed faintly as she rounded a corner, disappearing into the farthest part of the house.

"I'm going to go find them," Habi volunteered, already stepping forward, urgency tightening in her chest. She needed to warn Rafi—time was running out.

Before Hamza and Naji could even stop her, she had already taken off up the stairs, traveling into the unknown.

"Well, what now?" Naji sighed, shifting uneasily.

"We hope for the best, I guess," Hamza muttered with a shrug, his eyes flicking toward the hallway as Gwen's voice began to loop back around the home.

—

Some time earlier, Rafi and Tariq quickly reached the second floor, where they were met with more fabric decorations and relics adorning the walls. Just like on the ground floor, none of the items were worth their attention, given their size and the way they were prominently displayed in the hallways.

"We need to spread out. You cover this floor, I'll head upstairs," Rafi instructed, his voice low but firm.

Tariq nodded as he watched Rafi disappear up the stairs, then crept down the second-floor hall, testing door handles. As expected, most rooms were locked, and the ones he could enter were largely empty. He made a full loop of the floor, finding nothing of value.

Frustrated, he returned to the staircase—only to nearly jump out of his skin when Taliba suddenly emerged from the shadows.

"Holy—Taliba, what are you doing here?" Tariq whispered sharply, his pulse still racing.

"There was nothing worth taking downstairs. I came to warn you guys," Taliba murmured, her own nerves settling after the sudden encounter. "How's it going here? Where's Rafi?"

"Nothing here we can take," Tariq admitted. "Rafi went upstairs."

"We need to find him. This place might be a bust. Gwen could be back any moment, and she's going to realize something's wrong."

Tariq cursed under his breath, then jerked his head toward the stairs. "Right, let's go then."

Just as the two began to ascend the stairs, they heard the light tap of small feet climbing up from below. It was soon revealed to be Habi.

"Habi? What are you doing?" Taliba hissed, eyes narrowing.

"Gwen is back. I came to find you guys. She's searching the house for us right now," Habi panted, catching her breath from the climb.

"Well, there's nothing here worth taking," Tariq whispered. "We need to grab Rafi before this all goes south. Come on."

Without hesitation, the trio ascended to the third floor, where Rafi was supposed to be scouting.

—

Unaware of the chaos unfolding below him, Rafi had better luck than the rest. On the third floor, he came across several locked doors down a narrow hallway, except for one. When he tried the doorknob, it turned with ease, a smile spreading across his face. He gently pushed the door open just enough to peer through the crack. Inside, he saw a beautifully decorated vanity table with intricate wood carvings. The more he pushed the door open, the more he admired the room, which he suspected was Gwen's.

A queen-sized bed sat on metal frames in one corner, while three wardrobes with drawers lined the far wall. A magnificently carved nightstand stood by the bed, and a large gold-and-red carpet stretched across the floor, covering it from one end to the other.

Rafi gently shut the door behind him and immediately began to search the drawers and dressers. As he rifled through them, he mostly found prestigious dresses and undergarments. But in a few drawers, he struck gold—valuable trinkets, jewelry, and small treasures hidden away.

At the vanity table, Rafi opened a drawer to find several wooden boxes embroidered with gold and adorned with various gems. To his surprise, none of the boxes were locked with a key, which he'd expect from someone of higher status. Then again, he remembered that these people likely never had to worry about thieves in their homes—at least, not until now.

Rafi carefully opened the nearest bejeweled box, revealing an impressive array of rings, necklaces, bracelets, and watches—items he'd never seen before. Most jewelry from the middle hive was simple, lacking intricate details, embroidery, or proper craftsmanship. But the pieces in Gwen's box were the complete opposite. Each gold item was decorated with miniature, finely crafted designs, some even bearing the names of Gwen and Hizan. There were also a few pieces he couldn't quite identify, as they resembled silver, but something about them suggested they might be platinum—meaning he had stumbled upon items worth far more than gold.

Rafi swiftly tucked a handful of platinum pieces into his pouch, hoping their absence would go unnoticed when Gwen eventually discovered them. Moving quickly, he reached for the golden jewelry, carefully securing it–

Then, the doorknob behind him began to turn.

His body tensed. Instinct took over as he sprang into a defensive stance, his heart pounding, a cold shiver creeping up his arms and spine.

Fortunately for him, it was Habi.

"Habi?" Rafi whispered, barely moving. "Gently close the door behind you."

"What are you doing here?" he asked, his voice low, laced with urgency.

Instead of answering him right away, Habi waddled over to him and gave him a hug.

"I came to find you. Taliba and Tariq are on this floor too. We came to warn you that we couldn't find anything on the floors below, and Gwen is getting suspicious about us being gone," Habi whispered urgently.

"Then that means our time is nearly up," Rafi muttered through clenched teeth. He took a deep breath, steadying himself. "Right then, help me grab some of this stuff. This has to be platinum. This is it, Habi—we're getting out of the slums."

"Okay," Habi agreed, releasing her grip on him. Without hesitation, she stepped beside him, scooping handfuls of valuables from the box and stuffing them into her pouch.

"So Taliba and Tariq are searching the other end, I'm assuming?" Rafi asked, keeping his movements swift and efficient.

"Yeah, but I don't know if they're gonna be as lucky as we are," Habi pouted, her fingers brushing over a particularly heavy piece before shoving it away.

"That's fine. This should be enough to cover all of our citizenship. Hell, we still have more saved up back home." Rafi exhaled sharply, his mind racing. "I can't believe it's finally happening. Excited?"

"I'm very happy," Habi beamed. "Does this mean we can have beds, eat yummy food, and have clean water?"

"That's exactly what's going to happen," Rafi said, matching her smile.

The doorknob began to slowly turn again, catching Rafi and Habi's attention. This time, neither of them panicked. They assumed it was either Taliba or Tariq, already on the floor with them, checking in.

Without hesitation, they continued gathering as many valuables as they could, their hands swift, their minds focused. Every second counted—they had to leave without a trace.

"Taliba, Tariq, we're going to have a—" Habi began, turning her head with a bright, eager smile.

But the words died in her throat.

Her heart plummeted, her breath hitched, and her eyes widened in fear.

Even Rafi wondered why Habi suddenly stopped speaking, but as soon as he felt the shift in the room's atmosphere, he knew something was wrong. In one slow, deliberate motion, he turned to face the door.

Hizan Al'Za'im stood in the doorway, looking down at them with a menacing expression that struck fear into their hearts. Habi didn't realize it at the moment, but she probably was the reason he was there—he had most likely been lurking in the dimly lit hallways, spying on her.

"And so you finally show your colors," Hizan said coolly, shutting the door behind him with deliberate finality.

Rafi and Habi froze, their hands still halfway in their pouches.

"Do you both take me for a fool?" Hizan continued, his voice low and steady, but laced with quiet menace. "Well? *Do you?*"

The last words from Hizan's lips struck like lightning, booming like thunder. Habi was too terrified to look up at him, her gaze fixed on the floor. Meanwhile, Rafi slowly returned the goods to the drawer, never breaking eye contact. But even with his will and determination, he eventually dropped his gaze from Hizan's, silently accepting that they had been caught red-handed.

"So my wife unknowingly invited six slum rats into my home," Hizan growled, his fingers intertwining as he rested his arms across his waist. His eyes burned with contempt.

"She even fed you her cooking—food that none of you deserve," he continued, his voice darkening with fury. "And you probably thought I hadn't noticed you, golden-eyed child."

Habi stiffened, her pulse pounding in her ears.

"My wife believed you were a noble boy," Hizan sneered, his gaze drilling into her, "but I know an ugly, *disgusting* slum girl when I see one—especially the one causing havoc in the middle ring."

"I'm the damn commandant," Hizan pressed on, his presence suffocating. "I've lost many men in battle, which is considered *honorable*—but for them to die in *your* presence? That is something else entirely. That is *horrific.*"

Hizan advanced toward them, his footsteps slow and measured, eyes locked onto their every movement as if daring them to run.

Habi stood paralyzed, terror gripping her so tightly that she couldn't move. Her breath hitched, her hands trembling at her sides.

Rafi, however, instinctively shifted in front of her, his stance firm. His pulse pounded in his ears, but he held his ground, bracing himself between Habi and the looming threat.

"Brave boy," Hizan sneered, lowering himself to Rafi's height, his piercing gaze locking onto him.

Without warning, he seized Rafi's wrist, yanking his hand up between them. His grip was ironclad, unyielding.

"Do you know what we do to thieves, *boy*?"

Without even giving the chance for Rafi to speak, Hizan continued.

"We cut off their hands and feed them to the dogs," Hizan said coldly, his eyes narrowing. "Then we let the thief watch, as they witness their paws get devoured to the last bone."

Despite the horrific words, Rafi maintained his composure, keeping his eyes locked on Hizan's. Hizan chuckled, impressed by Rafi's courage. "But that's not going to happen to any of you," he added with a sinister smile. "We'll just kill you off instead. The Sultan has no time for you rats."

Rafi's breathing began to quicken, and Hizan's sharp eyes caught the subtle shift—how Rafi started to curl his fingers into a fist, his body tensing with the urge to act.

"You want to fight, *boy*?" Hizan snickered, his grip tightening. "That's all you slum rats do, yeah? Claw and bite for scraps?"

"Habi," Rafi said, his voice wavering ever so slightly, though his eyes never left Hizan.

Habi had never heard Rafi's voice tremble before. The fear in it was something new, something that sent an icy chill through her. It made her stomach knot, her fingers twitch.

Despite the terror gripping her, she managed a small whimper—a barely audible response in the suffocating silence.

"Run," Rafi instructed.

As soon as Rafi spoke his last words, he spat directly into Hizan's face, then headbutted him square in the nose. The force of the blow made Hizan recoil, his eyes flashing with fury.

"Ah! So we're doin' it!" Hizan roared, his fury erupting.

In an instant, he moved. As Rafi turned to run, Hizan drove his knee straight into his chest. A sharp, brutal impact—like a hammer striking flesh.

Rafi's breath vanished. His body buckled, gasping, choking, before he crashed onto the floor with a heavy thud.

As Rafi crumpled to the ground, clutching his chest, Habi was already sprinting toward the door, her every step fueled by desperation. As she reached for the doorknob, Hizan was already upon her. With a swift yank, he pulled her back by the shoulder. Without hesitation, he slammed her into the ground, her face hitting the floor with brutal force. Habi let out a loud, bloodcurdling cry, her tears streaming down her cheeks as she struggled to escape the merciless grip of Hizan's wrath.

Before Hizan could fully pin Habi down, Rafi surged forward, his adrenaline surging as he aggressively leapt onto Hizan's back. With a fierce snarl, he sank his teeth into Hizan's neck. Hizan let out a painful groan, the bite breaking his skin and drawing blood. Staggering from the unexpected assault, Hizan tried to shake him off, but Rafi held on tight, wrapping his arms around Hizan's neck. With a savage growl, Rafi bit down again, this time repositioning to secure a stronger hold.

Habi's eyes were clouded with tears, but she managed one last glance at Rafi, seeing him fight with everything he had to pull Hizan away from her. She wanted to help, but deep down, she knew—just by the sheer difference in size—that if she fought alongside him, none of them would make it out alive. Desperation fueled her decision. With trembling hands, she scrambled to her feet, threw the door open, and bolted. She ran, heart pounding, never once looking back.

Meanwhile, in the room, Hizan finally managed to loosen Rafi's grip by slamming himself violently against the walls, causing several decorations to crash to the floor. With a growl of frustration, Hizan latched onto

Rafi's arms, bent forward, and tossed him over, slamming him hard onto the floor. Rafi gasped, choking on blood and flesh as he struggled to breathe. Hizan, unrelenting, stomped into Rafi's chest and then kicked his face, leaving deep scratches, bruises, and blood smeared across his skin.

Rafi, heavily incapacitated, could barely move. With a cruel smirk, Hizan wrapped one arm around Rafi's neck and began dragging him across the floor like a lifeless corpse.

"You're done, boy," Hizan huffed, his breath heavy and ragged as blood trickled down his shirt from the bites on his neck. He looked down at Rafi with a mix of contempt and satisfaction, knowing the fight was all but over.

—

Responding to the chaos, Taliba and Tariq broke into a sprint, heading toward the source of the screams and crashes. It was then that they saw Habi, tears streaming down her face, crying her lungs out as she dashed toward them in pure panic.

"Habi? Habi? What happened!?" Taliba asked, her voice frantic as she gently cupped Habi's weary face, searching her watery eyes for answers.

"He took Rafi! He took Rafi! We need to leave!" Habi cried out in shaky tones, her body trembling with fear as she grasped onto Taliba, panic filling her voice.

Taliba froze for a moment, her heart sinking as she caught sight of the tall figure of Hizan, dragging Rafi's motionless body toward them. The sight of him, so lifeless, sent a wave of terror through her, and her body stiffened in disbelief.

"Run!" Tariq shouted.

With no more time to think, the trio sprinted toward the stairs, nearly tripping over each other in their haste. Fear pushed them forward, every step a desperate attempt to escape the looming danger.

As they descended, Gwen was ascending, drawn to the noise. She paused when she saw the frantic trio, confusion and concern flashing across her face.

"Little ones, what is–" Gwen started, but she stopped mid-sentence as the children barreled past her, nearly knocking her down. Not a single word was exchanged between them. Gwen stood frozen, shocked and confused, unsure of what was unfolding around her.

—

Back on the ground level, Hamza and Naji stood by the stairs, their curiosity piqued by the growing noise. They exchanged uncertain glances, wondering what was happening. But soon, their questions would be answered in the most unexpected and terrifying way.

Habi was the first to burst from the stairs, with Taliba and Tariq right behind her. All of them were hyperventilating, and Habi's tears flowed freely as she continued to sob. Not a single word was exchanged with

Hamza or Naji—there was no time for explanation. They simply shouted, "Run!" and charged for the door.

As if a sudden realization struck them, Hamza and Naji understood the gravity of the situation. Without hesitation, they scrambled toward the door, joining the others in their frantic escape. The children fumbled with the locking mechanism, their hands shaking as they twisted one knob, then turned the other. With a final push, the door creaked open, and they poured out into the streets of the higher hive, their breath ragged in the cool night air. The moon cast a pale light over their path, while the flickering street lanterns offered only faint guidance. Without a second glance, they ran, not daring to look back at the mansion they had just fled.

—

Some time had passed, and the door to the home remained ajar, the disarray of scattered furniture and broken decorations marking the chaos that had unfolded. Gwen stood in the main room, her heart racing, anxiety gripping her as she tried to make sense of what had just transpired. Her thoughts were interrupted when Hizan finally entered the room, his presence heavy with a dark satisfaction. In his arms, Rafi was limp, defeated, and utterly powerless. Gwen's breath caught as Hizan's eyes met hers.

"Hizan!" Gwen cried out, rushing forward, her voice sharp with panic. "What happened!? Why are you hurting the boy!?"

Hizan dropped Rafi onto the ground with a harsh thud, showing no care for his well-being. The wounds on his own neck, still bleeding from Rafi's earlier attack, dripped blood onto the floor. Gwen stood frozen, her heart racing as she took in the grim sight of both Rafi's motionless body and Hizan's bloodied form.

"You're bleeding," Gwen frowned, her voice trembling as tears welled in her eyes. She dropped to her knees beside Rafi, reaching out instinctively to tend to his wounds.

Before her fingers could touch him, Hizan's hand shot out, seizing her wrist. His grip was firm—unyielding, yet not cruel. Gwen froze, staring up at him in confusion and fear.

"Don't touch him," Hizan ordered, his voice as cold as steel. "He's from the lower hive, Gwen. *All* of them are."

Gwen's breath hitched.

"I caught them stealing from your room," Hizan continued, his tone unwavering. "Which is now a mess because of them."

Kneeling beside Rafi, he reached under the boy's shirt and ripped the pouch from his chest. With a flick of his wrist, he tossed its contents onto the floor.

The room fell silent as jewelry clattered against the tiles, the expensive trinkets scattering like fallen coins. Among them, a single item rolled away—Habi's doll.

Gwen's eyes flickered to it, her expression unreadable.

"I'll be taking him to the Sultan," Hizan declared, his gaze locking onto Gwen's. "To face his punishment."

As the events unfolded, Gwen's tears began to fall freely, her face contorted in sorrow. But it wasn't guilt over the thieves being in her home that weighed on her heart; it was the fact that they were just children. Children who had been forced into a world that terrified them, and now, they would pay the price. The helplessness of the situation overwhelmed her, knowing that they had been caught in a web they didn't deserve to be in.

"They're just *children*, honey," Gwen whimpered, her voice breaking under the weight of her emotions. "They—they just wanted a home—a place to eat—maybe even sleep! *They're just children*!"

Desperation clawed at her words as the reality of the moment sank in. She couldn't understand—how something so simple, so *human*, had been met with such cruelty. The realization gnawed at her, and she couldn't stop the tears from spilling down her cheeks.

"They *stole* from your room, Gwen," Hizan snapped, his voice sharp with fury. "They had no intention of being friends with you! You *let them in*—right into our home—because you can't stand the guilt of not giving me children! That's all this is, isn't it? Your little fantasy of a family!"

Gwen recoiled as if struck.

"That's *not* going to happen, dear," Hizan continued, his words like a blade. "And you need to accept that! You know nothing of the lower hive and its people. If you saw what those rats are truly like, you wouldn't dare look one of them in the eye again! Do you *understand*?"

"You didn't have to shove that in my face!" Gwen snapped back, her voice shaking with rage. "You're *disgusting*! Why did I even *marry* you!?"

She turned back to Rafi, her chest heaving. "Rafi is just a *child*! He's *human*! He's–"

Hizan embraced his wife, letting her cry into his shoulder.

"You understand that I'm trying to protect you, right? Not just you, but the entire city as well," Hizan said, his tone firm, as if reason alone could justify his actions.

"Are children from the lower hive not citizens, then?" Gwen cried, her voice raw with disbelief.

Hizan hesitated for a moment before answering.

"They are, but–"

"*Then why are you treating them as if they're not*?" Gwen hissed, her fury boiling over. "You're the *commandant* of the army! You swore an oath to the Sultan—to protect these people and Koura's lands. Those children were just *hungry*! We can always get more jewelry!"

Hizan exhaled heavily, rubbing his temple. "Honey, believe me—once you let a thief get what they want, they'll do it again. And again. And *again*. Maybe even from the same house if they're stupid enough."

He turned his gaze back to her, his expression grim.

"Tell me, dear—what is a world without justice? Answer that."

Gwen looked her husband in the eye, thought for a moment, and then shrugged.

"A world without justice would mean that no one learns what is right and wrong," Hizan explained, his voice steady, resolute. "Not everyone will like it, but it is necessary."

He leaned in and kissed Gwen on the lips, a gesture that felt more like reassurance than affection.

"He will be punished accordingly for his actions," Hizan continued. "For your sake, I'll do my best to ensure it is not out of malice. But in the end, it is the Sultan who decides."

Gwen's eyes burned with emotion. "*Swear it.*"

Hizan met her gaze without hesitation. "I swear upon the gods and under the Sultan's name."

A moment passed before he exhaled, rolling his shoulders. "Now... can we treat my neck wound?"

Gwen nodded and released herself from Hizan's arms, heading toward the dining area to gather the proper towels and ointment.

That was when Rafi groaned and finally opened his eyes, briefly met with a blur of unfamiliar surroundings. His vision swam, struggling to focus as his mind processed the pain and confusion. For a moment, everything felt disjointed, but the sharp realization that he was no longer where he had been jolted him back to full awareness.

"Stay down, boy. Your journey ends here," Hizan spat, his voice laced with finality.

Rafi let out a quiet chuckle, lifting his head slightly to meet Hizan's gaze.

"Yeah, I'm probably done," he admitted, his breath still uneven as he fought to steady himself. His vision sharpened, his chest still aching from the blow.

"But *they* aren't."

—

The children ran as far as they could, pushing their stamina to its limits, making a beeline for the shack with the tunnel system. Just before they reached its vicinity, they finally came to a halt, collapsing to catch their breath, each one trying to restore some semblance of composure after the chaos they had just experienced. Everyone was shaken, but it was Habi who felt it the most—she was the only one who had witnessed Hizan taking the boy she loved. As she took deep, ragged breaths, tears continued to pour down her face, her sobs uncontrollable.

"He took Rafi! Hizan took Rafi! *No, no, no, no!*" Habi sobbed, gasping for air as she wiped at her reddened eyes, her voice cracking under the weight of panic and disbelief. Each word felt heavier than the last, but she couldn't stop them—couldn't stop the tears, the terror, the crushing realization of what had just happened.

Her chest heaved, her heart racing, the world around her blurring as she struggled to process the unbearable truth.

"Habi, hey, look at me," Taliba urged, kneeling in front of her, her own breath unsteady. She reached out, steadying Habi with a firm but gentle grip.

"I know, I know—this is bad," she whispered urgently. "But we need to keep it down. We don't want to catch the attention of the citizens—let alone Ghazi. Can you do that for me?"

Habi buried herself into Taliba's chest, clinging tightly as sobs wracked her small frame. She pressed her face against Taliba's clothes, muffling her cries in the only comfort she could find.

"Okay," Habi sniffled, her voice barely above a whisper.

Once Taliba managed to calm Habi down, even if just a little, the group continued toward the shack. At this hour, most of the wealthy were already tucked safely inside their homes, preparing for the next day. The streets were quieter now, the city's upper tier falling into a calm that felt foreign to the children. Meanwhile, the band of thieves carried their dread with them, but at least they had made it to the shack, avoiding any more trouble for the time being. The fear of what had happened to Rafi weighed heavily on them all.

Tariq was the first to enter the shack, flipping the trapdoor open with an aggressive kick that echoed through the small space. The sudden noise startled Taliba, who was right behind him, causing her to stumble back slightly.

"Tariq? Are you okay?" Taliba asked, worry etched into her voice.

"No, I am not okay, Taliba," Tariq snapped, his voice tight with frustration and grief. "We just lost Rafi."

Taliba could hear his voice shake behind his words. If Tariq was losing morale, then that meant the rest of them were just as bad, herself included. When she looked back to see how Habi was doing, she was relieved to see that Habi had stopped crying, but that wasn't the worst of it. Habi was staring down at the floor, her eyes empty, as if she had just lost a piece of herself. Taliba knew that now that Rafi was gone, she would be the next one to keep the children in check and ensure they made it back home safely. Before they descended down the stairs, Taliba held Habi's hand, offering comfort, though Habi didn't react.

"Come on, let's go home," Taliba said to everyone, gathering her courage and leading the charge.

—

At first, the children were worried about finding the way back as soon as they lit the torch. Fortunately for them, Naji planned ahead and secretly dropped crumbs of food he had pocketed from the middle hive, which left a subtle trail. At the time, he was hoping to receive praise and credit from the others, but he didn't care for it at the moment, seeing as to how he was torn from the absence of Rafi. Thanks to Naji, the children safely made their way through the tunnels without running into any smuggler or squatter.

Throughout the entire trek, the children remained silent, their exhaustion mounting with each step. Their minds and bodies ached, and the weight of Rafi's absence hung heavily in the air. When they finally emerged from the trapdoor into the middle hive, there were no words between them. They simply moved quickly, shutting the door behind them, sticking to the detour route to avoid Ghazi patrols enforcing the curfew.

At this point, Habi was moving on auto-pilot, as she refused to react or speak. It was a miracle that she even drank from her canteen. However, when the children made it to the familiar water well to refill their supply, it was Taliba who had to retrieve Habi's canteen and fill it for her. Afterward, they continued their climb beneath a moon hidden by clouds, finally landing back in the lower hive.

They made their way through the Sleeping Complex without issue. The long journey back home felt shorter than it should have, as their minds swirled with dark thoughts, distracting them enough to make time seem to pass in a blur.

When they returned to the familiar street where their shed stood, Hamza was the first to shatter the dreadful silence.

"How are we going to explain this to Father?" Hamza asked, his brow furrowed in concern.

"I'll handle that," Taliba volunteered.

Naji stole a glance at Habi's weary face. Forcing a smile, he said, "Knowing Rafi, maybe he'll escape and find his way back, right?" His attempt at laughter came out hollow, hanging in the air between them.

"*Naji*," Taliba scowled.

Naji slumped in defeat, Habi's silence crushing any hope he had left.

"It's my fault," Tariq muttered, guilt weighing heavy in his voice. "I was the one who found the tunnel and told Rafi about it. If I hadn't, none of this would've happened."

"It's not your fault," Taliba said firmly, placing a reassuring hand on his shoulder. "We all know how Rafi is. He just wanted what was best for us, even if it meant taking risks. He *knew* the dangers that came with this gig."

She took a shaky breath. "I don't know what happened in that room with Hizan, but I do know that Rafi put his life on the line to get Habi out of there. That's who he is. And knowing him, he'd gladly take the blame if it meant keeping us safe."

She tried to steady herself, but the weight of her own words pressed down on her. Her voice wavered, and before she could stop it, tears welled up in her eyes. For as long as she could remember, Rafi had *always* been there—Father's first child, her first companion, the one who stood by her side through everything, from childhood games to heated arguments.

She clenched her fists, forcing herself to stay strong. "We'll see him again. Don't worry."

By the time they reached their shed, a heavy silence settled over them. Their stomachs twisted as they spotted the flickering glow of a lantern inside.

"He's home," Tariq muttered, exhaling sharply.

Taliba straightened her shoulders. "I'll go. Stay behind me," she instructed, her voice firm.

Without hesitation, she led the group forward, stepping toward the shed. Taking a steadying breath, she reached for the door and pushed it open.

Father was startled by the children's sudden appearance as he sat at his desk. What caught him off-guard most was the clothing they wore, but he quickly pushed that thought aside as he began counting them one by one as they entered the shed.

"Where's Rafi?" Father asked, smoke curling from his pipe as his logbook lay open in front of him, untouched.

The children stood frozen, their silence stretching. No one dared to answer.

Father took another slow drag from his pipe before repeating himself, each word sharpened with expectation.

"*Where. Is. Rafi?*"

Before he could ask a third time, he noticed how Habi appeared completely depressed, unwilling to even look at him. The entire time, Taliba kept her hand intertwined with Habi's, and after analyzing their faces and demeanor, he rephrased his question.

"Children," Father said, his voice unsteady. "What happened?"

"Father," Taliba began, her throat tightening. "I'm sorry—we're sorry."

Father set his pipe aside, his gaze steady as he shifted in his seat, giving her his full attention.

"Just tell me the whole story, Taliba."

Taliba took it upon herself to tell the truth, and nothing but the truth, given how dire the situation was.

"We traveled to the higher hive—and stole from a home. The lady, Gwen, invited us in, and we all thought we could take from her, but we didn't know her husband would come back. While we were stealing, Hizan caught Rafi, and then we—then we ran," Taliba said, struggling to hold back tears, especially as sorrow filled Father's eyes.

"Did you say—Hizan?" Father swallowed.

"Yes," Taliba whimpered. "We're so sorry, Father. I—I don't know what to do—I miss Rafi."

The children expected to be punished and scorned, but Father didn't say a word of reprimand. Instead, he rose from his seat and embraced them, understanding the weight of their feelings. He offered no words of comfort, only the warmth and shelter they needed. As they huddled together, the children could feel his hands shaking, which frightened them.

Habi knew that Father knew Hizan, and from his reaction, she also understood that Father was powerless against him. A deeper sense of despair washed over her as she realized she might never see Rafi again. The thought that she would never get to share the rest of her life with the boy she admired so much destroyed her.

"Where are the stolen items now?" Father asked, his touch still gentle around the children.

"I have them," Habi said shakily, pulling the pouch from beneath her shirt. It was the first time she had spoken throughout the ordeal.

She revealed the platinum jewelry and gold rarities to Father. As he examined the items, he noticed that some of them had Gwen's and Hizan's names engraved on them.

Once Habi surrendered her belongings, she broke away from the circle and slowly walked to her bedroll, lying down. The children wanted to comfort her, but Father shook his head.

"Give her time," Father murmured.

Habi dug through her bedroll and retrieved the gald coin that Rafi had marked with his kiss. She pressed it to her chest, closed her eyes, and silently cried, trying to force herself into slumber and escape the nightmare.

"What do we do, Father?" Taliba wondered, looking up at him.

Father grinded his teeth and dropped his eyes, saying, "Nothing. I can do nothing, Taliba."

After the interaction, Father released his hold on the children but remained kneeling.

"Get some sleep. No more of this nonsense, okay?" Father said, his voice firm but weary.

"Yes, Father," the children murmured in unison, their voices subdued.

Slowly, the children hunched over toward their bedrolls and tried to join Habi, wishing to forget that any of this had ever happened.

Before extinguishing the lantern, Father went to write in the logbook one last time before bedding down. With a deep sigh and shaky hands, he wrote a single sentence in Koumaic, fighting to hold back his tears.

Meeta timats kon cena.

I lost my son.

Chapter Twenty-two

Back at the higher hive the following day, the sun began to rise, setting the tone for a new morning. Wealthy citizens strolled in their luxurious outfits, going about their daily routines, while the children, dressed in their school uniforms, made their way to class. There wasn't a hint of chaos in the ring, aside from the occasional bickering between two children fighting over an extra bar of chocolate.

At the Al'Za'im mansion, Hizan slipped into his long coat, the medals and ribbons on it jingling with each movement. Bandages were wrapped around his neck, and he made one last check of his dark uniform to ensure he looked presentable. He retrieved his scabbard, where his sword still rested sheathed, and attached it to his sword belt. Afterward, he walked to the standing mirror in his room, running a hand from the front of his hair to the back, smoothing it into place.

As he admired himself, a few gentle knocks echoed from his door. When he opened it, his wife, Gwen, stood there in a red gown, looking up at him.

"So, you leave me again, and this time with the poor boy by your side," Gwen sighed. "You're not even fully presentable for an audience with the Sultan." She ran her hands down Hizan's chest, smoothing out the wrinkles in his clothes. Once satisfied, she kissed him and adjusted the ends of his mustache. "Better."

"Thank you, dear," Hizan said. "I shouldn't be gone as long this time. The training program for aspiring Mamluks takes about six months, and I'll return when there's time. I'll settle the matters involving the boy as soon as I reach the palace."

"His name is *Rafi*," Gwen reminded him. "And remember the promise you made."

"Of course, darling." Hizan kissed her again. "Is he awake?"

"He is—fed and with a full belly. Still in the same chains you left him in," Gwen informed him. "I pray the gods and the Sultan guide your trip and bring you safely back to me."

"Aye." Hizan pressed his lips to hers again, lingering in the warmth of her kiss. "It's time for me to go."

"Very well," Gwen said with a soft smile.

Once their personal matters were settled, Hizan and Gwen descended to the second floor of their home and unlocked a door that revealed an empty room. A single lock and chain were attached to a long metal bar positioned under a window. In those chains, Rafi's ankles were secured, and he was wide awake, turning to face the couple as soon as they entered the room.

"Oh, good morning to you, Hizan," Rafi said, his eye bruised from one of Hizan's strikes.

"You seem rather pleased to be escorted to the Sultan," Hizan said with a grin.

Rafi lifted the chain on his ankle, played with it for a moment, then let it drop.

"Beats being locked in here like a prisoner—though I do enjoy Gwen's company," Rafi chuckled.

"And you think you won't be locked up again once I turn you in?" Hizan scowled.

"I doubt that's up on the list," Rafi said with a smirk. "Now, are we going or what?"

Hizan nodded at Gwen, who held the key to the lock. She slowly walked over to Rafi and knelt beside him. Before inserting the key into its slot, she whispered, "Please behave, Rafi. I don't want you to get hurt any further."

Rafi chuckled. "You're too nice, Gwen. You don't know the stories of what they do to lower hive criminals—and your man over there is about to let them all know how you let some kids steal from a general."

"That's enough, boy," Hizan hissed.

Gwen sucked in her lips and stared at Rafi with pleading eyes. "I know there's good in you, Rafi." She inserted the key into the slot and twisted it open, freeing Rafi's ankle. "Otherwise, you would've had your siblings suffer before you."

Rafi glared at Gwen with his beaten eye, admiring her emerald beauty, full of innocence and goodwill. He didn't speak another word as Hizan lifted him to his feet and pulled his arms behind his back. Hizan retrieved a pair of iron-hinged cuffs from his coat pocket and locked them around Rafi's wrists. Once secured, Hizan kept a firm grip on Rafi's bicep, leading him out of the room.

"The moment you try to run, I'm planting you to the ground, got it?" Hizan whispered into Rafi's ear.

Rafi didn't speak, but he also didn't react to the threat.

As soon as Gwen locked the door behind them, they proceeded down the stairs and into the main room. Gwen opened the front door for them and watched as Hizan escorted Rafi out into the harsh sunlight.

"Stay safe and return soon," Gwen prayed, her voice barely audible before they moved out of earshot.

"Safety to you as well," Hizan replied.

With that, Gwen gently shut the door behind them and remained in her home, while Hizan kept Rafi in check, guiding him all the way toward the noble grounds—where the Sultan sat upon his golden throne.

—

The sun neared its peak as some of the higher hive citizens took notice of Hizan's approach toward the border that separated the rich from the Sultan's bloodline. They observed his steady, confident gait, their eyes also falling on the dirtied child in his grasp. The wealthy weren't as rowdy as those in the middle hive, where shouting profanities and throwing trash at a criminal were seen as ideal pastimes. In the higher hive, the citizens simply acknowledged the fact that a criminal had been detained before returning to their day. While such an event would be a spectacle in the lower hives, the escort itself was seen as a humiliation, a form of punishment deemed worthy of the Sultan by those in the upper grounds.

Passing several gardens, trees, and the luxurious smells of freshly cooked food, Hizan finally reached the border, Rafi still firmly in his grasp.

The two Mamluk knights standing at the gate immediately recognized Hizan and his status, opening the large iron gates for him before he could even greet them.

"Commandant," one of the Mamluks announced, saluting with his fist to his chest.

Hizan didn't speak a word, and Rafi didn't fool around either. Hizan was focused on keeping Rafi restrained, while Rafi, despite his situation, simply enjoyed the scenery. The two absolutely despised each other, but for now, they both worked in each other's interests.

Once the iron gates fully opened, Hizan marched right in with Rafi in tow. The two Mamluks on the other side of the wall took notice of Hizan's presence and saluted him accordingly.

Rafi, witnessing the noble ring for the first time, scanned the horizon. He could see every part of the wall that encased them in this layer, proving it to be the smallest ring in all of Koura, and for good reason. There were a few mansions, but mostly open land with lush green fields, livestock, and glistening pools of water. Aligning the paved walkway were numerous golden statues, molded into tigers, eagles, and bears—symbols of the three main nations to the west, east, and north, respectively. Further away, golden statues of the Sultan's likeness stood tall. His eyes were sharp, his chin strong, and even the rough stubble on his lower jaw was intricately detailed. Atop his head, he wore a crown adorned with foreign letters, and a third eye was tattooed in the center of his forehead.

Beyond the decorations and scenery stood the Sultan's tower itself. From below, it seemed as if the summit of the tower touched the clouds, with platforms jutting out from the main structure, offering ample shade to those below. There was even an angled section of this colossal tower that extended over part of all the hive rings, which explained the many stories surrounding the Sleeping Complex—from the sun's position to the tower's striking architecture.

As Hizan dragged Rafi closer to the tower, Rafi could make out details of the tower's walls, where the eight-pointed star was draped among several flags at the base. It was hard to miss the largest flag hovering several feet above him, proudly displaying the city's colors of purple and gold. The foundation of the tower was made primarily of sandstone, metal, and granite, with hints of golden embroidery outlining the bricks. While Hizan didn't terrify Rafi as much, the sheer presence of the tower alone sent shivers down his arms. He could only imagine how he would react when facing the Sultan himself.

While Rafi was taking in his new surroundings, Hizan had already guided him to the Sultan's front door, where two more Mamluks stood guard. Both of the steel-plated knights had decorations across their chests and pauldrons. Their armor bore scratches, and dents, proof of their experience and survivability in countless battles. But even these feared Mamluks didn't question Hizan, mostly because they were all acquainted with him, knowing he was the leader of their army.

One of the Mamluks glanced at Hizan, then down at Rafi, giving no thought to the situation Hizan had brought to the palace.

"Commandant," one of the Mamluks announced, his voice muffled beneath his helmet.

"How many recruits for your ranks today?" Hizan asked, making idle conversation.

"At least a hundred wish to become Mamluks, sir," the knight replied.

"How many do you think will make it?"

"Not many, sir."

"Aye," Hizan said before departing with Rafi.

"Sir," the Mamluk acknowledged.

As the Mamluks heaved open the tall iron gates to the Sultan's tower with an eerie creak, Hizan and Rafi stepped inside.

Inside, a long, tall hallway stretched before them, layered with red and gold carpet. The tall walls were adorned with decorations, armor, and portraits of the Sultan and his bloodline. Corridors branched off to unknown destinations on either side, but at the end of the hallway stood an open circular room, housing a spiral stairwell.

"Keep up, boy. We're going for a climb," Hizan said.

"Whatever, old man," Rafi muttered—only to receive a sharp slap to the back of his head.

From there, the duo marched toward the end of the hallway and began ascending the stairs—a thousand steps, it seemed, spiraling upward toward an unknown destination.

—

Both Hizan and Rafi were conditioned enough to make the lengthy climb without rest, thanks to Hizan's rigorous military training and Rafi's tough life in the slums. They passed several platforms that led to more corridors and mysterious doors, steadily nearing the top of the tower.

Finally, Hizan and Rafi stopped on a platform that held a single ominous corridor, with no doors on either side. The only way forward from this level was a large golden door at the end of the path, adorned with golden letters and molded heads of beasts. In the center of the pristine door was the eight-pointed star.

It was faint, but the duo could hear a conversation echoing from the end of the hallway, though it was indistinguishable. Standing next to the door were six Mamluks, three on each side, their presence imposing as they guarded the entrance.

Even though there was an important assembly taking place, Hizan continued forward with his young criminal in tow, approaching the Mamluks standing guard. All of the Mamluks were armed with halberds, yet none of them brandished their weapons to stop Hizan from entering. However, Hizan paused to ask a few questions.

"Commandant," the Mamluk furthest from the door announced. "Be advised, sir, the Sultan is conducting business."

"Brief me on the matters," Hizan requested.

"Sir, the Sultan is consulting with the Chief of Police, Ibrahim Hafeez, and the Head of the Kouran Intelligence Service, Elina Faheem."

"Ibrahim and Elina, huh? And why wasn't I invited?" Hizan clicked his tongue.

"I have no answer for that, sir. Perhaps it concerns domestic affairs."

"I appreciate the insight," Hizan said with a nod, continuing forward.

"Aye, sir," the Mamluk responded, stepping aside to let him pass the golden boundary.

As the golden doors thundered open, Hizan and Rafi stepped through. Inside, Rafi took in what he assumed to be the throne room. Rows of pews lined each side of the vast chamber, draped with the city's flags. At the far end, a golden throne rested atop a grand staircase, and in it sat the Sultan himself. From a distance, Rafi couldn't make out the Sultan's features, but as Hizan led him closer, his gaze shifted to the four golden statues towering behind the throne, facing the audience.

Recognition flickered in Rafi's mind—he had seen these figures before in the mythological books Taliba loved to share. They depicted the gods said to have shaped the world of Skania, the very beings who gifted humanity its existence. Arranged from left to right, the statues represented: Aiden, the God of Body and Battle; Shie, the Goddess of Mind and Knowledge; Helso, the God of Health and Spirit; and finally, Centi, the Goddess of Emotion and Fertility.

The Sultan sat upon his throne in front of the gods, as if he claimed himself to be the fifth. Rafi spat at the idea, because if the Sultan truly were a deity, then Rafi believed the lower hive should've been in much better condition.

Two tall individuals stood before the Sultan, just below the throne. One was an older, olive-skinned gentleman who, despite his age, carried himself with the poise and strength of a man still in his prime. His complexion was smooth and resilient, and his short gray hair, cut into a fade, revealed hints of black beneath. He wore a dark blue tailcoat over a crisp white dress shirt, partially concealing his dark slacks. A pair of square glasses rested on the bridge of his nose, framing his sharp hazel eyes.

The other individual was a pale woman, tall and slender. She wore a jet-black tailcoat, similar in style to the man's. Her round, protruding brown eyes contrasted with her sharp chin. Her long black hair was braided all the way down to her waist, and her slacks were tailored to fit her modeled figure.

The Sultan, now clearly visible at their distance, bore an uncanny resemblance to the statues behind him—if not an exact reflection. His olive skin was framed by dark stubble along his jaw, and like the statues, a third eye was tattooed at the center of his forehead, just above his piercing sky-blue eyes. He wore a regal purple robe adorned with golden scales across his chest, with intricate golden embroidery lining the fabric. His traditional harem pants were a deep charcoal hue, complementing the golden crown atop his head—a symbol of his dominion over the city and its people. His dark hair was slicked back and tied into a short tail.

This was the man who governed the hive—the same man who showed no regard for those struggling in the slums.

The Sultan noticed Hizan entering the room with the dirtied boy in tow, but he paid no heed to them, his attention focused on the ongoing discussion with the man, Ibrahim, and the woman, Elina.

"Tell me again, Ibrahim, how your Ghazi are failing to quell the rising crime rates in the middle hive," the Sultan growled, his voice a monstrous presence that filled the room. "How do you expect the middle ring to function properly if your police force can't prevent the rats from causing further disorder?"

"We are still looking into that, Enlightened One," Ibrahim replied, his voice raspy and measured.

"You're all doing a miserable job at simply *looking* if citizens from the middle keep informing my men that their belongings are vanishing. Have you even checked the walls? The gates? Hell, have you even searched the pipes below and the water table? This needs to be dealt with immediately, Ibrahim. I shouldn't be hearing rumors about a couple of brats outsmarting my people." The Sultan pinched the bridge of his nose in frustration before shifting his gaze to Elina. "Elina, deliver me your report on the hive."

"Yes, Enlightened One," Elina responded, her voice young yet composed. She retrieved a folded piece of paper from her coat pocket and began to read.

"On this day, reported from dawn's watch: the noble ring remains balanced. The higher hive remains balanced. The middle hive has seen an increase in burglary and larceny, with some reports of battery and murder. The lower hive remains unchanged. No public gatherings or riots have been observed there as of late, and no further evidence has been gathered regarding the Hassazi and their potential insurrection. Population numbers remain steady, with a slight increase in births. The middle hive has seen a minor decline, while the lower hive continues its steady decrease. That concludes the report, Enlightened One."

"At least the lower hive continues to kill each other off like the pack of wild dogs they are. That marks off the least of my worries," the Sultan grumbled. "As for the Hassazi, are you certain there's no new evidence of their whereabouts? Another uprising could be more fatal than the last."

Elina folded the report and spoke with unwavering poise. "Yes, Enlightened One. We've dispatched scouts and conducted thorough sweeps in the lower hive. There are no signs of organized movement from the Hassazi. However, their presence remains a persistent threat—elusive, but never truly gone. Surveillance along the lower hive borders has been heightened, and patrols in the sewers and tunnels have increased."

The Sultan leaned forward, his gaze sharp and calculating. "If they're hiding beneath us, what's to stop them from striking when we least expect it?"

Elina's composure remained intact, but she felt the weight of his scrutiny. "We are prepared, Enlightened One. Our agents are embedded in the lower hive, and any whispers of unrest will be dealt with swiftly. We won't let them gain a foothold again."

The Sultan's eyes flicked to Hizan, then back to Elina. "I trust you understand the consequences of failure. Continue your watch, but be ready. I expect results, not excuses."

"I understand, Enlightened One," Elina replied, her voice steady. "My agents have been working tirelessly, and none have reported any signs of Hassazi activity—or of Saif Sabbah's whereabouts."

"Dig deeper. The Hassazi aren't finished, and they're patient enough to burrow into the shadows like vermin until they decide to disrupt everything I've built," the Sultan said.

"Enlightened One, if you don't mind me asking—why not simply eradicate the lower hive? Crime would naturally dissipate if they ceased to exist," Elina suggested.

The Sultan's gaze darkened. "You're the Head of Intelligence, Elina, and that's the conclusion you land on? Use that brain of yours, *girl*," he growled, making her stiffen. "The lower hive was established to regulate resources and maintain stability. I ordered its severance when famine and economic decline threatened to collapse this city. If I were to wipe it out entirely, what do you think those in the upper hives would believe? That they're next? That another purge looms on the horizon? There would be an uprising—an insurgency I have no patience for.

"Or worse, they'd riot, knowing I sanctioned the slaughter of millions. Blood would flood the streets, and this city would burn. The lower hive remains, but its fate is its own. I have no intention of staining my hands further."

"Yes, Enlightened One," Elina said.

Rafi smirked, barely restraining his laughter, knowing full well he was part of the reason behind the Sultan's fury.

"Is this amusing to you, *boy*?" the Sultan roared.

While Ibrahim and Elina turned their attention away from the Sultan, Hizan smacked the back of Rafi's head again, hissing, "Show some respect, *boy*."

"Hizan, you have yet to disappoint me in your service, so tell me—why is this boy standing in my domain?" the Sultan asked.

"Of course, Enlightened One," Hizan answered, presenting Rafi almost as a gift. "I caught this boy within my dwelling. He was stealing alongside several other children, including the rumored golden-eyed child. I bring him before you, Enlightened One, for you to decide his punishment."

The Sultan's eyes gleamed with curiosity and amusement as they met Rafi's rebellious glare.

"How did this child get into your home?" the Sultan asked.

"My wife invited them in, mistaking them for children from the higher hive. It was our mistake," Hizan explained.

The Sultan burst into laughter, slapping the armrest of his throne with a resounding thud. Hizan stood firm, masking his embarrassment behind a stoic expression.

After regaining his composure, the Sultan fixed his sharp gaze on Rafi, relishing the child's simmering rage and the sting of his humiliation.

"*Toito yule blaka cha tuti,*" the Sultan hissed.

Rafi raised a brow, puzzled by the Sultan's cryptic words. The others around him, however, remained stoic, unfazed by the peculiar language. Rafi assumed it must be customary for the Sultan to speak in such a manner, but when the next question came, an unfamiliar sensation stirred in his chest and throat, something unsettling and unexplainable.

"You will speak the truth, child," the Sultan said, his smile sharp and menacing as his piercing gaze bore into Rafi. The room fell silent, all eyes fixed on the boy. "What is your name?"

Rafi tightened his jaw, intent on refusing the Sultan's demand. Yet, before he could muster his defiance, the words escaped his lips unbidden: "Rafi Sabbah."

Rafi's eyes widened in disbelief. His name hadn't even crossed his mind, yet it slipped out as though willed by some unseen force. *Demons*? *Djinns*? His thoughts raced. He could feel it—a crushing weight in his chest, as if an invisible hand gripped his heart, tightening with every beat, coaxing the truth from him. His head felt light, teetering on the edge of dizziness, but his senses remained sharp, fully attuned to the Sultan's unrelenting gaze and the silent onlookers around him.

"What did you do!?" Rafi shouted.

Hizan struck the back of Rafi's head once more. "Easy, boy," he said firmly. "The more you fight it, the worse it gets."

"Rafi Sabbah," the Sultan said, his smile stretching into a maniacal grin. "Do you know Saif Sabbah?"

"Yes, he is my father. He adopted me," Rafi revealed.

At this point, Rafi considered bashing his head against the floor just to escape the invisible grip of the Sultan's gaze. But the thought of hurting himself held no appeal. Besides, even if he tried, he wouldn't be able to tear his eyes away from the Sultan, as though some unseen string bound them together.

"Excellent!" the Sultan chuckled. "Now tell me, Rafi—where is he, exactly?"

"The lower hive," Rafi answered.

"That's it? Nothing more specific?"

"No. We just live in a shed. I don't know where we are."

The Sultan cursed and spat.

"How many children were with you? Tell me their names. Tell me about the golden-eyed child," the Sultan pressed.

"There were five others," Rafi admitted, his voice trembling despite his efforts to stay firm. "Taliba, Hamza, Tariq, and Naji—all under the same name. The golden-eyed child is Habi Sabbah."

"And why were you all stealing from Hizan's home?"

"Because we wanted to sell the stuff and buy our way into the middle hive!"

The Sultan coughed violently, breaking eye contact as blood splattered from his lips. Rafi gasped for air, finally free from the crushing pressure that had gripped his chest.

"Enlightened One!" Elina shouted, preparing to provide aid to the Sultan.

"No, step no further, girl," the Sultan coughed, throwing an arm out toward Elina. "No one steps up on this throne."

Elina stepped back, her eyes narrowing as she watched the Sultan expel the last traces of blood. The room fell silent, save for the quiet sigh that escaped the Sultan as he reclined into the plush backing of his golden throne.

"So you're guilty of stealing not just from a home in the higher hive, but from my commandant as well. The other children abandoned you, and you happen to know the man I despise. All of this—for riches?" The Sultan waved a hand toward his lavish decorations and treasures. "You rats from the slums are all the same, but this—this is far more intriguing, little Rafi."

Rafi didn't know what to say, still trying to grasp the situation and fully understand it. The Sultan had his answers, but the consequences had yet to be revealed.

"Let's get on with it, then, step by step," the Sultan grinned. "Little Rafi, based on everything spoken in this room, you are guilty of trespassing, burglary, and misconduct—not just against any of the Sultan's men, but against the commandant of Koura's army. That alone is one of the highest violations.

"You have two options, little one: lose both your hands and face life imprisonment, or trial by duel. Which will it be?"

"Enlightened One, may I intervene and ask, for the sake of my wife—she does not wish for harm to—"

The Sultan cut Hizan off before he could finish.

"Your wife isn't here, Hizan. Her words mean nothing to mine. Why does she even care for a lower being? A forsaken child that isn't even hers?" the Sultan hissed.

"But—"

"*Silence*, General. Speak no further. My decision is made—now, choose, little Rafi," the Sultan commanded.

At first, Rafi didn't want to choose, planning to give the Sultan the silent treatment. However, considering how much information the Sultan had already siphoned from him, along with the long walk to this tower, Rafi realized there was no point in resisting any longer. And so, he decided.

"Trial by duel," Rafi decided, unwilling to lose both his hands and be tossed into a dungeon for life.

"Smart boy," the Sultan chuckled, amusement flickering in his gaze. "Ibrahim, inform the gate guards to bring me a trainee. Hizan, keep the boy there. Elina, how about you look pretty and stand aside, clearing the dueling ground?"

"Yes, Enlightened One," the three leaders responded in unison.

Without hesitation, they each moved to fulfill their assigned tasks, setting the stage for the spectacle that was about to unfold.

—

Many moments later, one of the Mamluks at the throne's door finally returned with Rafi's contender. To no one's surprise but Rafi's, his opponent for the trial was another boy around his age, though slightly more built. The Mamluk also delivered two short swords, dropping one on either side of the pathway that led to the Sultan's steps. With that, the dueling ground was ready. All that remained were the introductions and the rules.

"This is Jafar, Enlightened One," the Mamluk announced, stepping aside to reveal the young warrior. "He is one of our finest aspiring recruits. He has been tested in several battles against his peers, demonstrating both his mettle and proficiency with the blade."

While Hizan began to unlock the bars confining Rafi's wrists, Rafi scanned Jafar from head to toe, sizing himself up against the larger boy. Jafar was a little taller than Rafi, covered in scars that complimented his toned muscles. He stood proudly before the Sultan, eager to prove himself in the Sultan's holy eyes. As Rafi sized up his opponent, Jafar did the same, snickering.

"Before this trial begins, I have an order for you both, Hizan and Ibrahim," the Sultan declared, his voice carrying undeniable authority.

Hizan placed Rafi on one side of the red carpet while the Mamluk positioned Jafar on the other. Both men straightened at the command.

"Yes, Enlightened One?" they responded in unison.

The Sultan's gaze swept over them, his expression unreadable. "Rally your men and activate the garrison. In a few days' time, you will descend upon the lower hive to deliver the final consequence of this boy's actions."

A chilling pause followed.

"For one whole day, you will bring them slaughter—teaching them the price of acting like animals and disregarding their place. Let their blood stain the streets, let their shelters burn to the ground. It will be done."

His words hung in the air like a death sentence.

Out of all the leaders, it was Elina who questioned the Sultan's order.

"Enlightened One, if I'm not mistaken—didn't we establish that destroying the lower hive would cause further disorder?" Elina asked.

"I *know* what we established, *girl*," the Sultan hissed, his gaze snapping toward her. "This isn't *eradication*—this is a *culling*. Just enough to cripple their foolish ambitions while keeping the upper hives content and unbothered."

His expression darkened as he leaned forward slightly. "That's where you come in, Elina. You oversee the media, do you not?"

"Yes, Enlightened One, but–"

The Sultan raised a hand, cutting her off before she could finish.

"Then you and your agents will spread the news," the Sultan commanded, his voice sharp and final. "Let it be known that the lower hive will suffer collective punishment for the crimes of these children. Let fear take root, so the more seasoned rats think twice before trespassing into the upper hives."

He exhaled slowly, a cruel smirk forming. "And if we're lucky, perhaps this will flush out Saif and his Hassazi once and for all."

His gaze bore into Elina. "See it done."

Elina held her breath, completely baffled by the Sultan's order. Just moments ago, he had been against touching the lower hive, but now, with the revelation of Rafi and his actions, his demeanor had shifted. Elina also knew that her actions were key to preventing the hives from turning on each other—and on the throne. Now that the Sultan had given her the order, she had no choice but to comply, fully aware that he would carry out his command regardless.

"*Leave*, Elina. Go inform the people—*now*," the Sultan growled, his patience razor-thin.

"Yes, Enlightened One," Elina replied, bowing her head before swiftly departing the throne room.

Once Elina had departed, the Sultan shifted his focus back to the spectacle before him.

"Did you two understand my order?" the Sultan asked, his gaze flicking between Hizan and Ibrahim.

"Yes, Enlightened One," they both acknowledged.

"I will see the task done," Hizan added, though there was the faintest tremor in his voice.

The Sultan smirked, satisfied, before turning his attention to the two young boys standing on opposite ends of the dueling ground.

"Rafi and Jafar—you will duel to the death." His voice was calm, almost casual, as if he were merely discussing the weather. "You are provided blades, and you may fight with no restrictions."

He leaned back in his throne, exhaling contentedly.

"See it done. *Now*."

And with that, the spectacle began.

Hizan and the Mamluk stepped away from the boys, watching from the pews. Rafi was prepared to fight, his eyes cold with resolve, but for a moment, he was confused by the Sultan's order, wondering if he had been given the chance to finally begin. However, it was Jafar who answered first.

As soon as the Sultan spoke his last words, Jafar swiftly retrieved the short sword from the ground and dashed toward Rafi. The boy was so quick that by the time Rafi began to reach for his blade, Jafar was already within striking distance.

Jafar's blade sliced through the air, barely grazing Rafi's chest. A sharp sting followed, forcing a wince from him, but he had managed to backstep just enough to avoid a deeper, more lethal cut.

His breath came in ragged gasps as he realized his predicament—his blade lay out of reach, gleaming on the ground.

Jafar noticed too. His stance shifted, positioning himself carefully between Rafi and the weapon, his grip tightening on his own sword.

Rafi was defenseless.

"Should've paid attention, boy," Jafar growled, pointing the tip of his blade at Rafi.

Rafi danced around Jafar, staying light on his feet, while Jafar crouched low over the blade, eyes fixed on Rafi, watching his every move.

"Hey, hey, I know you're trying to kill me," Rafi called out, his breath uneven, "but would you really consider yourself an amazing soldier if you killed an unarmed boy?"

His eyes stayed locked on Jafar, watching every twitch of his muscles, every shift in his stance. Both of their blood ran high, the tension thick between them.

Jafar snickered, a smug grin tugging at his lips. Then, without warning, he kicked the blade across the floor toward Rafi.

Rafi didn't hesitate. He lunged for it, his fingers curling around the hilt as he scrambled to his feet, brandishing the weapon in front of him.

"With or without a blade," Jafar taunted, rolling his shoulders, "you're still just a *rat*."

The clash of steel rang through the throne room as Jafar kept pressing the attack, hacking and slicing at Rafi with relentless precision. Rafi barely managed to evade the strikes, his blade meeting Jafar's only in desperate, clumsy blocks. Each step forward from Jafar forced Rafi to retreat, his breathing growing more labored with every passing second.

Jafar was no amateur—his footwork was tight, his control impeccable. Every strike was measured, every movement deliberate. Rafi, by contrast, was barely keeping up, skidding from side to side, rolling away from the pews to avoid being cornered. But no matter how fast he moved, exhaustion crept in, his limbs growing heavier. Jafar dictated the flow of the duel, approaching with a steady, calculating gait.

Rafi knew he couldn't keep running.

Gritting his teeth, he surged forward, going on the offensive. He swung wildly, forcing Jafar to defend. But every strike was met with a precise parry, every attack dodged or deflected with ease. Then, with one expert maneuver, Jafar countered—knocking Rafi's sword from his grip. The blade clattered to the ground. Before Rafi could react, Jafar struck him across the face with the pommel of his sword.

Pain exploded in Rafi's skull as he crashed onto his back.

He wasn't much of a swordsman, that much was clear. But Rafi wasn't just some helpless fighter either. If there was one thing he prided himself on, it was being a damn good observer.

Jafar was skilled—too skilled. His stance was textbook perfect, his focus unwavering, always targeting Rafi's collarbone, like a trained duelist would. His balance, his control—it was all by the book.

But Rafi wasn't a duelist. He was a brawler. A dirty, desperate, unpredictable fighter.

And that's what was going to save him.

As Jafar raised his blade for the final strike, Rafi lunged, slamming his body into Jafar's, knocking them both to the ground. In the scuffle, Rafi scrambled atop him, forcing his weight onto Jafar's sword arm, pinning it down.

Jafar thrashed, swinging a fist into Rafi's face—once, twice—his punches cracking against bone. Blood filled Rafi's mouth, but he didn't care.

Because he had other plans.

Ignoring the blows, Rafi shifted his grip—and latched onto Jafar's groin.

Jafar's entire body seized.

Then, Rafi squeezed.

A scream tore from Jafar's throat, high-pitched and raw, echoing through the throne room. His punches grew wild, erratic, but their precision was gone. His body bucked beneath Rafi, desperate to break free.

Rafi didn't let go.

As Jafar gasped for breath, his movements becoming sloppier, Rafi released his grip and mounted his chest, raining down brutal fists. His knuckles crashed into

Jafar's face over and over, until Jafar's grip finally slackened. His sword slipped from his grasp. His struggles grew weaker.

Then—he went still.

Rafi rolled off him, panting, his vision swimming. He grabbed his fallen blade, staggering to his feet.

And with his knuckles bloodied, his body aching, he leveled the tip of his sword at Jafar's unmoving form.

Both Hizan, Ibrahim, and the Mamluk were stunned, their eyes wide with amazement at Rafi's performance. A boy with no combat training had just incapacitated a skilled fighter. That was when the Sultan applauded and cheered, standing up from his seat.

"That's what I want to see!" the Sultan cheered, his voice ringing with excitement. "There is no fairness in real fights! Skill alone does not always determine victory! I saw your drive! I saw your desperation! I saw the way you cast aside your morals just to eliminate your enemy!"

His eyes gleamed with satisfaction as he stood, reveling in the spectacle before him.

"There should be no mercy!"

As his exhilaration settled, he eased back onto his throne, this time leaning forward, watching with keen anticipation.

"Right then, little Rafi..." his voice dropped, laced with command.

"*Kill him.*"

Rafi heard the order but hesitated. He had stabbed others in the lower hive, but he had never knowingly taken a life. Another thought gnawed at him: this boy was just another kid from the middle hive, someone who either got lucky or was conscripted. Rafi didn't want to kill him—because he was *human*—but he also wanted to press the blade to his throat—because he was *human*. A human who stirred his jealousy, a reminder of those who lived better off. But right now, his freedom hinged on his choice.

Ultimately, Rafi thrust the blade into the boy's throat, pushing past muscle and bone, twisting and gouging. Jafar let out several bloody coughs before finally going completely limp, the life fading from his eyes.

Rafi immediately dropped the blade and sat on the floor next to Jafar, breathing heavily as the pain and bruises on his face began to settle in.

Hizan, Ibrahim, and the Mamluk stood expressionless, darting their eyes between Rafi's battered body and Jafar's lifeless form. The Sultan simply smiled, watching a child murder another to earn his freedom in the bout.

"Hizan, Ibrahim, go carry out my orders as given. I shall see the culling done in a few days' time," the Sultan commanded. "You, soldier, clean up this mess and dispose of the body. You brought me a failure—now you must bear him."

"Yes, Enlightened One," the three replied, setting to their tasks.

Rafi, relieved to have earned his freedom, sat still next to the pool of blood as the Mamluk prepared to gather supplies to prevent the body from leaking throughout the throne room. However, he wasn't out of the chaos yet—the Sultan had other plans for the young, victorious boy.

"Rafi, you have proven yourself, and I have witnessed its end—as if the gods destined it," the Sultan said, rising from his throne and descending toward him. He knelt, meeting the boy's battered eyes. "This trial by duel is concluded, and you have earned your freedom. But now, little Rafi, the next step in your life hinges on this choice alone."

The Sultan smirked. "Do you wish to return to the lower hive and keep fighting for your life alongside brothers and sisters on their last leg?" He extended his hand. "Or are you interested in a personal offer?"

Rafi missed his friends, the familiarity of the streets, and the culture that had shaped him, but he knew that was never his ultimate goal. He was a boy of ambition, and deep down, he knew it. The Sultan could see it too. Rafi had no clue what the Sultan's offer entailed, but he had a hunch.

Before speaking his next words, Rafi began to imagine the faces of Father, Taliba, Hamza, Tariq, Naji, and Habi, smiling at him as if he had just returned home from this arduous journey. He loved them, after spending most of his life alongside them, but he kept asking himself:

How long? Just how much longer until we can finally be free and live the life we deserve? How long until we can earn our way to the middle hive? I miss them, but how long until we all die? I love them—but for how long? I love them—but will they even stay? Money won't give me happiness, but it'll solve most of my problems.

Finally, Rafi let out a pained groan and said, "What's the offer?"

Chapter Twenty-three

Three days had passed since Rafi was taken by Hizan Al'Za'im. Back in the lower hive, in the familiar shed now thick with sand and dust, the children chose to follow Father's teachings—behaving and avoiding reckless pursuits like stealing from the upper hives. Most had adjusted to Rafi's absence, with Taliba now leading their band.

Though they carried on with their daily routine, sneaking what they could within the lower hive walls, a heaviness lingered in their hearts, a quiet certainty that Rafi would never return. Only Habi clung to hope, praying for his return.

Taliba was moving things around and organizing the shed, cleaning the dust off of books and sweeping the floor, until she noticed a troubling trend. She paused, then turned to ask Hamza, who lazily lay on his bedroll, counting the cobwebs on the ceiling.

"Hamza, is Habi outside again?" Taliba asked.

"Yeah, she's been sittin' out there ever since Rafi got taken," Hamza muttered, lazily picking his nose.

"I'm worried about her. She's been out there every day, waiting for Rafi to come back," Taliba said, frustration creeping into her voice. She kicked Hamza's side to snap his attention away from whatever thoughts were distracting him. "Take this seriously, Hamza. She hasn't eaten properly, she hasn't gone to play in the hive once. While Tariq and Naji are out taking what they can, you just lay here like none of this matters."

"Can say the same to you, Taliba," Hamza sighed. "You keep cleaning things that don't need cleaning. It's almost like you're trying to keep yourself busy so you don't have to think about it."

"That's exactly what I'm doing, Hamza," she admitted, crossing her arms. "We can't just sit here and wallow in it, letting it eat us alive. How about you actually do something and go talk to her?"

"I *tried*. She wouldn't talk to me," Hamza grumbled. "How about you do it? You haven't even sat with her. All you do is wave every time you walk in and out of the shed."

Taliba hesitated. "I—I don't even know what to say."

"You think *we* knew what to say?" Hamza shot back.

Taliba sighed, leaning the makeshift broom against the wall, her gaze settling on Father's desk. A thought—reckless, maybe even foolish—crossed her mind. But it wasn't cruel. It wasn't meant to hurt.

Habi refused to talk, refused to engage, but Taliba knew one thing—Habi could read the foreign script Father wrote in. Maybe, just maybe, she could use that to pull her sister out of the suffocating grip of despair, even for a moment.

Her fingers drifted over the desk, brushing against scattered papers and books. Father had left at his usual time. She was in the clear.

With careful hands, she returned a few books to their rightful place, making the space look undisturbed. Then, with a swift motion, she swiped Father's logbook.

Tucking it close, she turned toward the shed door, stepping out into the light.

Once Taliba was outside, the sun glared directly into her eyes, causing her to shade her face with her arm. As usual, several homeless, undesirables, and citizens walked back and forth on the dusty streets, some heading for the pond, others for the flea market.

When Taliba turned her head, she immediately spotted Habi sitting right next to the shed door, looking down at the ground and playing with the sand with her finger as she cradled her knees. Habi seemed absorbed in her thoughts, but Taliba caught the quick side-eye the golden-eyed child gave. Without a word between them, Taliba hugged Father's logbook against her chest and seated herself next to Habi, who still wore the same frown she had ever since running away from the higher hive.

"Hey, Habi," Taliba said, forcing a smile as she approached.

She considered asking the usual, *Are you okay?* but swallowed the words before they could escape. She already knew the answer.

Not only would it be pointless—it would only make things worse.

Instead, Taliba presented Father's logbook, which slightly caught Habi's attention.

"I wonder what's written in here," Taliba mused aloud, deliberately flipping through the pages. "If only I could read it. Imagine all the *stories* and *secrets* Father has in here!"

She made sure her voice carried just enough intrigue, enough to plant a seed of curiosity.

Habi's eyes narrowed as she finally looked up. "What are you doing?" she asked, suspicion creeping into her tone.

It turned out that Habi wasn't reacting to the mysterious book, but rather, Taliba's horrible acting. Nonetheless, Taliba managed to draw out a few words from Habi, meaning there was at least some interest—depending on the topic.

"Trying to be a good sister, but failing miserably," Taliba grinned, hoping—*praying*—to coax even the smallest laugh from Habi.

But Habi didn't smile. Didn't react.

"I just want Rafi back," she murmured, her voice barely above a whisper as her gaze dropped back to the sand beneath her.

Taliba scooted closer to Habi until they touched shoulders. She hugged Habi with one arm, and proceeded to open the book to a random page, placing it on her lap.

"I want him back too," Taliba admitted, her voice softer now. She hesitated for a moment, then gently nudged the logbook toward Habi.

"Here, check this out though," she said, forcing a bit of intrigue into her tone. "These scribbles and letters seem interesting, no?"

At first, Habi wasn't interested in reading the book Taliba offered. That soon changed when she kept glancing at the page Taliba had opened, noticing a word in Koumaic that caught her attention. Her eyes widened when she saw Rafi's name written in Koumaic, and that sparked her curiosity. She leaned in closer to Taliba.

"Oh? See something you like?" Taliba asked, her smile gentle as she watched Habi's eyes scan the pages.

"What does it say?" she wondered aloud, her voice light with curiosity.

She rested a hand on Habi's shoulder—warm, steady, reassuring. In that small moment, she wasn't just a sister. She was something more—something softer. Almost like a mother.

Habi read the text that mentioned Rafi, slowly piecing together the mystical writing of Koumaic as she decrypted its message. She leaned in closer, holding the book in her hands to get a better look. While Taliba was pleased by Habi's sudden interest, she hadn't expected the answers Habi would read aloud.

"On this day, I found a nameless boy in the Sleeping Complex. He is the first to be adopted by me, ever since my recent disbandment. His name will be Rafi, under my surname," Habi read aloud, her voice quiet.

Her fingers traced the inked words as if trying to absorb them, as if they could bring Rafi back.

Taliba's eyes widened as Habi's neutral expression shifted into a frown, her thoughts turning to the boy she loved, now gone. Taliba quickly flipped through the next several pages, desperately hoping that none of them mentioned Rafi.

"How about this?" Taliba asked, gently pointing to a page filled from top to bottom with dense writing.

She leaned in slightly, her voice soft, as if offering a secret. "This one looks like it could be something important."

Habi sighed and took another look at the book, playing Taliba's game.

She scanned the page, but refused to read it all out loud.

"It's just a bunch of names of people we don't know," Habi muttered, her voice flat as she glanced over the page.

"Oh? Anything else? Maybe they're Father's friends?" Taliba pressed, eager to keep the conversation going.

"I don't want to play this game anymore," Habi groaned, curling back into her previous position, staring at the ground again.

"Oh, come on, Habi. Aren't you at least a little curious? This is Father's book we're talking about," Taliba urged, flipping to another page with a hopeful smile. "Oh, how about this one? This page is a drawing of something."

Habi decided to look at the book one last time before refusing any more advances from Taliba. This time, it was a drawing or a diagram of a large ring on the page, with several lines and circles branching out from it, leading to words in Koumaic. Both of the girls scanned the drawing, wondering what it could possibly mean, until Taliba made a deduction of the diagram.

"It's the lower hive," Taliba said, her finger tracing the small circles on the page, leading toward the words written in Koumaic. "What does this say?"

"Ally," Habi read aloud, her voice quiet but certain.

Taliba nodded, her finger moving to another circle. She followed the lines out to another word written in the same script.

"And this?" she asked, her gaze fixed on the next word.

"Neutral," Habi read again, her brow furrowing slightly as she processed the words.

Taliba continued to point out all the circles, letting Habi read them off. It turned out that the word 'ally' outweighed the words 'neutral' and 'foe'. There was one specific circle that Taliba remembered clearly, as it was the only shaded part of the large drawing of the ring.

"This has to be the Sleeping Complex. What's it say?" Taliba asked again.

"Neutral," Habi read, her voice dull.

Taliba paused, her finger lingering over the page. What had started as a simple game now felt more like a complicated puzzle.

"What could it mean?" Taliba wondered aloud, furrowing her brow as she tried to make sense of it all.

"I don't know. I don't care," Habi said, turning away from Taliba and the book, her voice tinged with exhaustion.

"Hab–" Taliba began, about to offer some comfort, but she was cut off by the screams of people echoing down the dusty road.

Both girls went still, the tension between them forgotten in an instant as they turned toward the sound.

A few moments later, a large crowd of lower hive citizens charged down the street toward the children. Some of the people, instead of fleeing, ran toward the chaos. This inadvertently caught Habi's attention, as sand and dust were kicked up into her face by the frenzied mob. From a distance, more screams rang out, followed by a series of crackles and a loud boom that echoed down the streets.

"What's happening?" Habi asked, clutching onto Taliba as the crowd surged past them.

"They're running from the market area—but why!?" Taliba shouted, trying to make herself heard over the mayhem, her voice barely carrying through the din of shouting and panic.

While the two huddled next to the shed door, they could see thick plumes of black smoke rising in the distance, curling toward the sky above the market area. The first cloud was followed by another, then another, until it seemed as though the entire lower hive was being consumed by chaos. People ran in all directions, some clutching at wounds, others wearing charred clothing, their faces painted with fear.

The screams and cries for help pierced through the air, mixing with the sound of crashing debris. The smoke thickened, darkening the sky, and the pungent smell of burning filled the air. The scene unfolding before them was unlike anything Taliba and Habi had ever seen, and the dread in their hearts only grew heavier with each passing moment.

Finally, Hamza jumped up from his bedroll and rushed to join Taliba and Habi outside. He squinted toward the source of the smoke, his brow furrowed with confusion and concern.

"Hey! Get inside!" Hamza demanded, his voice urgent as he flung open the door for Habi and Taliba.

The fear in his eyes mirrored their own, and the frantic pace of his movements made it clear there was no time to waste.

Without hesitation, the two girls sprinted into the dilapidated shed, slamming the door behind them to shield themselves from the outside world and its elements.

"Hamza?" Taliba whimpered, her voice shaking with fear. "What's happening?"

Hamza made a hush gesture to Taliba, signaling her to listen closely. As they stood there, the screams and shouts of the panicked crowd filtered through the thin walls of the shed. They could hear:

"Ghazi! Mamluks!"

"Run! They're going to kill us!"

"The gods have finally forsaken us!"

"Fire! There's fire!"

Taliba, with a shaky breath, said, "W-Why are the Sultan's men attacking?"

Habi began to shake as well, her despair shifting into a new form of fear. The ache of losing Rafi still gnawed at her, but now, there was a real possibility that all of the children could lose their lives in an instant.

"I don't want to die," Habi cried, her small body trembling as she clung to Taliba tightly. "Why is this happening!?"

"I don't know," Taliba cried along, her own heart pounding in fear. She wrapped her arms around Habi, trying to offer whatever comfort she could. "Just stay close to me, and we should be fine!"

While the trio huddled in their shed, letting the madness unfold outside, the door suddenly swung wide open, and a gust of sand poured in. Tariq and Naji rushed inside, covered in soot, their faces grim and exhausted. The moment they entered, the tension in the room thickened, as they quickly reunited with the others.

"Tariq! Naji! What happened!?" Taliba shouted, her voice filled with panic.

"We gotta get out of here!" Tariq urged. "There are hundreds, if not thousands, of Ghazi and Mamluks marching down the streets from all border gates, killing random people and burning the buildings. It's madness out there! If we don't move right now, we could be next!"

"While we were stealing stuff, the army came out of nowhere and sliced a man in half!" Naji cried, his voice trembling with fear. "We need to get out of here!"

Taliba was prepared to follow their advice, as she helped Habi onto her feet, maintaining Father's book in her grasp. Amidst the violence, the entire situation was confusing at first, without any viable reason for the sudden surprise attack on the lower hive. However, it suddenly dawned on Taliba, as she theorized as to why this was happening.

"This is happening because of us," Taliba said, her voice filled with a mix of guilt and fear. "We were caught stealing from a *general*, and Rafi got taken because of it. This is the Sultan's response."

"No time for thinking, Taliba! We are leaving. Now!" Tariq shouted, his urgency cutting through the tension.

"Okay! Fine! Habi, are you ready to move?" Taliba asked, her tone softening as she turned to her sister.

"Yes," Habi whispered, a soft whimper escaping her, a single tear slipping down her cheek.

"Right then. Hamza?"

"Way ahead of you," Hamza said, positioning himself at the door alongside Tariq and Naji, ready to act.

"Okay. Leave everything we don't need, here. We'll come back for it later, depending on whether this shed still stands or not," Taliba declared, holding Habi's hand tightly and guiding her toward the door.

"Get rid of that book, Taliba," Hamza said, his voice low but firm.

"No. This is Father's book. There's valuable information here that Habi can read. There's something bigger than all of us that's moving, and we need to understand it," Taliba replied, her grip tightening around the book.

"Let her keep the damn book," Tariq said with a resigned sigh. "Line up on me and stay close. Hang onto each other, because the crowd out there is getting real messy."

"Aye," the children responded in unison, gripping each other's ragged shirts as they steeled themselves for the escape.

"On three. One. Two. Three!" Tariq counted, pushing the door open and leading the way into the sea of bodies that surged outside.

Right away, several people bumped into Tariq, causing a brief disruption in the line they formed. However, he quickly recovered, pulling himself toward the side closest to the buildings and tents that cluttered the streets. The group followed the flow of the crowd, forcing their way between people who desperately tried to escape the onslaught of the Sultan's men. As they ran, the crackle of something igniting reached their ears, followed by a deafening boom. With each blast, the crowd grew more frantic to save themselves, shoving and jostling to get away from the source.

The children kept running, their path uncertain. Taliba frequently glanced back at Habi, making sure she was keeping up, relieved to see that she was still on her feet, despite the panic around them.

Within the cries and screams, Taliba yelled at Tariq, "Where are we going!?"

"Anywhere! As long as it's away from–" Tariq shouted, but his words were cut short when the front line of the fleeing crowd suddenly stopped. A formation of Ghazi soldiers emerged from an alleyway, blocking their path.

This time, the Ghazi looked different. They still wore their usual steel-plated chest armor and carried scimitars and bows, but now their faces were obscured by horrifying, featureless masks. The smooth, metallic surface barely revealed the color of their eyes, making it impossible to read any emotions. The blank, silver-gray masks struck a deep, primal fear in those who saw them. The Ghazi moved with eerie precision, executing their violence without a hint of humanity. Some of them carried lit torches and small, round metal balls with strings attached. No one knew what they were, until the Ghazi set the strings alight with their torches.

Immediately, the front of the crowd was cut down by a barrage of arrows from the Ghazi. The shrieks of the injured and dying were drowned out by the chaos as the arrows found their marks. Without hesitation, the Ghazi with the lit objects hurled them into the mass of fleeing bodies.

Crackle. Crackle. Boom!

The grenade detonated, sending several people crashing to the ground or turning them into charred remnants, with shards of metal flying in every direction. Fortunately, the children were shielded from the arrows by the mass of bodies in front of them. However, one of the explosions from a grenade hit nearby, knocking them to the ground and causing them to tumble over each other, or onto the bodies of those who had already fallen lifeless. As sand swirled up into thick clouds, the children found themselves briefly scattered. Once they regained their bearings, they began shouting for one another amidst the uproar.

"Taliba!" Tariq shouted, scrambling to his feet. He dashed over to Hamza as the Ghazi pressed their attack, now chasing those who had managed to flee their initial strike with scimitars raised. "Come on, big guy," Tariq urged, helping Hamza up.

Hamza loudly cursed and shouted, "What the hell was that!?"

"Shut up and find the others!" Tariq yelled.

At this point, the crowd began to thin, slowly revealing the children's presence. Tariq and Hamza scanned the area frantically, searching for any other child before they made their escape. They trampled over fallen bodies and stumbled across more, scrambling to find someone—anyone—from their group.

"Naji!" Hamza cried out, his voice panicked.

Tariq rushed over at Hamza's call, his heart pounding as he discovered Naji, his body covered in soot, his rags torn and singed. Naji's face was pale, and his chest rose and fell rapidly with each labored breath.

"Naji! Get up!" Tariq demanded, his tone harsh but filled with urgency, reaching out to help him.

However, Naji couldn't move a single muscle, his body paralyzed by the blast of one of the grenades. Tariq gritted his teeth, summoning all his strength to lift Naji, but it wasn't until Hamza joined in that they managed to hoist him onto Hamza's back. Together, they kept moving, desperately searching for the others. But their efforts were abruptly halted when more Ghazi emerged from the rear, cutting off their escape.

"We need to go!" Tariq shouted.

"What about Taliba!? Habi!?" Hamza worried.

"They'll be fine! We need to save ourselves now! Quick, down this alley!"

The remaining three declared that both Taliba and Habi were missing, and with the crowd thinning out and the Ghazi closing in, they could no longer search for them. To save themselves, the trio made the decision to follow the rest of the panicked crowd down a narrow alleyway, hoping to escape the deadly pursuit.

—

Taliba and Habi were unharmed, having managed to escape with another group of civilians fleeing the attack. The blast had thrown the boys in one direction while the girls were tossed in the other. They quickly regained their footing, their hearts racing from the shock, but the crowd around them surged with such force that they were swiftly swept away.

HABI

The frantic mob pushed and shoved, dragging them along in a desperate bid to avoid being trampled. The chaos around them was overwhelming—shouting, the sound of pounding footsteps, and the screech of distant cries filling the air as the group moved further into the sea of panicked bodies.

"Where are the others?" Habi cried out, as Taliba aggressively guided her through the crowd with Father's book in her other hand.

"They're strong boys. They'll be fine. We need to save ourselves right now," Taliba said. "I just want this to end!"

As soon as she spoke, the front of the crowd came to an immediate halt once again—this time, in a narrow alleyway. A smaller formation of Ghazi appeared, armed the same way as before, their haunting masks still covering their faces.

Just like the previous attack, the front of the crowd was pinned down by a barrage of arrows, while the Ghazi with the grenades lit their fuses.

Taliba and Habi hugged each other tight, knowing that they couldn't escape from this attack, seeing as to how everyone was packed in the alleyway like sardines. Habi let out one last whimper before she heard the crackle.

Boom!

Taliba wondered why she wasn't dead yet, so she poked her head back out from Habi's shoulder.

The grenade exploded in the crowd of Ghazi, taking down several of them as arrows targeted their carriers.

After the blast, more arrows rained down from the rooftops of the buildings lining the alleyway, striking other Ghazi and sending them to the ground.

"*Kopek*!" a man shouted at the top of his lungs from above.

After the shout, several assailants in dark clothing dropped from above, landing swiftly on the remaining Ghazi, driving their blades into them, and slicing through their throats. Some engaged in close-quarters combat, moving with a familiarity that mirrored how Father fought. They were ruthless, methodical—cutting through the Ghazi's defenses with precision. They exploited every weakness in the Ghazi's armor, targeting joints, stabbing underarm pits, and gouging their eyeholes.

The unknown heroes made quick work of the Ghazi, wiping their bloodied daggers and scimitars along their elbow creases before scavenging weapons and arrows from the fallen. Their faces were mostly shrouded in scarves, shawls, and shemaghs, some even donning the same metallic masks as the Ghazi, as if mocking their enemies by claiming the masks as trophies.

"Hear me out, you lot!" one of the rebels shouted. "You either keep running, or you fight alongside us! This is a culling! The wretched Sultan finally broke and decided to send his men to take our lives! To destroy our homes! To ruin our families! This damned city is run by the value of gald, and those damned gold tongues treat us like roaches beneath their feet! You fight, or you run! Come on!"

Some of the crowd hesitated, torn between saving themselves or joining the fight. A few broke away, rushing past the rebels, eager to escape. Meanwhile, another portion of the people let out battle cries, taking up arms alongside the rebels in dark clothing. As the rebels led the fighters out of the alley, Taliba and Habi, knowing they were no match for the overwhelming force, followed the rest of the fleeing crowd, focusing only on escaping the bedlam.

"Who were they?" Habi asked, her voice shaky as Taliba continued to pull her through the crowd.

"I don't know—but the way they fought—it reminded me of Father. Maybe those were some of the allies that were written in the book?" Taliba theorized, turning a corner with the others who fled.

"Taliba, what's a culling?" Habi asked.

"It's—It's a slaughter, essentially," Taliba answered, which rang a bell in her head. If this really was a culling, like the man said, then this wasn't going to last forever. This wasn't going to be the end of their story, but they still needed to be cautious and wary. That sliver of hope was what kept Taliba moving, and she had to share the information with Habi as well, just to ease the tension she was feeling. "If what the man said was true, then this isn't going to last forever, Habi. We just need to run or hide it out."

"Taliba," Habi called again.

"Yes?" Taliba replied.

"Why is it quiet?" Habi asked.

She was right. Aside from the heavy breathing and panic that filled the air, and the small crowd around them, there were no explosions or distant screams. The silence was unsettling enough for Taliba to believe the slaughter had finally stopped.

As the group exited the alley and stepped back onto the streets, they found no sign of the Ghazi. Instead, the air was thick with black smoke rising into the sky, like a funeral pyre marking the devastation. The ground was littered with the lifeless bodies of the fallen, their stillness a grim testament to the brutality that had unfolded.

Buildings that once housed goods and food were reduced to rubble, their charred remains jutting from the ruins like broken bones. Tents that had once provided shelter were now nothing more than ashes, burned to the ground.

A mixture of sand, dust, and ash blew through the empty streets, swirling slowly, settling over everything like a blanket of sorrow. The group Taliba and Habi were with carefully picked their way through the desolation. The remains of the few survivors around them began to calm, their voices rising in hushed conversation, full of disbelief. The sudden, eerie reprieve left them questioning what had just happened, and what might come next.

"Is it over?" Habi wondered, her voice soft as she hugged Taliba tightly. "I hope the others are okay," she said, her eyes filled with worry. "I hope Rafi is okay too."

"Over or not, we should find a spot to hide for the time being," Taliba suggested, glancing around nervously. "There's too much going on right now."

"But what if they come back and burn our hiding spot down?" Habi frowned, her concern growing.

"Then we run away before they can do that," Taliba replied firmly, pulling Habi closer to her. She kept a tight hold on Father's book, unwilling to let it go.

As some of the people grieved, mourning the sight of their loved ones among the sea of limp bodies, the children and others suddenly turned toward an unfamiliar sound. Whatever it was, it was moving quickly. The crowd heard the constant clash of metal against metal, accompanied by the rhythmic pounding of a thousand hooves. It didn't take long for the dust cloud to part, revealing what was approaching them with unnerving speed. Taliba stood frozen in fear, her eyes wide and mouth agape, as a long line of horses emerged from the smoke. Mounted on them were several fully armored soldiers wearing winged helmets, the eight-pointed star emblazoned on their chestplates. In their hands, they brandished halberds, aimed directly at the crowd, charging toward them at full speed.

"Mamluks," Taliba murmured.

At that instant, the crowd scattered in all directions, desperately attempting to flee from the charging Mamluks on horseback.

Taliba quickly yanked Habi off the street and sprinted toward the nearest alley, joining two men and a woman who had wisely taken the same route before them.

Out on the streets, the Mamluks trampled over the lifeless bodies and those of the living. They swung their halberds instinctively if someone got too close, but for the most part, most of the people who fled were immediately impaled and maimed by the tip of their halberd. The rest of the people who didn't escape in time were trampled by the horses, disappearing into the sea of hooves and sand as their cries for help and pain came to a disturbing stop.

"They're killin' everyone, man!" one of the men cried, who happened to be the tallest out of the current group.

"Get yer self together. There's children 'ere. What, you wanna show 'em how weak you look right now?" the other man growled.

"Stop fighting you two! We need to get out of here before the gold tongues see us!" the young woman pleaded. "Little ones, stay with us. We're gonna head down this alley and get away from this."

"Okay," Taliba agreed, still keeping Habi and the book in her hands.

After the brief exchange, the group dashed down the alley, leaving the screams of the dying behind them. Taliba knew the alleyways were likely their safest option, though not without risk. The Sultan's men often moved in groups, but even they couldn't block every path through the maze of streets. This entire massacre was nothing more than a show of power, a grim reminder of the consequences for defying the Sultan's rule.

After several turns and weaving through tight angles, the group occasionally glanced behind them, checking to make sure they weren't being followed. Some of them even laughed, convinced they had escaped the worst of it.

However, as the group reached a narrow intersection between four different alleyways, two men at the front were suddenly struck by a blur of silver, sent crashing to the ground. Before they could react, the attacker drove a short blade into one of the men's chests. The man let out a guttural cry as the blade sank in, his ribs cracking under the force. The other man scrambled to his feet, desperate to flee.

"Mamluks!" the woman screamed, her voice filled with panic. "Children, turn back! Turn—"

Her words were abruptly cut off as another Mamluk appeared from around the corner. With a brutal motion, he slammed her head against the wall, quickly pinning her in place. The force of the impact left her dazed, her body struggling to stay upright as the Mamluk maintained his grip.

The other Mamluk who had taken the life of the helpless man noted the other who ran, refusing to give chase. Instead, he squeezed himself past the other Mamluk who had the woman against the wall, who was also flailing her legs in the struggle.

In one swift motion, the Mamluk who held the woman delivered a series of brutal blows with his steel gauntlet, each strike landing with a sickening crunch. Her cries and flailing grew weaker with every hit, until they ceased altogether, leaving only the sound of her lifeless body slumping against the wall. Meanwhile, the other Mamluk, having forced his way through, turned his attention to the children who had already begun to scatter, preparing to flee.

"Habi! *Go*! *Go*!" Taliba screamed, pushing Habi back to get her to run.

Habi screamed in pure terror, her voice raw with fear, as Taliba followed closely behind her, heart pounding in her chest. The two Mamluks steadily closed the distance between them, their looming presence threatening to overtake them. Taliba could almost feel the breath of one of them, just inches from grabbing onto her long, flowing hair.

Just as the leading Mamluk reached out to yank her back, a heavy weight suddenly dropped down onto his shoulders. The force of the blow sent him crashing to his knees, throwing him off balance. The same fate befell the Mamluk bringing up the rear, as something unseen knocked him off his feet, sending him tumbling to the ground.

Two rebels happened to drop down from the rooftops, trying their best to take down the Mamluks and pull them away from the fleeing children. Although the assailants were mobile and lightly equipped, their strength alone could not match up to a single Mamluk. Their only saving grace was the fact that all parties were hindered by the tight space of this alley.

The rebel closest to the children was a woman who swiftly incapacitated her Mamluk by driving a knife into his throat, taking advantage of the element of surprise. Though she was briefly tossed around by the armored foe, her persistence and strength forced him to crumple to the ground. Unlike the other rebels, this woman didn't wear a mask, which caused both Taliba and Habi to instantly recognize her.

"Sara!" Taliba cried out.

"Stay back you two!" Sara ordered, shielding the children behind her as she witnessed the misfortune of her partner.

While Sara landed a devastating strike, her partner, who had dropped onto the other Mamluk, wasn't so lucky. As Sara dashed toward him, she saw the Mamluk toss the rebel over his shoulder with terrifying ease, slamming him into the ground. The impact knocked the wind out of him.

Without hesitation, the Mamluk stomped down on the rebel's head, using all his weight. The sickening sound of a cracking skull echoed through the air, and blood spilled from the man's ruptured head. His body went limp beneath the brutal force, his life extinguished in an instant. The scene was drenched in violence, the grim reality settling in as Sara's partner lay motionless.

The Mamluk had no time to celebrate or catch his breath as Sara closed the distance, her dagger flashing with expert precision. She drove the blade straight into the exposed gap of armor beneath his armpit, piercing through the weak point with deadly accuracy.

Even after Sara's dagger sank into the Mamluk's side, causing him to roar in pain, he retaliated with a brutal right hook to her side. The blow sent her staggering, her breath catching in a pained gasp. With the last of her strength, she yanked the dagger free and tried to drive it into his exposed neck, but the Mamluk was faster.

Fueled by pure rage, the Mamluk finally engaged in a fair fight, relishing the opportunity to face a worthy opponent. He forced Sara's dagger arm against the wall, using his shoulder to push her body along with it, pinning her in place. As she struggled, trying to break free, he launched a brutal punch into her gut. The impact knocked the breath out of her, and spit and saliva splattered against his helmet.

In an instant, he shifted his wrist, driving the tip of his blade deep into her abdomen. The cold steel pierced her flesh, and Sara gasped, her body seizing as the pain coursed through her.

Sara let out a bloodcurdling scream as she exhausted all of her remaining energy into her dagger arm, trying to free it and strike the Mamluk in his neck. Now, the Mamluk was ready to deliver the fatal strike, as he pulled his blade out of her stomach to have her bleed out. He pointed the tip of his blade toward her neck, angled perfectly for a deadly swing.

Suddenly, the Mamluk roared in pain.

The children mustered enough courage to act and save Sara. Taliba and Habi scavenged blades from the ground, driving them into the back of the Mamluk's knees, causing him to buckle. Their war cries were soft yet fierce, giving Sara just enough time to free her arm and drive the dagger into the Mamluk's neck. As he released her, she collapsed onto him, continuing to stab until his body went limp, his gurgles fading into silence. The children quickly dodged the Mamluk's falling body to avoid being crushed under his weight. As Sara finished off the Mamluk, Taliba and Habi, still trembling, fought to catch their breath, the adrenaline coursing through them.

"Did we kill him?" Habi worried, her voice trembling with fear.

"No, no, we only wounded him. Sara finished him off," Taliba reassured, placing a gentle hand on Habi's shoulder. She made sure Habi didn't carry the burden of feeling like a murderer.

Sara pulled her dagger out of the Mamluk's throat after delivering several fatal strikes. She coughed, rolling onto her back, and clutched her gut wound, which continued to leak blood. Her chest rose and fell with unnerving speed, and her face grew pale.

"Sara!" Taliba cried out, running over to Sara. Habi followed her trail and weeped alongside her older sister. "Wait, wait, wait, let me help you!"

As Taliba pressed down on Sara's wound to stop the bleeding, Sara gently pulled her bloodied hands away from her stomach.

"It's fine, Taliba," Sara groaned, her voice strained with pain. Tears ran down her cheek as she fought to stay conscious. "You and Habi can't stay here any longer. There could be more." She wheezed and coughed, her hands trembling from the strain, but her eyes locked on Taliba with urgency.

Taliba took Sara's hands and held them tightly, letting a few tears fall. Habi joined in, offering what little comfort she could with a gentle touch. All three of them cried, exhausted from the horrors they had just endured.

"I don't want to leave you, Sara," Taliba frowned, her heart breaking as she looked down at her friend.

"Then I'll tell you to leave me," Sara cried, her voice laced with desperation. "I can hear their march approaching us—please, take Habi and leave."

"Sara–"

"*Leave*, dammit!" Sara cried out. "I always knew I was going to die at some point in the slums, but I will not bring you two down with me! Please—just go!"

Taliba recoiled, pulling Habi with her. She was terrified of losing Sara, but just as afraid of being scolded by her on her deathbed.

"Sara!" Habi cried out, her voice choked with emotion as she reached for Sara one last time.

"Habi—please stay safe. You're too precious to be taken. I love you all," Sara whispered, her voice filled with a mixture of pain and tenderness. "If you two ever meet my child—her name is Rosa. Please tell her that mommy loves her when she grows up—please be friends with her. She should be safe with my husband at the outskirts of the ring. Please."

"We will, Sara," Taliba promised through her tears. "We love you."

"I love you girls too," Sara managed a weak smile, her eyes lingering on both of them with all the love she could muster. Taliba, with a heavy heart, had to pull Habi away, her arms firm around her as the ominous sounds of approaching steel grew louder. They needed to move, to escape, even as their hearts ached to stay.

Habi shouted out Sara's name until her voice faded away around the corner of another alleyway. Taliba refused to stop and look back, while her sister mourned the loss of a friend—a mother.

Sara shifted around and positioned herself against the wall, loosening her grip on her wound. Her vision blurred, and her hearing started to fade. One hand covered her wound, while the other still gripped her dagger. She faintly acknowledged the arrival of two Mamluks who had stopped their patrol and now observed the mess left behind.

"This one's still alive," one of the Mamluks mentioned, noticing Sara's shallow breathing. "She looks kind of cute. Still fresh if she passes for the picking," the Mamluk chuckled, his tone casual and cruel.

"You're a Mamluk. Sticking it into a slum dweller is madness," the other Mamluk joined, his voice laced with disdain, yet a hint of caution.

For one last time, Sara gritted her teeth and clenched the handle of her dagger, slowly lifting her head to meet the sunken eyes behind the helmet of the Mamluk kneeling over her.

"*Fuck the Sultan*," Sara hissed, using the last of her energy to swing the dagger into the Mamluk's neck.

She landed the strike, causing the Mamluk to roar and recoil away from her. But now that he was furious, he instinctively responded with a heavy straight kick into Sara's head. After that, there was a loud crack, and everything suddenly went dark.

Chapter Twenty-four

Naji took a deep breath as Tariq and Hamza shielded him from the harsh elements. Hamza gently slapped Naji's face to keep him alert, while Tariq offered him sips of water from his canteen. The children had taken refuge beneath an abandoned building on the outskirts of the ring, huddled with other lower hive citizens bearing the brunt of the attack. The sharp tang of fresh blood saturated the air, making many occupants wince at its metallic scent. At the front door, a man from the group stood vigil, peering through the cracks to monitor any sign of advancing enemy forces.

"The Mamluks and Ghazi are occupied with another group," the man murmured to those who had gathered behind him, his voice low as they watched the Sultan's forces wreak havoc on the unfortunate souls caught in their path. "Those poor souls."

"Why are we always running and hiding!?" another man suddenly yelled, his frustration boiling over. "There's more of us compared to them! We weren't raised in the lower hive just to cower away and piss our pants! We're fighters! Those men and women in dark clothing are trying to bring the fight to them, but they alone are outmanned and outmatched! What are we doing!?"

"Shut up!" a woman shouted back, her voice sharp with fear and anger. "A single Mamluk can cut a wave of us in half with a single swipe of their halberd! We may outnumber them, but they are well equipped! We will just feed the slaughter!" Her words echoed the grim reality of their situation, dampening the brief flare of defiance.

The people started to riot, taking sides as to whether they'll fight back or wait it out. Their in-fighting was beginning to erupt the building of its static sand and dust from the ceiling.

"Am I dead?" Naji murmured under Tariq's arms, his voice weak but audible.

Hamza chuckled, relief washing over him as he realized Naji had recovered somewhat from the blast. "Not yet, you ass. Nearly scared me and Tariq for a second there," Hamza replied.

"We're hiding out in a building right now that's furthest away from the center. We should be fine for now," he added, glancing around the makeshift refuge they had found. It wasn't much, but it was away from the immediate danger, giving them a momentary breath of safety as they regrouped and planned their next move.

Naji grabbed Tariq's collar, pulling himself close until their faces were inches apart.

"They're going to kill us all. We should just run for the dunes!" Naji panicked, his voice cracking with fear.

"Keep it down, Naji," Tariq growled, his gaze intense as he scanned their surroundings. "If they wanted to wipe out the entire hive, then we'd be dead already. Something else is going on—it's almost like they're trying to push us back and pick out the weak. Most of the buildings are still standing too. They're not razing us down."

"Then what the hell are they doing?" Hamza asked, his brow furrowed in confusion and worry.

"I don't know, but Taliba may have been right about why this was happening. We managed to piss off the Sultan by stealing from his general, and now that he probably has Rafi, he probably has all the information he needed."

"Rafi wouldn't sell us out like that," Hamza pouted, his voice a mix of hope and denial.

"We don't know that," Tariq shrugged. "But this isn't an extermination. This is a lesson, and the Sultan is the teacher."

Suddenly, a man at the door shouted, his voice urgent and filled with alarm, "Hide! Hide! Mamluks are coming!"

Immediately, the room was filled with a flurry of movement as everyone scrambled to find cover, their hearts pounding as the threat of discovery loomed over them once again.

The establishment plunged into panic as the pounding hooves of a large Mamluk force echoed down the empty streets, a thick cloud of dust rising in their wake. As if the Mamluks weren't threat enough, the thinning dust revealed the ominous shadows of Ghazi formations advancing behind them. Their march reverberated through the building's foundation, shaking both its structure and the fragile resolve of those hiding inside.

"We are *not* fighting *that*!" a man shouted over the indistinct crowd. "We need to run!"

"Run where, *fool*!?" another man retorted. "No matter where we go, we are either going to get cut down, or the desert will claim us! I say we fight! The gods are testing us!"

"The gods had already forsaken us if they allowed to let the blood flow this far and many!" a woman cried.

As always, the people of the lower hive failed to unite under a single decision, let alone a common banner. Panic and exhaustion had worn down every survivor, and it showed in their frayed tempers and strained bodies. The crowd erupted into clashing viewpoints—some calling for rebellion, others for passivity or prayer. Caught in the middle of the chaos, the three children found themselves swept into the growing turmoil.

"What do we do?" Hamza asked, turning to both Naji and Tariq, his voice thick with urgency.

Tariq shrugged, his expression stoic in the face of danger, while Naji pushed himself up from the rough floor.

"We brace. If we run, we'll be singled out in no time. When the gold tongues hit us, we got to use the crowd and the confusion to get away. That's my best bet," Tariq explained, his voice steady despite the rising tension.

"They're charging!" the man at the door shouted, his eyes wide with fear. He quickly bolted away from the entrance to avoid being crushed if the Mamluks broke through.

"Stay with me, guys," Tariq murmured to his brothers. "We'll get out once they strike."

The thunder of horses' hooves grew louder, prompting everyone inside to retreat from the front of the building, desperate to avoid being the first to face trampling or blades. Tension thickened as they braced for impact—some squeezing their eyes shut, others whispering prayers for mercy from the gods.

Suddenly, a loud war horn blared, its echo reverberating through the entire lower hive. The piercing sound caught everyone off guard, including the children, who braced for the order to raze the next row of buildings. To their astonishment, the horde of Mamluks and Ghazi came to a gradual halt. A single, elaborately adorned Mamluk rode to the front of the formation, his imposing presence accentuated as he raised his halberd high.

"Cease the assault!" the Mamluk ordered loudly. "The horn calls! Round it back! Cease the assault!"

"*Cease the assault! Round back!*" Several of the Sultan's men repeated.

To the people's surprise and relief, the Sultan's men began to split off to either side of the wide street, marching back the way they had come. Their disciplined retreat left the helpless onlookers untouched. The war horn sounded once more, its deep bellow signaling the riders to pull their reins and withdraw. The Ghazi soldiers held their position, waiting for the Mamluks to fully clear to the rear before following suit with the same measured precision.

"Round back!" a Ghazi commanded, his voice sharp and authoritative. The order was quickly echoed by several others, their shouts ringing out in unison.

The people watched as the Sultan's men redirected themselves up the hill, fading into the blur of sand clouds they kicked up.

"What just happened?" a man murmured from the crowd, his voice filled with disbelief as he watched the retreating soldiers.

"We're saved! The gods have graced us!" a woman nearby cheered, her voice rising with hope as relief washed over the onlookers, replacing the fear that had gripped them moments before.

Once the streets were clear of the Sultan's men, the people began to cautiously emerge from the building, still wary of their surroundings. Survivors from nearby buildings also stepped back into the sunlight, some cheering, others lost in despair. Those who refrained from joining the celebration felt no cause for joy. While they had saved their own lives, the lower hive was in ruins—countless businesses, homes, and lives had been torn apart in the blink of an eye.

The children carefully made their way out the door, taking in the scene before them—people cheering, praying, and mourning the dead scattered across the landscape. They, too, felt relief, but it was tempered with the weight of the devastation around them. Their emotions were not as joyous as the others; the sight of the destruction stilled any celebration in their hearts.

"It's actually over," Naji murmured, his jaw hanging in disbelief as he surveyed the aftermath.

"Yes—but look at what they took with them," Tariq said, his voice heavy, frowning as he gestured toward the lifeless bodies scattered across the ground. His expression was grim but unshaken by the horror surrounding them. "*We* caused this."

"Don't say that, Tariq," Hamza spat, his voice rising with anger and frustration. "This is the doing of the gold tongues and the Sultan. They're goddamn evil."

The children scoured about, trying to orient themselves in the disarray of the lower hive. Everywhere they looked, those who had been bickering moments before were now helping each other—putting out lingering fires and responding to cries for help from those trapped beneath fallen debris. People scooped handfuls of sand to douse the flames, while others rushed to the nearest pond, carrying water back in a desperate bid to extinguish the fire.

As the citizens scrambled to provide relief, the children kept their eyes on the land of bodies that had not been so fortunate. They saw men, women, and children whose guts had been gouged out, some charred, others missing limbs. Some of the children were still clutched tightly in their mothers' arms, their faces frozen in expressions of fear.

"I hope Habi and Taliba are alright," Hamza pouted, his voice laced with concern as he scanned the surroundings nervously.

"I just hope we don't find them among these bodies," Tariq frowned, his gaze sweeping over the chaotic aftermath with a heavy heart.

"Let's not think about that," Naji suggested, trying to inject a note of optimism, even though his own voice trembled slightly with fear.

Tariq froze when he spotted a child face down, her long hair resembling Taliba's. The girl was mangled, tangled among a heap of other victims. With careful steps, Tariq navigated over the piles of bodies, gently rolling the child onto her back. A wave of disgust washed over him as he gazed at the horrific, disfigured face, but a deep sense of relief followed. It wasn't Taliba who had perished.

Tariq cursed under his breath as he continued to guide the others through the wreckage, his gaze occasionally flicking to the bodies scattered around him. With each stumble, he prayed he was wrong about Habi and Taliba—hoping, against all odds, that they weren't among the dead.

"Let's get out of here," Tariq sighed, his tone heavy with exhaustion.

"Aye," Hamza and Naji agreed, nodding solemnly as they prepared to move, eager to leave the devastation behind and find their friends—or at least, a safer place to regroup and plan their next steps.

—

Some time before the ceasefire, Habi and Taliba remained huddled within the narrow confinements of the alleyways, convinced it was their best chance to stay safe and survive. Both were still mourning the decision to leave Sara behind, but they knew they had no other choice. The occasional clash of steel against steel rang out through the maze of alleyways, a constant reminder that danger was never far off.

"Ta-Taliba, I'm tired," Habi cried, her small voice quivering with exhaustion.

"I know, Habi, but we can't stop moving! Just a little longer!" Taliba said, her voice also strained from fatigue but firm with determination, encouraging her sister to keep going despite the overwhelming odds.

As Taliba tried to comfort Habi, the latter suddenly collapsed from sheer exhaustion, tripping and falling hard onto the ground. She barely managed to catch herself, her hands scraping against the rough sand beneath her.

"Taliba—help me," Habi whimpered.

As soon as Habi dropped, Taliba spun around and rushed back to her. With all her remaining strength, she pulled Habi to her feet, silently thanking the gods for making her light enough to lift. As Taliba helped Habi to her feet, a sudden, sharp clank of metal echoed directly behind her. She froze, her heart racing, before jumping in sheer terror.

A Mamluk had stepped into their small sanctuary, his short sword hanging menacingly by his waist. As the armored giant turned toward them, the children scrambled away, their hearts pounding in their chests, breath coming in desperate, uncontrollable gasps.

The Mamluk gave chase, his heavy footsteps echoing as the two girls darted in frantic, erratic directions down the winding alleyways. It wasn't until Taliba abruptly stopped that Habi realized, too late, they had run straight into a dead end. Piles of trash towered before them, blocking any escape. Habi's heart seemed to stop as she turned to face the looming figure of the Mamluk closing in.

Before Taliba could even suggest hiding inside the trash pile, the Mamluk had already closed the distance.

"Taliba!" Habi cried out, wrapping her arms tightly around her sister.

"I'm sorry!" Taliba cried along, her voice breaking as she hugged Habi back, her body instinctively moving to shield her younger sister with a protective embrace, demonstrating her unwavering resolve to keep her safe.

As the Mamluk drew and raised his sword, poised to strike the children down, a deep, resonant war horn suddenly blared, echoing across the lower hive and bouncing off the walls of the narrow alley. The Mamluk froze, his attention momentarily torn as the sound filled the air.

When the horn sounded again, the Mamluk hesitated, his grip loosening on the hilt of his sword. With a swift motion, he retracted the blade, sheathing it at his hip, his eyes scanning the alley as if waiting for further orders.

Habi, still clutching Taliba tightly, dared a glance at the slits in the Mamluk's helmet. Through the shadows of the visor, she saw a pair of green eyes, almost haunting in their intensity. For a fleeting moment, Habi thought she was imagining things, but she could've sworn the eyes reflected regret and sorrow—so vivid, it almost seemed as if the man were on the verge of tears.

"Round back!" other voices shouted from the alleyways.

The Mamluk gave the two girls one last, lingering look before lowering his head. Without a word, he turned and retreated, his heavy footsteps fading as he disappeared around the corner.

"I was right," Taliba let out a sigh of relief, her voice trembling with emotion. "It was temporary—we survived! Habi, we made it!" Her words were filled with hope and relief as she hugged Habi closer, grateful for their escape from imminent danger.

While Taliba quietly celebrated their narrow escape, Habi remained still, wiping the remnants of tears from her cheeks. Her frown deepened, not just out of pity for those who had fallen, but for the Mamluk they had encountered as well. She couldn't shake the haunting image of his sorrowful eyes.

"Habi, are you okay?" Taliba asked, reaching down to help her sister to her feet.

"I'm okay. I'm happy that we are alive," Habi responded, managing a small smile despite the turmoil around them. "But I can't help but feel bad for that knight."

"Why would you feel bad for him? He nearly killed us if those horns didn't sound off," Taliba remarked, her tone reflecting her confusion and slight irritation. "But he could've still killed us even after the horn went off," Habi frowned, her expression thoughtful. "I think he was nice—maybe he was just following orders."

"Following orders and committing to the slaughter is still a bad thing, Habi. Don't worry about them," Taliba advised firmly, giving both herself and Habi a quick pat down to ensure they were unharmed before cautiously peeking around the corner. "Come on, I think it's clear. We need to find the others."

"Okay," Habi replied, nodding in agreement. However, her mind couldn't help but drift back to Sara and Rafi. The thought of them sent a wave of quiet, gnawing despair through her.

—

After the ceasefire, an alleyway was littered with the lifeless bodies of Ghazi and Mamluks, their forms crumpled and packed between the walls. The walls themselves were deeply scratched, some sections missing large chunks. One Mamluk groaned weakly as he removed his helmet, desperate for air. He slumped against the wall, clutching the dent in his armor where the blow had landed. He knew he was dying—blood coughed up and spat out in thick, red splatters. The brutal strike to his lower abdomen had fractured his ribs, likely puncturing his lungs. Breathing had become a laborious task, and he recoiled when he saw an elderly man looming over him.

"The horn sounded—the fight is over. Please, I was just following orders," the Mamluk pleaded, choking.

Saif Sabbah knelt down, bringing himself eye to eye with the wounded Mamluk. In his right hand, he gripped a bloodied short sword, its dark crimson stain glistening in the dim light of the alley.

"Did it ever cross your mind—that this order would question your morals? That thousands of innocent lives would perish under your hands?" Saif hissed, his voice dripping with contempt. "All for what? The Sultan's praise? A few ribbons across your pauldron? You're not a soldier—you're a puppet."

"Please, I have a family. If you know the Sultan, then you know the consequences," the Mamluk begged, his voice breaking as the weight of his actions and their implications suddenly became too much to bear.

Saif paused for a moment, his gaze cold and unyielding. He showed no pity for the man before him, his expression hardening as he took in the Mamluk's suffering.

"Shame—shame to know that your wife will be without a husband, and your children without a father—as I have a family too—a family where you people just raided and slaughtered," Saif said, his voice low and heavy with bitter reproach. His eyes bore into the Mamluk, reflecting a deep well of grief and anger from the losses he had endured.

Before the Mamluk could search for any sign of humanity in Saif's eyes, Saif drove his blade up under the man's jaw, the steel piercing through to the other side of his cheek. With a brutal twist, Saif wrenched the blade and the man's head, using the handle as leverage. The sound of cracking bones filled the air as the man's neck snapped. In that instant, the Mamluk's life was extinguished, and he slumped, lifeless against the wall.

After the last of the patrol had been dealt with, Saif stood up, wiping the blood from his blade before sheathing it under his sash beneath his dark cloak. He straightened, his eyes hardening with resolve as he continued down the alleyway, moving with a clear purpose. His gaze swept the area, vigilant and sharp, searching for any sign of his loved ones or anyone he held dear. Each step was measured, his senses alert to any further danger or the possibility of finding those he hoped were still safe.

Almost immediately, a small group of rebels emerged from a nearby alley, startled by Saif's sudden and nonchalant appearance. Their hands instinctively moved toward their weapons, but they froze when they recognized the cloaked figure. A tense silence hung in the air as they assessed the man before them.

"Saif, praise thee," one of the rebels said, releasing his hand from the handle of his blade as he approached. "It seems that their slaughter has come to an end."

"How many of our people suffered?" Saif asked.

"Many brothers and sisters were lost, Saif. The attack was sudden, but they all fought valiantly. This will delay our future efforts," the man explained, his face marked with the grief of loss yet tempered by the resolve that defined their struggle.

"Aye," Saif nodded solemnly. "They knew what they signed up for. They are lucky to dine with the gods for fighting against such tyranny."

"Aye," the rebels agreed, their voices a chorus of weary determination.

Saif rubbed his beard thoughtfully, his eyes scanning his loyal followers—those who had sworn to help disrupt the Sultan and his forces. He took a moment to steady himself before preparing to ask the next question.

"Have any of you seen any children as of late? Three boys and two girls. One girl has gold eyes," Saif tensed up a bit as he asked, his voice betraying a hint of urgency.

The rebels exchanged uncertain glances, silently questioning one another, as they tried to recall any details that might match the broad descriptions Saif had provided.

"We have not seen any living children or a golden-eyed child as of late. Most of the children we saw had already fallen," the man answered somberly.

"I see," Saif frowned, his concern deepening. "Any word from Sara?"

"Sara has yet to report back to us," another rebel spoke up. "She was in charge of this district, as you ordered. We have not seen her."

"Very well then," Saif sighed, the weight of his responsibilities pressing heavily on him. "Go provide aid to the citizens and help them recover what life they can. I will continue on my own."

"Aye, Saif. Stay safe," the man said, offering a nod of respect.

"As for you all," Saif replied, his tone firm yet inspiring, "stay vigilant and be ready. We must be prepared for what may come next. The fight is far from over."

The group dispersed in several directions, each of them searching for survivors, while Saif continued down the path where the alleyways twisted into a maze. The deeper he ventured, the more he encountered a growing number of dead bodies—rebels and Sultan's men alike, often piled on top of one another in the narrow corridors. Innocent men, women, and children lay scattered among them. Saif's gaze lingered on the fallen, his eyes filling with sorrow. He wished he had known about the Sultan's sudden, brash decision. He had not anticipated a slaughter of this magnitude.

As Saif turned the corner, he stumbled upon a small group of bodies—two of his own people and two Mamluks. He glanced over most of them, but his attention was drawn back to the woman who leaned against the wall. He held his breath, a tightness in his chest, and dropped to a knee to get a closer look at her mangled face. The sight was haunting, the once familiar features now distorted beyond recognition. His heart sank as he tried to make sense of what he was seeing.

"Sara," Saif murmured in dread.

Sara lay exactly as she had been left, her hand still resting on her stomach, the other loosely gripping a bloody dagger. But the once fierce and determined woman was now barely recognizable. Half of her head had been caved in, exposing bone and brain matter beneath the shattered skull. Her jaw hung limply, dislocated, and her eyes, empty and lifeless, stared vacantly at the ground. The sight was a grotesque reminder of the brutality they faced, and Saif's breath caught in his throat as he struggled to process the image before him.

"I'm so sorry," Saif frowned, his voice thick with emotion as he struggled to hold back his tears. "I'm so, very sorry."

As Saif mourned, the soft scuttle of little feet reached his ears. His head snapped to the side, and he caught sight of two small figures in his peripherals. His dread, which had weighed heavily on him, slowly began to lift, replaced by a surge of unexpected joy. His heart quickened as he recognized the familiar shapes, hope stirring once more.

"Father!" Taliba called out, happily rushing over to him.

"Father!" Habi shouted along, joining her sister in the reunion.

"Taliba! Habi!" Father called back, opening his arms and embracing the both of them as they relished in his warmth. "Oh, thank the gods that you're both safe!"

Father, after finally reuniting with some of his children, broke down in tears.

"Where's Hamza, Tariq, and Naji?" Father asked, his voice shaking with concern.

"I don't know. We got separated when everything went off," Taliba replied, trying to maintain a hopeful tone. "I'm sure that they're okay though!"

"Father—is that Sara?" Habi suddenly asked, her eyes widening in horror as she noticed a lifeless body behind Father.

Father sucked in his lips and answered, only because there was no point in hiding the truth in this grim reality they lived in.

"Yes—that is Sara. Do not worry, little one—she fought bravely," Father said, his voice thick with grief but steady, as he tried to reassure Habi.

"Sara saved us," Taliba whimpered, tears welling up in her eyes. "She took out the Mamluks and told us to get away. I wanted to help, but–"

"Say no more, child," Father counseled Taliba gently, placing a comforting hand on her shoulder. "It was her wish. Knowing her, she didn't want any harm to come to you two. She did what she felt was necessary to protect you."

Habi whimpered softly, her hand trembling as she gently placed it on Sara's thigh. She kept her gaze fixed on the ground, unable to look at the terror still etched on Sara's face. The sight was too much for her to bear, and she sought comfort in the small, familiar touch, trying to block out the horror around them.

HABI

"Thank you, Sara," Habi murmured, her voice soft and filled with gratitude as tears streamed down her cheeks.

Father rubbed Habi's back soothingly, his grip firm yet gentle as he lifted her onto his shoulder. He took Taliba's hand in his, guiding her away from the gruesome scene.

"Are we just going to leave her there?" Taliba asked, her voice laced with worry.

"No, I will return to give her a proper burial. We need to find the others right now," Father reassured her.

"Okay," Taliba responded, her expression still troubled but accepting her father's plan.

As the trio departed, Habi cast one final glance at Sara's body, her hand lifting in a slow, somber wave. Unbeknownst to Father and Taliba, Habi's eyes lingered a moment longer, and in that fleeting moment, she saw something that made her heart skip—Sara, standing beside her own lifeless form, waving back with a smile that was both warm and bittersweet.

"I'll see you soon," Habi lightly whispered.

—

Tariq, Hamza, and Naji found themselves in one of the market areas of the lower hive. Once a bustling hub of trade and life, it was now a grim landscape, littered with trash, ashes, debris, and the bodies of the fallen. The air was thick with the sound of mourning—mothers weeping for their children, husbands for their wives.

Children, their faces streaked with dirt and tears, called out for parents they couldn't find, their voices lost amidst the chaos.

"Just how many of us died?" Naji frowned, his eyes scanning the devastation around them.

"I don't want to know," Hamza said, shaking his head, his voice thick with unease.

"It doesn't matter right now," Tariq interjected, trying to keep the focus on their immediate survival.

"Tariq, come on man, there's so much death and blood everywhere. Other kids are cryin' for hell's sake," Hamza gestured towards the mess surrounding them, his frustration evident.

"Let's be *real* here," Tariq growled, his voice hardening as he jabbed a finger at Hamza and Naji. "We're not dead, even though sometimes we wish we were. We're still stuck in the slums. The fewer people alive, the more goods there are for us. The fewer enemies we make. Every single one of us got screwed over by the Sultan's law, and we feel it every damn day. Sure, I mourn for the dead—but that doesn't mean I want them back. All we can do now is clean up and accept that, maybe, we'll have more food for our bellies." His words, harsh and pragmatic, cut through the air, a stark reminder of their harsh reality.

Hamza and Naji pouted, shocked by Tariq's statement. It may have been a morbid take, but he was right.

"If there's less people, then there's less people who can fight the Sult—" Naji began, his voice carrying a hint of desperation, but Tariq cut him off.

"Who's going to fight the Sultan, Naji!?" Tariq erupted, his frustration boiling over. "Those folks took Rafi! A single Ghazi can wipe out dozens of us! A single Mamluk—hundreds of us! We're screwed! Just accept it. Rafi's dream is down the drain—it left with him."

"Still assertive against little Naji as always, aren't you, Tariq?" a familiar voice chimed in, a man carrying a golden-eyed child on his shoulder, with another child holding his hand.

"Father!" the boys called, their faces lighting up with joy as they rushed over to him, carefully avoiding the debris scattered across the ground.

"You're okay! You're all okay!" Hamza cheered, his voice breaking with a mixture of joy and relief as he embraced his family. The heavy burden of fear and uncertainty that had clung to him dissolved in the warmth of their reunion.

"Aye, son," Father said, his face stern yet relieved. "Yet there's no time to rest. If our shed still remains standing, you will all take shelter while I provide aid to the others who need it. I expect all of you to handle yourselves when I am away."

"And if the shed is gone?" Tariq asked, his tone serious, anticipating the worst.

"There's several vacancies," Father replied succinctly.

—

After a long detour toward the street that housed their shed, the family finally arrived, passing several citizens who were laboring to carry bodies into organized piles. It would take time—perhaps never—to fully cleanse the streets of their grim waste. As they walked, the children noticed familiar buildings and tents, many of which had either been reduced to ashes or collapsed entirely. Yet, against the odds, their shed had only suffered a few burns, with small pieces of shrapnel embedded in its walls. It stood as a small, fragile haven amidst the devastation.

Father took the lead, knocking on the door to make sure no squatters had taken shelter during the raid. He waited a few moments, his ear pressed to the door, before slowly pushing it open. The interior of the shed was empty, the familiar clutter of their home in disarray. The desk and shelf had tipped over, scattered across the floor. A thick layer of sand, carried in by the endless stream of passersby, littered the room, covering the floor and their bedrolls. It was a mess, but at least it was still theirs.

"And so she stands," Father commented as they approached their still-intact shed. "You children know what to do. I will return as soon as I can—maybe even with food and water if there's any left."

"Aye," the children acknowledged, ready to hunker down and maintain their makeshift sanctuary.

"Oh, and Taliba—return the book to my desk." Father's tone was firm, emphasizing the importance of keeping the book safe, a silent acknowledgment of its value beyond just paper and ink.

Taliba, still clutching Father's book in her hand, had managed to keep it safe. Though she hadn't had time to go over it with Habi—constantly on the move, with little time for anything else—she was relieved that the vital information it contained was secure. She also felt a small sense of comfort knowing that, despite everything, Habi seemed to be returning to herself. Though Taliba was sure Habi still carried the weight of Rafi's absence, for now, she appeared to be distracted by other matters, allowing a brief moment of normalcy amidst the turmoil.

As soon as Taliba returned the book to its rightful place, Father gave a small smirk and nodded approvingly. Without saying a word, he turned and left the shed, his steps purposeful as he disappeared into the haze of the chaotic streets.

"I can't believe we're alive," Hamza said, his voice carrying a mix of relief and disbelief as he aimlessly kicked at the piles of sand that had gathered around their feet.

"That's what we do. We survive," Tariq responded.

"Hey, help me clean this place up," Taliba demanded, her voice assertive as she pulled a broom out from under the layers of sand and debris. She was ready to restore some order to their battered shelter.

After Taliba barked orders, the children immediately set to work. Taliba swept the floor, pushing the thick layer of sand aside, while Tariq and Naji worked together to fix the books and shelf, returning some semblance of order. Hamza took to the exterior, inspecting for any major damage, while Habi focused on the bedrolls. As she shook them free of sand, she lifted Rafi's small wooden board, confirming the safety of his stash beneath it. Though the box was partially submerged in sand, when she opened it, the valuables inside were intact and untouched.

As Habi shook out her own bedroll, the Rafi-kissed gald coin slipped from its folds and landed softly at her feet. She paused, her heart skipping a beat, before gently placing the bedroll back down. Kneeling, she retrieved the coin, carefully cleaning it with her thumb before pressing it to her lips in a quiet, tender kiss. The simple act brought a fleeting moment of comfort, as if Rafi's presence lingered just a little longer with her.

"Got a live one 'ere!" a man yelled from outside, his voice sharp and urgent.

Following the man's shout, a crowd began to gather, their voices rising in an uproar, filled with contempt and harsh slang. The children instantly halted their work, adrenaline kicking in as they ran toward the door. They peeked their heads out, where Hamza was already standing, observing the scene outside with quiet intensity. Habi was the last to join them, her movements slow as she carefully secured her beloved gald coin in her pocket.

Out on the streets, a mob of citizens quickly gathered, their voices rising in fury as they surrounded a single Ghazi soldier. One man, seething with anger, kicked the soldier relentlessly in the ribs and back, forcing him to stagger forward. The soldier, beaten and exhausted, struggled to stay on his feet, his armor clinking with each blow. The crowd's jeers and curses filled the air, as the mob's growing tension made it clear that they had no mercy left for the enemy.

"They're going to string him alive," Taliba murmured, her voice tinged with a complex mix of emotions.

"Good," Tariq responded coldly.

The Ghazi soldier was a young man, his clothing tattered and his broken chest plate barely hanging on. His face was a grotesque canvas of bruises, blood, and tears, the pain of his ordeal evident in every line. He raised his arms in a desperate, trembling plea, his voice cracking as he begged for his life. Despite his broken form, he looked out at the mob, hoping for mercy that seemed unlikely to come. His eyes darted nervously, scanning the crowd for any sign of compassion, but all he found was contempt.

"Found this gold tongue hiding under some rocks!" the man shouted, his voice filled with cruel amusement. With a final kick to the young Ghazi's ribs, he sneered, "Boy's cryin' for his mommy!" He mimicked the pathetic cries of a toddler, his voice high-pitched and mocking. The crowd erupted into laughter, their jeers and taunts growing louder as they circled the helpless soldier. The mob's restlessness was palpable, their anger fueling the cruel spectacle, while the young Ghazi, barely able to keep himself upright, trembled under the weight of their ridicule.

"Mercy!" the young Ghazi pleaded. "I'm still young! I was just following orders! I was–"

"Shut yer stupid ass up, gold tongue!" a woman shouted. "You lot took my son away from me!"

The crowd roared, their voices a chaotic mixture of rage and twisted excitement, as they reveled in their cruel dominance over the Ghazi. They spat on him, their insults blending together into a cacophony of hate and mockery. The soldier was drowned in the chorus of voices, his cries unheard beneath the crowd's relentless chanting. The mob savored every moment, tormenting him for their own satisfaction, until a man suddenly emerged from the throng, a gleaming dagger raised high. The blade gleamed in the harsh sunlight as he hovered over the Ghazi, his intent clear—this was no longer just a mockery; it was a sentence.

"I say that he gets a stab from every man, woman, and child 'ere! Yeah!?" the man bloated, waving his arms to entice the crowd.

"Yeah!" The crowd yelled.

"Stab the ass hat where it hurts without killin' 'em quick, yeah!? Make the slob cry for his stupid mama and papa, yeah!?"

The crowd surged with manic energy, their cheers deafening as they pressed in closer, eager for their turn. Each person seemed to crave a piece of the brutality, eyes wide with a mix of fury and exhilaration. The dagger gleamed ominously in the air, a symbol of their vengeance. They jeered and shouted, urging the man with the blade to strike, hungry for blood, their bodies jostling with anticipation.

"Wait, wait–" the Ghazi pleaded, but the man had already driven the dagger straight into his gut, immediately pulling it back out.

The young Ghazi screamed in agony as the crowd cheered, spitting on him as he writhed in pain.

"That's for me wife and son!" the man roared, his voice thick with rage as he pointed at a random woman in the huddle. "Come on, lass! You next!"

A young woman stepped forward, her face partially burned from shrapnel and a grenade blast. The man handed her the bloodied dagger, and the crowd urged her on, their cheers growing louder.

Four men held the Ghazi down by his limbs as he cried and whimpered, his eyes locked on the mutilated face of the woman approaching him.

"For my child," the woman hissed, striking the man's gut with the dagger.

The crowd continued to roar as the woman handed the dagger to a boy, stepping to the sidelines to watch.

"You took all of my friends!" the boy growled, stabbing the Ghazi in the gut as well.

The trend continued until every last person in the mob had their turn. With each scream and cry from the young Ghazi, the crowd drowned out his agony with their cheers and laughter.

"Let's go back inside," Taliba suggested, her tone firm as she turned away from the escalating scene.

"But I want to watch," Hamza protested, his curiosity outweighing his unease.

"Go back inside and clean the shed," Taliba growled, not giving him a choice as she retreated into the shelter.

Hamza cursed under his breath, dragging his feet as he followed the others inside. "Okay, but I was already outside, jerk," he muttered, begrudgingly accepting his fate.

With that, the children spent the rest of the day tidying up the shed, restoring it to its former state. Sooner or later, the mob that had formed in the streets would dissipate, returning to their duties of rebuilding and rescuing, leaving the young Ghazi to rot.

Father returned with bags of scavenged potatoes and buckets of water as promised. Together, the family watched the day turn into night, eating, cleaning, and comforting each other. As the hive slowly returned to its usual state, the children finally found peace under the familiar shelter of their home. All of them fell into a deep slumber, including Father, exhausted from the long and difficult day. Habi, however, struggled to sleep, her mind racing with thoughts. But as she clenched the small gald coin in her hand and cleared her thoughts, she eventually drifted into a peaceful rest.

Galdi opta ki-le, the whispers crooned.

Chapter Twenty-five

Habi woke up to a familiar dark plain of existence. She wasn't afraid, nor at peace—she was simply tolerant. The air was thick with the presence of something otherworldly, and as soon as she heard the whispers, she knew the dead were returning to her. There were more of them now, more than ever before, ever since *The Culling*.

Instead of panicking as she usually would, Habi chose to patiently wait for a visitor. Over time, since discovering her ability to speak with the dead, she had begun to notice the unwritten rules they followed—rules that governed their visits and interactions with her in this eerie void. It was a strange, unsettling system, but it was one she had come to accept.

Habi had learned over time that the dead only appeared when they wanted to be seen. In her waking hours, they required a great deal of energy to manifest, and their presence often felt heavy, lingering in the air. But in her dreams, she was vulnerable—at rest, with no way to resist their visits. The dead spoke in either the common tongue or Koumaic, often telling their tales, but leaving no solid answers behind. Sometimes, they spoke in riddles that left Habi confused and unsettled. From what she understood, the dead could only manifest in the state they had perished in, trapped in the form they had been when they died.

She was about to learn how wrong she was.

The air around her shifted, and dark, grainy sand began to swirl, twisting around her in erratic patterns. Habi felt a strange pull in the atmosphere, as if something—or someone—was about to reveal itself in a way that defied the rules she had come to understand.

One moment, Habi was patiently awaiting the familiar visit of the dead, but in the blink of an eye, everything changed. The grains of sand around her twisted and contorted into shapes that made her blood run cold. The forms took shape—deformed figures with gaping jaws and long, jagged claws. Their limbs were unnaturally thin, skeletal, their bony fingers stretching toward her like the claws of predators.

As the creatures gathered around her, their grotesque forms looming ever closer, Habi's breath quickened. Fear surged through her body. She fell to the ground, scrambling backwards, her heart pounding in her chest. Her body trembled, her eyes wide with terror as the creatures reached for her, their hollow eyes filled with hunger.

Her mind screamed for her to run, but she was trapped in the void, her surroundings as hostile and unfamiliar as the creatures closing in on her. Panic took over, and she whimpered, her voice barely a whisper in the vast emptiness. There was no escape, no way out.

"Help me!" a creature cried out desperately. "Help me! Help me!"

As the creatures closed in on her, some began to cry out in distorted, pleading voices, their calls echoing through the void. Their wails were maddening—sharp and unearthly, each cry more desperate than the last. The sound pierced through Habi's mind like a dagger, threatening to tear her apart. Some of the creatures, twisted and broken, reached out for her with clawed hands, while others let out blood curdling screams that vibrated the very air, their voices warping into something neither human nor alive.

"*Galdi opta ki-le*! *Necromantia*! *Yariz moite*!" the creatures screamed.

The grainy figures crawled over Habi, smothering her, their sand flooding her nostrils and mouth as she tried to scream. Their screeches echoed through the void until she lost consciousness, fading into black. But when she opened her eyes again, she could breathe. The creatures had vanished, and the void before her began to shift into a peaceful garden, lush with greenery.

"Little Habi," a woman sang, catching Habi's attention.

"Sara!" Habi cried, rushing over to her and wrapping her arms around Sara's waist.

Sara bent down, wrapping her arms around Habi, her face lighting up with the same beautiful smile she always wore.

"I see that you are fine, golden-eyed child." Sara smiled. "All of you are. I am grateful."

"Sara, are you okay?" Habi asked, looking up at her with tears in her eyes.

"I am well, Habi. I feel no pain. As for you, little one—your journey is not over yet."

"What do you mean? Taliba says we're stuck here, and Rafi—well, I feel lonely without Rafi."

"You are only stuck if you truly believe you are." Sara cupped Habi's face. "And Rafi—I must tell you, he is safe and far from harm. As for loneliness—well, you have a loving father, many brothers, and a sister who cherish you dearly. Any one of them would give their life to protect you."

Habi smiled, hopping in joy.

"I love them all too!" Habi cheered. "But Rafi—I love him the most. He's always been there for me since I came to this home."

"And that's good, little one, but—even though he is free, he still needs help."

Habi's brow furrowed with worry.

"Huh?" she murmured.

"The Sultan is—" Sara began, but her voice suddenly faded, her lips still moving. "Do not—you—please—"

"Sara, I don't know what you're saying." Habi clung to her, frowning.

In an instant, the garden twisted into darkness, and Sara began to change. Her limbs contorted at unnatural angles, her skin darkening and roughening as a guttural scream tore from her throat. Her form warped into one of the sand creatures, its presence overwhelming. A surge of terror seized Habi, and she scrambled back, heart pounding, eyes wide with shock at the horrifying transformation.

"My child!" Sara wailed, her dark jaw gaping wide. "My child needs me! Help me! *Galdi opta ki-le, yariz moite*! I don't want to die!"

Sara's high-pitched cries suddenly ceased as Habi jolted awake from her nightmare. In that single dream, Habi felt she had uncovered a new rule of the dead.

Habi believed that if the ones who visited her had died recently, they never had time to properly rest or forget that they were no longer among the living. Each creature she encountered seemed trapped in a constant loop of their own death, crying and screaming as if their torment never ceased. Their desperate pleas for her to save them were unsettling, as if they weren't fully aware of their fate. All of these creatures were victims of The Culling, still burdened by the worries they carried in life. Hearing Sara, a woman Habi loved like a mother, scream for her child and beg not to die nearly broke her heart.

As Habi stood from her bed, lost in a trance-like state, Taliba watched her from the shadows, carefully lifting the blanket that covered her nose and mouth.

"You okay, Habi?" Taliba whispered, her soft words cutting through Habi's trance.

"Taliba, you're still awake?" Habi whispered back, blinking as if pulling herself back to the present.

"Yeah. Couldn't stay asleep. Still trying to accept the fact that this entire mess happened," Taliba whimpered, her voice raw with exhaustion. "How about you? You look like you've seen a ghost."

Habi turned her head toward Taliba, giving her a look that screamed, *Really*?

"Oh, right," Taliba murmured, pulling herself halfway out of the bedroll to chat with Habi, ignoring Hamza's snoring. "So, what did you see?"

"I saw Sara and many others who recently passed," Habi frowned, her voice barely above a whisper. "All of them were crying for help, and I could do nothing to save them."

Taliba crawled out of her bed and joined with Habi, hugging her.

"I don't know what to say," Taliba frowned, rubbing Habi's back gently. "What did Sara say?"

"She said that you all love me and that Rafi is fine—but he needs help," Habi explained, her voice uncertain.

"Rafi is fine? What?" Taliba blinked in confusion.

"Yes, she mentioned Rafi being free of danger, but then she—she—mentioned the Sultan before she—" Habi trailed off, struggling to put her experience into words, but Taliba understood without needing further explanation.

"You don't have to force yourself, Habi," Taliba comforted, giving her a reassuring squeeze. "Is that all you needed to get out?"

"She said that Rafi needs help, but I don't know how we can help him," Habi whimpered. "I want to help. I want him back, Taliba. But–"

"I don't think we can do anything, Habi," Taliba admitted, her voice heavy with reluctant acceptance. "If Sara mentioned the Sultan, then that means one thing—which means it's nearly impossible for us to help Rafi."

"Rafi is in the Sultan's tower?" Habi's voice quivered.

"Yes, exactly that."

Suddenly, Hamza stopped snoring and groaned, "Hey girls, I'm tryna sleep 'ere."

"Shut up, you," Taliba hissed, swatting Hamza on the nose with her palm.

"*Ow*! What the hell!?" Hamza cried, grabbing his nose.

The friendly banter was enough to make Habi let out a soft giggle, which in turn made Taliba smile.

"Let's go back to bed. We can chat about this later," Taliba whispered, kissing Habi on the forehead.

"Okay," Habi whispered back with a smile across her face.

While Hamza continued to groan and sob, drifting back to sleep, Taliba returned to her bedroll, trying to settle back into slumber. Habi spent a few moments staring at the ceiling, her thoughts swirling, before her eyes grew heavy, and she finally surrendered to the peaceful embrace of sleep.

—

Many moons had passed since The Culling, and the streets of the lower hive were slowly returning to their usual state, now free of the masses of bodies and debris. The air still carried the weight of what had transpired, but life, as it always did, pressed on.

Ghazi soldiers had once been stationed at every border gate, maintaining order through their imposing presence. But now, they no longer stood within the lower hive. Instead, they had withdrawn to the middle hive, sealing the iron doors behind them to prevent further conflict with the restless and enraged slum dwellers. Reports had already surfaced of Ghazi patrols being ambushed, attacked, and maimed, forcing the Sultan's forces to take precautions.

As a result, the soldiers were now positioned behind fortified walls, standing in disciplined formations rather than openly patrolling the lower hive. Without this quick reaction force, the slum's residents might have had a real chance to breach the middle hive, an outcome the Sultan's men would not allow. For now, the iron doors remained shut, keeping the two worlds divided.

Approaching along the middle hive's stone roads toward one of the border gates was a young, light-skinned woman, dressed in the tattered rags typical of a slum dweller, with a leather corset wrapped around her breasts, accentuating her figure. She wore ragged pants and a pair of dirty brown leather boots. In her hand, she held a rolled scroll, and a small ink jar with a quill was attached to a belt around her waist. Her brown, shaggy bob cut and sharp hazel eyes caught the attention of the guards on watch.

"Halt there, ma'am. I advise you go no further," one of the Ghazi commanded, holding his arm out in front of the large iron gate. His stance was firm, his gaze sharp with suspicion.

"I work with the Intelligence Service. I would advise that you let me through, soldier," the woman responded, her voice soft yet edged with authority.

The Ghazi narrowed his eyes, hesitating. "You *do* understand the dangers, right?" He raised a brow, unwilling to send a young woman to her demise. "The lower hive is not kind to outsiders, especially after The Culling."

"I do, and I'm on private business," the woman hissed, her patience thinning. With a swift motion, she revealed a silver pin tucked beneath her belt—an emblem shaped like an eye with a needle piercing through it.

The Ghazi stared at the pin, then shifted his gaze back to the woman, hesitating as he ran his tongue across the back of his teeth. After a moment, unwilling to argue further with an agent, he nodded at the other guard and signaled for the reaction team to keep watch as the gate creaked open, just in case the lower hive citizens were feeling bold today.

"Thank you, sir," the woman smiled and bowed, her demeanor polite yet calculated.

"Do you need an escort?" the Ghazi asked, his tone still carrying a hint of concern.

"No. That will draw too much attention, but thank you," she replied smoothly, adjusting her belt as she stepped forward.

"Aye."

As the soldiers positioned themselves around the gate, the operators pulled on the chains, slowly lifting the door. While the soldiers braced themselves, the woman showed no sign of concern, as the other side of the gate revealed only a dusty street and a lone homeless man scrambling away from the door that had disturbed his rest.

The woman walked through and crossed the boundary, waving a small smirk over her shoulder at the Ghazis as she passed. Once she was safely inside, the guards decided to seal the gate behind her, locking her within the ruined streets of the lower hive. The woman shot the homeless man a stern look as he spat in her direction before crawling away into a dark alley.

The woman rolled her eyes and unfurled the scroll, quickly darting her eyes over the words and keeping it angled away from the curious onlookers. She clicked her tongue in frustration as she rolled the scroll back up and tucked it into her belt, then began her trek through the dirty streets.

It wasn't long before she came into contact with other dwellers, many bearing wounds and burn scars from The Culling. To the citizens, she stood out like a sore thumb, an outsider among the ruined streets. None of them shied away—their eyes bore into her, full of hate and spite.

Though she may have looked the part, her gait, scent, and cleanliness betrayed her origins. She moved with too much purpose, her steps too controlled. She smelled of fresh linens and oils, untouched by the filth that clung to the lower hive.

The further she marched, the more the crowds began to reveal themselves to her Some sat in hushed conversation, others patched up their homes with whatever scraps they could salvage. A few fought over the remnants of a discarded meal, their desperation turning savage. The air was thick with the weight of survival, and every passing glance toward her carried the unspoken question—*why are you here*?

"You dun belong 'ere, girl!" a man shouted from the ruins of a crumbled building, his fingers gripping a burnt wooden pillar for balance. His voice was rough, slurred with either exhaustion or malice.

"Unless you wanna? Yeah?" he chuckled, his cracked lips stretching into a grin as he lewdly licked the air with his tongue, his eyes gleaming with something vile.

The woman ignored the man, not even sparing him a glance.

"Oi! Yer good 'nuff to work a brothel!" a woman cackled from the side, her voice thick with mockery.

"Keep walkin' like that, and the boys'll come pickin' you apart! Where's yer sword, *whore*!?" she sneered, her laughter mingling with the low murmurs of those who had taken notice, their eyes trailing the outsider with growing interest.

The woman ignored the woman as well, as she began attracting the gaze of nearly everyone down the street. Their eyes burned with feral intent, and they taunted her with warnings of the dangers that lay ahead if she continued on her path.

Another woman crossed her path, and out of nowhere, the local spat in her face, causing her to stagger back.

Everyone laughed and pointed at her, some even throwing trash and feces in her direction. As she panicked and wiped the spit off her face, she started running down the street, desperately trying to escape the growing mob. After some time, she glanced over her shoulder to confirm that no one was following her—and to her relief, there was no one in sight. However, she knew she wasn't out of danger yet, for that was the nature of the lower hive.

She tried to steady her breathing as she stopped to rest, hiding behind a ragged tent. Her body began to shake, and in response, she pulled a silver coin necklace from beneath her shirt, revealing the face of Shie, the Goddess of Mind and Knowledge. She whispered a prayer to it, her words soft and indistinct, until she was interrupted by two young boys standing right in front of her.

"Hello there, lady, whatcha doin'?" one of the boys asked, picking his nose.

The woman slowly regained her composure, kneeling down to the level of the children and forcing a small grin.

"Why you two look like nice ki–" the woman started, but before she could finish, the boys slapped her face and shoved her to the ground, seizing the pouch of gald tucked inside her belt. The woman was caught by surprise, unable to react quickly enough to recover and stop them. By the time she got back to her feet, the boys were already laughing and disappearing down an alleyway.

Everyone knew better than to give a stranger their initial attention. In this place, if someone approached another, it was usually for business—otherwise, it was most likely an altercation.

"*Stupid*!" one of the boys mocked, his laughter echoing as it faded into the distance.

"Oh Sultan, help me," the woman mumbled to herself, patting herself down.

"The hell you even doin' 'ere?" a bulky man growled, causing the woman to flinch in surprise.

The woman raised her arms, quietly pleading for her life as she slowly backed away from the man, who clearly had the scars of several knife fights.

"Oi, get back 'ere. I'm not a bad man, mid 'iver," the man waved, his hands open in a show of supposed goodwill.

"I'm not from the middle hive," she lied, her voice trembling just enough to sound uncertain. "How do I know I can trust you?"

"Well—you'd be dead, and I'd be ridin' ya. Think 'bout that," the man replied with a crude grin. "Youse too cute to be a slummy. I'd put a baby in ya if I wanted to. Though, ain't got nothin' 'gainst mid 'ivers. Some helped me back then when I was wee smaller."

"How do you know I'm from the middle hive?" the woman asked, slowly lowering her arms as she cautiously approached the man, keeping her guard up.

"Rich folk don't come down 'ere, less they want them sniff sniff, yeah?" the man chuckled. "The Culling, so everyone says it, gots everyone on edge. Surprised you ain't dead when you walked the gate."

"I didn't expect it to be—this bad," the woman frowned, glancing at the ruins around her.

The man burst into laughter, his voice hoarse but amused. "Oh girl! You ain't even seen the bad yet! Ha!" He wiped a tear from his eye before focusing on her again. "Say then, the hell you doin' 'ere? You a trader? Got family? Thoughts them gold tongues got them walls on hold."

"I'm with the media," the woman answered carefully. "I—I actually came down here to see if I could get some insight and document the people's experience—the ones who suffered from the Sultan's decision. Since you're the first *nice* person I've met, I was wondering if I could get your take on it."

"What's yer name?" the man asked, his eyes narrowing with interest.

"Raja Samaha. How about you, sir?"

"Folks call me 'Tiny.' Fittin', yeah? Ha!"

"Yeah, fitting," Raja faked a chuckle, eyeing Tiny's biceps, which were the size of her head. "So, are you willing to write a statement for me?"

"Dunno how to write," Tiny revealed. "Can tell ya, though, but for a price. If ya don't know how it works down 'ere, then maybe ya ought to feel that glimmy on yer ear, yeah?"

His grin widened, the implication clear.

Raja brought her hand up to her earlobe, rubbing one of her silver earrings. She knew exactly what Tiny would want in exchange for a fair trade of information, and at this point, she was desperate enough to do whatever it took to secure at least one cooperator.

"Oh, that's fine," Raja said, removing her silver studs and handing them to Tiny.

Tiny smirked, admiring the shine of the earrings in his palm. He couldn't wait to pawn them off for a decent amount of goods, but he was a man of his word. With a grunt, he secured the earrings in his ragged pocket and placed his large hand on Raja's back, guiding her down the side of a wide, sandy road.

"Thank ya fer that—but not 'ere though. Folks stab yer boob out if not careful. Come with me, I know a good place," Tiny suggested, his tone casual but laced with an underlying warning.

"Oh, okay then. Will I be safe?" Raja asked, her voice measured, though her fingers twitched slightly at her side, ready to react if needed.

Tiny bolstered another loud laugh, "Oi, Raja, you be safer than ever! You stay with me and no buddy will shank ya, yeah? They know me—I know you, easy, easy."

Raja, finally able to relax her shoulders for a moment, closely followed Tiny as they turned into an alleyway that wound through the lower hive, taking them away from the public eye and potential danger.

—

After some time, Tiny escorted Raja to a large establishment buzzing with life—people cheered, laughed, and sang, their voices mingling with the clinking of glasses. Armed guards stood at the entrance, keeping the rowdy crowd in check, their stench of alcohol thick in the air.

"What is this?" Raja asked, her eyes scanning the building and its surroundings with cautious curiosity.

"The Tavern, silly," Tiny laughed.

Raja rolled her eyes as Tiny pushed his way through the crowd, guiding her toward the front door.

"Make way! Make way! Gots a cutie behind me!" Tiny shouted, shoving and pushing the intoxicated patrons aside, who merely laughed in response. At least none of them were getting violent.

Once the two were inside, the cheers and music grew louder than ever. People danced on tables, gambled in the corners, and drank to their heart's content. A show was in full swing on stage, where a band played drums, cymbals, tambourines, and stringed instruments. On stage, five women adorned with gold and jewels swayed in their belly dancing outfits. All of them were beautiful, their figures sculpted like models—a sight that even made Raja feel a twinge of jealousy.

"Sexy, yeah!?" Tiny shouted over the roaring crowd, making sure Raja could hear him above the noise.

"Yeah—how is this a good spot!?" she yelled back, struggling to make out his words through the chaos.

"It safe! Trust me!" Tiny bellowed, flashing a grin as he pushed through the throng of people. "Follow, yeah!?"

Raja hesitated for a brief moment before sighing and weaving through the packed room after him, unsure whether to trust his definition of *safe*.

Tiny guided Raja to a secluded table in the far corner of The Tavern. Though it was away from the organized chaos, the sounds of laughter and music barely faded. It was when Tiny encountered a man with a pot belly, someone he seemed to recognize, that Raja started to wonder what kind of place she had walked into.

"Oi! Boss man! How goes it!?" Tiny smiled, spreading his arms out with joy.

"Tiny?" Gunther said. "I was wondering where you were. You were supposed to help the boys with the crowd. Now the place is overflowing!"

"My bad, boss man! Least gets the goods flowin', yeah!?"

Gunther rolled his eyes as he noticed Raja, then gave her a sly grin.

"And who are you, fine lady?" Gunther said with a smirk, bowing slightly as he lifted Raja's hand and pressed a light kiss against it.

"I'm Raja. I work for the media. Tiny brought me here so he could tell me his side of the story—his experience during The Culling. How about you, sir?" Raja asked, keeping her tone polite but professional.

"Oh? Nice to meet you, Raja," Gunther said with a grin, his eyes gleaming with interest. "My name is

Gunther Blythe, the owner of this fine establishment. Tiny here is a good friend of mine and part of my security team. A friend of Tiny is a friend of mine." He leaned back slightly, studying her with curiosity. "So, you want to know about our feelings toward The Culling? Well—mind if I join in too?"

"I don't mind, sir," Raja smiled, maintaining her composure.

"Drop the 'sir', Raja. Just call me Gunther," he said smoothly, flashing a more relaxed smile. "Please, please, let's take our seats. Shouldn't be long, yeah?"

"No si—Gunther, shouldn't be long at all," Raja corrected herself, offering a small nod.

Tiny happily pulled a chair out for Raja and Gunther, seating himself last. Raja unraveled the scroll once more, setting up her jar of ink and retrieving her quill. Instinctively, a barmaid walked over to the table, noticing her boss seated with two other guests.

"May I provide anything, sir?" the barmaid asked with a warm smile, her hands deftly adjusting the tray at her side.

"Glasses of water for all of us, Yasmeen. Thank you," Gunther requested, his tone casual yet firm.

After that, Yasmeen bowed and made her way to the bar, weaving skillfully through the crowd.

"Right then, I'll get started," Raja said, sitting up straight in her chair. "How was this establishment not affected by The Culling? Did your people fight off the threat and chase the soldiers away?"

Gunther chuckled. "The Sultan's men didn't even make it this far into the hive. From what people say, most of the lives and homes lost were closest to the walls, with some spreading to the outskirts. We're right next to the Sleeping Complex, and those folks—well, they take good care of us. I'm sure they did plenty of fighting, too."

Raja dipped her quill into the ink jar and wrote, moving on to the next set of questions.

"What's the Sleeping Complex?" Raja wondered, her curiosity piqued.

"You don't want to know," Gunther replied, his tone shifting slightly. "And I think they prefer those outside the lower hive not to know." He leaned in just a little, lowering his voice. "Just know that if it starts getting dark while the sun's still up, you're probably there."

Raja furrowed her brows, sensing the weight behind his words. Whatever the Sleeping Complex was, it wasn't just a place—it was a warning.

During the session, Yasmeen returned to the table with three glasses of water, and the patrons thanked her. Once they were satisfied, she moved on to the next wave of guests and customers.

Raja sipped from the glass as she took more notes.

"Were any of you affected in any way due to The Culling? If it's too sensitive, you don't have to share," Raja asked, careful not to push too hard.

"The Culling took out some of the folks that kept callin' me nasty words! Good riddance to them, ha!" Tiny laughed, slapping his knee.

Gunther, however, didn't share his amusement. He exhaled through his nose, his expression dimming. "As for me, I wasn't affected directly. But I know some of the people who lost their lives were regulars here. All of them were good folks." He drummed his fingers against the table before shaking his head. "People who didn't deserve it."

"I see," Raja said, taking note of their differing perspectives. "How do both of you feel about the Sultan's decision?"

Tiny laughed, spitting out some of his water and nearly splashing it on Raja and her scroll.

"He a bad man, but hell, don't mind some of us missin'," Tiny frowned, scratching at his chin. "Gettin' too crowded down 'ere, but sad to lose the good ones with it, yeah."

Gunther leaned back in his chair and sighed. "It was bound to happen sooner or later, but the rumors are all over the place. No one really knows why he did it. Some say it was his way of thinning the population. Others think he just did it because he wears the crown. Some claim it was the act of the gods." He paused for a moment, his gaze darkening. "And there are even rumors that a bunch of kids started the whole mess."

Raja's eyes darted up, sharpening at Gunther as the mention of kids caught her attention, even as she continued writing.

"You say one of the rumors may have been started by a bunch of kids. Do you happen to know their rumored names? Maybe even their descriptions?" Raja wondered, keeping her voice casual despite the weight of her question.

"Hell, Raja, I just hear things," Gunther chuckled, shaking his head. "Don't think anyone knows what the kids looked like, even if they were the reason. Just whispers in the dark, you know?"

Raja tapped a finger against the table, thinking for a moment before pressing further. "Then do you happen to know of the golden-eyed child that lives around here?"

Gunther's smile faded just slightly. Tiny stopped picking at his nails. The air between them shifted.

Gunther squinted at Raja, leaning forward in his seat and staring her dead in the eye. That alone made Raja realize Gunther was acquainted with the golden-eyed child.

"Why's that a question?" Gunther wondered, his gaze sharpening as he tried to read Raja's face.

Raja swallowed, shocked by Gunther's sudden change in demeanor. However, she decided to challenge him, leaning forward onto the table herself to ensure he didn't catch any suspicious changes in her expression.

"I've been receiving reports that the golden-eyed child was seen at every major incident and disaster, like The Culling—almost as if she's bringing bad luck with her," Raja said, keeping her voice steady. "I don't mean any harm to anyone—I just want to chat with her and see if those rumors are true. I'm not a superstitious person, unless it involves the gods themselves. Consider it one of those 'wonders' people love to read about on the side," she lied, maintaining unwavering eye contact with Gunther.

Gunther raised an eyebrow, still gauging her. "So she's just gonna be part of a side story?" he asked, his tone casual, but his eyes still searching hers for any hint of deception.

Raja noted in her mind that the golden-eyed child was a girl.

"Yes, that's all. I apologize if this is personal to you," Raja said, raising her palms in a gesture of reassurance.

"Sort of," Gunther admitted, exhaling through his nose as he leaned back in his chair. "I met the little one only once. A good friend of mine adopted her when she was young. To think that stories are already gathering around her is crazy to me." He chuckled, shaking his head, his tension easing slightly.

"Well, tell you what—I don't know where she lives, or if she's even alive, but I do know most of the kids like to play on the streets over there," Gunther said, gesturing toward The Tavern's wall. "If you want to hear about her and her 'bad luck' stories, you might find her around there. Whatever gets you the scoop, I guess."

"Oh, the work in media," Raja giggled, prompting the other two to chuckle along.

"Well, that concludes our session. I thank you both for your patronage. It was a pleasant experience." She gave them a polite nod, keeping up her friendly facade, though her mind was already working through her next steps.

Raja smiled and extended her hand, hoping to get both Tiny and Gunther to shake it. Both men instantly obliged, and they all stood up from the table as Raja gathered her belongings.

"No problem. It's always entertaining to know that stories from the lower hive can reach the uppers. At least someone cares. Hell, I heard the folks in the higher hive don't even know we exist," Gunther smirked, shaking his head.

"As long as people have their ears, eyes, and minds—stories from every corner of the world are a delight to hear," Raja smiled, keeping her tone light. "May I have an escort out?"

"Of course," Gunther said, nodding at Tiny. "You have a wonderful day, Raja."

"And to you, Gunther," Raja replied, offering a respectful bow before turning to follow Tiny.

"Okay, pretty lady, boss man has me sendin' you out," Tiny said, leading her toward the exit. "You want me around longer for more of that news stuff?"

"It's okay, Tiny. I think I'll be fine," Raja assured him.

As soon as she spoke those words, a man slammed a glass bottle over another man's head. The glass shattered, and both men immediately broke into a brawl, causing several patrons to cheer while watching both the stage dancers and the unexpected spectacle.

"On second thought, yeah, please stay with me," Raja requested with pursed lips.

"Ha! Say no more, lady!" Tiny laughed, pulling one man off the other with a single hand.

—

Tiny escorted Raja out of Gunther's establishment, heading toward the general area Gunther had indicated. She knew it wasn't much of a hint, but she figured it was better than trying to ask others who might not be as polite as Gunther. At every turn and narrow path, Tiny took the lead, scaring many of the inhabitants away while Raja tucked herself closely behind him. It took some time, but with enough persistence, she finally heard the sound of children playing.

She quietly nudged Tiny to change paths, guiding him toward the sound of the children, which seemed to come from around the next corner. As Tiny stepped onto the street, Raja stayed slightly behind him, peeking her head around the turn to observe the children. A handful of boys and girls were playing with a makeshift ball made of intertwined sticks and trash, kicking it back and forth while cheering each other on. However, none of the children stood out to Raja, as none bore the distinct golden eyes of the child she sought.

Once she confirmed that none of the children were connected to her search, she nudged Tiny to continue forward, guiding him along the side of the street to keep their distance from the group.

It wasn't long before Raja spotted another child waddling out of a dilapidated shed, who seated themselves on the sand. The child wasn't engaged in any particular activity, instead slowly shifting their gaze across the horizon, as if searching for something—or perhaps waiting for someone. When the child turned their head in Raja's direction, that's when she saw it: a beautiful pair of eyes that glinted like the shine of a gald coin.

"The golden-eyed child," Raja whispered to herself, slipping behind Tiny. "I found you."

Chapter Twenty-six

Raja tapped Tiny's shoulder and whispered, "Hey, Tiny, I found the golden-eyed child. Mind if we stop here for a bit? I need to chat with them."

"O' course, lady. Wants me to stand the watch?" Tiny asked, chuckling as he cracked his knuckles.

"Yes, please. The child is right across the street, and I shouldn't take long."

"Yeah, right on, then," Tiny smirked, leaning casually against the sandstone wall that lined the foundation of the alleyway they had just exited. His eyes flicked lazily over the street, but his posture remained relaxed, giving Raja the space she needed to approach unnoticed.

Raja gave Tiny a small grin before slowly making her way toward the child. She shot him one last look of concern before pointing at him, prompting Tiny to smile and give her a thumbs-up. Raja unraveled the scroll, doing her best to navigate through the crowded, dusty streets without bumping into the bustling pedestrians, gradually closing the distance between her and the child. As she opened the scroll, her notes were scrawled at the bottom half of the sheet, while other words—unrelated to her penmanship—were already written at the top. Raja's eyes darted to the statement above, reminding herself of the instructions that read:

Golden-eyed child, Habi Sabbah.
Info. provided by Rafi Sabbah.

Ordered by the Enlightened One, Sultan
Befriend them.
Inform them of Rafi's safety.
Grant Habi and their friends safe passage to the
tower, use extra copy of sigil. Advise them, subject
to attest alongside Rafi Sabbah.
Advise to arrive from dusk to darkest hour on the
following day. Return and report.
Signed,
Elina Faheem, Head of Kouran Intelligence Service.

Raja kept the order vivid in her mind as she gently rolled the top half of the scroll, concealing it just before she approached the golden-eyed child sitting on the sand—Habi Sabbah.

"Hello, little one," Raja calmly greeted, waving and smiling at Habi.

Habi flinched slightly when Raja surprised her. She looked up at the mysterious woman, noting her unusual demeanor for the streets of the lower hive. Habi scanned her expression carefully, her eyes flicking to any strange objects in her hands.

"Papa told me not to talk to strangers," Habi said.

As Habi politely recited her common mantra, she stood up and began to walk back toward the shed, hoping to avoid any conflict.

"Wait, wait, little one, you're Habi Sabbah, correct?" Raja called, knowing that using Habi's full name might not have been the safest choice, but it was enough to catch her attention. "Sorry, let me introduce myself. I'm

Raja Hakim. I work with the media, and I happen to be a friend of Rafi Sabbah. You know the boy, yes?"

As soon as Raja mentioned Rafi's name, Habi's eyes lit up with surprise and curiosity. In that moment, Raja knew she had Habi's full attention.

"You know Rafi?" Habi's jaw dropped. "Is he safe? Is he coming home? Is he here with you?"

From the initial interaction, Raja quickly deduced that Habi was overly obsessed with Rafi, which made the job a lot easier for her.

"Yes, I know Rafi," Raja lied smoothly, keeping her expression neutral. "Actually, I am here to inform you that the Sultan requests both you and the rest of the kids to attest for your previous actions at his tower.

"Rafi's freedom is guaranteed, but he will not be released until the Sultan is satisfied with a full apology from all parties. Afterwards, you will all be released back to your homes without any further consequences. The Sultan is a caring man, after all."

Habi hopped in joy, only listening to half of the words Raja had spouted. All she paid attention to was *Rafi's freedom is guaranteed*, and *The Sultan requests both you and the kids—full apology—release back to your homes*.

"Do we come now?" Habi asked, excited to be reunited with Rafi.

"Not quite yet, but tomorrow night, you can," Raja said, peeling a part of her belt back to retrieve another sigil, the Intelligence Service pin, hidden behind her original copy. "I'm supposed to give you this. Keep it safe and show it to the guards at every border gate. They should let you pass, and then you can make your way to meet Rafi. The Sultan just wants to see you all. That's all."

Raja handed the copy of her silver pin to Habi, who happily accepted it. Habi inspected the sigil, rubbing her thumb over the silver eye with a pin piercing through its pupil, astonished by its simple yet morbid design.

"I use this and we get to see Rafi?" Habi asked, seeking confirmation of the instructions.

"Yes, just like that. Remember, it's just you and the other kids," Raja continued. "I know you have a father, but he's not invited, unfortunately, since he wasn't involved in your previous actions.

"Rafi has already confessed to his crimes, mentioning you and the others as his acquaintances. The Sultan has a window for your assembly from dusk till the darkest hour. I hope this decision pleases you," she explained, her tone calm and reassuring.

"Okay, we will come," Habi smiled brightly. "Thank you!"

"You're welcome, little one," Raja smiled back, keeping her voice gentle. "Now, as I told you, I am part of the media. I'm trying to obtain information on how The Culling affected everyone. Since we're already here, do you mind answering a few questions? It won't take long."

Habi nodded and secured the silver pin in her ragged pocket.

"Right then, Habi," Raja coughed as she squatted down, using the top of her thighs as a platform. As she started to pull out the quill and ink jar, she decided to ask the questions while doing so. "Habi, were you affected by–"

As Raja was speaking and setting up her equipment, the shed door suddenly flung open, and Hamza walked out.

"Hey Habi, do you–" Before Hamza could finish his sentence, he noticed a young woman kneeling in front of Habi. Habi didn't seem threatened or scared, but wore her usual expression, one that looked lost or confused. Even so, after a quick glance, Hamza's concern was clear.

"Oi! Who are you!?" Hamza shouted, pointing his finger at Raja. As he caught both of their attention, he noticed the needle-like object in Raja's hand, which he immediately assumed was a weapon—but it was just her quill.

"Oh, hello, I'm–" Before Raja could finish her introduction, Hamza didn't hesitate to throw rocks and handfuls of sand at her, trying to protect Habi from the malicious quill.

Raja fell onto her bum and scrambled to her feet, spreading her arms in a defensive gesture as she pleaded her innocence.

"Wait, wait, wait, I–" Raja tried to explain, but once again, as she claimed her innocence, Hamza continued closing the distance, cursing at her.

The entire scenario unfolded too quickly for Habi to react. Habi would've joined in to defend Raja, but she ultimately decided that being exposed to a large amount of verbal words wasn't going to work well with her head.

Besides, Habi's neutrality had already been established, and she had received the valuable information about Rafi that she needed. As far as she was concerned, Raja no longer held any significance.

"Get! Get!" Hamza roared, throwing another handful of sand at Raja in a threatening motion.

Raja panicked, keeping her distance from the children as she choked on the sand, patting it off her clothing. She turned to Tiny, her temporary bodyguard, hoping for help. However, when she spotted him, he was too busy entertaining himself with another woman who had stopped by to talk to him. He was blushing, and all Raja could think about was how absurd the entire situation had become.

After quickly calculating her retreat, Raja ran to Tiny and yanked him away from the random woman, forcing him to meet her eyes.

"I'm *done* here. Get me out!" Raja growled, dirtied with sand.

"Oi! I thought you said you didn't have a mate!" the woman shouted from behind.

"You be quiet! We are leaving!" Raja shouted, dragging Tiny away from the scene. Tiny blew a kiss at the woman behind them as he carelessly stumbled in Raja's grip. It didn't take long for the two of them to vanish into the alternating foot traffic up the street.

Hamza stood proudly next to Habi, placing his hands on his hips and shouting, "Good riddance!"

Habi simply applauded, as if Hamza had just chased a witch away.

"Okay, now who was that? Why were they tryna stab ya?" Hamza asked, turning to face Habi, his expression still tense from the confrontation.

"She was a nice lady who wanted to talk with me," Habi answered innocently.

Hamza raised a brow, then pinched the bridge of his nose with a sigh. "She was—*nice*!? Why didn't you say anything!? Now I look like the bad guy here!"

"She talks too much, it's okay," Habi said with a small shrug.

"Oh, so she's an adult-sized Taliba," Hamza chuckled, shaking his head.

Both of them laughed at the joke, and Habi retrieved the silver sigil from her pocket, showing it to Hamza.

"What's that?" Hamza wondered, eyeing the small object in Habi's hand.

"The lady gave it to me. I think her name was Raja. She said we've been invited to meet the Sultan and help get Rafi out of the tower. She said that the Sultan just wants us to apologize for what we did, and then we can all go home together—with Rafi!" Habi beamed, her golden eyes shining with excitement.

"Wait, so let me get this straight—this lady, *Raja*, gave you a pin and just straight up told you that we can actually meet Rafi and bring him back home? And all we have to do is say how bad of children we are?" Hamza asked, trying to make sense of it all.

Habi nodded eagerly and explained further, "She said that this pin will let the guards open the gates for us, and we are supposed to be at the tower tomorrow night.

She said only you, me, Tariq, Naji, and Taliba have to go. Father wasn't invited because he didn't do bad things."

Hamza's brow furrowed in suspicion. "And how exactly did Raja know where to find you, let alone what you look like?"

"She said Rafi confessed to everything and described me," Habi replied, pointing to her golden eyes.

"Fair point," Hamza muttered, though he still felt uneasy. "I mean, none of it really sounds fishy. I'd believe that the Sultan is pompous enough to want some kids to grovel at his feet. We still have to run it by the others, though."

"I can't wait," Habi smirked excitedly. "Rafi is coming home!"

—

Raja finally reached her breaking point and decided to fully retreat back into the middle hive. She had enough of being assaulted, harassed, and constantly pestered by snobby kids. Despite the multiple instances of misfortune, she had ultimately completed her main objective: contacting Habi and informing her of the Sultan's decision.

With Tiny as her escort, Raja was able to safely make her way to the gate and thank him for his service. Tiny was happy to oblige, waving farewell to the cute lady he had the pleasure of leading around in such a dangerous place. Once Tiny returned to whatever activities piqued his interest, Raja spoke to the guards behind the gate and waltzed back into the middle hive, finally allowing herself a sigh of relief.

Raja spent the rest of her time walking to an outpost stationed on the outskirts of the middle ring. It was a small sandstone home that blended seamlessly with its neighboring buildings.

When she reached the door, Raja knocked three times in rapid succession, followed by three slower knocks, signaling the code. The door unlocked and swung open, revealing a young man dressed in attire suited for the middle hive lifestyle.

"Raja, welcome back. Oman will be waiting for your report in the briefing room," the man said.

"Thank you, Basim," Raja replied, stepping fully into the building as Basim sealed and locked the door behind her. She took a steadying breath, preparing herself for the debriefing ahead.

As Raja walked through the small building, she greeted her coworkers, who were either writing reports or discussing their next meal. They were glad to see her return but concerned about the dust and sand clinging to her disguise. She eventually made her way to the briefing room at the back of the house, where Oman, the lead agent, was waiting, engrossed in another report.

"You look like someone ran you through a trash pile and rolled you in sand like flour," Oman said, his expression unreadable as he noticed Raja's presence. "Were you compromised?"

"Yes, sir," Raja answered, aware that her familiarity with lower hive culture was lacking. It didn't help that the lower hive had been one of her first missions. "I-I wasn't aware of how–"

"It's the *lower hive*, Raja. Everyone knows how they live. You've spent too much time sucking on your mother's teat in the confines of the middle hive. You only made it into the service because you scored high in academics at the schoolhouse, but unfortunately, you lack the knowledge of the streets and its dwellers. It's not all flowers and smiles out here, girl—especially not in the lower hive," Oman scolded, making Raja lower her head in shame.

"Sir, if I may ask, why was I chosen for this assignment? As you've pointed out, I have zero experience in the slums," Raja pouted, her insecurities evident.

"That's exactly why I chose you, Raja," Oman stated. "It's because you have no experience and you've never stepped foot in there. If I send any of my experienced agents, there's bound to be a conflict. The slum dwellers aren't as dumb as you think—they lack literacy, but they know faces—and they remember them. Word spreads quickly down there, and especially after the recent incident, the people are going to be on edge, thirsty for blood.

"But unfortunately," he continued, his tone sharpening, "you thought the lower hive was a walk to the beauty parlor, so you're already compromised. You won't be returning there anytime soon."

Raja was disappointed to be pulled from her assignment so quickly, but she found some comfort in the fact that she wouldn't have to deal with the people who lived there—at least for a while.

"So tell me, Raja—did you accomplish the task?" Oman asked, resting his arms behind his back, his gaze steady.

"Yes, sir. I relayed the information to the child, Habi Sabbah, while maintaining my cover as an investigative reporter for the media. I believe she's more than excited to follow the orders I've given her," Raja answered confidently.

"Golden-eyed, correct?"

"Yes, sir."

"Very well then," Oman said, retrieving an empty scroll from the shelves behind him and handing it to her. "Proceed to write your report while the events are still fresh in your mind. Afterwards, clean yourself up and await further instructions for your new assignment. These are busy times, indeed."

"Yes, sir," Raja acknowledged, taking the scroll. As she held it, a thought lingered in her mind, one that had been nagging at her ever since she crossed the border gate.

"Sir, may I ask a question?"

"Say it," Oman ordered, lowering his gaze to the reports in front of him.

"Why does the Sultan worry about small matters involving children? Doesn't he have hundreds of other important affairs to tend to?" Raja asked carefully.

Oman's eyes snapped back up, his expression darkening. "Are you questioning the Sultan's order?"

"No, I would never," Raja pleaded, quickly waving her hands in front of her. "I was just wondering how this matter took precedence over many others, that's all, sir."

Oman sighed, his scowl easing into something more measured. "Raja, I received this order from the district lead agent. The district lead agent received it from the hive lead agent. The hive lead agent received it from the head of the service herself. Do you think I actually know why the Sultan cares so much about this? We are here to work, gather information, and counter threats—not to pry into matters above our sanction and delve into conspiracies."

"I-I apologize for my rudeness then, sir," Raja said, bowing her head slightly.

"But if it makes you feel better, after your *disastrous*, yet successful day—I've heard rumors that the ordeal you were dealing with involved the Commandant of the Army, Hizan Al'Za'im himself. You should be honored, Raja, if that's true."

"Thank you, sir," Raja bowed again, accepting his response, though it only left more questions lingering in her mind.

"I'll get to the report then."

—

Elina Faheem climbed the spiraling stairs as the sun began to set behind the glass windows layered across the tower walls. Once she reached the floor of the Sultan's throne room, she walked down the long corridor. The

Mamluks standing guard at the throne door did not stop her, but they did warn her of the potential consequences should she choose to enter.

"Lady Faheem, I advise you that the Sultan is handling another matter at this time, but you are free to enter," the Mamluk explained, his voice steady and respectful.

"Thank you, soldier," Elina said, offering him a small smirk as she strode past, inviting herself into the Sultan's throne room without hesitation.

Upon entering, Elina saw the Sultan leaning back in his seat, unamused by the words of the man who had spoken before him. Beside the man stood a Mamluk knight, closely observing his movements, listening to his speech, and carefully gauging his demeanor.

"Enlightened One, please—I only wish to know the safety of my wife in the lower hive," the man begged on his knees, his voice trembling. "I haven't received any letters from her since The Culling, and I am unable to step through the gates because the Ghazi are locking down entry from all fronts. Is this too much to ask, Enlightened One?"

The Sultan let out a long sigh, resting his chin on his hand. "This, to me, sounds like a personal matter," he mused. "Yet here you are, groveling at my feet, because you are too impatient for the cordon to be lifted. Mamluk, take this man away."

"Aye, Enlightened One," the Mamluk obeyed, stepping forward and grabbing the man's arm. But as soon as the soldier pulled, the man resisted.

"This is not just a personal matter!" he shouted, his voice raw with desperation. "You were the one who made the decision to slaughter the lower hive! The people have yet to receive an answer, and I fear my wife is in danger! You ruled the severance! You ruled The Culling! You ruled the lockdown!"

The Sultan's expression darkened, his fingers curling over the edge of his throne. "You should be thankful to even have food in your belly and the ability to speak like that, boy. Not everyone can win."

"*Fuck you*, Sultan!" the man spat, thrashing against the Mamluk's grip. "I heard the Hassazi were reforming, and they'll beat you down! I just want to see my wi—"

Before he could finish, the Mamluk yanked him off his knees with one hand and slammed him onto the marble floor with bone-crushing force.

"You do *not* sully the Sultan's name!" the Mamluk roared, pinning the choking man beneath him, his hand wrapped mercilessly around his throat.

The Mamluk, following the laws and his codex, unsheathed his short sword and drove it into the man's chest. The man screamed in unimaginable pain, tears streaming down his face, his agony clear. Over countless trials, the Mamluk had perfected the strike, aiming for the heart and ending the man's life nearly instantly. At the front of the throne room, Elina turned away from the murder she had just witnessed, but she reminded herself that the man had indeed sullied the Sultan's name—which was a death sentence.

"Try not to dirty the carpet and pews too much now, Mamluk," the Sultan said, shaking his head without any regard for the man's life. "Clean up your mess and behead him at the palace grounds. Display it in the middle hive, so he can return home and serve as an example to those who wish to follow."

"Yes, Enlightened One," the Mamluk replied, leaving the blade embedded in the man's chest to minimize further stains.

The Mamluk walked toward the throne door to exit the room, his bloodied gauntlets and chest plate glinting in the light as he passed Elina, towering over her. As he brushed by, he simply said, "Lady Faheem."

"Soldier," Elina replied.

The Mamluk exited the throne room and sealed the door shut, heading to retrieve the necessary supplies to clean up the bloodshed. With the Sultan no longer occupied, Elina stepped toward him, carefully tiptoeing over the body and its remnants.

"Please tell me you have good news for me, Elina. I tire of these trivial matters the people keep requesting an audience with me for," the Sultan sighed, rubbing his eyes with visible frustration.

"It is good news, Enlightened One," Elina stated, standing poised with her hands resting behind her back. "One of my agents has successfully informed Habi Sabbah and her friends to meet with you on the following day at the stated time. I was advised that Habi seemed rather excited to see Rafi again."

HABI

The Sultan smiled menacingly as he leaned forward on his throne.

"And she was told not to invite Sai—her father, correct?" the Sultan said, his tone laced with amusement.

"Correct, Enlightened One," Elina affirmed with a slight nod.

"Good," the Sultan chuckled.

While the Sultan smiled to himself, Elina pondered a question that had lingered in her mind since reading Raja's report, and she couldn't resist voicing it.

"Enlightened One, if I may ask, how do *you* feel about The Culling? The agent who finished the task mentioned how the lives of those in the lower hive have either been devastated or remained unharmed. Hundreds of thousands of people are unaccounted for. Just a little idiosyncrasy of mine to delve into numbers," Elina asked, hoping she wouldn't end up like the man on the ground.

The Sultan maintained his smile as he leaned back in his throne.

"If one person dies, it's a tragedy. If hundreds of thousands die, it's a statistic. People will come to accept and learn from those who ran through fire and suffered from it. It's human nature, Elina—and nature doesn't care," the Sultan answered, his voice cold and unwavering.

"I see, Enlightened One," Elina said, slowly lowering her head to avoid his gaze.

—

Back in the lower hive at the children's shed, Tariq and Naji finally returned from their scavenging trip, while Habi and Hamza busied themselves drawing on scraps of paper and in books, deliberately trying to rile up Taliba in her absence.

"Well, you two seem to be in an awfully good mood," Tariq said, dropping a bag of bread and potatoes onto the floor. "What's up?"

Father's ink jar sat between Hamza and Habi as they scribbled on their palettes with quills. Hamza was defacing one of Taliba's favorite books by drawing an ugly face on its pages, while Habi was sketching the family again—Rafi holding her hand, with Father at the center of all the children. Beside her artwork lay the silver pin Raja had given her, its delicate design catching Naji's eye.

"Hey Habi, what's that?" Naji asked, pointing at the pin.

Habi was too busy humming a song to herself when Naji finally asked the question.

"Oh, a lady gave this to me," Habi said. "She said that this pin will let the guards open the gates and we can go see Rafi and bring him back home!"

"What?" Tariq asked cautiously, his eyes narrowing.

"Let me explain. Habi's not really good with words," Hamza offered.

Hamza recounted the entire event, detailing Habi's interaction with the woman named Raja. The revelation caught Tariq and Naji by surprise, but they were eager to see the decision through. To them, the order made sense—believing the Sultan merely wanted the children to kiss his feet and leave with Rafi in hand. However, Naji remained uneasy about the decision to exclude Father. He believed they would need guardianship to stand before the Sultan himself. When Hamza elaborated on Raja's reasoning, Naji chose not to press further, reasoning that the children alone were held accountable for their actions.

"I mean, it could be a trap, no?" Naji wondered, his voice laced with hesitation.

"But for what, though? It's not like the Sultan is going to string us by the feet because we made a little *oopsie*," Hamza said with a smirk. "Rafi already confessed to our crimes, and all we have to do is say, 'whoops, teehee, we're sorry'. Don't think there would be anything else to it, yeah?"

"We still need to run this with Taliba. Maybe even Father too," Tariq pointed out.

"I feel like Father is just going to tell us to reject the offer if we told him," Hamza shrugged. "Hell, we could even make it a surprise! Imagine that! *Boom*! Rafi is home, and we're all back together!"

"Happy together!" Habi cheered, beaming.

"See? Habi gets it. Imagine the look on Father's face when Rafi suddenly comes back. Priceless, I say!" Hamza laughed.

"That's a devious plan—I like it," Tariq chuckled.

"I mean, if you all say so," Naji sighed, rubbing the back of his head. "Where is Taliba anyway?"

"She left right after you two did," Hamza explained, folding the defaced book he had been drawing in and shoving it back onto the shelf. "She said something about helping with relief efforts—working with the homeless shelter near the market area, I think. But honestly, I feel like she'd be up for walking straight to the Sultan's doorstep if it meant getting Rafi back."

"But you're *not* Taliba. Who knows what she thinks," Tariq said.

"I can be Taliba if you want me to," Hamza grinned mischievously.

"Please, no," Tariq grimaced, prompting the rest of the children to burst into laughter.

Almost as if the gods had heard the children, Taliba returned to the shed with an exhausted look on her face. She secured the door behind her, dusting herself off before pausing in front of the others, who were all giving her playful looks.

"Oh hey, look who it is," Hamza chuckled, pointing at Taliba as she approached.

"Wait, what?" Taliba sighed, immediately suspicious. "Were you all talking behind my back? Why are you all so giddy?"

"Rafi is coming home!" Habi cheered again, bouncing excitedly.

Taliba turned to face Habi, her expression shifting to pure shock. "What?"

"Here, let me explain it, since Habi isn't telling the story accurately," Tariq offered.

This time, Tariq explained the full story to Taliba, covering the delivery of the order, the pin, the circumstances, and Rafi's condition.

"It's a trap," Taliba stated firmly, crossing her arms. "Why would the Sultan even care to invite kids to *his* court? If it's too good to be true, then it probably is."

With Taliba's answer, Habi frowned at her pessimism, causing the others to erupt in protest.

"Okay, but why would he *not*?" Hamza countered. "He's the Sultan. He probably has all types of people just begging for forgiveness, including kids. Think about it, Taliba. It all makes sense!"

"And you're telling me that he made a large window for us to arrive at night?" Taliba shot back. "Either the Sultan has way too much time on his hands—which is very unlikely—or he's trying to jail us. Simple as that. We're not going."

"Oh, come on, Taliba, this is *Rafi* we're talking about!" Tariq growled. "Rafi already confessed for us, and now all we got to do is say how sorry we are!"

"Rafi already confessed for us—so why do we need to show up if the matter is already settled?" Taliba placed her hands on her hips, her glare unwavering.

"Taliba, you're not listening!" Tariq groaned, dragging a hand down his face in frustration.

While the children began arguing among themselves again, Habi stood up from her drawing and walked toward Taliba. In pure Habi fashion, she looked up at

Taliba, clutched her ragged shirt, and gave her puppy eyes.

"I want to see Rafi, Taliba," Habi whimpered, her voice small but insistent.

"Please don't give me that look," Taliba whined, staring into Habi's mesmerizing eyes. "Don't do this to me."

The entire room fell silent as everyone watched Habi's gifted tactic unfold on Taliba. It was the same look Habi used to distract merchants while the others snatched items, the same gaze she employed to get what she wanted. A tool of mass destruction, and Habi knew it all too well.

"I miss Rafi, Taliba," Habi cried, her golden eyes shimmering with desperation. "The Sultan invited us to see him and bring him home. I want to go see him. So does everyone else."

After gazing into Habi's eyes for a few seconds, Taliba had no choice but to surrender, giving in to the trick and the unanimous vote to visit the Sultan.

"Okay, okay! We'll go! You're all lucky that I miss Rafi just as much as anyone else! Now stop glaring at me like that!" Taliba shouted, throwing her hands up in surrender.

Content with her answer, Habi pulled away and hopped triumphantly as the other children cheered for Taliba's change of heart.

"Victory!" Habi roared.

"I'm totally going to tell Rafi that you just said you miss him," Hamza teased, smirking.

"Yeah, you better not," Taliba hissed, shooting him a glare.

"Hey, remember not to tell Father," Tariq warned, wagging a finger at her.

"Yeah, yeah," Taliba rolled her eyes, already regretting her decision.

The children laughed and traded jokes, their spirits light as the shed once again filled with joy and cheers. It felt as though months had passed since the last time the air was so full of happiness. The news of their opportunity to freely walk to the noble ring and return home with Rafi brought them all to tears of joy. They eagerly discussed the things they'd want to talk about and do once Rafi was home. And since Habi had been given the silver pin, she now led the charge. Habi hummed joyfully to herself as the others tidied up the shed, preparing for Father's arrival since it was getting late. She played with the silver pin and placed the family drawing on top of Father's desk, so it would be the first thing he saw when he opened the door.

Later, as the children's laughter faded and the desert night crept in, Taliba lit the ceiling lantern and pulled one of her favorite novels from the shelf. As she flipped through the pages, she immediately spotted the drawing Hamza had defaced her book with. Anger flared, and she prepared to confront him. Meanwhile, Tariq and Naji lay on their bedrolls, munching on raw potatoes. Taliba shouted at Hamza, who tried to plead his innocence.

Habi, lying on her bedroll, brought both the silver pin and the kissed gald coin over to the lantern's light.

She admired the two gifts—one a reminder of the boy she loved, and the other the token to bring him home. She couldn't help but smile.

Habi carefully tucked the trinkets inside her bedroll, pulling the blanket over herself as she turned to face Rafi's empty bedroll. She kept staring at it, her thoughts drifting as she imagined Rafi finally being by her side again.

As the night went on, Habi and the others happily drifted away into a deep slumber, except for Taliba. Taliba continued reading her book under the light of the lantern, enjoying the story she had finished countless times, since the other children were opposed to acquiring books from merchants and libraries. She found solace in her quiet reading.

When the moon was high in the sky, Father finally returned home. Taliba, her eyes lighting up at the sight of him, gladly welcomed him back.

"Hello Father," Taliba smiled, turning her attention away from her book.

"Hello, Taliba. Not tired yet?" Father asked, puffing on his pipe as he placed his logbook on his desk. After returning the book, his gaze fell on the drawing placed at the center of the desk. The art style was unmistakable, with two stick figures holding hands, and he immediately knew the culprit. He chuckled softly, shaking his head, and leaned the drawing against the wall of the shed, alongside the other previous drawings tucked in the corner of his desk.

"Not yet," Taliba said. "I'm at the most intense part of the book right now."

"You seem to enjoy that novel a lot, little one. Maybe I should make a trip to purchase more, just to keep you entertained," Father mused. "What is that one about that catches your attention so?"

"It's a story from the west," Taliba said, her voice filled with excitement. "It's about a boy—turned man—turned hero. He trained in the way of the sword, earning his fame, power, and riches by slaying invaders who were once his friends. He even defeated the dragon that threatened to end all of humanity!"

"I took you for a romantic reader. This is surprising," Father chuckled.

"Romance is okay now and then, but romance doesn't play with my emotions like this book does. I can feel the happiness, anger, sadness, fear, and mystery in this one, even though parts of it are starting to bore me."

"Romance novels make you feel all of those emotions you listed as well, you know."

"Father, you know what I mean!" Taliba pouted.

"I do know what you mean, and I think it's time for you to go to bed," Father said, snapping his fingers. The sound was meant to make Taliba flinch, but she was too tired to react, her eyelids heavy as she let out a small yawn.

"Okay, Father," Taliba sighed, folding the book and placing it back on the shelf. She hunched over to her bedroll, and before slipping into it, she turned to him and said, "Good night, Father," waving a tired hand at him.

"Good night, little one," Father replied, his voice warm as he prepared to extinguish the ceiling lantern, casting the shed into soft darkness.

Before Taliba buried herself in her bedroll, she was tempted to share the news of Rafi's possible return with Father. However, she decided against it, wanting to keep the surprise for the others. Too exhausted for a confrontation, she closed her eyes, slipped into her roll, and prepared for sleep, pushing aside the bubbling excitement for the journey ahead. As soon as the faint light from the extinguished lantern faded from her closed eyes, she fell asleep in an instant, joining her family in the land of dreams.

Chapter Twenty-seven

Habi woke up in a pile of black sand, the entire environment around her as dark as a starless sky. She recognized the place once more, but this time, she scrambled to her feet, shaking the sand off her and bracing herself for any sudden, contorted creature that might decide to lunge at her. She waited, heart pounding, expecting an ambush—but nothing came. The sand remained motionless, and the air felt thin, void of any presence aside from herself.

At first, she hadn't wanted to wake up in this dream world again, refusing to confront the restless dead. But now, as the silence stretched on, she found herself yearning for someone to visit—it was becoming lonely.

She never asked for the powers of Necromantia, and if she could, she'd rid herself of it, even if it meant losing the ability to communicate with those she loved. The dead, in her mind, should remain dead—at peace. There were times when the spirits, like Assad and Talia, had come to her aid, offering valuable guidance. But there were also times when the dead had frightened her or spoken in riddles, their words never making sense. Lost in thought, alone in the silence, a hand gently settled on Habi's shoulder. She flinched, instinctively spinning around to face the source of the touch.

Habi tensed, her fist raised instinctively to strike whatever threat loomed behind her. Her heart raced as she prepared for another terrifying encounter. But when she turned and saw the familiar, calming face of the person who had touched her, her hand fell.

"Sara!" Habi shouted, wrapping her arms around Sara's waist. The embrace lasted only a moment before Habi gently pushed herself away, looking up at Sara. "You're not going to become a monster, right?"

Sara laughed, flashing Habi her beautiful smile, the one that all the children loved.

"No, no, little one. I'm fine. I've come to accept the truth over time," Sara said, rubbing Habi's head gently. "How are you, my dear child?"

"I'm happy. Happy to see you, and happy to see Rafi tomorrow!" Habi beamed, her smile wide and full of excitement.

"Rafi?" Sara repeated, her expression unreadable, as if the name was unfamiliar to her.

"Yes, you know Rafi. He's coming home tomorrow!" Habi cheered, bouncing slightly on her feet.

While Habi was jubilant about Rafi's return, Sara blinked rapidly, as if something was caught in her eye. Her smile slowly shifted into a horrific frown, her jaw beginning to drop. When she finally stopped blinking, her eyes widened in fear.

"Habi," Sara gasped, her expression twisting with panic.

"Sara, what's wrong?" Habi frowned, fear creeping in at the thought that Sara might transform into a creature.

"Habi. No. No, no, no, no. You *can't* go to Rafi," Sara pleaded, dropping to her knees, gripping Habi's shoulders tightly as she met her gaze.

"W-Why?" Habi whimpered, shrinking under Sara's desperation. "You're scaring me. I want to see him!"

"Habi, Rafi is—" Sara began, but before she could finish, the entire void suddenly erupted in flames.

Both Habi and Sara shielded themselves from the scorching flames and intense heat as a ring of fire encircled them, trapping them in place. A strong wind howled, feeding the flames and making them grow even fiercer, spreading their destructive reach closer to the duo.

As Sara reached out to hug Habi, shielding her from the flames, a dark hand shot out, grabbing Sara and pulling her into the blinding blaze. Sara screamed in agony, her voice fading as it was swallowed by the crackling fire.

From the flames, a tall, dark silhouette emerged, wielding a sword in his hand. It was the same figure that had haunted Habi in her previous dreams, always ending in nightmares.

As Habi cowered, backing into a wall of flames, she managed to make out a small detail on the silhouette's face that hadn't been there before. Within the vast emptiness where its eyes should have been, two dim blue lights flickered, glimmering as if they were eyes.

For a split second, Habi could've sworn she recognized the color somewhere, but she had no time to dwell on it. The more she hesitated, the closer the silhouette drew, dragging the tip of its blade across the black sand.

Habi had no way to escape. She was left with two choices: burn alive or face the wrath of the blade wielded by an unknown being—one brimming with malice.

Before Habi could even make a choice, the silhouette had already decided for her, bringing its blade down into her collar with a swift, forceful strike.

—

As with every other nightmare, Habi jolted awake, drenched in sweat. With labored breathing, she immediately reached for her neck and shoulder, checking to make sure they were still intact. Her eyes quickly scanned the dark interior of the shed, searching for smoke or flames, but there were none. However, she felt a warm presence in her bedroll. It was damp, and a fear gripped her—believing that she was bleeding out. She touched the wet fabric and brought it to her nose, hoping it wouldn't smell of iron. After sniffing her hands, she let out a sigh of relief, thankful it wasn't her blood. But then, a wave of embarrassment washed over her—she had soiled herself.

Habi decided to dry herself off by stepping outside into the cold air of Koura's night. After checking the safety of her kissed gald and silver pin, now stained with urine, she dragged herself out of her bedroll and waddled toward the door, careful not to wake anyone.

When she turned the knob and opened the shed door, she froze immediately.

The dark silhouette that haunted her dreams was now standing right outside the door, looking down at her. As soon as she caught sight of it, the shed door slammed shut with a force that shook the entire structure. Habi stood frozen, speechless, but the same couldn't be said for Father and the children, who had just awoken from their slumber, startled by the deafening sound of the door.

"Habi, what the hell!?" Hamza groaned, barely able to make out her figure at the door in the darkness. The only reason he knew it was her was because of her short stature.

"Habi, are you okay?" Father asked, his voice groggy as he sat up from where he had been asleep next to his desk, which was near the door.

The children began rustling in their bedrolls, curious about the sudden, violent slam of the door.

"It wasn't me!" Habi cried. "There's a ghost outside! A monster! I swear!"

In situations like this, the family would normally have dismissed her plea, but now that they all knew of Habi's ability—or curse—to see the dead, they believed her without question.

Father quietly moved to the door, gently positioning Habi behind him as he prepared to open it. The other children stayed in their beds, tense, waiting for some kind of monster to appear the moment Father opened the door. But when he slowly pulled it open, there was nothing. Aside from a cold breeze that brushed against his face, no monster stood outside. Still, he didn't take Habi's intuition lightly.

"Remain here, children. I'll search the perimeter," Father commanded, stepping outside the boundary before the children could even respond.

The shed fell into silence, save for the breeze howling through the crack in the doorway and Father's soft footsteps. They could hear him moving around the shed, his feet grinding against the sand, his steps slowly fading as he turned a corner. He never stopped for a single second.

"Okay, this is creepy," Naji whispered, curling up inside his bedroll to hide.

"Habi, are you *sure* you saw a ghost?" Taliba whispered, her eyes darting toward the door.

"I swear it!" Habi whimpered, stumbling as she tried to find her way back to her bedroll in the dark.

A few moments later, Father returned to the shed door and sealed it behind him as he stepped into the darkness of his home. The children couldn't see him clearly, but they felt his presence all the same.

"There are no monsters, aside from the usual squatters that lay on the road across the street. It is safe, little ones," Father stated firmly.

"What if the squatters saw something?" Taliba asked, her curiosity piqued.

"That matter has already been dealt with," Father said. "Most of them were asleep. The ones who were awake saw nothing in the night, other than hearing the door slam from across the way."

With Father's declaration, the children wanted to call Habi crazy, but they knew better than to mock her visions. After all, those very same dead people had guided them through the maze of a narcotics tunnel and steered them away from certain misfortunes.

Father, too, understood the gravity of the situation. If Habi was right about a monster or spirit at their door, then it might have already invited itself into their home. He had read enough scriptures and past accounts about spirits and demons to know that, while many dismissed them as superstition, there was often a kernel of truth to the belief that opening a door to a spirit meant inviting it into one's domain.

Yet, aside from the cold breeze still lingering in the air, nothing seemed out of place in the shed. Father hoped his suspicions remained just that—suspicions. But that was what he had thought about the legend of Necromantia, who, of all people, had placed her curse on Habi from the moment she was born.

The more Father thought about it, the more restless he became. In the end, he decided it was better to ignore the supernatural—if it was even real. His focus now was on the safety of his children and ensuring they could rest peacefully.

"Let us return to sleep, little ones. Let's not let this small instance haunt our minds," Father recommended, settling back at his desk.

"Yes, Father," the children murmured, though some cast wary glances toward the door before curling back into their bedrolls.

Unfortunately for Habi, instances like these did haunt her mind, and she was growing weary of it. But since Father had assured them there was no immediate danger, she pushed the thought aside and crawled into her bedroll, the smell of urine still lingering. She hadn't even had the chance to dry herself off.

As the family closed their eyes, the shed finally returned to its natural state, filled with peace and quiet under the moonlit sky. For the rest of the night, Habi had no visitors, and she feared that no spirit was willing to speak with her, deterred by the lingering presence of the dark entity forged in fire. She may have fallen asleep, but she couldn't shake the feeling that someone—or something—was watching her.

—

Ever since the taking of Rafi and The Culling, the family had returned to their usual routine. When the sun rose, Father would distribute food, and the children would bathe at the pond before going about their day. As usual, Father left early in the morning for his activities, which both Habi and Taliba now speculated were focused on reforming a rebellion and building connections throughout the lower hive, after translating parts of his logbook. But at that moment, none of that mattered, because today was the day all the children had been waiting for, and they needed to properly prepare for it.

"I can't wait! I can't wait!" Habi cheered, hopping with excitement, already brushing aside the haunting memory of the possible entity from last night. "Rafi is coming home!"

"Let's not get too excited, Habi," Tariq chuckled. "We've still got a long way to go before we can actually see Rafi. A trip to the noble ring is definitely going to take up our entire morning, afternoon, and evening." He sighed as he packed a piece of bread into his neck pouch, wrapping it around himself. "Though, I'm not sure if our access to the gates will make the trip any shorter. It'd be nice if it did."

"It should," Naji agreed, packing a piece of bread into his pouch as well. "The main roads are all straight shots to every border gate, and they keep going until they connect to the noble ring. The only downside is that it's a small incline."

"Does this mean we have to play dress-up again? Those clothes are itchy," Hamza whined.

"Shouldn't be necessary," Taliba joined. "If what Habi said is correct, then the silver pin she has should give us free passage and free roam."

"Free roam? So you're telling me that we can just mess around in the upper hives without any punishment? That's crazy," Hamza laughed.

"Do you want to see Rafi or not?" Taliba scowled at him. "Even if we did roam, using the pin to our advantage, the woman who gave it to Habi knows where we live now, and I highly doubt the Sultan will let us go freely if we kept such a trinket to ourselves."

She helped pack a piece of bread into Habi's pouch, ensuring that Habi's precious gald coin was still secured. As she turned, she noticed the silver pin lying on the ground next to Habi's bedroll. Clicking her tongue, she quickly retrieved it and handed it to Habi, pointing a finger at her.

"You *can't* be forgetting something like this already," Taliba scolded, securing the pin into Habi's pouch. "This is how we get Rafi back."

"Sorry," Habi murmured, lowering her head in shame.

"Man, Father is gonna be stoked when we come back," Hamza chuckled. "This is gonna be awesome!"

After Taliba checked the children's equipment for a second time and confirmed the presence of the silver sigil, she was satisfied that they were all ready to set off on their grand adventure.

"Right then. Let's go see Rafi," Taliba said, pulling the shed door open.

—

Just like old times—though only weeks had passed—the children traveled through the streets of the lower hive. This time, however, they stuck to the main road, where most of the foot traffic was.

As they walked, they passed slum dwellers going about their day, their faces weary but resolute. Among them were a handful of citizens still marked by scars and burns, grim reminders of The Culling. Since the children's shed was positioned closer to the center of the lower ring, much of what surrounded them had been left relatively unscathed. But as they pressed forward, the landscape gradually changed. The rough, makeshift homes and tents gave way to charred ruins and scattered debris, the scars of destruction growing more severe the closer they got to the border wall.

Taliba was the only one who had seen the worst of it firsthand. She had volunteered to help in the inner districts, tending to those left with nothing. But soon enough, the others would witness the full aftermath as well—for they were now approaching one of the main market areas.

What used to be a bustling area filled with secondhand merchants and shady food stalls had now transformed into a large encampment, home to the sick, wounded, and homeless. With supplies scarce after the devastation, the citizens were forced to barter, trading items of equal value for food, water, and goods. Nearby, the large homeless shelter the children had visited before had also been affected by The Culling. Once a thriving building that housed and cared for millions, it now lay in tatters, a shell of its former self.

Several locals rushed across the square, carrying corpses and tending to the wounded who had yet to receive aid, overwhelmed by the sheer number of those still suffering. In the cramped architecture of the lower hive, cemeteries and burial grounds were scarce. Bodies were often left on the streets unless their loved ones—if they had any—could afford funeral services.

But now, with the looming threat of plague following the slaughter, priorities had shifted. The people had no choice but to act swiftly, dragging the dead away from standing buildings and stacking them in designated spots. The makeshift funeral pyres dotted the square, some already set ablaze. Once a pile reached its limit, torches were lit, and whatever tinder could be found was used to reduce the bodies to ash.

Thick plumes of gray and black smoke coiled into the sky, mixing with the ever-present dust of the lower hive. The acrid fumes stung the children's noses, burning their throats with every breath. Around them, people rushed in frantic bursts, their feet kicking up clouds of sand as they scrambled to control the despair engulfing them.

At the center of the encampment stood a makeshift wooden stage, illuminated by countless candles that surrounded its edges, flickering in the breeze. In the middle of the stage were hundreds of thousands of names—either carved into wood, etched into stones, or written on scraps of paper. The stage had essentially become an altar, a solemn place of homage for those who had lost their lives during The Culling. It was the people's way of paying tribute and remembrance to their loved ones, a symbolic gesture to honor the dead in a time of overwhelming grief.

There were several citizens gathered around the altar, some praying, others in tears, and many bowing deeply to the ground. Though The Culling had occurred only some days ago, its weight still pressed heavily on the people, as though the tragedy were ongoing. Perhaps, in some way, they believed it had never truly ended, given the dwindling resources that continued to claim more lives. Some screamed at the top of their lungs, overcome with grief or the effects of drugs, while others retreated into dark corners and alleys, refusing to interact with anyone. The scene was chaotic and heartbreaking, a stark contrast to the children's own situation. They couldn't help but feel grateful that they hadn't been as severely impacted by the disaster surrounding them.

Suddenly, Habi ran off from the formation and made her way to the altar, squeezing in between those giving prayer.

"Hey, Habi, wait up!" Taliba shouted, chasing after her. The rest of the children quickly followed, closing the distance as they hurried to catch up.

Habi climbed onto the altar without hesitation, her eyes scanning the scattered trinkets and inscriptions left behind by grieving souls. The wooden platform was littered with tokens of remembrance—rings, beads, cloth scraps, and hand-carved names etched into its surface. To her, it resembled a merchant's stall, a collection of sorrow displayed without order, each piece carrying the weight of a loss she couldn't yet comprehend.

Realizing she had nothing tangible to offer, Habi followed the example of those who had come before her. She reached for her silver pin, gripping its dull needle between her fingers. It wasn't as sharp as she had hoped, but it would do. Pressing the tip against the wood, she began to carve, her small hands trembling as she tried to leave her mark.

Just as Habi was about to finish her carving, the children caught up, climbing onto the platform behind her. Taliba, ready to scold Habi for her impulsive actions, froze when she saw the name etched into the wood. The sight of it stopped her in her tracks, and her expression shifted from anger to something more uncertain. The name—familiar, yet haunting—was enough to silence her. The other children stood still as well, the gravity of the moment settling over them.

In large, scratchy lines, Habi etched 'Sara' into the wood. When she finished, she secured the pin back in her pouch and brought her palms together in a prayer, despite not knowing exactly how to pray. The others, uncertain at first, followed her lead, their actions a silent show of respect. The name, 'Sara', could have been carved by someone else before, but now, the children were certain—a tribute to a good friend.

After a moment of quiet reflection, the children slowly recovered from their gesture, hopping off the platform with careful steps to avoid disturbing any of the candles.

"All right, Habi, you're forgiven," Taliba whispered, gently holding her hand as she guided the group back onto the main road.

"I miss Sara," Habi pouted. "Why do we have to die?"

It was a dark question from the youngest, but Taliba chose to answer it directly, given their living conditions.

"It's just life, Habi," Taliba said. "That's how the gods made us. We live, laugh, and learn until it all comes to an end. Besides, living forever doesn't sound that great. If you live too long, you'd get bored of everything—you'd have already done it all. Death gives life purpose. So live a life worth remembering, that's what I say."

Habi pouted again, unsure of what to make of Taliba's complicated words, but she understood the gist of it. However, she soon came to the conclusion that death was inevitable. If there was life, then there was death. If there was a language for the living, then there must be a language for the dead—Koumaic.

As the children continued toward the border gate, Habi munched on her piece of bread, already feeling hungry. Unfortunately, Taliba ruined her fun.

"Habi, we have to ration it," Taliba scolded again, patting Habi's chubby face. "This trip will take all day, and we don't have any gald. Eat small pieces and make it last."

"Okay," Habi frowned, tucking the bread back into her neck pouch.

"Wow, Taliba, you're starting to sound a lot like Father," Hamza snickered.

"Thank you," Taliba smirked.

"That wasn't a compliment."

With the children mixing up their conversations with theory, excitement, and bickering, they soon encountered the first obstacle of their journey: the border gate that separated the lower ring from the middle. The number of slum dwellers resting nearby was sparse, and the absence of the Ghazi guards at the gate made the children uneasy. It was ironic, considering how much they despised authority and the Sultan's men.

Taliba gestured for the others to stay close as she slowly approached the iron gates, where a few vagrants watched her from a distance, intrigued by her actions. Keeping Habi close by, Taliba held her hands, scanning both directions down the adjacent alleyways before deciding to knock on the gate. Taliba knew there were always guards at a gate, but even with her knowledge and the courage she gathered, she couldn't help but feel a tremble as her small hands reached for the cold metal. With an open palm to avoid injury, she slapped the iron gate three times in quick succession, waiting for a response.

The sound of metal scraping against each other from the other side of the gate signaled the opening of a small peephole, through which a Ghazi soldier's eyes appeared. He scanned the area, his gaze darting up, down, and side to side, unable to spot the small children who stood below his line of sight. As he began to cover the peephole, the screeching of the metal door still echoing in the air, Taliba swallowed her nerves and called out, "Wait! We're down here!"

The Ghazi soldier slowly reopened the peephole, his eyes narrowing as he scanned the ground to locate the source of the voice. Taliba quickly motioned for the others to step back a few feet, positioning herself so that the soldier could finally meet her gaze.

"You kids shouldn't be playing up here. Access is restricted to citizens at this time, and I doubt that you lot have citizenship up here," the Ghazi growled, preparing to seal the peephole again.

"Habi, show him the pin," Taliba commanded, urging Habi quickly to prevent the soldier from leaving.

Habi scrambled through her pouch, wedged between a piece of bread and a gald coin, but luckily managed to pull the pin out just in time. She raised it toward the sky, shouting, "Wait, we have this!"

The Ghazi soldier squinted hard to make out the object in Habi's hands. Once he registered the details, he immediately sealed the peephole and consulted with his partners.

"Those kids have the seal of the Intelligence Service," the Ghazi said to his companion.

"What do you mean? How the hell did they get that? Let me see," the other Ghazi groaned, opening the peephole. Habi stood outside, arms trembling as she held the silver pin high. The Ghazi's eyes narrowed as he examined the sigil—an unmistakable silver eye pierced by a needle. The pin's color and design were correct.

He shut the peephole and turned back to his partner. "Holy Centi, you're right. But how did they get it?"

"There's only one way. An agent must have given it to them. That means it's an order from the Sultan."

"Well, let's get them through then," the Ghazi said, his tone shifting. "I'm not losing my ass because we turned away a group of kids the Sultan invited."

"Aye, already on it. We still have to confirm its authenticity."

"Aye—Alright, men, form up at the gate! We're opening it!"

Following the command, the reaction team of Ghazi soldiers positioned themselves at each end of the gate, while the guards pulled on the chains and slowly raised the iron gates.

The children couldn't believe their eyes. The gates that had kept them locked inside the lower hive their entire lives were actually opening for them. They couldn't help but watch in awe as the gates rose, particles of sand drifting off its weathered structure.

When the gates locked into place at their highest point, the children waddled into the middle hive and confronted the Ghazi face to face. Habi kept the silver pin close to her chest, yet still exposed to the soldiers' view. The formation of soldiers slowly closed in, their blades and eyes fixed on the open gateway.

"Why did those kids get to go through, huh!?" a vagrant man shouted angrily. "Let me at it! Keep the gates open!" He rose from his sandy patch, hunched over, and moved toward the formation of Ghazi without a trace of fear in his eyes.

"Get back, or we will strike you down!" a Ghazi soldier commanded.

The Ghazi formation pointed the tips of their scimitars at the approaching man, while some notched arrows on their bowstrings. The soldiers who weren't in a defensive stance moved to secure the children, gently pushing them away from the entrance. More slum dwellers began to gather at the gate, shouting profanities about how the Ghazi had allowed lower-class children to pass so casually.

"We'll tear you gold tongues to pieces!" a man from the lower hive yelled. "You lot caused all this!"

"Keep that gate open! Watch what happens!" a dirtied woman shrieked.

"This is by order of the Sultan! Get back!" a Ghazi shouted, marching forward with his comrades to display a show of force, stopping just before the gate.

"Close the damn gate!" another Ghazi ordered.

As the guards rushed to the pulleys at each side of the gate, housed in small gate shacks, a large rock was hurled from the lower hive, striking a Ghazi soldier in the forehead. The impact sent the soldier reeling, breaking formation. As a deterrent, one of the soldiers fired an arrow into the chest of a man, presumed to be the rock thrower.

The small mob in the lower hive continued shouting and screaming at the fortified Ghazi, who kept barking commands. Once the gate guards unlocked the chains around their pulleys, the iron gate dropped rapidly, slamming against the ground and kicking up sand and dust into the air. The rattling chains came to an abrupt halt, and the mob's riot faded, now distant and muffled through the iron threshold.

"Give me a head count and check on the wounded!" a Ghazi officer demanded. "Are the children secured?"

"Aye, sir, the children are with me," another soldier said, resting his hands on Tariq's and Hamza's shoulders as the rest of the group huddled between them.

"All accounted for, sir. Asim took a blow to the head, but he'll be fine," a soldier reported, wiping the blood trickling from another soldier's forehead.

"Aye, tend to him and get him back up," the officer ordered before turning to the children—his gaze settling on Habi and the sigil in her grasp. "I'll be damned. If it isn't the rumored golden-eyed child. We all thought it was just some ghost story about a little brat running around, but here you are."

Tariq and Hamza took up a fighting stance, tensing as they locked their gazes on the Ghazi who had identified Habi.

"Now, now, little ones. It would behoove you all to comply with our customs," the officer warned. "I'd rather not harm the Sultan's potential guests, but if it came to a fight, you wouldn't stand a chance. That silver pin you're holding—hand it over."

Habi complied with the man's order, gently raising her arm with the pin in hand. But instead of treating the pin with the same care, the Ghazi aggressively swiped it from her grasp and brought it to his face for a closer inspection.

"Where'd you get this?" the officer asked.

"A-A lady gave it to me. Her name was Raja. She said she was with the media and told me to bring the pin to the gates. She said the Sultan wants us to visit his tower for a meeting," Habi explained, trembling—unused to facing the authorities in a direct conversation.

The officer maintained his tired expression as he rubbed his thumb across the silver sigil, picking at it to see if any of its material would flake off.

"Sir, it's the K.I.S.," another soldier whispered to the officer. "I was on watch at one of the other gates when the agent requested permission to pass during the blockade yesterday. She was under orders directly from the Sultan and the Head of the Service. It's valid."

The officer sighed and handed the pin back to Habi, who gratefully retrieved it.

"I was informed there'd be visitors, but I didn't expect children. And of all the gates, they chose this one," the officer snickered, gesturing to two men from the reaction team. "Malik. Jalal. Take two horses and escort the children to the higher hive border. Hand them off to their watch, then return and finish your shift."

"Aye, sir," the two soldiers acknowledged.

"You little ones have fun with the Sultan now," the officer chuckled, his smirk menacing as he eyed the group. "All right, gents, back to work! Show's over! Nobles ain't payin' us to just stand around!"

"Sir, that's exactly what they're payin' us to do," a soldier jested.

The soldiers laughed together at the friendly banter. The officer joined in with the cheer, fixing his composure and making sure his men were in their proper positions.

When the children saw the interaction between the Ghazi, they believed they had just witnessed a spark of humanity in them. The children had always thought the Sultan's men were nothing more than evil puppets, but the men's smiles made the hairs rise on their arms. The men were close, much like the children were. It made them wonder why everyone had to keep fighting each other, even though everyone was human. Most of the children were oblivious to the underlying truth, but Taliba knew that in any structured civilization, conflict was inevitable—especially among different classes and political perspectives. It was human nature, and it was bound to happen.

"So much for free roaming," Hamza whispered to Taliba as the two Ghazi pulled the reins of two brown horses stored next to the gate shack.

"Shut up. We're lucky to have even made it this far," Taliba hissed.

The Ghazi soldiers helped the children onto the saddles of the horses. One soldier mounted a stallion with Hamza, Tariq, and Naji behind him, while the other carried Taliba and Habi. Once everyone was seated, the Ghazi pulled their reins, gripped the sides of the horses with their legs, and leaned forward as the horses began to move. The children, feeling the sudden inertia of the swift forward motion, immediately steadied themselves and cheered to each other. They couldn't believe it—they were traveling through the middle hive on horseback.

"This is fun!" Habi laughed, tightly nestled between the Ghazi and Taliba. "So this is a horse!"

"That it is, Habi!" Taliba laughed along.

Habi kept the silver pin tightly in her small hands as the group moved through the crowds of middle hive citizens, going about their day. Some of the citizens gazed toward the clouds of smoke rising over the lower hive. With their mighty horses, the Ghazi easily parted the throngs of people like a wave. Unfortunately, the children didn't have the chance to run about and steal their favorite types of food. The guards weren't the only hindrance; time was against them as well. The sun was already past its highest point. It was afternoon, and the children could feel the brunt of the desert heat at its peak. The only way they could stay comfortable now was by rationing their bread and sipping from their canteens as the gallop quickened their journey.

Never having traveled the main road of the middle hive before—or had the opportunity to—the children saw structures and fields they had never witnessed. The closer they got to the next border, the more fences, crops, and animals they encountered, with citizens working the fields. The group could smell a mixture of hay, manure, soil, spices, and other scents they couldn't quite identify. It was a sensory buffet that filled their nostrils, but they much preferred it to the stench and rot of the lower hive. Other than international trade, the children figured this production district was the main source of Koura's life, comfort, and stability.

Habi gazed at a large brown creature on four legs, munching on grass, curious to know what it was.

"Taliba, what's that?" Habi asked, pointing at the mysterious creature behind the fences.

"That's a cow," Taliba answered, recalling the descriptions from the books she had read. She was confident that it matched the characteristics and description of one.

Moo!

"Moo!" Habi mimicked, causing the Ghazi to shake his head. "What do they do?" she asked, still curious.

"Well, from what I know, we drink their milk, harvest their leather—and we also eat them," Taliba explained.

"We what?" Habi asked, her jaw dropping in disbelief.

—

By the time the children reached the border gate to the higher hive, the sun was creeping toward the horizon. Two more Ghazi stood watch at the border, and Habi could see the look on their faces as they saw two of their cohorts bringing in a trove of children.

"By order of the Sultan," Malik, one of the children's escorts, began, pulling the reins to bring his horse to a halt. "These children are to meet with the Enlightened One, brothers. One of them carries the pin of invitation, bestowed by an agent," Malik continued. "Child, show them your sigil."

On cue, Habi raised the silver pin toward the two guards, catching their attention. Both paused for a moment, then nodded to each other, preparing to deliver their verdict.

"Aye, we will ensure the children are delivered to the noble ring," a border guard said. "You may return to your post, brother. We'll handle it from here."

"Aye. May the gods bless you and the Sultan grant you guidance. The Sultan is great," Malik said, dismounting and helping the children down. His partner did the same with his group.

"The Sultan is great," the border guards repeated.

Once the children's escorts returned to their horses and galloped down the slight incline of the hill, heading back to their post, a border guard slapped his hands on the iron gate behind him and shouted, "Open the gates! By order of the Sultan, we have children who bear the Eye of Shie!"

A few seconds of silence passed between the children and the guards, until the chains began to rattle around their pulleys from the other side of the wall. This iron gate, which separated the middle and higher hive, was cleaner than the previous one. When it lifted, only a few drifts of sand fell from its rims, and its iron foundation was well-maintained.

The children remained quiet, appreciating the unexpected kindness. Not long ago, they had been mere rats to the slaughter, overlooked and forgotten. Now, they were the Sultan's esteemed guests, granted the rare privilege of walking past the higher hive border without conflict. Habi couldn't help but smile as she daydreamed, imagining how she would return home with Rafi and continue their lives together, alongside the others.

"Present the pin, child," another guard said from the other side of the wall.

Habi didn't realize it at first, but the iron gate was already locked in place, hovering above her and the children. Two more Ghazi introduced themselves as the opening cleared, waiting for the proper evidence that Habi carried.

As instructed, Habi raised the pin once again, allowing the guards to inspect it from arm's reach.

"Aye, I'll escort them to the noble ring," one of the Ghazi said.

"Very well then, Qasim. Trying to get your steps in?" his partner chuckled.

"Nothing ever happens on this ring. A little walk won't hurt," Qasim said with a smile, gesturing for the children to follow. "Come now, little ones. The Sultan waits."

Silently, the children waddled closely behind their escort, while the three remaining gate guards bade each other farewell, sealed the gate, and returned to their watch.

The higher hive at this hour saw children and young adults returning home from their schools and lessons.

608

Though it was a busy time, the well-maintained streets were still less crowded than those below.

As the Ghazi escorted the ragged children, the citizens couldn't help but watch in awe and curiosity. For most who lived in this ring, they had never seen such a stark display of torn clothes, scars, bruises, and dirt on an individual—let alone children. As the group moved forward, some of the citizens whispered amongst themselves about trivial matters the children would never have thought to concern themselves with.

"Who lets their child wear rags like that?"

"Wow, they really stink."

"When was the last time they had a proper meal?"

Some of the wealthy children, dressed in the finest garments, even waved at the passing group, as if it were some kind of game. However, the only ones who waved back were the Ghazi and Habi, both of whom seemed genuinely excited to be there.

By the time the children reached the next border gate, dusk was settling in, with the sun slowly sinking behind the dunes, casting a red glare across the sky. The moon began to rise, greeting the dimming heavens once again. At this point, the children were exhausted from all the walking. They had essentially trekked away half of their day, savoring the little food and water they had left. They could only hope that either one of the Ghazi soldiers might spare some rations, or that the Sultan had prepared a grand feast for their arrival. Both outcomes seemed unlikely, but the children couldn't help but admire the thought.

The escort followed the same protocol as those before him, but instead of Ghazi at the gates, there were two Mamluk knights. Both Mamluks noticed the approaching soldier, leading a group of children behind him. They knew that the only reason a Ghazi would bring such citizens—if they could even be called that—to the noble ring was because the children had matters pertaining to the Sultan. The Mamluks, trained for such situations, knew exactly how to handle it.

"Present the sigil," a Mamluk barked.

Habi flinched slightly at the Mamluk's deep, muffled tone. She had thought the Ghazi were intimidating up close, but witnessing a Mamluk—who towered over both the children and the Ghazi soldier, and wasn't actively trying to maim her—was truly horrifying. When Habi lifted the pin for the knight, the Mamluk gently plucked it from her hand and inspected it. Instead of returning it like the others, he kept the pin and tucked it into one of the satchels across his waist.

"You may go, Ghazi," the Mamluk ordered. "I'll lead them to the tower."

"Aye," the Ghazi obeyed, turning to head back to his post.

Habi, judging from their brief interaction, believed that the Ghazi and Mamluks weren't as cohesive as when the Ghazi chatted amongst themselves. It felt more like a parent scolding their child, and the children could sense the overwhelming presence of the single Mamluk escorting them to the tower.

When the children passed the boundary, two more Mamluks were stationed on the other side, simply noting their presence. From afar, lit against the night sky, the Sultan's tower seemed closer than ever. With each step forward, the children could make out the countless lanterns glowing along its walls and platforms, illuminating the flowing flag of Koura. As they drew nearer, they noticed golden embroidery along the rims of the stones and bricks that formed the tower's foundation. The colors shimmered softly in the light of the lanterns. A large, angled platform high above ominously loomed over one side of the city. Granite homes dotted the noble ring surrounding the tower, making it the most spacious of all. But the only figures visible roaming the royal grounds at this hour were Mamluk knights, sworn to guard the Sultan and his bloodline.

The moon was near its peak, casting a bright, illuminating light on those beneath it. The walk from the border to the tower was the shortest journey the children had experienced when it came to making a beeline across a ring. When they reached the imposing gates of the Sultan's tower, two decorated Mamluks stood guard beneath it, hailing their brother who guided the children.

"Open the gates," the armored escort commanded. "These children have an audience with the Sultan."

"Aye," his armored companions acknowledged, slowly pushing open the large iron doors, their hinges groaning with an eerie creak.

A.G. MANNY

"Welcome to the tower, little ones," the Mamluk escort said.

Chapter Twenty-eight

The iron gates slammed shut behind the children as soon as they entered the premises of the Sultan.

"We're close to Rafi! I can smell him!" Habi cheered, hopping up and down in the corridor lined with armor, decorations, and paintings.

"Habi, settle down! We're in the Sultan's home. We need to show respect," Taliba scolded, trying to calm Habi. The rest of the children laughed, but the Mamluk who volunteered to escort them through the dimly lit halls remained unfazed.

As instructed, Habi calmed down, though her smile never wavered. To distract herself from the excitement, she focused on the rich red carpet beneath their feet, its golden trims glinting in the light. Her gaze flitted between the vibrant decorations, ancient suits of armor, and paintings she assumed depicted the Sultan and his ancestors. The air was faintly stuffy, yet fragrant with perfumes and the scent of fresh fabric. It felt as though she had stepped into a museum dedicated to the history of Koura.

The children thought they were finally free from the endless walking, but as soon as they reached the open circular room at the bottom of the spiral stairwell with its seemingly infinite steps, all of them groaned in dismay.

"Well, let's think about this," Hamza chuckled. "One last hike up these stairs, and sooner or later, we'll see Rafi!"

"My legs are never going to recover from this," Naji groaned, gazing up at the spiral stairs twisting into a dizzying vortex.

Tariq patted Naji's back as the Mamluk began the ascent, saying, "Come on, buddy, almost there. Look, you gonna let little Habi outshine you? She's already halfway up the steps with Taliba."

"Habi is literally built differently," Naji sighed, joining Tariq on the steps.

The Mamluk didn't utter a single word to the children, only occasionally turning his head slightly to ensure they were all keeping up. Some of the children climbed with the last of their energy, while others, particularly Habi and Hamza, bear-crawled up the stairs, having fun but making sure not to pass or hinder the Mamluk guiding them. The children expected the climb to take longer, but the Mamluk paused at a platform halfway up the tower and then led them down a tall, dimly lit corridor. To avoid getting lost and jeopardizing their chance to see Rafi, the children followed closely behind, gazing at the empty granite walls on either side.

There were only a few wooden doors on either side of the hallway, and at the end of the corridor stood a large double door made of solid steel. As the children gazed at the imposing doorway, they knew Rafi was near—and so was the Sultan.

"I'm so excited, Taliba," Habi whispered with a giggle, resting her head against Taliba's arm.

"Me too, Habi," Taliba said with a smile. "Maybe after we get him back, we can rest a bit, enjoy some good food, and share stories."

"I would love that," Habi murmured, her smile unwavering.

The Mamluk stopped in front of the double steel doors and placed a hand on them, preparing to push them open. Before he did, he turned to the children and said, "This is your destination, little ones. The Sultan awaits your arrival."

The children braced themselves, containing their excitement as the Mamluk slowly opened the doors with both hands. The heavy doors creaked and groaned as they were pushed back, finally locking into place with a loud thud. Habi tried to peek past the Mamluk's body, but all she could make out were more lanterns illuminating a vast, empty room. Once the Mamluk led the children inside, another Mamluk stood post just a few feet from the entrance. Once all the children had entered, their escort sealed the steel doors behind them and took up a position on the other side with his companion.

The children couldn't decide whether to feel frightened by the dimly lit room or joyous knowing Rafi was near. As they settled in, they began to map out the space, piecing together what they could see. The room was an open rectangular hall with multiple stone pillars, each mounted with candle-lit lanterns. The pillars also supported a walking balcony above, hinting at another floor directly overhead. The flooring shared the same design as the rest of the tower, draped with a red carpet trimmed in gold.

If Taliba had to guess the room's purpose, she wouldn't have called it a courtroom. Instead, it felt more like a ballroom, akin to the dancefloors she had read about in her novels. The ornate decorations and statues lining the walls, though shrouded in shadow, added to the impression of a space designed for grandeur rather than formality.

From above, a loud stomp echoed through the room, followed by the synchronized step of several Ghazi soldiers moving forward in unison. Each soldier wore the haunting masks the children recognized from The Culling. In their hands, they held wooden bows, and though barely visible from the children's perspective, the feathered ends of arrows in quivers at their hips caught their attention. The children flinched at the soldiers' sudden appearance, their numbers easily overwhelming the small group below. Despite their unease, they assumed it was merely the Sultan's way of showcasing his troops.

At the far end of the balcony, a tall figure emerged from the shadows, accompanied by a much shorter one. As the lantern light illuminated their faces, Habi's eyes lit up, and she burst into a cheer, her smile stretching wide.

"Rafi! Rafi! You're safe!" Habi shouted joyfully toward the two figures above.

Rafi, his gloomy blue eyes fixed downward and his face expressionless, noticed Habi calling out to him but did not respond. Beside him stood the Sultan, adorned with a bejeweled golden crown resting above his tattooed third eye. The Sultan placed a hand on Rafi's shoulder, his piercing gaze falling on the children as he silently waited for one of his men to reprimand them for speaking out of turn.

"Silence yourself, as you are in the presence of the Enlightened One! You do not speak unless told to do so! You are to kneel! Do so, now!" a Ghazi soldier commanded sharply, his voice booming from behind his iron mask.

Startled, Habi let out a small whimper and joined the other children in kneeling to the ground as commanded. With their heads lowered, Habi subtly tilted her gaze toward Taliba, her expression filled with sadness and concern.

It's okay, Taliba silently mouthed to Habi.

After a moment of silence, the Sultan finally spoke, his voice firm and authoritative: "Stand."

As commanded, the children rose to their feet, while the Ghazi and Mamluks remained motionless and silent.

Before starting the session, the Sultan decided to consult with Rafi.

"Are these the children?" the Sultan whispered to Rafi.

"Yes," Rafi said with a hoarse voice.

"Very well then," the Sultan chuckled lightly before turning his attention to the children huddled in the center of the room. Spreading his arms in a gesture of warm welcome, he said, "I appreciate you children for going out of your way to attend this audience. For that, I thank you all. Now, which one of you is Habi Sabbah?"

The children exchanged confused glances, hesitant to identify Habi under the intense gaze of the Sultan. After a moment, Habi timidly raised her small hand into the air, still too afraid to speak, not wanting to incur another reprimand.

"Please, you may all speak freely," the Sultan clarified. He then turned his attention to Habi. "As to you, Habi, I thank you personally for receiving the order and advising your family. It is also a great honor to finally be in the presence of the golden-eyed child."

"T-Thank you," Habi stuttered, barely audible to the Sultan's ears from afar.

"Ah, of course, I can't ignore the rest of you," the Sultan smiled, gesturing toward the children. "Please, introduce yourselves accordingly."

"Taliba," Taliba started the roll call.

"Hamza."

"Tariq."

"Naji."

The Sultan nodded, his gaze sweeping over the children as he continued.

"Pleasure to meet you all. You do know who I am, yes?" the Sultan grinned, amusement gleaming in his eyes.

"Yes, you're the Sultan," Taliba answered swiftly.

"In the presence of their greatness, you will address them as *Enlightened One*! Do so, now!" a Ghazi bellowed, his voice echoing through the room.

Taliba flinched at the sudden burst of noise from the Ghazi, which shook the quiet room. She quickly corrected herself, her voice steady but tense, "Yes, you're the Enlightened One."

"Aye. Then you all know why we gather here at this hour?" the Sultan asked, his tone steady and piercing.

"Yes, Enlightened One," Taliba answered for the children.

"Good, now let me explain," the Sultan said. "Rafi here, as you all know and love him, has confessed to his crimes in regards to attempted burglary in the confines of my Commandant's home, as well as several counts of petit and grand larceny throughout the city. He has proved himself worthy to live another day, and all that I ask from you all is a simple apology. Speak it so when you are all in agreement."

The children nodded at each other and, nearly simultaneously, said, "We're sorry, Enlightened One."

The Sultan smiled and nodded, satisfied with the apology. He then gestured to the Mamluks who stood at the steel doors to open them, and the two knights did just that. The doors creaked as they swung open, locking into place with a resounding thud. The Mamluks then stood at both sides of the frame, silently observing.

"Apology accepted," the Sultan said with a smile. "You are all free to go."

"Rafi!" Habi cheered again, while the other children exhaled in relief.

However, Rafi didn't react to Habi's call. Instead, when the light shined on his face, it almost seemed like he was about to quietly tear up, which made Habi worry.

"Except there is one last thing," the Sultan menacingly grinned, snapping his fingers.

With the snap, both Mamluks at the door raised their halberds and crossed them over the doorway. The Ghazi soldiers above nocked arrows to their bowstrings, gripping them with both hands, ready to draw.

The children immediately whimpered, glancing up at the Sultan, who chuckled to himself like a maniac.

"You see, little ones," the Sultan hissed, his voice rising. "That doorway is not how you'll be *free*. Time and time again, I've received reports of lowly hive rats causing turmoil in the upper hives, stealing from honest citizens, even assaulting them. Do you think the people would forgive—think *I* would forgive—you, especially after you dared to *steal* from one of my leaders? *Do you*!?"

From the Sultan's voice alone, the children could tell he was furious. They shivered, desperate to flee. But when they glanced toward the far end of the room, two more Mamluk knights guarded another exit. With soldiers at both ends and above, the children realized they were trapped. Helpless, they remained silent, frozen in fear.

The Sultan patted Rafi on the shoulder and began to laugh. "You see, little roaches—Rafi decided to cut a deal and take up my offer. In exchange for your lives, which will stop a good amount of crime reports from the people, Rafi will live under *my* roof and enjoy *my* riches. He chose to live a good life, rather than be stuck with you fools. Isn't that right, Rafi? You've always wanted the life you deserve, haven't you?"

Rafi hesitated, his fists clenched, as his voice began to shake.

"Yes," Rafi whispered, his voice breaking.

"Louder, Rafi. They can't hear you," the Sultan demanded.

"Rafi! It's not true, right!?" Taliba shouted, her voice trembling as if her life depended on it.

"Rafi! You little shit! You better be fuckin' around!" Tariq roared.

Habi stepped forward, hands clasped tightly to her chest as she gazed up at Rafi.

"Rafi, I don't know what he said, but—you'll come home with us, right?" Habi asked, her innocent eyes filled with hope.

"Silence the room for the Enlightened One!" a Ghazi soldier commanded loudly.

"*You* silence, soldier," the Sultan retorted angrily, causing the soldier to withdraw. "Let the children blabber. Let them speak, let them cry. Let them scream their last words."

"We're gonna die," Naji murmured, his voice trembling with panic. "My god, we're gonna die."

"Hey, hey, man, we're still breathing," Hamza said, trying to comfort Naji. "We can still–"

"No, Hamza, you don't understand! We're trapped, and the Sultan practically ordered a death sentence on us. We're gonna die!"

Naji crumpled to the ground, wrapping his hands over his head, whimpering and crying. Hamza and Tariq tried to help him up, but Naji resisted, violently flailing, sparking a struggle between the three children.

"Rafi, you get down here right now! Or I'll–" Taliba shouted, but an arrow landed right next to her feet, warning her to step no further. She froze, staring at the arrow that had narrowly missed her.

Habi scrambled away from where she stood, terrified of the arrow that had landed between her and Taliba. She whimpered, running into Taliba's arms, her skin growing cold from horror and distress.

"Taliba, what's happening?" Habi asked quietly, fighting the tears that threatened to spill from her distraught voice.

Taliba remained speechless, the weight of her fears now a harsh reality. Her breathing quickened as she steeled herself, preparing to speak some sense into Rafi once more.

"Rafi—please, we have a home, you have a family. Please," Taliba pleaded, her voice breaking as she burst into tears.

The Sultan smirked as he patted Rafi again, murmuring, "Go ahead, speak, child. Express your inner desires, and let them realize that one should put themselves first at all costs. Speak it."

Rafi, finally gathering the courage through his tears, shouted, "I'm sorry—This is my home now! I don't want to go back to the lower hive, living day by day, fighting to survive! This was my ticket out, and the Sul—the Enlightened One—gave it to me!" He broke into tears, his voice cracking as he forced out the rest. "I'm sorry! You all know I wanted to get out, but—none of you can come with me. I–"

"That's enough, boy," the Sultan said, patting Rafi on the head as the boy sobbed. "Now, bear witness."

The Sultan raised his right hand with an open palm, and at his signal, all the Ghazi archers notched arrows into their bows, aiming them at the children below.

The children at the center of the room whimpered, panicked, and filled with absolute terror. They could do nothing but cling to each other, attempting to crawl away from the scene—but it was futile. They considered hiding behind the stone pillars, but they knew they wouldn't make it in time when the arrows flew. The children screamed, curling into themselves in sorrow, with some begging the Sultan for mercy.

"Habi," Taliba whispered softly, holding her tightly in her arms. "Close your eyes."

"W-Why? What's happening?" Habi whimpered, tears streaming down her cheeks. Without waiting for an answer, she obeyed Taliba's command, closing her eyes and hugging her tightly.

"We need to run! We need to–" Tariq shouted frantically at his family, but before he could finish, the Sultan extended his arm forward with an open palm.

Tariq's voice was barely audible as the arrows were released with the snap of the bowstrings.

—

From pitch darkness fading into a blur of colors, Habi slowly opened her eyes, feeling excruciating pain in her legs and back. One moment, she was hugging Taliba, and the next, she was on the ground, barely able to move a muscle. All she could feel was agony, sharp objects lodged in her body, and warm liquid flowing down her skin.

As her vision slowly cleared, Habi was able to make out the horrific sight that lay before her.

Naji was hunched over, his face pressed into the ground. Several arrows jutted out from his back and head.

Hamza lay on his back, his face expressionless. Arrows were lodged in his chest and neck, and his blood began to stain his rags.

Tariq was on his knees with his head lowered and his arms limping against the ground. He suffered arrows from all directions.

Taliba lay on her side, right next to Habi. Unlike the others, she was still able to move, though only slightly. Arrows protruded from her back, shoulders, and legs, her face etched with grief and agony. Habi, noticing the extent of her own injuries compared to Taliba's, realized that Taliba had shielded her from most of the volley.

"I-I don't wanna die!" Taliba wailed, tears and saliva choking her throat. "Papa! They're hurting me! Papa!" she cried out in desperation.

Suddenly, another arrow flew loose, striking Taliba in the head, and she went immediately silent, her body going limp.

Habi, witnessing the death of her brothers and sister, felt a deep pain in her heart. She wanted to go and check on them, but her strength was at an all-time low. Not only that, she was terrified of suffering the same fate as Taliba, who had cried for mercy and for Father. Habi was on the verge of surrendering to the pain, but when her eyes landed on the open doorway where two Mamluks stood, she knew what she had to do—survive.

Habi's instincts kicked in instantly, and a surge of adrenaline flooded her veins, driving her to survive. She hyperventilated, sweating, leaving a trail of blood behind her as she scrambled to her feet and dashed toward the exit, praying she wouldn't be struck down.

"We got a runner!" a Ghazi shouted, quickly preparing to notch another arrow.

"Stand down! Let her go!" the Sultan ordered, and the soldiers immediately obeyed. Instead of letting them deal with the sole survivor, the Sultan patted Rafi on the shoulder once more, who had just witnessed his entire family slain before him. "Go. She's yours."

Rafi hesitated, but in the end, he spoke with a soft, painful voice, "Aye, Enlightened One."

The Mamluks, following the Sultan's order, stepped back from their post and allowed Habi to sprint down the corridor in pure panic. Behind her, a liquid red trail marked her path, leaving Rafi to follow.

—

Habi ran in agony down long, dark corridors, each stride sending the tips of the arrows twisting deeper into her muscles. She had no idea where she was going, but she knew she couldn't afford to stop moving until she was safe. Occasionally, the paralyzing, stinging pain would overwhelm her, and she'd trip, crashing to the floor. But with every ounce of energy left in her, she scrambled back to her feet and continued running. It felt like she was only running from the inevitable, and she could've sworn there was a spiral stairwell up ahead. But instead, the dark corridor led her to a pair of wooden doors, sitting alone at the end, with no other exit in sight.

When Habi reached the doors, she turned the knobs as quickly as she could. To her relief, they were unlocked, and without hesitation, she stepped through. But though the door was an exit, it wasn't the kind of freedom she had hoped for.

Habi was pelted with strong desert winds that chilled her to the bone as she limped forward. The doorway had led her onto a balcony with no railings or safety measures, and she hoped there might be a way down. Unfortunately, when she peered over the edge of the jagged platform, all she saw was an empty space and a long drop to the city grounds below.

She froze, staring down from the ledge, feeling her heart sink and her bones tremble. From this absurdly high vantage point, she could see every hive ring, from the bright noble mansions to the dark lower slums. The entire city, carved into the sand, sprawled before her in its marvelous multi-ring foundation. The desert dunes surrounding the city were dark, only the tips illuminated by the high moon, sparkling faintly in the night. The platform beneath her swayed slightly side to side, rocked by the strong winds and the height.

If she had to guess exactly where she was on the tower, it would be the angled platform that loomed over a section of the city. The platform jutted out near the peak, and from here, she could see how the city was swallowed by the night, with scattered lanterns lighting the paths of those below. Directly beneath her, the platform cast a shadow over the already darkened part of the city. She was above the noble ring, and the only thing standing between her and the nobles was hundreds of feet of open air.

Habi knew she couldn't turn back, convinced the Sultan's men were still pursuing her. However, she couldn't go forward either, unless she wanted to be battered by the winds as she ran to the end of the platform—for who knows how long. She had always thought nightmares were confined to her dreams, but now, she was living in one—and she was at her breaking point.

She still couldn't believe that her family—Taliba, Hamza, Tariq, and Naji—were all gone. She refused to accept it, fighting the urge to run back and see if they were okay. She couldn't fully grasp what had happened during the encounter between Rafi, the children, and the Sultan; she could only hope that Rafi was still the same boy she had once loved—because hope was all she had left.

She flinched and quickly turned to look at the door that had locked open behind her, fearing it was a Ghazi or Mamluk preparing to strike. To her remaining shred of hope, she saw Rafi instead.

Nearly tripping and falling after a brief respite, Habi burst into a small, limping jog toward Rafi, who still wore the same frown across his face.

"Rafi!" Habi cried out, latching onto his chest. "Please, I wanna go home! I want you and me to go home! I'm scared, Rafi!"

Rafi tried his best to suppress his emotions in response to Habi's pleas, but a couple of tears escaped despite his efforts. He gave Habi a warm hug, momentarily shielding her from the cold winds, before releasing her and gently gripping her shoulders. His eyes met hers as he spoke.

"Habi, you know I love you," Rafi murmured genuinely, fighting back the tears flooding his eyes. "Part of me was really hoping that none of you came," he frowned. "But the other part of me—is glad that you did."

Habi didn't know what to say. She had never seen Rafi cry in front of her before, and it made her heart ache to see him like this.

"Rafi, I love you too!" Habi cried. "Let's just go home! If you don't want to go home, then I can stay with you! You know I'm a good girl!"

"I can't do that, Habi!" Rafi lashed out. "You're not part of the deal! I tried to convince him, but—he doesn't believe any of you deserve to live. Meanwhile, I had to fight for my life in front of him. He chose *me*, Habi."

Habi sobbed, her tears flowing uncontrollably, pain written all over her face. She couldn't believe what was happening. Her entire world had just fallen apart. She believed everything had gone wrong because—she had led the children here—led them to their doom, and in the end, she blamed herself for it all.

"Rafi, no—please," Habi cried. "Money—money doesn't matter! You and I can go home, spend time together, and be happy with what we have! Remember what Father said as one of his rules? 'Take care of those next to you'. Please, Rafi!"

Rafi brought Habi close for another hug as both children sobbed and whimpered. He gently rubbed her back, trying to comfort her. Habi, still shaking profusely, retrieved the kissed gald coin from her neck pouch and held it out to him, hoping to spark something in him—to knock some sense into him.

"Remember?" Habi whimpered, her voice trembling. "This is the same coin you kissed and gave to me during our first trip out. I still have it. This is how much you mean to me, Rafi!"

Rafi stared at the coin, his tears falling onto its carved surface. He was deeply hurt, and Habi knew that this was the only way to reach him—the only way to bring him back.

Rafi grimaced in agony and gently pushed Habi away from his chest, placing his hands on her shoulders once more. He couldn't bear feeling this way any longer. It was time to put an end to this dread, to make a choice, and to stop being consumed by the weight of it all.

"I'm sorry, Habi," Rafi apologized, his voice shaking. "I'm sorry for everything, but—Saif is no longer my father. And think about it, Habi—you are taking care of me, as I am taking care of you."

Habi stared at Rafi, her brow furrowed in confusion and concern, unsure of what he meant. The gravity of his words hung in the air between them, leaving her feeling both lost and anxious.

"You are taking care of me because you gave me this chance to live a better life. And I am taking care of you—because soon, you won't feel pain anymore," Rafi said, his lips quivering.

"W-What do you mean?" Habi whimpered.

Rafi quickly kissed Habi on the forehead, holding the warm touch as long as he could. After the kiss, he rested his forehead against hers, their eyes only inches apart. He then turned his face away and let out a deep sigh.

"I'm sorry, Habi," Rafi murmured.

Suddenly, Rafi's blue eyes glowed. A surge of energy rushed from his arms into Habi's chest, making her shiver from the unfamiliar power. With one swift push, Rafi sent Habi tumbling off the edge of the platform.

But instead of falling, she was propelled toward the sky with overwhelming force.

Habi, still struggling to grasp the situation, watched Rafi's face grow smaller and smaller as she shot upward at an insane speed, past the tip of the platform, before rapidly descending. She felt as if her insides were trying to burst from her chest, and there was nothing to hold onto. She didn't even know where her precious kissed gald coin had gone. All she could focus on in that moment was the overwhelming certainty—she was falling to her death.

When she realized she was falling, Habi let out a bloodcurdling scream so powerful she thought she'd rupture a lung. She flailed, crying out repeatedly, "Rafi! Rafi!" She screamed and shouted throughout her entire descent, releasing the last of her strength, pleading for anyone—whether it be a mythical creature or the gods—to save her. She kept crying until her voice abruptly cut off. A wave of excruciating pain spread through her back and body. Everything inside her went numb, and her vision darkened as her last breath wheezed out of her limp jaw.

—

Rafi lowered his head and quietly sobbed as the glow in his eyes faded, staring at the abyss where Habi had landed. He now had to live with the haunting thought that he had sent his family to die while personally killing Habi. It was the only way to fulfill the Sultan's offer, and had he defied the Sultan's command, he would have been the one to die, alongside the others.

He knew the Sultan had been watching the entire time, following his every move. The Sultan was waiting to see if Rafi would falter and give in to his emotions. In the Sultan's royal eyes, Rafi had proven himself worthy to live under the crown. The deal was settled.

The Sultan gave Rafi a brief moment to mourn before stepping into view from the doorway, flanked by two Mamluk knights. He placed a hand on the boy's shoulder and offered a cold, calculated comfort.

"You've done well, boy," the Sultan crooned. "Extinguish your meaningless ties, and you will emerge from your new shell without weakness. Grieve now, for that pain you feel is temporary. Tomorrow, you will stand tall, knowing your success will last a lifetime. What's done is done."

Rafi heard the Sultan's words, yet he kept his eyes fixed on the deep, dark abyss below, imagining how helpless and horrified Habi must have felt when she realized she was falling. The entire way down, he could almost hear her screams, slowly fading until they came to a disturbing, silent stop.

The Sultan kneeled next to Rafi, trying to see what Rafi was seeing. While Rafi saw grief, the Sultan saw change.

"You understand that it had to be done, right, boy?" the Sultan murmured.

"Yes, Enlightened One," Rafi mumbled.

"You'll come to learn," the Sultan continued. "You will understand that people need to be led, and that some must be put down. You will understand that with great riches, power, and stability, there will always be those who try to take it from you. You earn your keep, and you ignore the beggars. Not everyone can be saved—and not everyone deserves to be saved. I will teach you all of this, little one."

After his lecture, the Sultan stood and offered Rafi his hand, a gesture not many would receive. Rafi looked up at the Sultan with sunken, red eyes, the remnants of his flood of tears still visible. He gritted his teeth and clenched his fists, as if ready to strike the Sultan. But instead of lashing out, he forced himself to swallow his despair, straightening his posture to present himself properly for the Sultan's presence—and the new age ahead of him. The Sultan smirked as he watched Rafi's gloomy expression shift into one of anger and ambition. After giving Rafi a moment to regroup and accept the new reality he had thrust upon himself, he took the Sultan's hand.

The Sultan smiled from cheek to cheek, satisfied with the boy's grit and determination.

"Heavy is the crown." The Sultan grinned, leading Rafi away from the windy platform and into the dimly lit corridor beyond the wooden door.

Chapter Twenty-nine

Saif Sabbah felt a sudden, sharp pain in his chest as he walked the dark streets of the slums. He brushed it off, attributing it to his age, and continued smoking his tobacco pipe while carrying his logbook. Every step was instinctive—either suppressing his presence or standing tall, ready for any potential ambush. It was muscle memory, and he kept his pace steady as he made his way back to his shed.

The moon was still young, and by this hour, the children should have been home, playing near the lit lanterns. But when he reached the shed, there was no noise, no laughter. The cracks and creases in the structure offered no trace of light either. He assumed they were either asleep or hadn't returned yet. To his dismay, when he opened the door, he found the latter to be true.

Saif placed his book on the desk, took a draw from his pipe, and kindled the ceiling lantern. Everything in the shed was well-maintained, the bedrolls lying empty—flat and wrinkled.

Saif remained silent, piecing together theories about what the children might be up to at this hour. He expected them to return soon and chose not to dwell on it. Instead, he continued writing in his book, the only sounds around him those of wanderers on the streets, their voices fading with the wind and sand.

As he took notes, a leaning piece of paper in the corner of his desk caught his eye. It was one of Habi's drawings, and he couldn't help but chuckle at how silly yet earnest it looked. He recognized every child in the sketch and smiled at the image of himself that Habi had included. Everyone was smiling in the picture, and each time he looked at it, he found himself wishing the children would return home soon—just to know they were safe, just to know he was a good father.

A couple of hours passed, and there was still no sign of the children. Saif believed they were up to no good again, likely meddling in the affairs of the upper hives. He was already preparing to scold them as soon as they returned, but for now, he knew he needed rest.

Saif organized his workspace and extinguished the ceiling lantern. He then returned to his corner and lay down, expecting the children to open the door at any moment. However, his exhaustion overtook him, and he soon drifted into a deep slumber.

When Saif woke up in the morning, he expected to see the children lying in their bedrolls, but to his consternation, they weren't there. He even waited outside the shed, leaning against the door, keeping an eye out for any children running amok—but he didn't see any, at least none that were his.

It was unlikely that the children would skip a day of being home, and that alone alarmed Saif. Something was wrong, and he could feel it in his old heart. He refused to go back to work, deciding instead to remain at the shed and wait for his children to return.

Hours passed, and Saif even went out of his way to gather the usual provisions of food and water for them—but they weren't there. He simply munched on a raw potato alone outside the shed, watching several slum dwellers, young and old, pass by. None of them were his beloved children.

Saif took a deep breath and looked up at the clear sky, his voice unsteady as he whispered to the gods, "Where are my children?"

—

At the Sultan's tower, Ibrahim Hafeez, the Chief of Police, thundered up the spiral steps until he reached the throne room. Ahead of him, two Mamluks, standing sentinel at the golden door, noticed his approach.

"Sir Hafeez," a Mamluk said.

"Please tell me the Sultan is not busy. This is urgent," Ibrahim spat, his voice edged with anger.

"The Enlightened One has no audience at the moment," the Mamluk answered.

"Good. Open the doors."

As commanded, though Ibrahim wasn't their commander in chief, the Mamluks pushed the doors open and made way for the tall, elderly Ibrahim. On the other side of the boundary, two more Mamluks stood watch, unfazed by Ibrahim's sudden appearance, despite his outburst. The Chief of Police marched down the red carpet, passing the pews, until he reached the Sultan.

The Sultan was occupied with admiring his statues of the gods that sat behind his throne when he heard the familiar footsteps of one of his leaders. Without turning to face Ibrahim, the Sultan calmly said, "Ibrahim. Why the sudden visit?" He gently rubbed his finger across the golden face of Shie, the Goddess of Knowledge, clearing a few specks of dust from her cheek.

"What did you do?" Ibrahim growled, sensing the impending argument with the Sultan.

"I do many things. You should be more specific," the Sultan grinned, turning to face the chief who stood at the base of the steps.

"Four of my Ghazi—my men—took their own lives last night," Ibrahim stated. "Their superiors and some family members had to contact me about the incident. From what I understand, those men who are now dead were under your command from dusk 'til the highest moon. I understand that some of our people will give up and take their own lives, but this—this isn't a coincidence. What happened last night? I demand to know the answer. Their families need clarity!"

"Chief of Police! I advise that you *do not* speak to the Enlightened One with that demeanor! Under our pledge, you may be slain! This is a warning!" a Mamluk knight shouted from the doorway.

Both of the knights marched toward the throne, hands resting on the hilts of their swords, but Ibrahim did not falter in the face of their show of force.

"*Stand down*, Mamluks," the Sultan ordered, causing the knights to immediately come to a halt. "Let Ibrahim speak freely. He has done nothing wrong."

"Aye, Enlightened One," the Mamluks acknowledged.

After calming the obedient knights, the Sultan returned his attention to Ibrahim, who refused to break eye contact.

"So, you wish to know what occurred last night?" the Sultan asked.

"I do not wish. I *demand*," Ibrahim spat.

"Very well then. You have the right to know, since these were your men, after all," the Sultan chuckled, showing no regard for the sudden deaths of Ibrahim's soldiers. "There was an execution last night. A band of thieves was lured into my domain, and I gave the soldiers the command to dispose of them. That is all."

"You're not speaking the whole story, Selim. I've known you ever since you were sucking on your mother's teat. I helped you get a seat on that very throne you plant your hands on. Speak the truth without omission," Ibrahim retorted.

"The thieves were children from the lower hive," the Sultan blurted out.

Ibrahim, shocked by the answer, paused and pinched the bridge of his nose, trying to take in the sudden revelation.

"You, made *my* men, execute children?" Ibrahim asked for verification, holding back his rage. "Some of those soldiers you recruited had yet to spill blood, and the first task you give them is the murder of children? Forget the fact that they're from the lower hive, Selim—my men are human—and no matter their training, this isn't an ideal task to start with. You literally plucked fresh recruits who recently graduated from the academy! Do you understand what this means? Not only did you have my recruits slaughter little ones, but if this word gets out to the public, there will be—"

"I *know* what there will be, Ibrahim," the Sultan interrupted. "That's why your job is to make sure it doesn't leak. Besides, hundreds of children die in this city every day, and there is no law that bans their slaughter in regard to committed crimes. You know this, Chief of Police."

"That's not the point, Selim," Ibrahim said. "You lured children in without proper trial—you made it a personal matter. Their execution was one thing, but the suicides that followed after, due to that action—this wasn't justice, Selim. This was murder. You skipped an entire process, just because *you* wanted these children off the streets, because you believed they were the main reason for your rising numbers in crime. I'll let you know right now, and I went over this with Elina prior to being here, but those numbers have not changed one bit. We're supposed to be an economic and cultural leader in the world of Skania, but if information gets out that we're having new recruits murder children—why? Why did you do it?"

"They were Saif Sabbah's children," the Sultan answered. "This was a sacrifice that had to be made. I did not expect some of your men to falter and take their own lives. I thought we trained and desensitized them better than that, but history is history. With this blow, Saif Sabbah will no longer wish to move forward with his rebellion—with his Hassazi. A few lives to save millions—what is so wrong with that?"

"You don't even know if this will stop Saif," Ibrahim growled.

"Oh, I do," the Sultan laughed. "Saif had already attempted to take the throne once, but he ended up failing miserably. He gave up once, and tried to rebuild. Imagine him giving up once more, because his beloved children are now all dead. I'm just digging deeper into a wound that was already there."

"What makes you think he'll just stop and give up because of losing his children?"

"A father who dearly loves their children would never want anything to happen to them. As they say, a child should never die before their parents. I know how he is, Ibrahim."

"It almost sounds like you personally knew him."

"In a way, yes. After all—his wife and daughter fell to the blade of my men."

Ibrahim stood in silence as he stared at the mad king, unsure of what to say next. It was obvious to Ibrahim that the Sultan did not care for trivial matters. The Sultan was too busy handling a grudge with his greatest threat, Saif Sabbah and his insurgency. His next priority was the overall health of the city, seeing as it was the largest trading center in the entire world of Skania, attracting millions of foreigners and international goods. He couldn't care less about the people—especially those from the lower hive. Ibrahim had taken the mantle of chief for a reason, driven by a passion for the city's people and its culture.

"Are we finished, Ibrahim?" the Sultan asked, breaking Ibrahim's trance.

Ibrahim tried to think of any other topic he wanted verification for, but nothing came to mind. He also believed it wouldn't matter in the end, because the Sultan, who believed himself to be all-knowing, would strike down his concerns.

"We are finished, Enlightened One," Ibrahim affirmed, returning his composure. "How is your health?"

"I feel—*rejuvenated*," the Sultan said with a wide grin. For a split second, Ibrahim could have sworn the tattoo of the Sultan's third eye blinked.

—

In a dark, empty void, a small figure curled up, hugging their legs and burying their head into their knees. In the land of vast black sand, with no stars in the sky, the little one was but a dot in a sea of emptiness. They felt no physical pain, yet they continued to cry, drowning in thoughts that were now lost.

When the child looked up to wipe their tears, they saw a tall woman standing over them. Her long white hair cascaded over a flowing black dress that accentuated her slender, curvy figure, with slits revealing glimpses of her pale thighs. Her face was the epitome of eternal youth, marred only by the dark circles beneath her eyes. She was beautiful and gentle, gazing down at the child who bore the same curse she had once suffered.

"W-Who are you?" Habi whimpered, staring at the woman's golden eyes.

"I am you," the woman replied softly, her voice monotone.

"Where am I?" Habi asked again, struggling to gather her thoughts.

"*Muto o cha Cadeave*—You're in the land of the dead, little one," the woman answered. "It seems you've met your end."

"I don't want to be dead. Where is everyone? I-I don't feel anything. I can't think of anything!"

"It is a haunting experience," the woman sighed, her voice heavy with grief. "Know this: your physical body may be gone, but your soul—your energy—your mana, lives on in this world we walk in. You are not dead."

"You just told me I was dead, though," Habi frowned, burying her head again in despair.

"Oh, you are," the woman confirmed. "But as long as this world still has veins, you are not truly dead. *You*, specifically."

"Why me? You never even told me who you are! Tell me!"

The woman stepped forward, her bare feet silent on the ground, and kneeled down, gently taking Habi's hand. Caught by surprise, Habi looked up at her, and their golden eyes locked.

Although Habi couldn't feel any pain, a strong surge of pressure flowed from the woman's hands into her hollowed bones. The pressure continued to grow, yet Habi didn't pull away. She could feel the force—the power—behind this woman. That was when she realized who she was dealing with.

Before Habi could speak her name, parts of the black sand beneath them began to glow a brilliant blue, revealing long lines of veins branching out from where they stood. She felt the tremendous aura radiating from the sapphire-colored veins, and it was as if she had been given a breath of fresh air.

"Necromantia?" Habi murmured carefully.

"So that's what they call me," the woman smiled gently. "My name is Evan, but I am the one you speak of."

Habi forced her small hands away from Evan, causing the veins to subside and fade back into the black sand.

"*You* gave this to me," Habi said, pointing at her golden eyes. "I never wanted this. So many scary things happened!"

"But, good came out of it as well, did it not?" Evan asked.

Habi didn't answer that question.

"Where there is life, there is death. Where there is death, there is knowledge and rebirth," Evan crooned. "We learn from those who have passed, from days long gone, and with that knowledge, we give birth to the new.

While life may be prominent, death is just as present—if not more so. Many stories have been told, and many have ended. Everything will die—it's another world.

"Skania has witnessed much, and many souls of the old still wander. Think of it this way, little one—life is one race, and death is another. That is why I created the language of the dead, Koumaic. New souls arrive every second in *Muto o cha Cadeave*, and none of them can communicate, because what was once taken for granted is now gone. I granted them that opportunity."

"You talk a lot, lady," Habi said.

Evan laughed. "Perhaps I do. It's been so long since I've spoken with another being—let alone, one I chose."

"And why did you choose me?" Habi asked, beginning to feel annoyed. Her first impressions of Evan had started off well, but now it seemed like Evan was just pestering her.

"You were a perfect option," Evan said. "The two who gave birth to you abandoned you because you were not a part of their plan. Then a man with a desire for change finds you in the rain, takes you into his care. The same man who longs to eliminate the very one I want gone—the one you know as the Sultan."

"Wait, are you saying I wasn't born this way?"

"No, you were not. You were perfect to be chosen because you had no attachments at birth, and the man who cares for you is the same man who would leave you his legacy. Everything lined up."

"And *how* did you know to choose me?"

"The dead are everywhere, little one. I'll know," Evan smiled. "You have a destiny to fulfill."

"I don't wanna. Besides, I'm dead. I hate it here," Habi whined.

"That *is* a problem," Evan agreed. "Ever since the Heaven's Roots fell, magic has been dormant, even though mana flows through the blood in all our veins. Without the catalysts from the gods, we are just—human."

"So much for your big plan. I'm gonna continue being dead," Habi stated, limping down onto the sand.

"You act like your story is over," Evan pouted, squatting down over Habi.

"It *is*," Habi barked, closing her eyes and pretending to be asleep.

"The dead don't sleep," Evan clarified.

"*The dead don't sleep*," Habi mimicked, mocking her. "Rafi killed everyone. Rafi killed me. You tell me I have a destiny, but here I am—dead. And then you say our power doesn't work because one big tree fell down. You stink!"

Evan wasn't sure whether to feel offended or appalled by Habi's outburst, especially considering she was dead. As far as Evan knew, the dead weren't supposed to generate their own emotions, only feeling their last thoughts from when they departed. That meant something else was at play here, and Evan knew exactly what it was.

"*All tales have an origin*," Evan sang.

"I can't hear you, I'm dead," Habi clarified, rolling around in the sand.

"You do know of the tales behind the world of Skania, don't you? Especially in Koura?" Evan continued.

"Yes, Father told them to us all the time," Habi said, accepting that Evan wouldn't leave her alone.

"Then you know the tale of the djinn? One of Skania's many mystical beings that spawned from the Heaven's Roots?"

"And how evil they are? Yeah," Habi groaned. "Why?"

"You'll see. Just remember, little one—life begets death, and death begets life. The cycle never ends," Evan smiled as she began to fade away, leaving Habi alone in the void.

—

Somewhere in the dark corners of the Sleeping Complex, piles of trash littered an entire district, nestled against a wall of ruins. Most of the mess was worthless debris, but among it lay discarded relics and pieces of jewelry the Sultan had cast away from above. Though not particularly profitable, these remnants stood out against the surrounding refuse. Scavengers from the slums would sometimes dig through the mounds, sifting through disease and decay in hopes of uncovering something of value.

As dawn drew to a close, a young boy who scavenged for leftovers and goods from the pile searched for his next meal, shaded by the jagged platform connected to the Sultan's tower, which loomed like a dial. He was a true slum dweller—dirty, ragged, and accustomed to using both hands to dig through piles of excrement and rotten food. When he unearthed a small, broken bronze watch, he tucked it into his pocket and continued his hunt.

He moved to another pile and prepared to dig, but then he stopped in his tracks.

He saw the mangled body of a young girl, her organs spilling out from her cavity. She was limp, her eyelids half-open, barely revealing the lifeless golden eyes she once had.

The boy wasn't scared, as he was accustomed to death and decay, but he refused to search that area—moving a body would take too much effort. Instead, he scoured away from the corpse and began digging through another pile. His brash movements caused the stacks of trash to shake, sending several items tumbling down beside the lifeless body, some of them relics he had missed.

A small, hand-sized bronze jar tumbled down the piles of filth, coming to rest at the feet of the corpse. It appeared to be a simple container, likely meant for holding small doses of sand or trinkets. Having been discarded, it was clear the Sultan had deemed it worthless.

Suddenly, the jar began to act strangely. It rolled side to side, as though a small animal were trapped inside, then even hopped onto piles of trash, as if someone had kicked it. It continued to roll, occasionally correcting its direction due to its oval shape. The jar seemed aimless, but it had a specific target in mind.

The jar rolled over the remains of the golden-eyed child and came to a full stop on their chest. It took some effort, but the jar managed to slip into the pouch that hung around their neck. Once it secured itself inside, the lid of the jar swiftly flipped open and then sealed itself. A quick flash of minty green light shot out from the jar, phasing into the child's body. The force of it unsettled nearby debris, almost as though a gust of wind had swept past.

On the child's lifeless face, a black mark slowly began to form beneath their left eye, high on their cheekbone. The inky substance gradually molded into a small black circle with a curved dash beneath it. The child's chest started to rise and fall gently, and their organs began to retract back into their body. The cracks in their bones melded together, and the body attempted to realign itself, forcing limbs into position while pushing arrow shafts from its wounds. As soon as the cavity was sealed by some mysterious force, the child's eyes snapped open, blinking rapidly. They took a deep breath and choked. Trying to scream, only raspy hisses escaped their throat. Their entire body was in agony, and despite the healing, they couldn't move a muscle.

The boy from before decided to make one last search before heading home, wherever that might be. When he returned to the site where the corpse had been, he froze in shock. With his jaw agape, the boy could've sworn to the gods that the body he had seen just minutes before was mutilated and torn apart. Now, that same body was whole, and his heart seemed to stop at the sight of it. He was used to the dead—just not the dead coming back to life. In panic, the boy sprinted away with a horrifying scream, dropping some of his goods just to move faster.

By the time the boy disappeared into a nearby alleyway, the recovered child was able to move their arms, and then seconds later, their legs. Their raspy hiss slowly transitioned into a growing scream as they felt their entire body morph back together. Once the last bone snapped back together, the child stopped crying in pain. They attempted to push themselves into a seated position, but they ended up tumbling down the piles of trash, meeting the sandy ground below. They groaned and pushed themselves off the ground, proceeding to alternate their head and take in their surroundings.

"W-Where am I?" Habi murmured to herself. "W-Why am I–?"

Habi only remembered being in a dark space, and she couldn't recall any of the previous events. She gripped both hands to her head, feeling her brain twitch and ache. She tried to stand and walk, but she couldn't even remember how to do that. Instead of fighting the headache, she lay down and gazed toward the sky, noticing the tower's platform several hundred feet above.

"Did I—fall?" Habi asked herself. "I'm Habi—Habi Sabbah."

Habi continued speaking to herself, trying to piece together any information. Over time, she began to recall fragments of her life. She was aware that she was in the lower hive—she had lived here. She knew she had a home, a small shed, but she couldn't remember where it was. With only that scant information, desperation took hold. Despite her aching head, Habi gathered whatever strength she had left and slowly made her way toward an alleyway, leaning her hands against the walls for support.

Her lips were dry, and her mouth felt like cotton. She was both hungry and thirsty as she limped down the tight web of alleys. She wanted to find answers, but with an empty stomach, her efforts felt pointless.

When she stumbled upon a small animal carcass, she fell to her knees and quickly scavenged what was left of the rotten meat. The dead rat wasn't filling, but it was enough to quiet the rumble of her stomach—at least for a moment. However, her body rejected it. She regurgitated the pieces of the rat along with chunks of stomach bile, her body heaving in disgust.

Once she caught her breath, the stinging pain in the back of her throat still lingering, she crawled back to her feet and followed the alley walls until she reached a more populated area. To her relief, she found a small pool of dirty water, surrounded by people who dipped their feet and bathed in it. Desperation overtook her as she scrambled to the sandy shores, dropping to her knees and frantically cupping handfuls of the water to her lips.

The water tasted like sand and urine, with small grains of dirt slipping past her tiny teeth. Nonetheless, she was grateful to quench her thirst, despite the conditions. To clean herself, she briefly dunked her face into the water, lifting it back up before continuing to drink from the pond.

The small crowd around the pond suddenly became wide-eyed, their jaws dropping in a mixture of awe and disgust. Most of them quickly ran away from the scene, clearly disturbed by Habi. She became concerned, thinking there might be a dangerous presence nearby. But when she scanned the area, there was no one behind her.

Turning back to the pond, she found that everyone had already disappeared. Staring at her murky reflection in the water, she wondered if something was wrong with her face. The only difference she could spot was a small black mark under her left eye, which she tried to scratch off with little success. Frustrated, she gave up and lowered her head back into the pond.

A couple of locals who had run away stood around a corner, peering at the mysterious child from a distance. They were used to seeing the dead, but they weren't accustomed to witnessing a living child with the back of her skull cracked open, exposing parts of her brain. One of them blinked rapidly and squinted, unsure if what he was seeing was real. He may have stood a safe distance away, but he swore to his partner that the child's skull was slowly threading itself back together.

—

After a victorious drink, Habi wandered through a maze of alleys, eventually emerging onto a street teeming with foot traffic. The sun was still young, and the air brimmed with the scent of spices as merchants called out their wares. She limped toward the nearest wooden stall, eager to glimpse what was for sale.

As she moved, some citizens recoiled in disgust, their gazes fixed on the back of her head. Her hair was growing back at an alarming rate, an unsettling sight they couldn't ignore.

As Habi squeezed herself between potential buyers, her eyes glowed with a strange intensity. She spotted cooked rat meat skewered on sticks, and despite her recent unsettling encounter with a carcass, this was the real deal—cooked, seasoned, and ready to eat. Her stomach growled at the sight, the smell of the meat making her mouth water.

"I-I want one," Habi begged, pointing at a skewer.

One of the merchants responded to her request and lifted a skewer from the fire.

"What do you have to trade, kid? Unless you've got gald?" the merchant asked.

Habi rummaged through her sleeves and pockets, searching for something to trade. That's when she felt an unfamiliar object against her chest. She reached into the strange pouch of her necklace under her shirt and pulled out a small bronze jar. She had no memory of it being there, but given the circumstances, she wasn't in a position to question it.

Habi, without a second thought, handed the bronze jar to the merchant. She was hungry, and that was all that mattered.

The merchant inspected the relic with a practiced eye, aware that this type of trade would usually cost him three skewers. But to preserve the product, he kept that information to himself and handed Habi a rat skewer, watching the joy spread across her face.

"Thank you!" Habi smiled and walked off, munching on her meal.

The merchant grinned and was about to drop the jar into the crate of traded goods between him and his companions when he felt it begin to shake. He froze in awe as the jar trembled violently. A few shakes later, it slipped from his grip and darted away from the stall.

"Damn child tricked me!" the merchant roared, flailing his arms in a desperate attempt to catch the flying jar.

"Shoulda expected it, buddy," his partner laughed. "You know how it be down 'ere. Gotta keep an eye on that shit. That kid probably attached a string to that jar and played you, ha!"

Meanwhile, Habi limped down the street, searching for the familiar shed she had pictured in her mind while savoring her cooked rat meat. As she reached for another bite, a strange object struck her, knocking her down and causing her to drop the precious skewer. Suddenly alert, she spun on the ground to face the culprit, but there was no one—at least no one who seemed suspicious. The streets were crowded with people, and some of them chuckled quietly after witnessing the child being struck. It reminded her how the citizens in the lower hive rarely cared for the lives of others, too absorbed in their own struggles.

Habi searched for the object that struck her, but found nothing significant—only sand kicked up into her face. Refusing to waste any more time, she retrieved her dropped skewer and pushed herself up. As she stood, she felt an insubstantial weight pressing against her chest. She reached for it and found an object there. When she dug into her pouch, she was dumbfounded to see the bronze jar again. She didn't give it much thought, assuming she had hallucinated parts of her transaction with the merchant. Instead, she bit into the last rat on her stick, tossed it aside, and continued down her wayward path.

During her journey, Habi passed by several dilapidated sheds, but none of them drew her attention. The sheds were either occupied by unfamiliar faces, or their structure and details didn't seem familiar. Despite this, she refused to give up. Her determination was reignited when she discovered a local pond, offering a refreshing drink to regain some strength.

The sun was preparing to set, and Habi's search had yielded no results. Just as she was about to settle into a dark corner for the night, a shed caught her eye. She believed it to be her home, as every detail seemed to match the image she had in her mind. There was even a small pathway leading to a yard in the back, reminding her of the many times she had used the restroom there.

Sparkling with hope, Habi limped toward the shed and tried the door, which to her surprise was unlocked. She was eager to regain her memories, but instead, she stumbled upon an unexpected scene.

When she opened the door, she saw a naked woman bouncing on a naked man lying on the floor. To Habi, it looked as though the woman was trying to harm the man. Meanwhile, the couple realized their intimate moment had just been interrupted by a child.

"Get out, kid! Get lost!" the man growled furiously, panting and moaning.

"Another street rat! You forgot to lock the door again!" the woman shouted, still moaning. She then grabbed her dirty undergarments and hurled them at Habi, trying to chase her out while keeping her connection with the man.

Habi, being pelted with clothes, ran out of the shed and back into the streets. It was not only unfortunate that she couldn't stop the woman from harming the man, but also because the shed didn't seem to belong to her. In the brief moment she had to glimpse the interior, it felt completely unfamiliar.

As darkness began to engulf the hive city, Habi had no choice but to camp somewhere. She refused to stay in the ruins or buildings, fearful of the squatters and residents who might harm her. She wasn't sure where she was in the lower hive, but throughout the day, she had regained some memories of its people and culture, which only deepened her fear. Part of her felt like she was missing something important, but she couldn't piece it together. All she could do was find a dark corner blessed with solitude and lay down for the night, trying to push her worries aside.

Even though she tried to sleep after her exhausting search, Habi couldn't. The nights in Koura were ruthlessly cold, despite the swarms of people living there. The alleys of the lower hive formed small wind tunnels that chilled any living being to their core. Lying on the sand and dirt, Habi could feel the warmth of her body slowly being drained away. If she didn't find shelter soon, she was going to freeze to death.

Groggy, Habi picked herself up and set out in search of a better place to sleep. The streets still carried some foot traffic, though far less than before. She had no sense of how long her eyes had been closed or how many hours had passed. Pushing aside her uncertainty and restlessness, she focused only on finding somewhere comfortable and warm.

Habi remained in the winding alleyways, observing several dark spaces where citizens more accustomed to the cold ground huddled together. Some gathered in groups, using their body heat to stay warm, while others wrapped themselves in filthy rags and torn blankets. Habi was tempted to steal a rag for herself, but she knew that if she got caught, the trouble would only multiply. She couldn't afford to attract more attention.

Within the dark alleys lit by dim candles, Habi spotted something promising. After searching for a suitable place to settle down, she came across the ruins of a house with a wooden platform for a foundation. A few planks were broken and missing, creating a small gap just big enough for Habi to slip through. She immediately seized the opportunity, claiming the hole as her own.

She dug some of the sand out from the opening to smooth the entry, and once satisfied, she slipped into the gap. Aside from her head and butt catching a few loose planks, she managed to fit into the crawlspace successfully.

There may have been cold sand on the ground within the dark confines, but at least she was shielded from the elements. She only hoped the building wouldn't collapse on her or that a rat colony wasn't hiding with her. While the chance of another squatter being in the crawlspace seemed unlikely, she didn't completely rule it out. With her vision useless in the darkness, all she could hear was the occasional howl of the wind outside, pressing against the wood and shifting the sand. She wasn't warm, but she was at least comfortable to some extent.

Habi lay on her side, embracing the chilly sand beneath her. Before deciding to doze off, she retrieved the small bronze jar from her neck pouch and ran her fingers over its engravings, trying to make sense of its curves and details in the pitch darkness. What struck her as most strange was when she tried to open it. No matter how much force she applied, the lid remained sealed. However, to her surprise, the jar felt relatively warm, despite the cold surroundings. It wasn't scorching hot, nor was it lukewarm—it felt as though she was being touched by another human being.

Baffled by her discovery, Habi wrapped her tiny hands around the jar, hoping it would warm her cold, numb fingers. She yearned to understand more about the mysterious object and, more importantly, to remember everything about her life. The only things she recalled clearly were that she was from the lower hive and had lived in a shed. Everything else remained shrouded in mystery.

She wasn't sure whether the ache inside her or the numbing cold was worse. But as she closed her eyes, fingers curled around the jar, none of it mattered. She would try again tomorrow.

Chapter Thirty

As the light of the rising sun crept into the crawl space, Habi was relieved she hadn't been eaten alive by rats during the night. However, she jolted awake when she felt cockroaches crawling all over her arms and legs. She shook them off in a panic, only to bonk her head on the ceiling of the den. Her body was still cold and aching, but her palms were somewhat warm, thanks to the mystical jar she held. She couldn't feel her feet, as the cold had siphoned all warmth from them, so she had no choice but to drag herself out of the hole and greet the sun.

Once she climbed out of the darkness, Habi basked in the sunlight, sitting in the sand and waiting for her body to regain some warmth. After securing the jar back into her pouch, she felt her stomach rumble, demanding food.

Once she could feel her limbs again, Habi resumed her search. She tried to recall the path she had taken from the streets into the alleyways, but her sense of direction was weak. However, it seemed the gods answered her call, guiding her with a parade of enticing scents—spices and freshly cooked ingredients wafting into the alley. Instinctively, Habi followed the smell, not only hoping to fill her belly but also to find answers.

—

Thankfully, the walk wasn't as far as she had expected. The movement helped her recover some warmth, though the aches wracking her body lingered, unrelenting. As she traced the source of the smell, she found herself in a large, bustling square filled with people, merchant stalls, and black smoke curling into the air. Her eyes fixed on a wooden platform at the center, illuminated by countless candles, and a memory struck her sharply, as though something had pinched her mind.

She wept, reliving the harrowing events of The Culling in vivid detail, recalling the lengths she went to save herself—and the others who were with her. The faces of the children in her memory remained blurred, but she knew one was a girl and three were boys. She also glimpsed a gentle woman who had protected her and a tall, bearded man who had given her shelter. It was a partial answer, but far from complete. The memory was agonizing, and to quell her grief, she forced herself to accept that what happened was now part of the past. This revelation splintered into countless fragments of potential clues, leaving her overwhelmed and directionless. Yet, she clung to one certainty: she had to find the shed. She believed it was the key to unlocking everything.

After wiping away her tears, she reminded herself of the pressing need to quell her hunger. There would be no point in searching if she perished before uncovering the answers to her journey. Steeling herself with newfound resolve, Habi straightened and marched toward the encampment nestled in one of the main squares of the lower hive.

Habi entered the square, her gaze catching a handful of slum dwellers marked by scars, burns, and missing limbs. They were grim reminders of the horrors the Sultan's men had inflicted on her home, stirring vivid flashes of death and fear in her mind. Nearby, piles of bodies burned, the source of the black smoke that lingered in the sky. She wondered if the smoke had been there when she first awakened but realized she hadn't looked up—her focus had been fixed straight ahead.

Burned and crumbled ruins dotted the main square, where some citizens toiled to rebuild its foundations with the scarce resources available. Hundreds gathered at the central altar to pray, while others struggled to survive, salvaging what little remained unscathed. Some offered humanitarian aid, while others bartered goods in desperate exchanges.

Amid the unrelenting turmoil of The Culling's aftermath, Habi's attention narrowed to a stall displaying raw potatoes. The enormity of it all pressed down on her, and she could only begin to fathom how vast the world of Skania must be, having known nothing beyond Koura her entire life. Yet, she clung to two resolute goals: to satisfy her thirst and hunger and to piece together the fragments of her shattered memories.

Habi did her best to weave and squeeze through the crowd of loiterers, but her short stature made her an easy target for shoves and jostles, forcing her off course from the potato stall. Still, her determination paid off, and with enough persistence, she finally reached her destination.

The merchants were swamped, their stalls surrounded by citizens eager to trade whatever they could—scraps of cloth, shards of wood—for the merchants' meager offerings. Despite her efforts, Habi couldn't catch their attention amid the chaos. She felt like a small pebble lost in a sea of stones.

The temptation to steal a potato triggered another memory. She recalled how she used to loot merchants and passersby alongside a group of friends—a family. Their faces remained indistinct, but the recollection of her skill in thievery was vivid. It felt like second nature as she deftly swiped a single raw potato from the stall without drawing any attention. With her prize in hand, she slipped away toward the streets branching out from the square.

After weaving through the throng, Habi found herself back on a dusty street, continuing her journey with a bitter, starchy raw potato to gnaw on. As she walked, her attention was drawn to a group of children playing with a ball fashioned from entwined twigs. Their laughter echoed as they kicked the makeshift ball between them, carefree and joyful. For a moment, Habi longed to join in—it looked like so much fun—but she reminded herself that she had no time for such diversions. As she moved on, trying to ignore them, one of the children broke away from the group, waved at her, and ran in her direction.

It was a boy, not much older or taller than Habi. His olive skin, like hers, was streaked with dirt and sweat, and he beamed at her with a bright smile, revealing yellowed teeth.

"Oi! I've seen you 'round 'ere before!" the boy said happily. "Aren't ya usually with them other folk? Why ya lookin' lost?"

"W-Who are you?" Habi asked, her voice faltering as she instinctively clutched the potato tightly to her chest.

"I'm Asim! Nice to meet ya, uh?"

"Habi," Habi answered. "Aren't you playing with the others?"

"I was, but none thems passin' the ball to me. Talk about borin' yea? Where you been?"

"I-I don't know. I don't remember anything. I don't even remember where I live," Habi frowned.

"You don't know!? Girl, I see you come out of that shed all the time. Ain't far from here!"

Habi's eyes lit up as she realized that Asim might hold the answers she had been searching for. She should have guessed it sooner, especially since the boy had recognized her. If he remembered her, it meant she was getting closer.

"Can you show me!?" Habi requested joyfully, stepping closer to Asim.

"What, ya fell from a buildin' and cracked yer head open or somethin'? Fine, I'll show ya, but you gotta come by and play ball with us, got it?" Asim said.

"I will," Habi happily agreed.

"Nice! Follow me then! Tis a good ways away!" Asim cheered, starting to walk off with a hopeful glance over his shoulder, ensuring Habi was close behind, which she was.

They walked further from the heart of the population, descending the uneven hills and steps that formed the lower hive's architecture. The children navigated a few corners, sticking to the main streets and avoiding the alleys to keep from getting lost. Every so often, Habi would offer Asim a piece of her raw potato as a gesture, but he always politely declined. Together, they steered clear of danger, stopping to drink from nearby ponds to quench their thirst. Habi felt that the journey was taking longer than she had anticipated, but to her surprise, the sun hardly moved in the sky, suggesting her sense of time was a little off.

Fortunately, certain parts of the street jogged Habi's memory, bringing a few more details into focus. She recognized the same homeless figures sprawled on the sides of the road. The familiar stench of rot, blood, and urine, though far from pleasant, was strangely comforting. Asim led the way, and with each step, Habi's gaze fell on a shed that sent a chill down her spine. This time, she was certain it was the shed she had envisioned in her mind, and she could only pray that Asim hadn't led her astray. The last thing she wanted was to encounter another naked woman killing a man.

"That one ring a bell, ya?" Asim asked, pointing at the shed across the street.

"I think that's the one!" Habi said, stepping ahead of Asim to get a better picture of the shed. "Thank you As–"

When Habi turned to face Asim, she was dismayed to find that he had suddenly vanished. She scanned her surroundings, but all she could see were squatters, rats, and the dull outlines of dusty buildings. The emptiness around her served as a stark reminder of her strange ability to see the dead, though their guidance had often proven useful.

"Thank you, Asim," Habi whispered softly, hoping her words would find their way to wherever his soul might be.

After a brief moment of grief, Habi felt a sense of relief wash over her as she finally neared what could be her home. She moved cautiously across the street, careful to avoid the steady stream of pedestrians. When she reached the shed door, she paused, took a deep breath, and turned the knob.

She expected to visit those from days gone, but to her dismay, the interior of the shed was empty, filled with the haze of sand and dust, likely a result of the strong winds earlier. Despite the emptiness, she was certain this was her shed. In one corner sat a desk, and in the back, an empty bookshelf—both covered in cobwebs. It wasn't a definitive answer, but the familiar layout stirred memories of the years she had spent there. She recalled the bearded man, always seated at the desk, writing endlessly, and the hazy children who played on the floor where bedrolls used to be. Yet, there was one more detail that Habi nearly missed: a loose plank in the floor, now fully exposed.

Habi rushed to the plank and lifted it, disturbing the sand that had settled on top. As she dug through a small pile, memories slowly returned to her. She pulled out a wooden box and opened it, a smile spreading across her face as she found pieces of jewelry inside. The sight of the contents reminded her of the hard work she and her friends—her family—had put in to achieve their dream: to escape the lower hive and live in the middle hive.

"Father. Taliba. Hamza. Tariq. Naji. Rafi," Habi whispered, the faces of the bearded man and the children reanimating in her mind.

She may have found a crucial piece of her memory, but it still didn't explain why they were all absent. Now, her next goal was to find them. Her first plan was to stay in the shed, hoping someone would return. To pass the time, Habi ventured back to the streets, stealing scraps of food and gathering rags that littered the area. She made several trips to the shed, setting up a makeshift mat and blanket while nibbling on bread. As the moon rose, she continued to wait, her energy draining from the work until exhaustion overtook her, and she dozed off alone in the dark shelter.

Morning greeted her again, and she awoke alone once more. Though she was more comfortable within the confines of the shed and her rags, the absence of her family weighed heavily on her, leaving her to brood.

Habi stuck to her routine for at least a week, stealing food and gathering supplies while keeping a watchful eye out for anyone she recognized. But with each passing day, no one came to her lonely shed. Her only companion was the jar around her neck, its warmth a comforting presence—but it wasn't the same as the touch and laughter of those she loved. It was then that she realized waiting was no longer an option. She had to find them herself.

Before leaving, Habi was tempted to take Rafi's stash with her, but she knew that carrying such treasure would only bring conflict with the other slum dwellers. Instead, she helped herself to a sapphire ring, slipping it into her pouch alongside the jar. The ring reminded her of how much she loved Rafi, knowing that his fingers had once touched it. She left most of the rags in the shed, taking only the largest one to use as a cloak that fit her size. It would also serve as a blanket when she needed to rest. Once she was satisfied with it, she draped the rag over her head and looped the rope of her neck pouch around it, creating a makeshift hood. For her safety, she kept the pouch inside her shirt. Now, she was ready to continue her search for her family.

All the missing pieces were beginning to fall into place. With every step she took since leaving the shed, Habi reminded herself that she was from the lower hive, living with six others who had all endured The Culling.

For the following days, Habi roamed through several alleyways and streets. When it was time to rest, she searched for the nearest shelter or corner, wrapping herself in her cloak and cuddling with the warm jar. With every journey, she reminded herself of the harsh reality of the lower hive: its filth and violence. Fights were constant, often ending in death. Citizens would relieve themselves wherever they pleased, and trash piled up in some alleyways, making them nearly impassable. To survive, Habi made a mental note of the local ponds and the common spots for food and goods. The lower hive was vast, and she never knew exactly where she was. She kept a particular eye out for children, but those she encountered were either ignoring her or too engrossed in illicit activities.

One day, Habi found herself near the outskirts of the lower hive, where the desert dunes stretched out along the horizon. Amidst the vast expanse of sand, a single dead tree stood, oddly out of place. She swore she had seen this tree before.

She decided to walk up to the tree, wondering if it held any significance in her memory. The branches were bare, and some of the bark had peeled away. When Habi looked down at the trunk, she noticed an iron slate embedded in the tree, its surface worn and weathered. It read:

Here lies Assad Sabbah. May he rest. Never forgotten.

After reading that name, Habi felt a sharp pang in her head and a sudden chill that seemed out of place given the scorching sun overhead. She recognized the name Assad; he had been part of the old family that lived under Father. The memory of the others who had been part of that family returned to her, stirring feelings of warmth and longing amidst the unfamiliar desert landscape.

"Assad. Karim. Lena. Sara," Habi murmured to herself again.

As far as Habi knew, Sara had been the closest to her and the others, especially since she had acted like their mother. Habi recalled moments spent with Sara, but her current fate remained a mystery to the young girl. Frustration bubbled inside her from not having the answers, yet she couldn't shake the overwhelming desire to uncover what had happened.

Frustrated, Habi gently slapped the side of her head and hissed, "I can see dead people. Why won't you help me!? I'm lost! Help me! Help me!"

"*Yat koolay sa nenet yi ta govo*. All truths are not to be told," a man's voice said behind her.

Alarmed, Habi quickly turned around to confront the sudden intruder. She tensed, ready to run, until she saw a young man standing next to a frowning woman, both towering over her.

"Assad? Sara?" Habi called out, seeking confirmation.

"It is us, *li ah-te*," Sara confirmed sorrowfully.

"Wait, Sara—are you–?"

"I am," Sara answered. "Me and Assad have been with you ever since you awakened, but after realizing that you're not seeing everything as it should be, we decided to remain dormant. I'm sorry for that."

The information Habi received sent another sharp tingle through her head, causing her to reimagine the entire scene of Sara's death during The Culling.

"*That* is why," Assad added, noticing Habi's wince.

"What do you mean?" Habi asked, scratching the side of her head. "What do you mean by that? Why did none of you help me? I just want to find my family." This time, Habi wasn't begging; she was demanding. She broke into tears, her body shaking as she leaned against Assad's tree, overwhelmed by the unanswered questions. "Tell me, please! I'm tired of looking!"

Sara and Assad exchanged a glance before lowering their heads, their eyes filled with sorrow as they faced the grieving girl.

"Your power seems to have grown, *galdi opta ki-le*," Assad said. "You called for us against our own desire, and now you've given us no choice but to answer. A demon is at work, and you are a host."

"Just answer me! Where are they!?' Habi demanded furiously, her voice trembling with frustration and pain.

Sara and Assad remained unfazed by Habi's sudden outburst. However, obeying the silent command of the golden-eyed child, Sara took a step forward, ready to share the painful truth.

"Little one—Habi—" Sara said sorrowfully. "I love you like a daughter, and you must know that once I speak these tales, you will be hurt. Your mind will twist, and your heart will sink into a pit of despair—that is why we kept silent. But now, by some strange force, you've left me no choice."

"I-It can't be that bad, right?" Habi whimpered as Sara knelt to meet her eyes, hesitation and sorrow etched across her face.

Up close, Habi could see Sara's gentle face, forcing a smile in an attempt to comfort her. Sara's chest didn't rise and fall, as she had no need to breathe. Her eyes, too, remained still, not needing to blink. After locking eyes with the beautiful ghost, Habi braced herself for the words that Sara was about to speak.

"To answer your command, Necromantia—" Sara began. "After The Culling, you and the other children departed for the Sultan's tower to rescue Rafi, who had been taken. When all of you arrived, the Sultan ordered his men to take your lives. All of them have passed, and you died by the hands of the boy you loved—Rafi Sabbah. Trading your lives for his, Rafi now lives comfortably with the Sultan's riches. As for Saif Sabbah, your father—he waited for his children to return, but he soon came to accept that his beloved little ones suffered a terrible fate. Saif departed the city and left for the dunes. That is all."

During Sara's tale, Habi winced, cried, and growled as her entire memory flooded back. She felt a chaotic mix of joy, fear, helplessness, and rage, and both Sara and Assad could only watch as Habi crumpled to the ground, clutching her tiny aching heart. She remembered how each of her siblings had died, pierced with arrows. She recalled how her excitement to bring Rafi back had turned into a desperate fight for survival. She remembered the exact moment when Rafi kissed her forehead, only to push her off the tower, ending in her own demise. Habi didn't know what to feel. All she understood now was pain, and she cried until tiny puddles of tears formed on her dirty rags. Part of her wished she had never asked for the truth about her family, while another part was slightly relieved to finally have closure.

"Little one—" Assad began, trying to comfort Habi, but she wailed and screamed, rolling in the dirt as agony seared through her entire body.

Her cries began to draw the attention of some locals, but none of them paid her any real notice. They assumed another citizen had simply abandoned their child. No one wanted the responsibility of caring for a child—especially if they didn't share the same blood.

With labored breathing and a throat choked with tears, Habi gasped, "W-Where's Father?"

"He ran, Habi. We do not know exactly where he is. He's out of our jurisdiction, somewhere in the dunes. That's all we know," Assad answered.

Unable to bear any more pain and grief, Habi lashed out at her two friends from the past, shouting, "Go away! Go away! Leave me alone!"

Without another word, both Assad and Sara dissipated, fading away right before Habi's eyes. As commanded, she was left alone, and she refused to interact with the dead any further. Her entire world shattered the moment she remembered that her family was broken, torn into a million pieces. What made it worse was the fact that she had died and been resurrected, now forced to endure the agony of life all alone.

"I don't want to," Habi cried to herself. "I don't want to be alone. I don't want to keep going. I want everything back to normal. Why? Please, just let me go. I don't want this."

Habi curled into a ball, her body trembling as she continued to whimper, shrouding her face with her knees. The despair was overwhelming, and she had no idea how to move forward. She didn't want to be another child on the streets, scavenging for scraps and trying her best to avoid death or kidnapping. She never wanted Necromantia's powers. She wished she was still rotting away in the complex, far removed from this cruel reality.

"Oi, stop cryin'!" a squeaky voice roared.

Habi, tears still pouring from her eyes, looked up from her knees and shouted, "I said leave me alone!"

"Ya, I'm not leavin' you alone, kid," the high-pitched voice spoke again.

Immediately, Habi searched around, wondering if another living child was nearby, but to her surprise, there was no one within arm's reach—only the dead tree.

"It's takin' lots of energy just for me to talk, kid. I'm down here!" the voice squeaked.

Habi, following the voice's directions, looked down at the sand, only to see nothing but wet spots formed by her tears.

"In your pouch!" the voice redirected.

This time, Habi retrieved the pouch from under her shirt, expecting it to be the strange jar. She was right. As soon as she opened it, a minty green cloud of miasma seeped from the lid, and in her fright, she quickly tossed the jar away from her, repelled by its eerie appearance.

The jar landed and rolled in the sand, only to start rolling back toward her, as if a small animal was running inside of it. When it closed the distance, Habi scrambled away, backing herself into the tree, her heart racing in fear.

"Ya, don't do that," the voice suggested. "I made a contract with you. Be happy that you're alive."

The jar stopped at Habi's foot, and its lid fully opened, releasing a small cloud of green mist that floated in front of her.

"What are you!?" Habi frantically shouted, shielding her face with her hands.

"Hey, take it easy. I'm just a djinn. I'm a friend, believe me. I'll even tell ya my name. It's Rashid. Nice to meet ya," the green mist said.

Habi peeked between her fingers and tried to kick at the miasma lingering in the air, but it did nothing, the mist swirling harmlessly around her.

"Djinns are—real?" Habi asked through a sob, her voice trembling with disbelief.

"All tales come from somewhere. Of course we're real! What, you think the gods made a magical tree and decided that humans should be their only plaything? Okay, kid," Rashid chuckled.

Habi, accepting the fact that the Djinn was real, aggressively picked up the jar and growled at it, the floating cloud of mist following the jar's movement.

"Are you saying *you're* the reason I'm alive!? I hate you!" Habi scolded, throwing the jar to the ground and slamming a hammer fist onto it.

Habi's strike had no effect on the small jar. Instead, she cried out in pain and recoiled her hand, rubbing it with the other, her frustration mounting.

"Ya, no, that's not going to work. Also, you're pretty weak, not gonna lie," Rashid stated.

"Shut up! Leave me alone!" Habi cried out.

The locals who passed by gave Habi concerned glances, wondering who she was talking to. Most simply concluded that the child was influenced by drugs or other substances.

Habi squinted at Rashid and asked, "Do they not hear or see you?"

"Nope. Only the one bound by contract can hear and see me," Rashid clarified.

"I never accepted a contract!" Habi growled.

"Ya, being dead doesn't really give you any consent—just saying."

"Okay, then why did you choose me? Why not someone else more deserving?"

"You think I'm going to miss out on the chance to look over *the* Necromantia? There's no way I was going to expose myself to that wicked Sultan guy up there. I thank the gods that he tossed me down into the dumps, and all I had to do was conceal my mana. Wish I could say the same to my brothers though," Rashid explained.

"What do you mean?"

"Oh, the Sultan has two djinns under a contract. No big deal."

"What?" Habi scowled at Rashid. "Isn't that a bad thing!?"

"To you guys, ya. Not really for me," Rashid chuckled. "Might bed down soon. Lack of mana and all. Talking is a lot of work."

"Wait, wait, wait," Habi begged.

"Oh, *now* you're interested to chat with me. Go on then, meat skin."

"Wow, you're *mean*," Habi hissed. "You never answered why you made a contract with me."

Rashid sighed, "I literally answered that. You're Necromantia. Everyone has a destiny set for them, and it all depends if you want to be smart about it, or if you want to be dumb and get yourself killed. Well, destiny says that you should die by falling and find me in the pit. That simple."

"I don't think it's that simple," Habi said.

"If you ain't dead, then death isn't through with you yet. As long as you wake up, you're still in the game. Even though some of us are against Necromantia, it's probably a big sign to find her kin lyin' dead. That means you got a big job ahead of you, buddy."

"What's the job? What's the contract? Please, tell me."

"You're gonna have to ask Necromantia herself for the job. She chose you for a reason, which means something big is about to happen. As for the contract, I keep you alive, and all you gotta do is feed me mana. I'm also a good catalyst to help unlock more of your powers. That's about it."

"How do I feed you mana? How do I—" Habi began, preparing to ask another question, but before she could finish, Rashid dissipated, and parts of his green mist returned to the jar, sealing the lid behind it. "Rashid? Rashid, please talk to me."

Habi shook the jar, clutching onto its warmth in an attempt to wake the sleeping spirit, hoping for more answers—hoping to fill the void of loneliness. Just moments ago, she had been glum and miserable after recalling her entire story, but since Rashid had started speaking with her, she felt a strange sense of ease. Despite not knowing the full details of Rashid's origins as a djinn, she found herself intrigued and even willing to keep him around. Even if she wanted to get rid of him, he would likely return, bound by the alleged contract made during her death. But right now, with Rashid absent and the dead hiding, Habi had no idea how to continue.

She held Rashid's jar in her hands as she leaned against Assad's tree, staring into the bright blue sky with a blank expression. She wished she could fly like the birds above, but unfortunately, she was only human—a human given a second chance at life, and apparently a role to accomplish. To her, this second life wasn't a blessing; it was a curse. She had lost everything in the blink of an eye and was forced to relive that painful reality, suffering internally from the traumatic events all over again.

"Rashid?" Habi whispered, her eyes still glued to the sky. She wanted a response from the djinn, but as the little spirit had foretold, he must have been out of mana, and Habi had no idea how to provide it. Not only that, but she was desperate for company.

The more Habi stared blankly into the sky, the more her joy began to fade away. It was a big world, and she felt like just a crack in a castle of glass. She could feel her life slowly draining as she sank deeper into a depression. If what Rashid had said was true, if she were to die again, his magic would bring her back, since her power dealt with the dead. It was a lot to process, and all Habi wanted was to sleep forever, to forget about living altogether. That was when her stomach rumbled, the hunger reminding her that she was still alive, still breathing, feeling the ache in her belly for food. Despite everything, she was still afraid of death itself. She didn't want to face that pain again. She refused to suffer.

Habi decided to stand up, securing the jar into her pouch and donning her hood, her gaze sweeping across the endless alleyways ahead. All her life, she had nearly perfected the craft of surviving with the help of others, but now, she craved something more. If the gods had chosen to punish her, then the best thing she could do was to perfect another skill. She didn't want to merely *survive*—she wanted to *live*.

With a dreary expression, Habi returned to the bustling, rotten streets of the lower hive, disappearing into the crowds.

—

Many moons passed, and Habi continued to wander aimlessly through the slums. She stole food when she could and sought shelter whenever possible. Most nights, sleep eluded her, leaving her to stare into the darkness with empty eyes. She lacked dreams, and the absence was more unsettling than comforting. Rashid had not spoken a word since introducing himself, and as she had ordered, the dead kept their distance from her. But during one of her walks, something felt amiss.

"Taliba. Hamza. Tariq. Naji. Where are you? Why won't you visit me?" Habi whispered to herself as she followed the flow of traffic. "Visit me, please," she ordered, hoping her powers would summon their presence.

Unfortunately, there were no visitors. Believing her powers weren't working properly, she called for another name.

"Asim, visit me," Habi whimpered.

As commanded, Asim appeared from thin air, walking beside her.

"Oi, ya ready to play?" Asim asked.

"Go away," Habi ordered instantly.

And with that, Asim immediately faded away.

It was true that with Rashid's help, Habi had become more proficient in using her abilities. However, she still didn't fully understand its extent and wasn't willing to test it. She was left with confusion, wondering why her deceased siblings didn't appear, but Asim did. Aside from the surrounding dead and the demon in a jar, she was truly alone. Sara would've been a comforting presence, but ever since she passed, she seemed different. It was as if Sara had lost all her motherly emotions, which, by Necromantia's standards, was an accurate effect of being dead. All Habi could do was frown, cry, and carry on.

With every passing day, Habi stole food and ate it, relieved herself, and attempted to get as much sleep as she could. She became attuned to traveling alone and learned to navigate the hot spots for danger, but the invisible weight on her shoulders remained heavy. Not only did she carry the burden of Necromantia's desires, but she also carried the guilt of knowing that she had led her siblings to their deaths. Ever since the revelation, she blamed herself every day for what had happened. She just wanted to live a normal life, full of smiles and laughter, but that dream felt increasingly out of reach.

One evening, Habi hunkered down beside a noisy establishment, nibbling on a mix of looted nuts, cooked scorpions, and roaches. She watched with envy as laughter and music spilled into the streets. Citizens had gathered outside the building, singing, dancing, and drinking their worries away. Some sang of The Culling, while others vented their frustrations—grievances of life, a wife's infidelity with a Ghazi. The lyrics were foreign to her, but it didn't matter.

She couldn't bring herself to care for their merriment. All she wanted was to feel that way again—to laugh without effort, to carry a heart that wasn't so heavy.

"Hey, kid, no squatters on my property," a man growled from behind, making Habi flinch.

Habi turned to face the man, her hood casting a shadow over her features as she met his gaze, despite his taller frame. He had a familiar jolly potbelly, hidden beneath his gray garb and red overcoat. His well-kept brown mustache twitched when his jaw dropped at the sight of Habi's golden eyes and the strange, unfamiliar mark beneath her eye.

"Wait—aren't you Saif's kid?" Gunther asked, crouching slightly to get a better look. "Holy *shit*—you are!"

Habi refused to speak, still unacquainted with the memory of the man who owned the establishment. Instead, she kept her eyes locked on him, wondering if he had other implications in store for her.

"Relax, little one. I'm not here to hurt you," Gunther reassured, holding out his palms. "I don't remember you being so angry, but then again, it's been a long time. Aren't you usually with other children? I haven't seen Saif around for a while either. How's he been?"

"My family is dead, and Father left town. Leave me alone," Habi said sharply, her tone a clear warning.

"Wait, what? Did The Culling take their lives? I'm so sorry, little one–"

"Don't be sorry. Neither you nor The Culling killed them," Habi said, trying to maintain a brave face.

Gunther raised an eyebrow, taken aback by Habi's bluntness and intensity. To ease her irritation, he kneeled down to her level. It was clear to him that the loss of her siblings was a sensitive topic, so he shifted the conversation, focusing on Saif instead.

"Saif left the city? Why would he do that?" Gunther wondered.

"I don't know," Habi muttered, her legs trembling with a mix of fear and rage.

"Are you telling me you've been on your own ever since then?" Gunther frowned, pitying the child.

Habi didn't respond. She merely stared at the concerned man as she packed her belongings, preparing to flee.

"Wait, let me help you," Gunther said, noticing Habi's shift in posture. "It's the least I can do, after what Saif did for us. I'll give you a roof over your head, and better yet, a job if you're interested. Nothing shady, I swear it. Saif would vouch for me if he were here."

"I don't trust you," Habi whimpered, though the heartfelt offer tempted her.

"That's fine if you don't trust me. Trust is hard to come by down here. If only I had known about the fate of Saif and his family sooner, maybe I could've done something. To see another of his children still alive—I can't turn a blind eye to this," Gunther said.

"Saif never came to consult me, but that's just like him. Maybe he left because he was heartbroken, reliving the same pain he felt before, only worse, only growing.

You don't have to trust me, little one, but please—give me a chance and time to prove it to you."

"You don't have to do this," Habi said.

"You're right. I don't *have* to—I *want* to. There's not many children out here that I'd understand, but Saif himself raised you. I know that you'll fit right into The Tavern," Gunther said, offering a helping hand to Habi. "Tell you what—I'll show you around and have you meet the crew. If you don't like it, then you're free to leave whenever you like. Good?"

Habi struggled to find purpose in her life lately, reluctant to take Gunther's offer. She refused to experience betrayal from another person she cared for, afraid Gunther might turn out to be just like Rafi. But as she stared into his green eyes, she saw genuine sorrow and pity, nearly brought to tears by the reality that her family was gone. If she accepted the offer, there was a chance for a decently normal life, but if she refused, she'd only continue to survive, never truly live. She wondered if this was what the gods had granted her—maybe this was her chance, a chance for purpose and a way to move forward. Either way, she was still young and had nothing to lose—she couldn't even lose her life.

In the end, Habi slowly placed her tiny palms into Gunther's hand, accepting the conditions.

"Very well then," Gunther said, smiling. "Let's show you around. I'm sure you'll love it. Also, I'm sorry for not remembering your name, little one, but please let me introduce myself again—I'm Gunther Blythe, owner of The Tavern. How about you?"

A.G. MANNY

"Habi Sabbah," Habi murmured.

Chapter Thirty-one

The smell of booze and freshly cooked meals filled the air of The Tavern. Laughter, dancing, and singing swirled in time with the band playing on the main stage. Several wooden round tables at the center were packed beyond capacity, and the barmaids squeezed between the standing patrons, all caught up in the revelry. The round bar to the right of the stage was just as crowded, with the two bartenders unable to catch their breath. To the left of the stage were secluded tables reserved for important guests, the same area where Habi dined with her family. Behind the closed seating area was a backdoor, and various games played out in front of the reserved section. If paradise ever existed for both locals and foreigners, this was it.

Gunther carefully guided Habi through the crowds, making sure to alert everyone of his passage with a guest. Habi kept her hood on, holding Gunther's hand and keeping her head low, her mood grim. Most patrons noticed Gunther's arrival, cheering for him and ensuring they didn't bump into the child trailing behind. But as the drunken revelers let loose, a few splashes of beer landed on Habi's rags as they danced. She wasn't accustomed to being crammed into such a small space with so many people, and the splashes only fueled her annoyance.

Finally, Gunther stopped at the bar, positioning himself a few feet away so the bartenders could see Habi clearly.

"Oi, Samir! Yara!" Gunther called out to the bartenders, who were filling up drafts. "This little one is Habi. Honored guest for the day."

"Nice to meet ya, Habi!" Yara blurted out, waving while drenched in sweat.

Samir gave a quick nod to Habi, too busy to spare any words.

After the bar greeting, Gunther guided Habi to an open space between the main stage and the bar. This was where the barmaids came to deliver orders and relax for the few seconds they could spare.

As Gunther walked by with Habi, he called out, "Ladies! Honored guest Habi here!"

The women giggled, some immediately darting into the sea of bodies, carrying a cooked platter handed through a small gap in the wall.

"She's a cutie!" one of the barmaids exclaimed, causing Habi to shy away and pull her hood lower.

Next up was the band, but they were too caught up in their current melody to do more than nod and wink at Gunther and Habi as they passed by.

Passing the closed-off seating area, Gunther led Habi into the backrooms and down a dark hallway, which triggered a flash of memory from her past journey. This was the place where she had seen Father incapacitate a couple of Ghazi soldiers, back when the building had been cordoned off.

A few moments later, the pair emerged from the dark pantry and walked down another hallway lit by flames, with smoke lingering in the air and drifting out through a hole in the ceiling. This was where the cooks handled food and supplies.

"Hey, boss man!" one of the chefs called out, slicing through raw meat with practiced ease. "Heard the blockade's lifting soon. Should make our imports a little easier again, yeah?"

"Correct," Gunther answered. "Also, this is Habi, our honored guest for the day. I'm just showing her around right now."

The chef laughed and said, "Oi lil girl, you should be honored! Boss man here is one of the greatest businessmen you'll find down 'ere!"

"Not like there's much business to begin with, yeah?" another chef laughed, causing the entire kitchen to burst into an uproar.

Gunther laughed along as well, then quickly regained his composure while guiding Habi toward the exit door next to the pantry—the very spot where Father had defended his children.

"Tis true, but remember—never underestimate your competition, ya?" Gunther said, pointing at the line of chefs.

"Aye, boss man," the chefs acknowledged in staggered unison. After the comment, they returned to their dishes, chuckling at the thought of there being another strong business like The Tavern in the lower hive.

While the cooks fried and boiled their orders, Gunther opened the backdoor and carefully escorted Habi out of the dark pantry, leading them back onto the streets of the slums, into an alley. Directly across from them stood a long wooden building with a solid sandstone foundation. It wasn't as spacious as the main establishment, but it was enough to provide bedding for a few inhabitants.

"Next up are the dancers. They get their own dorms, but there are still some restrictions. Got one of my security boys posted at their door at all times. If the front of the house is meant to make you smile and the back is meant to fill your stomach, then these ladies fill your heart. Come on, the dorms are just around this right corner," Gunther explained.

"Okay," Habi murmured, slightly overwhelmed by the sheer scope of Gunther's domain. It was hard to fathom how so many people coexisted under the same roof without conflict, especially compared to the chaotic open streets of the hive.

As Habi tried to snack on some of her scorpions, Gunther had already escorted her to their destination. Gunther spoke the truth—the door to the dorms was indeed right around the corner, and a bulky man covered in scars stood guard outside the sealed entrance.

"Hello there, Tiny," Gunther greeted, gently pulling Habi into view.

"Oi boss man! Who the lil' 'un?" Tiny replied.

"This is Habi, my guest of honor for the day. Habi, this is Tiny. He's my lead security man. Can't really introduce you to the rest of the team because they're all spread out in The Tavern, but if you need something done, you can count on Tiny," Gunther explained.

"Hello, lil' 'un," Tiny smiled and waved, his hand larger than Habi's head.

"Hi," Habi simply replied, standing her ground as if she had already accepted defeat from a fight that never started.

"Lookin' a lil' sad there, ya?" Tiny said.

Gunther immediately crossed his hand over his neck, silently signaling Tiny to drop the topic. Tiny, understanding the cue, sealed his lips and gave a look that said, *Oh*.

"Anyways Tiny, mind if me and Habi enter the dorms? I want to show her the dancers," Gunther resumed.

"Oh ya, of course! You the boss man. Go 'head, ya?" Tiny nodded nervously, stepping to the side to allow Gunther to enter.

"Thank you," Gunther smiled proudly, turning the knob while holding Habi's hand.

Habi had assumed the muffled echoes of music came only from The Tavern behind her, but as the door swung open, she realized drums and chimes were playing inside as well.

A row of beds lined one side of the room, each with a nightstand, mirror, and wardrobe nestled between. The other side was open space, where five tall, toned, and slender women played instruments, their eyes fixed on four girls around Habi's age as they choreographed their dance. The women wore their respective belly dancing outfits, while the girls were dressed in small black gowns.

Each woman wore a fitted top that highlighted their toned midriff, adorned with colorful sequins and gold jewelry along the lining of their clothes. Some wore skirts that flowed with their movements, while others had on form-fitting harem pants and leggings that exposed parts of their thighs.

"One, two, three, *belly roll*! One, two, *twirl*!" a lady called out to the girls, snapping her fingers to the rhythm.

When the women called out numbers, the girls shook their hips in unison from one side to the other. At the command for a belly roll, they performed the move with precision, even though some of their spines cracked within the rhythm of the song. When the order to twirl came, all the girls spun around, but as soon as one lost her balance, she tumbled into the others, breaking the lesson and stopping the music.

"Basara, you suck!" a blonde girl cried out, sitting on the floor.

"Shut up! I'll crack yer head open!" the dark-skinned girl roared.

"Girls, stop fighting and get back in line!" a woman demanded, pointing at the girls.

While the dancers were scolding their apprentices, Gunther cleared his throat, catching the attention of everyone in the room.

"Boss man!" one of the dancers called, turning to face the door that let in the outdoor light.

The girls on the floor immediately scrambled to their feet and stood at attention, eyes fixed on the man in the top hat. Meanwhile, the women bowed and smiled at him, their gazes shifting to Habi as they noticed her presence.

"Oh, she looks *cute*," one of the women remarked, gazing at Habi's golden eyes. "Come on, little one, show us a smile. We don't bite."

Habi continued to frown as the women treated her like a lost puppy. The girls huddled together, trying to catch a glimpse of the unfamiliar girl hiding behind Gunther's legs.

"Ladies, girls, this is Habi, my guest of honor. I'm just showing her around. Mind if you continue with your lesson? Let her see the whole exercise," Gunther said.

"Of course, boss man, we don't mind," a woman agreed, stepping into the center of the line of musicians preparing their drums and chimes. "Girls, look good for the boss!"

"Yes, ma'am," the girls responded, lining up in formation. Before the session began, they extended their right arms toward the adjacent girl's shoulder, checking their spacing. In one swift motion, they snapped their arms back to their sides and placed their hands on their hips, poised to begin.

Once everything was set, the women at the drums began clapping their palms against the instruments, building a rapid rhythm. As practiced, the girls started shimmying their knees and hips to the beat, alternating sides in sync with the bass drum. When the chimes joined in, the girls vibrated their bodies, transitioning into gentle hip circles as the rhythm became more upbeat.

"One. Two. Three. *Circle*!" a woman commanded.

On cue, the girls dramatically swirled their hips before resuming their shimmying to the beat.

"*Ha's up and feel the beat*!" a woman sang out.

The girls began moving their hands and arms in a flowing motion, mimicking the movement of water. They gently bent and angled their arms as the chimes rang out in prominence. Whenever the bass sounded, the girls burst into abrupt, dramatic motions with their hips and arms, accentuating the music's tone. One of the women began to hum a beautiful melody, prompting the girls to shake sporadically and stomp in rhythm. As they spun slowly, they shimmed their shoulders back and forth, perfectly in sync with the music.

Gunther admired the performance and the dedication his dancers poured into training the next generation. While everything was business to him, he held a deep passion for those committed to his vision. In most cases, the dancers were the main reason patrons returned—the hospitality was merely an added bonus.

Curious, Gunther glanced down at Habi to gauge her reaction to the experience. Though her hood obscured her face, he noticed her gently tapping her feet to the rhythm. Gunther smiled, realizing the lost girl he had found now seemed captivated, particularly by the art of music.

Habi, still wearing a restless expression, continued tapping her feet, never having experienced an event like this where she could fully immerse herself. Music had always been present in The Tavern and on the streets, but she could never enjoy the atmosphere with crowds gathering around the shows. This time, she had her own private performance, and though she didn't show it, she loved it. For most of her life, friends and family had filled the empty space of loneliness. But now that they were gone, music found the chance to touch her heart. She felt the thrum of the drums resonating in her chest as the dorm came alive with an exhilarating melody.

"It seems the little one is enjoying herself, yeah?" one of the women laughed, noticing Habi's small bouncing motion. "Want to be a dancer? We have a slot open. Boss man is pretty picky when it comes to choosing us."

At the woman's statement, Habi immediately stopped her small dance, and the music began to fade as the short session came to an end. The women hesitated, worried that they had somehow frightened the golden-eyed girl, especially when she lowered her head and hid her face beneath her hood. The girls, meanwhile, stood in silence, simply observing the situation unfold.

To break the awkward silence, Gunther gently patted Habi on the head, causing her to look up at him. As soon as she caught his eye, Gunther grinned.

"So, what do you think?" Gunther asked. "I'm willing to take you in as one of my own. The ladies here would be delighted to look after you as well, and the girls would probably be excited to play with you. You'll have a place to sleep, eat, and forget about your worries. How about it?"

Habi remained silent, lost in thought. She wished she could ask Rashid or a reasonable spirit if this was the right path for her, but one was out of mana, and the other was far from reliable. Talking to herself in front of people she barely knew wasn't an option.

Still, the positives outweighed the negatives. Though being surrounded by crowds unsettled her, the music and the privacy of the dorm offered a sense of comfort. If she accepted the offer, she could start anew, leaving behind the burdens of her past. The temptation grew stronger as she realized that music might not only help her forget but, over time, perhaps even heal her broken heart.

The only thing holding her back was trust. Having lived in the lower hive and endured Rafi's betrayal, she had learned its value the hard way. She wanted to believe she could build a life here, but something kept her from fully embracing it. Her heart was fragile, and her trust was thin.

"Ladies," Gunther calmly called, catching the attention of the dancers. "Can we talk outside?"

"Of course, boss man," one of the women replied, slowly leading the others toward the exit in a single-file line. Some of them politely waved at Habi, while others gave her space, quietly acknowledging her grief.

When the last dancer walked out the door, Gunther turned back to face Habi and said, "I'll go have a chat with them really quick while you think about your decision, alright?" He grinned. "You can go talk with the girls if you want. I'm sure they're excited to speak with you. Believe me when I say this—out of all the departments I manage, I'm positive the dancers have the best cohesion. They're like sisters."

Habi didn't respond, even as Gunther walked out the door and secured it behind him, leaving her alone with four other girls she didn't know. As soon as the door closed, the girls slowly approached her, their eyes wide with curiosity as they carefully examined the hooded figure from head to toe. Habi's instincts told her to prepare for a fight, but the girls had other plans. Instead of advancing, they huddled around her, maintaining a respectful distance.

"Why do you have yellow eyes?" a light-skinned girl asked.

"You already have a tattoo? That's crazy!" another girl joined, pointing a finger under her eye.

"Why do you look so down?" another added.

"Girls, girls, girls!" the blonde girl shouted, her height making her stand out among the quartet. She looked like a foreigner, judging by her appearance. "This is Gunther's guest! Treat her with respect!" After scolding the others into silence, she turned to face Habi, standing tall and confident. "Habi, right? My name's Hailey! Nice to meet ya!"

Habi blankly stared at Hailey, as if she had a fly on her nose.

"The short one is Shakila. The smiling one is Mariam. The one with a screw loose is Basara," Hailey continued, pointing to each girl in turn.

"What did you just say?" Basara growled.

"The honored guest deserves to know the truth!" Hailey stated.

After Hailey's remark, Basara shoved her way to the front and yanked Hailey by her long hair, drawing cries for help. The other two girls, witnessing the altercation, quickly intervened to separate them. Watching how swiftly the dispute was resolved, Habi surmised it was a common occurrence, as the other girls seemed unfazed.

Habi started to have second thoughts about accepting Gunther's offer.

Hailey cleared her throat theatrically, as if her show had been momentarily interrupted, then smirked as she rubbed her head. "Anyways, we overheard that you might be interested in becoming a dancer. Do you like dancing?"

"I've never danced," Habi frowned.

"Well, we saw you tapping your feet earlier. That's technically dancing," Hailey pointed out. "Do you want to try it while the tall people are gone? It's fun, I promise! Shakila and Basara can play the drums and chimes while Mariam sings. Come on, let's do it!"

Feeling pressured, Habi lowered her head and slowly stepped away from the girls, but Hailey giggled, clearly enjoying herself. With a swift motion, Hailey grabbed Habi's hand and pulled her away from the door, gesturing for the other girls to take their spots at the instruments. Habi, too exhausted to resist, couldn't pull herself free in time. By the time she was released, the drums had already begun to play. Moments later, the chimes joined the rhythm, and Mariam started to hum a melody as she shimmied in place.

"Follow my lead," Hailey instructed, her voice cutting through the growing rhythm of the music.

Hailey shimmied to the rhythm, bending her knees and dropping her hips in time with the beat, her movements inviting Habi to join. Habi hesitated, wishing to escape the moment, but as she exhaled and let the drumbeats pulse through her, she surrendered to the inevitable.

Habi began to mimic Hailey's movements, her tentative steps gradually flowing into a gentle shimmy. Noticing her progress, Hailey twirled, waved her arms, and giggled with delight. Following Hailey's lead, Habi repeated the motion, the rhythm vibrating through her bones. When Hailey transitioned to circling her hips, arching her back, and shaking her hands toward the ceiling, Habi followed suit, drawing smiles from all the girls.

Habi couldn't bring herself to smile, but joy still welled within her. The music seemed to lift her spirit, sweeping away her worries and transporting her to a place free of pain, envy, and anger. Despite the weight of her trauma keeping her expression blank, she found herself immersed in the moment. When Hailey returned to shimmy, Habi followed, soon moving to her own rhythm. To everyone's surprise, her arms flowed with grace, as though she were pouring her emotions into the dance—a quiet, haunting tragedy. She pushed her hips left and right, her knees slightly bent, eyes closed as she surrendered to the music, shutting out the world around her.

A sudden applause jolted Habi out of her serene trance, her eyes snapping open as the music ceased. For a moment, she thought the ovation was from the girls, but her gaze shifted to Gunther and the women standing at the door. They all smiled warmly, having witnessed her performance. Hailey, awestruck, could only manage a wide grin and a firm thumbs-up in Habi's direction.

Embarrassed, Habi lowered her head and stepped away from the girls, centering herself in between the two parties.

"Don't be like that, Habi. You were great!" Gunther praised, his clapping gradually subsiding. "There was passion in those movements. I thought talking to the ladies would be enough, but you done gone ahead and proved it yourself. *Bravo*, little one."

"She was just showing me how to dance," Habi said, hoping it would serve as a valid excuse.

"Your comfort zone is killing your potential, little one," one of the women said. "You'd make a fine apprentice—I'm sure the girls would agree. You have the heart for it, and all of us here will help you nurture it. What do you say, Habi?"

"Do it!" Hailey cheered, her voice full of encouragement.

As Hailey chanted, the rest of the girls joined in, their voices blending together in a chorus of encouragement, each one trying to lift the lonely girl's spirit.

"Remember, Habi," Gunther said, his tone soft but sincere. "You don't have to do this, but it would break my heart to see you return to the streets. If Saif is gone—let me take his mantle. I know you've been through tough times, but please, let us be there for you. We're all in this together—down in the lower hive. What say you?"

This decision alone could change Habi's life for the better, but the pain she felt still weighed heavy. As Gunther attempted to convince her, Habi could only rerun the thoughts of Taliba, Hamza, Tariq, and Naji losing their lives right in front of her. She ran the image of Rafi pushing her over the ledge over and over again until her jaw trembled with sorrow. She could only imagine how Father felt, since he now believed that his beloved children were now gone. If she accepted this offer, her life would start over. She didn't want to forget the names of those she lost along the way, nor will she allow it.

But then she asked herself, *What would her siblings want for her*? She knew that they didn't want her to live on the streets fighting for her life. If anything, the stars seemed to be aligning, and Gunther's offer was the next step in her journey. It was what her siblings would've wanted. It was what Father would've wanted. Even Rafi, who had betrayed her for his own gain, would've wanted her to take this chance.

"I accept," Habi said, her voice steady as she fought to hold back her tears.

A brief pause followed her answer before the entire room erupted in cheers. The girls celebrated, welcoming another sister into their fold, while the women eagerly anticipated having another student. Gunther beamed with pride, knowing he could now offer a proper home to one of Saif's children.

"It is done then," Gunther smiled. "You're now a part of The Tavern."

"I can't wait to do lessons with you! You're a natural!" Hailey cheered.

Habi wanted to smile, but she couldn't. The hurt still clung to her, and she loathed herself for it. The dread twisted in her gut, but at least, for the first time in a long while, she was able to rest. She held the warm jar under her shirt, the one that housed Rashid, and thought of her future in this new place. She had been given another family. The comfort of music now eased her pain. There was warm food, a bed to sleep on, and a roof over her head. Though her siblings never made their presence known, she could almost feel their smiles, watching over her from the heavens.

Aside from the scarring memories, Habi couldn't help but wonder what Necromantia had in store for her. She found herself repeatedly asking, *What do you want me to do*? and *What is my purpose*?

She shrugged off the thought, grounding herself in the present as she accepted the embrace of her new family.

"I can't wait as well," Habi said.

It was time to start over.

Special Thanks

This book would not have been possible without the support and contributions of some truly incredible individuals.

To Loren, your encouragement, insights, and unwavering belief in me meant more than words can express. Your friendship has been a guiding light throughout this journey, and I am endlessly grateful.

To Muhammad Kaleem, whose artistic talent brought the cover of this book to life—thank you for capturing its essence so beautifully. Your work adds a visual dimension that perfectly complements the story within these pages.

And to everyone who has supported, inspired, or believed in me along the way—this book is, in part, yours too.

With gratitude, A.G. Manny

HABI

A.G. Manny is a passionate author who has spent a lifetime crafting short stories and tales, many of which remained unpublished—until now. Their debut, Habi: Book One, is a powerful testament to resilience, drawing inspiration from themes of struggle and tragedy. Based in the United States, A.G. Manny balances their creative pursuits with a love for drawing, video games, marksmanship, and personal fitness. With an unyielding commitment to storytelling, they continue to expand the intricate world of Skania and the epic tales that unfold behind the lore of the Heaven's Roots.

www.ingramcontent.com/pod-product-compliance
Lightning Source LLC
Chambersburg PA
CBHW060208030726
47499CB00004B/957